THE SHIMMER ON THE WATER

ALSO BY MARINA MCCARRON

The Time Between Us

THE SHIMMER ON THE WATER

Marina McCarron

HEAD
of ZEUS

An Aria Book

First published in the UK in 2022 by Head of Zeus Ltd,
part of Bloomsbury Publishing Plc

9 7 5 3 1 2 4 6 8

A catalogue record for this book is available from the British Library.

ISBN (PB): 9781801104449
ISBN (E): 9781801104432

Cover design: Leah Jacobs-Gordon

Typeset by Siliconchips Services Ltd UK

Printed and bound in Great Britain by
CPI Group (UK) Ltd, Croydon CR0 4YY

Head of Zeus Ltd
First Floor East
5–8 Hardwick Street
London EC1R 4RG

WWW.HEADOFZEUS.COM

For Joan McNutt, a gifted English teacher and a lovely
soul who changed my life.

Thank you, Miss McNutt, for everything.

And

For Andrew Lawrence, the best travel buddy ever.

Prologue

Portland Times and Record
July 5, 1997

Girl Missing

Police in Fort Meadow Beach are searching for a missing six-year-old girl.

Daisy Wright went missing last night during the town's annual Fourth of July celebrations. She was with her family when she disappeared in the crowd gathered to watch the fireworks at Sunset Beach.

The girl's father, Len Wright, says the family had spent the day at the beach. She was less than ten feet away from her parents when the old pier collapsed. 'The first thing I did was to look for my daughter. She's never been good with loud noises. I knew it would frighten her,' he said, his voice breaking.

The old fishing pier that has stood at the center of Sunset Beach collapsed just before the fireworks were scheduled to start. It is believed drilling for the new pier nearby may have weakened the structure.

Police and concerned citizens searched the beach and the surrounding areas all night but found no signs of the missing girl. Officers from neighbouring jurisdictions have been called in to help.

'We've never seen anything like this in the Fort,' said Chief of Police Tom Langley. 'We won't stop searching until we bring Daisy home.'

Daisy Wright is the chief's niece. He was not with family when Daisy disappeared, but his son John, nine, was.

Fort Meadow Beach has a yearly population of 6,000 which almost doubles during the summer months. The Fourth of July celebrations brings people from across the state, attracted by the sand and the seafood.

Fred Donnelly, former owner of Donnelly's Candy, has offered a ten-thousand-dollar reward for information leading to the recovery of Daisy Wright.

'This is not what this town, this community, is about. We're safe here. Our kids are safe here.'

Daisy was last seen wearing a pink and white striped swimsuit and pale blue shorts.

Anyone with information is urged to contact Fort Meadow Police.

I

Peyton

Spring, Maine, Present day

May is an awkward month to start over. September and January make the most sense. But the sun is shining when her plane lands and she takes it as a good sign, a promise of brighter days in Maine after the rainy darkness of Seattle.

Her father is waiting for her. He's always the tallest man in any crowd, so she sees him immediately and is happy. He had told her he would pick her up, but Peyton knew his job came first, and he could have been called into the hospital on an emergency. It had happened before. Lots of times.

'Dad!' she says when she's sure her mother isn't with him, rushing forward and throwing her arms around him. Her mother wouldn't approve of shouting, or public displays of affection.

If he's shocked by how she looks, he doesn't say anything. But then, he wouldn't. Her mother's reaction will be another story.

'Hello, sweetheart,' he says, leaning down to return her hug and take the huge suitcase she is wheeling and the bag from her shoulder.

They walk past the few people arriving on a Tuesday afternoon. Business travellers, mostly. Her father is wearing a suit and fits in with the crowd. Peyton, on the other hand, does not. She is wearing black trousers, a black turtleneck and white Converse sneakers. She looks like a funeral director ready to take to the court.

'It's so nice to see the sun.' Peyton is trying her hardest to be cheerful, to make up for the fact that she's returning under a frowned-upon cloud of failure. She's dreading seeing her mother. They haven't spoken since Peyton called and asked if she could move home for the summer.

The excuse she gave was that Seattle was too expensive, too far from home. Too much everything. In truth, it was too little. Or maybe a mixture of both. She hated her job as a pharmaceutical rep and was almost relieved when she'd been fired. Her boyfriend hadn't so much as broken up with her as he had slithered away, ghosting her. Then, her fabulous older sister had come to town, taken one look at her and shaken her head, not hiding her opinion, much like their own mother.

'You look terrible,' she said.

'I'm thinking of going home for the summer,' Peyton told her.

'So on top of everything else, you've lost your mind?' Caroline replied.

She knew what her sister had meant. She moved home anyway. She didn't have a choice. Not really.

'Thanks for coming to get me,' Peyton says to her dad.

'Did you manage to rent your place?'

'I can't. It's against the condo bylaws.'

'Shame to be losing rent money,' he says.

Peyton can see him figuring out the loss in his head. Yup, she's back home.

It's a forty-minute drive to Fort Meadow Beach. Peyton always thought it was a stupid name for a place. Is it a military garrison? Does it have an orchard? Both her parents work in Portland and they have an apartment there. Peyton hopes she has the house to herself a lot.

She feels herself both relax and grow anxious as they approach the turn that takes them to the main road through town. The sights of childhood begin to appear. The place that used to sell fried chicken. She remembers vividly the rare occasions she got to go with her dad. Her mother would not let them eat fried chicken, and from a cardboard box! The candy factory where all her friends had worked at one time. They made hard candies in a million different flavours, and some caramels, too. She's never seen the distinct pink packaging outside of Maine. Never really looked. She never liked hard candies. But it's comforting, now, to see the old factory that has stood since 1911.

They hit an intersection. It's probably the biggest in the Fort. A gas station on one corner, the Catholic Church on the other, a T-shirt shop and a drugstore rounding it out. Behind it is an old subdivision. She's never liked this area of town. The Fort doesn't have a seedy section, but this is as close as it gets.

Her dad turns left without even signalling. There are no other cars on the road.

'How's Mom?' she asks, looking out the window, away from both her dad and the answer to her question.

'Fine.'

'How does she feel about me coming home?'

'Peyton, this is your home. It always will be.'

It doesn't answer the question, but she lets it go. She knows not to push, where her mother is concerned.

They leave the town center and head up the hill that leads to her parents' home. It's twisty and it would be impossible to give someone who didn't know the area directions, but everyone local knows where their house is – the sprawling white mansion on a cliff overlooking the beach. It was once the summer home of a New York financier, before the Depression cleaned him out. Her great-grandfather bought it and many other properties for nothing and restored them. It had been passed down to her father, the only one who wanted to live in the Fort.

She can feel the engine in her dad's old Jag labouring up the hill.

'Maybe time to buy a new car,' she teases.

'Hush. You'll hurt her feelings.'

They park in the drive, where there's room for four cars. She's forgotten how much space there is in her home state. She hears the ocean – the water mind-numbingly cold even during the hottest summer – when she steps from the car. It's almost twilight now and the house has an eerie glow about it under the changing tones of the sky. She remembers the summer she read *Rebecca* by Daphne du Maurier and started calling the house Manderley. Her mother didn't find it funny.

She looks out at the water. She's travelled from one side

of the country to the other, her life is a mess, she's back home, but the view, this view somehow makes it better. Her father walks ahead of her, then stops to look back.

'Everything OK?'

She nods and follows.

He opens the door and she steps inside. Her entire apartment in Seattle could fit in the entranceway.

'The house is so big. There's so much space. I'd forgotten.'

Her father closes the door behind them.

Peyton has always hated the entrance to the house. The floor is black-and-white tile and it makes her dizzy to look at it. It feels like it might rise like a Pierrot doll and attack her.

'Where's Mom?' she asks, looking at her shoes and making sure she doesn't track anything inside.

She unlaces her sneakers and holds them, unsure where to put them. In the end, she rests them on top of her suitcase. She can hear the grandfather clock ticking in the dining room. Most families gather in the kitchen, but Peyton knows her mother won't be there. She'll be in the dining room or the conservatory, which are next to each other. She looks at her suitcases and thinks about going to her room to unpack but decides to get it over with.

She moves through the entrance, past the stairs, cuts through a corner of the kitchen. The dining room is empty – the small one, just for the family. They never use it. The main one is on the other side of the kitchen. They never use that one, either. She moves into the conservatory and sees her mother sitting in a chair by the window.

'Hello, Mom,' Peyton says.

Her mother, sitting in profile, turns slightly at the sound of her voice.

'Peyton.'

She sees her mother's eyes widen. Peyton has put on weight, hasn't had a haircut. She knows she looks bad. This will be a sin in Dr Lydia Winchester's world.

She moves towards her mother, bends and brushes her cheek with her lips. Her father comes in behind her.

'There will be a nice moon tonight.' He walks to the bar in the corner and pours himself a Scotch. 'Lydia?'

'I'm fine, Octavian.'

'Peyton?'

'A glass of red, Dad.'

'A glass of red, please, Dad,' her mother corrects.

'Sorry,' Peyton says. Five minutes and she's offered her first apology. Caroline's words echo in her mind.

Still, Peyton needs to be here now. She's not sure why, but she's sure of it.

Peyton sleeps most of that first day back. When she wakes in the evening, she sees the housekeeper, Mary, has left a plate of salad in the refrigerator for her. The house is empty and she takes it to the patio door, thinks about sitting by the pool to eat, but in the end just sits at the island in the kitchen, like she did so much growing up. Mary would talk to her as she ate.

When she's done, she rummages for a treat of some kind, perhaps ice cream or cheese, but can't find anything. There's nothing in the pantry, either. No one in the house. She figures both of her parents are in Portland and she's stung by this. She hasn't seen them in months – couldn't they have stayed home that first day? Found out why she wanted to move home so suddenly, out of the blue?

She leaves her plate by the sink. Goes back upstairs, past the same painting that's hung there since she can remember, and she stares at it. Asked to describe it, she'd have said it was a bunch of flowers in a field. But now, she sees it differently. The field that should be green is a dark blue. The flowers aren't typical flower colors. They have green stalks, with leaves like irises, but the flowers seem twisted. One is black. One is orange, looks like a flame. One is white. The sky is red, like the world is burning.

She's seen it a hundred times, but only now does she see how wrong it is. She looks for a name but can't see one. No doubt some artist her father wanted to support. She finds it unsettling and looks away.

She switches on the overhead light in her room, pale lavender walls appearing. The same walls she's had since she was ten and wanted to paint the room purple. Her mother refused.

'Ugly color,' she said. 'Garish.'

They'd settled on lavender. More of a gray, Peyton sees now.

She starts pulling open the drawers in her dresser, looking at her old clothes, wondering why she kept the things she has. Old jeans, ancient hoodies, the uniform of her high-school years. She finds a black one-piece and gets an idea. She pulls it on. It's too tight, far too tight, but no one will see her. She drags on a white T-shirt and trackpants and, leaving her feet bare, steps outside. The door beeps, has since they upgraded the alarm system years ago. Still, it startles her.

It's cool, almost cold outside. The kind of night you get in New England when you pull a hoodie over your shorts and shirt as the sun goes down. The grass is damp but soft and she loves the feel of it.

She walks to the edge of their property, then heads down the wooden steps leading to the beach. Each year, the winter does a number on them and each year, her father has them repaired. The splintered boards show he hasn't done this yet and she's careful, not wanting a shard in her foot.

The sand is cold under her feet. She wishes she'd brought a towel, but she doesn't really need one. She pulls off her T-shirt and her trackpants, leaves them where they fall. Then she walks to the water's edge. With each step, she can feel the wind off the Atlantic. It feels like it's working with the waves to pull her forward. But she doesn't really need to be enticed.

The sand gets colder and damper, turns to sludge, her feet dissolving in its murkiness as the first waves cover her feet. She gasps at the iciness of the water, but she doesn't stop.

When she was young and scraped her knee, her elbow, her father would say a dip in the sea would heal it right up. She thinks of that now as the water passes her knees, her thighs. The frigidness of it is both too much and not enough. When it hits her waist, she counts to three, dunks under, holding her breath.

Getting dumped. Getting fired. Losing friends. The embarrassment of all her failures.

But there's more. Something she can't put a label on – something that was wrong before she left the Fort, all those years ago. Something that hurts too much to think about. Something both vague and deadly, pulling at her like the floor of the ocean.

The chaos of her life is pressing down on her as much as the cold Atlantic. It feels like her lungs might explode, and her heart. The water mixing with her misery. Everything is starting to burn.

She breaks the surface, the night air even colder against her wet skin. It makes her gasp and she lowers herself, water getting in her mouth as the waves flow.

She looks around. Can anyone see? Even she knows what she's doing is dangerous, crazy. But she keeps thinking about her father's words when she was a kid. A dip in the ocean will fix that right up.

She dunks herself again. A baptism of sorts. Anointing herself with the salt of the ocean. Cleansing herself of her past sins – the ones she knows about, the ones she doesn't.

She turns in the water, floating on her back, looking up at the sky. Stars appear, hazy in the not-yet-dark sky. She wishes on one, for things to make sense, a broad wish. It's so cold now, she can't get her arms to do what she wants. Time to go in, to face dry land and real life.

She swims toward home. She's further away than she realized and the shore is dark, the only light the glow from where she thinks is her parents' house.

She can't feel her feet when she stands. She knows she's touched the bottom because the water settles at her hips. She moves forward, the cold biting at her, pinching at her now. She wraps her arms around herself, shivering, then finds her clothes. It's work to pull them on, her hands shaking violently from the cold. It isn't the smartest thing she's ever done, taking this evening swim. But she feels better for it, somehow.

It takes effort to get her legs going, but she makes it up the steps, across the lawn. She opens the door and stops. The house feels different. Someone's here.

Her mother appears, an apparition in a navy pantsuit.

'Jesus, Peyton. Have you lost your mind?'

2

Eualla

July, Tennessee, 1965

It's a hot day and Eualla Tompkins is playing in the back field behind her house with her best friend, Debbie. They're sitting with their feet in buckets of water, cold to start but quickly warming up. All morning they've been working on making a shelter, taping broomsticks to their lawn chairs then fastening old umbrellas to the tops. It seemed like a great idea, but no matter how much tape they use, the umbrellas tip over. They laugh each time it happens. It's the first full day of summer vacation – two whole months to do nothing but swim, sit in the sun, read and talk and laugh with Debbie. They're gonna have so much fun!

Eualla's mama is walking towards them carrying big plastic glasses of sweet tea. Her dress, faded from having been washed too many times, is further bleached by the relentless, pounding sun. She almost seems like a ghost coming toward them.

'You girls having fun?' she says, handing them both their drinks.

'Yes, thank you, Mrs. Tompkins,' Debbie says, sitting awkwardly under the tilting umbrella.

Eualla looks in her glass and sees her mom put fat slices of lemon in Debbie's sweet tea and one thin slice in hers. Both have ice cubes that make a plinking sound as the drink sloshes in the big plastic cups.

'Looking very tropical,' Mama says, eyeing up their creation. 'Like the South of France!'

Eualla has read about the South of France, a place called Saint-Tropez, in a book. Now, she says that's where she's going when she gets married. On her honeymoon.

Her mama reaches over and fidgets with the umbrella. It's straight, offering shade for a few seconds until it dips again.

'You girls can't sit out in the heat all day. You need some shade.'

'We're fine, Mrs. Tompkins,' Debbie says.

'You're starting to burn,' she says, looking at first Debbie, then Eualla, then squinting at the sky, as if trying to judge the sun's intent. 'That's it. Come in now. It's the hottest part of the day. You need a break from the sun.'

They reluctantly troop behind Eualla's mother, across the field and through the back door of the small clapboard building the Tompkins family call home. It's even hotter inside, but at least they don't have to squint. They both have dirty feet, from soaking in the cold water then walking across the land. Debbie stops and tries to brush it off, but Eualla walks straight in.

Minnie, Eualla's baby sister, runs to them. She's five,

excited for the summer and for school in September, and nervous, too. But then Minnie is nervous of everything. Eualla figures she's excited now because Debbie often brings her old toys she's outgrown, like the rag doll Minnie is currently holding.

Eualla and Debbie race to the room at the front of the house that Minnie and Eualla share. Minnie starts after them, but Mama calls her back. Eualla can hear her whine.

'So, what we gonna do all day?' Debbie looks around Eualla's room. She's seen it dozens of times, but it's like she's seeing it anew.

Eualla looks around, wondering what's out of place.

'I say we duck out of the sun for a spell to please Mama, then try to fix up them chairs again.'

'Doesn't seem to wanna work, the chairs,' she says. 'Besides, what I mean is what are we gonna do all summer?'

'Dunno,' Eualla says, stretching out on her bed.

Debbie sits carefully on the edge of Minnie's.

'I was thinking it would be fun to go to Pigeon Forge.'

Eualla sits up.

'There's shops. We could get some new clothes for the summer and for school,' Debbie says.

'School is way off,' Eualla says. ''Sides, who cares about clothes?' She lays back down in her bed.

'I do,' Debbie says softly.

Mama makes biscuits for lunch, and they take more tumblers of sweet tea back outside.

'The sun has melted the tape,' Debbie says as she tries to fix the umbrella.

Eualla jumps up from her hot plastic chair. 'Ouch! Wait here. I have an idea...' She runs inside, grabs a sheet from the closet and runs back out. 'Here! We can take down the umbrellas and put this over the broomsticks.'

Debbie grabs an end and they drape it over then climb underneath.

'It's a bit like a teepee,' she laughs.

They drink their tea and giggle. They don't need plans to have fun. They just need to be together.

Debbie turns up the next day with a bag of cookies her mama made for them and four bottles of Dr Pepper. Eualla tells Mama and Minnie the drinks are for her and Debbie, with strict instructions not to drink them.

'Can't I come play with y'all, puh-leeze?' Minnie begs.

'Mama?' Eualla says.

'Minnie, I need your help in the house,' she says.

That afternoon, they walk to the nearby creek and go for a swim. Eualla flings herself straight into the water, but Debbie hesitates.

'Whatcha waitin' for?' Eualla asks, floating on her back and tipping her head to look for Debbie, still on the side.

'I dunno. I mean, it looks kinda gray. Is there snakes?'

Eualla laughs. 'It's Tennessee! There's snakes everywhere. Come on in.'

It takes Debbie a spell, but she gets in.

'The pool in town is nicer. The water is... I dunno, cleaner or something.'

'But it costs fifty cents,' says Eualla.

'So?'

Eualla can't ask for fifty cents every time she wants to go swimming.

'This is free,' she says, waving an arm around the space. The water is clear, mostly. It makes a happy gurgling sound as is moves over the rocks resting on the bottom. The trees that line the bank seem to bend towards it, as if they too need a drink of the water on this hot day.

'But it's just us.'

'I like that it's just us. The last two summers it was just us.'

Debbie doesn't say anything, just walks out and sits on her towel.

When they get back to the house, Euella's brother, Jimmy, is there. Debbie doesn't want to go inside.

'What's wrong?' Euella asks.

'I-I just… I'll wait out here.'

'But why? You come in all the time.'

'I'll wait here. You go.'

'Suit yourself.'

Jimmy is sitting at the kitchen table, smoking. Euella ignores him. It's the best way to deal with her moody, crazy brother. She opens the refrigerator and sees two of the Dr Peppers are gone. Euella turns round, mad.

'Hey. What happened to our drinks?'

Jimmy responds by belching. Euella almost laughs, then remembers Debbie is outside. Euella is starting to notice that Debbie's family is different. Their house is real nice and all their dishes match. Her mama wears pretty dresses around the house and her daddy wears a suit for work. They have two cars even though they live in town and can walk pretty much everywhere. All the Tompkins have is Daddy's truck, and town is a long walk away. But it's something else. Something unseen but very real, that is different. No one in Debbie's house would ever belch.

Eualla takes a big drink of water and carries a Dr Pepper out to her friend. She'll leave the other one in case Debbie wants two, hiding it this time so Jimmy won't find it.

'Where's yours?' Debbie asks when she hands it to her.

'Drank it in one go,' she fibs.

Debbie sips her drink and looks out at the sunburned field around them.

Eualla wakes the next morning to a hammering sound. She looks out the kitchen window to the back field and sees Daddy banging in fence posts. Barefoot, she races out to see what he's doing.

'Whatcha doin', Daddy?'

'You fine young girls need a better place to call home,' he says. 'With a real roof.'

Eualla sees old planks on the ground around them.

'You watch yourself in your bare feet,' he says.

'You gonna make me and Debbie a roof?'

'Sure. Now go inside and tend to Minnie.'

'Where's Mama?' Eualla scratches some old mosquito bites on her arm.

'She's in bed. The heat has her feeling sickly.'

'OK, she says, running back to the house. A roof! She can't wait for Debbie to see it.

Their villa, as they've started to call it, takes shape. Daddy gives them a Styrofoam cooler he found by the side of the road. He fills it with ice and two Dr Peppers. One magical day he buys them animal crackers. Eualla can't wait for

Debbie to show up, to share this treat with her friend, but the morning comes and goes with no sign of her. Then the afternoon. She waits most of the day, finally giving up when the three o'clock sun drives her inside to start dinner, since mama is still minding the heat.

Debbie doesn't show up the next day, either. When she finally does appear, she's wearing new clothes.

Eualla looks at her pink top and her blue skirt, so new they still have the crease lines from being folded at the shop.

'Take it you've been to Pigeon Forge?' Eualla says.

'Mama took me,' Debbie says, doing a twirl. 'Oh, Eu, it was so much fun! We bought new clothes, and we had lunch at this real nice restaurant. I had the best fries ever.'

Eualla wonders why she didn't ask her along.

'Daddy bought us animal crackers, to eat in the villa,' she says.

'I don't wanna sit in there all day, it'll ruin my new clothes.'

Eualla looks at the yellow box of crackers. She'd been so excited about them just a few minutes earlier. Now, they seem like nothing, especially when compared to lunch at a fancy restaurant in Pigeon Forge.

The lazy July days pass with Eualla getting up early to feed herself and Minnie. Mama gets up some mornings, but not others. One morning she has a black eye, and Daddy doesn't come home that night. When he does appear, he gives her two one-dollar bills and tells Eualla to go swimming in the county pool, and to take Minnie and Debbie. Eualla starts to complain about taking Minnie but stops herself. The air is heavy with secrets, with unspoken questions. It's been too long since they've had rain and it's starting to make everyone a bit crazy. Debbie hasn't been coming over as much. Things feel strange. Funny-like. Unsettling.

Eualla packs a bag for her and Minnie and they walk into town, straight to Debbie's. Her friend's mama opens the door wearing blue shorts and a tan top, her hair pushed back with some sort of cloth band. She looks real nice.

'Hey, girls,' she says.

Debbie appears behind her.

'Daddy gave me money to go to the pool. You coming?' Eualla says.

Debbie looks at her watch. 'It's only nine o'clock. Isn't it a bit early?'

'Oh, I guess it is,' Eualla shrugs.

'Come on in. I'll need to find Debbie a swimsuit that fits her. She keeps growing. You're taller than when I saw you last too, Eualla.' Debbie's mom bends down to Minnie. 'And how are you, sweetie? You're as cute as ever, yes you are.'

Minnie takes a step back, leans closer to Eualla.

Debbie's mother straightens. 'Take a seat at the table, girls. I'll pour you some tea.'

There's a bowl of fruit in the middle of the table and Eualla thinks about how nice an orange must taste. As if Debbie's mama can read her thoughts, she offers one to each girl.

'Thank you,' Eualla says. She nudges Minnie to say the same.

'Thank you, ma'am,' she adds in her small voice.

Eualla digs her thumb into the skin and starts to peel the orange. Warm, sweet, sticky juice runs down her hands. She gives a section to Minnie and they share one between then. When no one's looking, Eualla puts the other in her bag for Mama.

Debbie's mother hands them each a paper napkin, the kind you buy at a store. It has little flowers in blue and green on it, and Eualla watches as Minnie stares, tracing them with her finger.

Debbie appears in another new outfit – blue shorts and a gingham top.

'Y'all got towels? Mama wants me to ask.'

'We do.'

The pool is fifteen minutes from Debbie's house, but the walk feels longer in the heat. They pass all the new houses just built, sparkling white under the sun, the green lawns trimmed and dewy looking, despite the heat. They look like palaces. One day she will live in a pretty house, just like them.

Feeling very grown up, she pays for the three of them. Inside the gate, she sees a crowd. Debbie heads straight for them, and Eualla sees it's their friends, Darlene and Pam and some others from school. Eualla hasn't seen them all summer, but Debbie starts talking to them like she's seen them lots. Eualla is confused, shooting looks at them all as she finds some chairs and lays out the towels. When she walks over to them, the girls stop talking, look at her funny. She's wearing an old swimsuit, faded and a bit frayed; it used to be mamas. But it fits.

'Hi,' she says, but they just nod.

'How's everyone's summer?'

When no one replies, she starts again.

'Hot enough for ya?'

Pam, who mama once said was not a nice little girl, rolls her eyes.

Eualla walks away, confused by what is happening. She jumps in the pool, swims to the side, and sets about coaxing Minnie into the water.

Eualla spends most of the day in the pool, but Debbie seems to move between her and Minnie and the girls from school, who make a big scene out of entering the water, all shivery and cold, while the boys splash them. Eualla watches, feeling like she's missing something but not sure what.

When Eualla is ready to leave, Debbie says she's going to the diner for pie. Eualla can't afford it, so she takes Minnie by the hand and they start the long walk home.

That night, Eualla crawls into bed sunburned and sore. Confused, too. Minnie creeps in beside her and Eualla reads her a story.

She hears Mama and Daddy talking, their voices different, rough and mean. They've been talking real loud a lot lately, but tonight they're shouting. Daddy sounds mad and Mama sounds sad. Both scare Eualla, and she turns on the small radio on her nightstand to drown them out. She pulls Minnie closer and kisses the top of her head. Her baby sister is sensitive to noise and gets upset. To Eualla, she's as fragile as the china dolls Debbie has at her house. She suffers from asthma and is small for her age. In winter, Minnie is often full of cold. She's everything that Eualla, who's strong, fearless and tall for her age, is not.

Eualla is used to Mama and Daddy fighting. It comes

and goes. They fight for a few weeks, then they're all lovey-dovey. But the summer is moving by, and they seem to keep fighting. And there's long patches of silence, too. Jimmy's been disappearing for days on end and then reappearing, with red glassy eyes. Something is wrong. Real wrong. And it's starting to scare her: strong, smart Eualla, who's not afraid of anything.

3

Peyton

May, Maine, Present day

Peyton's mother is staring at her like she's never seen her before. An alien sitting on a dining room chair wrapped in a robe and heavy socks, the heating cranked up. Her mother, after asking if she'd lost her mind, opened the front door, told her to shower, not to track mud in the house.

'And throw that swimsuit out!' was the last thing Peyton heard as she went up the stairs.

Peyton did as she was told, the hot water hitting her skin, making her feet throb. It had been too hard to dress, too exhausting, so she'd pulled on yoga pants and a sweatshirt, her robe over top.

Walking down the stairs, she heard the furnace, felt the welcome heat. Still, she was trembling, but she wasn't sure if it was from the cold or her mother. She slips on the marble floor, her socks too big on her feet, her limbs not entirely under her control. Maybe the swim wasn't a good idea, but she's glad she did it. She feels lighter, somehow.

Her mother is sitting in the lounge. She points for Peyton to sit. On the table next to Peyton is a snifter of brandy. She picks it up and takes a drink. It's sweet, thick. She's never had brandy before. She takes another drink, a long one.

'That's enough, Peyton,' she says.

Peyton sets the glass down, too hard. It makes a jarring sound in the emptiness of the large room no one uses. Usually they sit in the conservatory and she's not sure why they aren't now.

'What was that all about?' her mother says.

'What?' Peyton realizes her mistake. Saying what instead of pardon. Answering a question with a question. 'Swimming? I felt like going for a dip.' Even to Peyton's own ears, her answer sounds ridiculous.

'In water that still had ice chunks in it a few weeks ago?'

Peyton doesn't respond. She has no way to answer this.

'What would people have thought if they'd seen you?'

Ah, her mother's real concern.

There's a pause. She can feel her mother studying her.

'Were you trying to hurt yourself?'

'No. Of course not.'

'What about hypothermia? Did you not feel the cold, with the extra padding you've accumulated?'

Peyton's mother has always been as thin as a wand. So has Peyton – or was – and Caroline, who's almost six feet tall and built like a runway model.

'I just felt like a swim,' she says quietly, trying to hide her pathetic excuse.

They're silent, again – at least, no words are spoken, but the air around them seems to pulse with accusations, angry words, unshared feelings.

'I don't know what to say. If you were a patient...'

'I'm not a patient. I'm your daughter.' Peyton reaches for her glass and takes a gulp. She thought brandy would burn, but it's sweet. She swirls it in her mouth, liking the feel.

'Caroline told me you looked bad, but I wasn't prepared for this.'

'And what did Caroline say?'

'You had dinner. She met that boy you were so taken with and said he was a creep.'

Peyton remembers it now. She'd chosen the restaurant, thinking it looked charming from the street, like a Parisian bistro. Inside, it had been more *Lady and the Tramp* than *Maxim's*. She'd laughed too much, drank too much. Pushed too much. Sitting in her parents' home a year later, she sees it was the start of the end, for her and Marco, at least.

'So he broke up with you.'

'Yes and no. He just disappeared, if you must know.'

She doesn't tell her mother how many times she called him, texted him. She's embarrassed by this now.

'What about your job?'

'I didn't like it.'

'Jobs aren't meant to be enjoyed,' her mother says. 'They're a necessity.'

'So you dread going to your office each day? Dread talking to your patients? Find it hard to get out of bed and face the day?'

Her mother looks at her if not with concern, then slight alarm. Then Peyton sees her eyes narrow and the psychiatrist in her take over. She wishes she had more brandy. The whole bottle. Maybe even the whole cask.

'How is your sleeping?'

'Well, I did a lot of it in Seattle. Entire weekends sometimes.'

'And your eating?'

'Ice-cream based, mostly. Entire bags of cookies. I've financed an entire new wing for the Keebler elves treehouse.'

'That stops now. You don't put sugar and fat and artificial garbage in your body. I think it's situational, this depression, not clinical. We'll get you eating better. You'll exercise more, but if you want to swim, wait a month and use the pool. No one will see you. And it's heated.'

Peyton's unsure if her mother is making a joke or not. Still, she smiles.

'I'll write you a prescription.'

'What for?'

She tells her and Peyton laughs. 'That's the competition's brand.'

'What did you sell?'

Peyton barely has it out when her mother is shaking her head.

'Too many side effects with that drug.'

'Like what?' Peyton feels herself tense. She prescribed it for herself, took the samples she had for months.

Her mother looks at her shrewdly. 'You'll take the one I'm prescribing. It's a low dose.'

She waits to see if her mother wants to talk about anything. Isn't that what psychiatrists do? What *parents* do?

'There will be no more arctic dips. And Caroline told me about Marco. Arrived late, didn't pick up the bill.'

Peyton is dizzy from the brandy, maybe her earlier swim. Definitely from the change in direction of the conversation. Caroline told their mother about it? Peyton can't see that, although she knows they talk, are closer than she and Peyton.

'I thought I raised you better than that. But don't you let anyone treat you badly or push you around again.'

Peyton nods, remains quiet. But she's realizing something. The person who pushed her around most was the woman giving her this mandate. She feels her back straighten with the knowledge, the power it brings. She's getting to know the enemy. And the enemy is closer than she thought.

Her mother dips her head slightly and Peyton knows she's being dismissed. She stands up, her legs more solid underneath her now. She looks around the lounge they never use and suddenly knows why her mother chose this room for their powwow. The lounge is warmer. And there are no windows, like the conservatory. No one to see what is happening, should someone happen by.

She picks up her glass. 'Can I pour another of these?'

'A small one. And no snacks.'

Peyton walks to the bar in the corner and pours. She can feel her mother watching her or she'd take more. Then she climbs the stairs to her bedroom, closes the door, sealing herself in. She sits on her bed, thinks about what's just happened. Wouldn't a hug have been normal? A declaration of love? To her knowledge, no one in this family has ever said those three words to one another – I love you.

She looks around her childhood room, like she's observing it for the first time. As bedrooms go, it's nice. A big window looking out on the water, a walk-in closet, a double bed, two dressers for her clothing. On top of one, she sees a beige-colored spine and knows immediately what it is. Her high-school yearbook.

She pulls it down and flips it open, more for something to do than from any sense of nostalgia or interest. Looks for her grad picture, finds it easily. Her hair is poker straight, as was the style. She might have had it done for the photo. She can't remember. She flips through the glossy pages – twelve years of public school she spent with most of these people. Now, she's not in touch with any of them. She never wanted to be. Caroline still has high-school friends. Caroline's year was different. A different generation. Or maybe it was just her.

Peyton looks at some of the things written to her. Sees a picture of Todd Harcourt. She remembers kissing him one summer, behind that old, abandoned house where they all hung out, drank beer. She wonders if it's still standing. The Stick House, they called it, for some reason. It always crept her out.

She puts the book down and walks over to the desk where she sat doing endless schoolwork and starts opening drawers. She finds old pencils, pens, erasers. A pad of paper. She pulls it out. She's always liked paper, liked to scribble notes to herself. To doodle words that might be a poem, might be the start of a story. She takes out a few pens and tests them. Most are dry, but she finds one that works. She sets it aside and continues looking.

Underneath, she sees something else, something familiar. A coil-bound scrapbook. She hasn't thought about it in years, but she knows what it is immediately. Pulling it out, she starts flipping through the pages, heavy with clippings and tape, with memories and dreams. She'd started keeping scrapbooks in junior high, mixtures of journaling, stories cut from magazines she liked, photos. She sees one of New York. That had been the dream: Journalism school at New York University. Her mother had torpedoed that pretty quick. She feels it squeeze at her, rub at her, now.

She looks at the few things she tried to draw. A butterfly that was passable if you were six. She was twelve, maybe thirteen at the time. A wineglass that looked like she'd had a few herself before attempting it. She wanted to draw because her brother Scott could. He must have got the skill from his father, who wasn't Octavian.

A book report she wrote on *The Catcher in the Rye* by J. D. Salinger that earned her an A plus and the comment: 'Written with considerable flair and insight. Well done!' She remembers the feeling of reading those words. Remembers pulling the paper to her chest, sleeping with it beside her.

When she showed it to her mother, she said, 'Good, but your math skills aren't what they could be.'

She remembers that vividly, too. She might have had a way with words, but her mother did, too.

She flips another page, sees an article the local paper had written about her father paying for lights and scoreboard and uniforms for the Little League field. She scans the photos to see if Scott is in the group of kids, all in their uniforms. But he'd have been too old for the team. She wonders why her father was involved.

Pictures from a family trip to Disney World. Caroline

already a head taller than her mother, Peyton standing in front of her, squinting from the sun. She thinks they had fun, but she can't quite remember, even though she'd been eight at the time.

Next, she sees a copy of a poem she wrote about an empty room that was published in the school paper then picked up by the newspaper. She still knows it by heart but reads it anyway, the words moving on her lips as she turns the page.

A photo appears. She knows it's not possible, but it feels like her heart skips.

Everyone from the Fort knew the picture well. A little girl smiling up at a camera. It's cropped, but Peyton has seen so many versions of it, she knows she's holding a puppy in her lap. This version is black-and-white, clipped from the paper, but in her mind she clearly sees the pink of her T-shirt. That picture had been everywhere one summer. On telephone poles and in shop windows. If she closes her eyes, she can go straight back to that weekend in July when Daisy Wright, who was the same age as Peyton, disappeared.

She remembers her father sitting with the paper, shaking his head, the disappearance a betrayal of the land he loved so much. Remembers Scott going out searching. Both her parents had been gone a lot. She remembers that, too.

She's cold again, a different kind of cold than when she stepped from the water. This is a cold that comes from inside, from a memory of a bad time, a confusing time. A scary time. Peyton fears falling into it. It's been twenty-five years since she disappeared, and still no one knows what happened to Daisy Wright.

She looks around the room as though someone might have appeared, be getting ready to grab her. She lets out a breath.

Setting down the scrapbook, she crawls into bed with her phone. And she starts to search for updates to the Daisy Wright case.

4

Eualla

August, Tennessee, 1965

At the start of August, Debbie stops coming to the house. Eualla waits for her, saving the Dr Peppers her daddy bought, but after a week of walking to the road and looking into the distance for her best friend, she opens them one afternoon and shares them with Minnie.

Mama and Daddy are fighting so much, it's good Debbie isn't here. Eualla has her hands full taking care of Minnie, trying to protect her from the loud words, the crashes from their bedroom, the door slamming and Daddy peeling out the drive, kicking up dust and rocks. She wishes she had someone to talk to, but what would she say? She's not sure what's happening anymore.

It's mid-August when Mama and Daddy stop fighting. Mama seems to stay in her room a lot, so Eualla takes Minnie to the quarry or they sit in the villa. Daddy never did finish the roof, so Eualla draped the old sheet over the part he didn't do. It's now brown from dust, the cotton thin from the relentless sunshine.

Mama seems to be getting skinnier and skinnier. She doesn't talk much anymore, never laughs. Mama, who used to put on a record and dance around the kitchen. When Eualla takes her meals to her, she sees dark smudges of purple under her eyes. She thought at first they were bruises, but they're getting worse, not better.

Eualla has taken over the cooking. She's getting good at making grits, but that's like making oatmeal, adding stuff from a bag to boiling water and stirring. Today she thinks she'll do something else. Maybe she'll fry some chicken and make some coleslaw. She rummages around in the kitchen and gets to work. There's not much cabbage, so she adds some cucumbers and tomatoes. She's looking for pepper, when Mama comes into the small kitchen, sits at the table and watches.

'Are you feeling better, Mama?' Eualla asks.

'A little, Eualla, thanks.' There's a pause and then she says, 'I wish I hadn't named you that. I should have called you Kimberly. Or Susan. A nice, real name.'

'But my name is real,' Eualla says.

'I thought it so pretty at the time.'

'It is. I like my name.' Eualla's heart is banging in her chest. Mama sounds like she's talking in her sleep, not making any sense.

Her mama stands and walks over to her. 'I'm sorry there's no money for school clothes.' She kisses the top of Eualla's head. 'I'm sorry,' she repeats, before turning and shuffling back to her room.

Eualla hears the door shut.

*

It's Labor Day weekend, the start of September, and Eualla is scared. Something isn't right. Daddy seems to be drinking more. Jimmy's gone most of the time, working at the mill, filling in when they're busy. Eualla hates it when he comes back. Each time, he seems bigger. And he's always so angry, everyone tiptoes around him.

What scares her most is that after a summer of not doing much, for the last week Mama has had more energy than ten people. She's moving around the kitchen like she's in a race. The house is clean. All their clothes, what they have at least, too.

The night before school starts, Mama calls Eualla into her room and tells her to sit down.

'Your Daddy isn't good with money. Makin' it or keepin' it.'

Eualla nods, unsure what to say or what she's being told.

She pulls out an envelope. 'I'm giving you this money. It's not much. I want you to hide it with your schoolbooks. Keep it safe and tell no one. Not even Minnie.'

Eualla feels something cold dance across her shoulders.

'You're a good girl, smart. Smart is more important than pretty. Use your brain. You got it from my side of the family.'

Eualla doesn't understand how she can use her brain outside school.

'And look after Minnie, hear? She's not like you or me. She's delicate.'

'Are you sick, Mama? You're scaring me.'

'No, I'm not sick. Well, yes and no. But no, you don't need to worry about my health. I just want you to grow up strong and right. Not waste yo' life on no man. Starting right now. So go take out the big skillet. I'm gonna show you how to make fried pies.'

'That's Minnie's favorite,' Eualla says. 'Mine, too.'

'Shoo now. I'll be there in a minute.'

Eualla hesitates, unsure if she should leave her. Something isn't right.

'What are you waiting for? Go.' Her mama waves her away.

Fear grows with each step as she heads for the kitchen. She's just not sure what she's afraid of. Then she remembers the envelope in her pocket. She goes to her room and hides the money in her school bag. Minnie is sitting on the floor in their room drawing a picture, singing to herself. Eualla watches her for a moment, then she goes back to the kitchen and assembles everything they need to make fried peach pies.

When they're ready, she calls Minnie to the table and they eat in silence. Eualla can't bring herself to swallow the soft peaches, the golden crust. She pushes the food around her plate as she waits to see what will happen next.

Mama makes breakfast for her and Minnie and packs them lunches. She walks them to the school bus stop, holding Minnie's hand. Eualla keeps looking at her mama, a sick feeling in her belly.

They stand by the side of the road, the three of them, Eualla watching their mama like she's trying to solve a riddle or commit her to memory. Mama has her hand on

Minnie's head, like she's blessing her youngest. As the bus comes into sight, her mother puts her arms around Eualla.

'Mama, don't.' She twists away, embarrassed, not wanting her friends to see.

'You watch out for your baby sister.'

'She'll be fine, Mama. First grade is about coloring and singing and having fun.'

'Take her hand on the bus steps,' she continues, her tone anxious.

Eualla has never heard Mama like this before. Something feels off. Feels wrong. She takes her sister's hand, steps onto the bus, but turns, looks back at the woman who is their mother, standing there, as indistinct as the breeze. She's afraid to go to school, to let her out of her sight.

'Go now,' Mama says. 'Go.'

Eualla nods, climbs the last step, feeling the stifled, sticky, heavy heat inside. She walks past the bus driver, pulling Minnie along behind her. Hears the door close. Feels the bus start to move as she sits in the last row of seats. It's just her and Minnie right now. She looks through the window, already coated with dirt from the roads. Standing in the middle of the dirt road is Mama, shielding her eyes from the sun and the dust as they pull away. She wants to tell the bus driver to stop, to run to her mama. But she can't do that. Why would she do that? Mama slowly disappears as the bus rattles along, picking up speed.

Eualla puts her arm around Minnie as she turns around in her seat, facing forward.

'When's Debbie's stop?' Minnie asks. 'I can't wait to see her again!'

But Debbie doesn't get on the bus. Eualla, who hasn't seen her best friend in a month, finds her suddenly missing her even more.

The sun is noticeably warmer after the half-hour ride. There's a lot of noise, kids excited to see one another, racing around the playground. Minnie isn't good with noise.

'I don't want to go, Eu,' she says.

Eualla bends so she can look her baby sister in the eyes. 'You're gonna have so much fun! You won't want the day to end. Trust me.'

'I'll come check on you at lunch and Mama will be here before you know it.'

The teacher walks over to them and takes Minnie's hand. 'She'll be fine,' she says over her shoulder.

Eualla feels her heart squeeze. She hopes so. She waves to her one last time, then walks to her own classroom, on the other side of the school.

Eualla is as nervous as Minnie. Mama acting strange, Daddy being gone, Minnie being so scared, and now, she has no idea if her friend will sit with her or not.

In the classroom, Eualla sees them all gathered, laughing, and it hurts. She tells herself it'll be OK. The days of Pigeon Forge are over and they're all together again. Mama had been sad lately, but she'd be fine. She was Mama – funny, happy, full of life. Eualla bet when she got back from school, she'd be sitting there with sweet tea and a plate of cookies.

At least, she hopes so. They're packing up their books and getting ready to catch the bus, when Eualla's homeroom teacher appears beside her.

'The principal wants to see you,' she says.

Eualla, whose been nervous all day, is scared now. She feels Debbie look at her, everyone looks at her. But her friend stays away. Has all day, despite sitting in the desk beside her.

'Now, Eualla,' her teacher says.

Eualla throws her bag over her shoulder and walks down the hall as fast as she can without running. When she gets to the principal's office, she sees Minnie's teacher. She gives Eualla a concerned look. One of sympathy. Eualla is terrified something has happened to her sister.

'We called your house, but there was no answer. No one came to pick her up,' the principal says.

And there, sitting in the corner in the too-big chair, eyes red and tearful, is Minnie.

The sick feeling she had earlier in the day returns and intensifies. There's no way they could have called home – they don't have a phone. But Mama was supposed to pick up Minnie. She was gonna walk, if Daddy wasn't home.

'Come on, Minnie. You'll take the bus with me,' Eualla says. 'We're gonna have to run, though.' She grabs her small hand, half pulling Minnie along, racing through the halls to the exit, the parking lot, the bus stop. She feels sick, from the running, from the heat. From the fear. Mama, so skinny, acting so strange, on her own all day. Forgetting Minnie.

'Eu, not so fast.'

'We gotta run or we'll miss the bus.'

The bus is pulling away as they walk out the door.

'Scratch that. We're gonna have to walk,' she says.

They set off, Eualla carrying both their bags. It's early September, but the sun doesn't know that and is still frying everything in its path, including the two girls, both scared but for different reasons, walking along the side of the road.

'Why didn't Mama come?' Minnie asks.

Eualla can hear the sniffles in her voice. Part of her wants to comfort her, part of her is tired of her weakness and part of her just wants to get home and find out what's happening.

'I'm thirsty, Eu,' Minnie says.

'I know. Me, too.'

'Can't we get a drink?'

'Can't. Don't have any...' Eualla stops, remembering the cash in her bag. It's supposed to be for emergencies. She figures dying of thirst counts. 'Come on.'

They go into the diner, take seats at the counter. Dot, the waitress, shuffles over to them. She's old but works at the diner most days.

'Can we each have a sweet tea and a slice of peach pie for Minnie, please?'

'For real, Eu?' Minnie sits up in her chair.

'For real.'

As Minnie eats her pie, Eualla thinks about home. She doesn't want to go back. While they're here, eating pie, life is the same as it ever was. But once they get home, she knows it's going to be different. She doesn't know how, but she knows.

'You girls want anything else?'

'No, ma'am. Just the check, please.'

Eualla carefully looks in the bag and retrieves the envelope. She takes out a bill and pays.

'Golly. Where did you get that, Eu?'

'Hush, Minnie. It's my birthday money. Run and use the bathroom before we go.'

Minnie hesitates, scared.

'OK, I'll go with you.' She picks up both their bags and they walk through the diner to the small bathroom at the back.

Minnie is washing her hands when she says, 'Do you think Mama will be there when we get home?'

Eualla's insides seem to lurch and scramble at the same time.

'She'll be home,' she says, smiling too brightly.

'But what if...' Minnie takes her hand.

Eualla's heart squeezes.

'Let's just see, OK?'

They walk in silence, enveloped in a cocoon of scorching heat and fear of what's to come. With each step, Eualla tries to reassure herself – of course Mama will be there. Or maybe she's at the school now, wondering where her girls are, worried about them. But there's only two roads in this town, so it's impossible they missed each other.

'I need to go potty again,' Minnie says when they're halfway between the diner and home.

Eualla looks around.

'Go in the field.'

'They's snakes.'

'Shuffle your feet. They'll scoot. If you have to go, then go.'

Eualla turns her back to her sister and looks toward home – a faint, hazy box in the distance. For the first time, she looks at it critically, like someone driving by might see it. She can't see the porch from here, but she knows it sags in the middle. The paint is only a memory, the wood warped by time and weather. It's not so much a house as a shack. She's never seen it this way before.

Minnie walks up to her.

'Did you wipe?'

'Didn't have nothin'.'

They keep walking. Eualla hears her heart beating louder with each step. Can almost feel it. Daddy's truck is gone. That doesn't mean much, though. Mama's always around even when Daddy isn't.

But as they walk up the lane, Eualla knows. The house has an empty feel, even from the outside. She opens the back door, goes inside. They're quiet, Minnie almost pressed to the back of her as though she, too, knows something is wrong. Or maybe she's just being her normal frightened self.

Eualla walks through the entire house, doesn't take but a minute but each step feels like it takes hours, days even.

No Mama. No one.

'Go sit at the table. Draw me a picture,' she says.

Eualla takes out one of her books and pulls out a sheet of paper. She sets it in front of her sister and watches as Minnie pulls her new crayons from her school bag.

'Draw me something pretty,' she says.

Minnie nods, looking at her crayons carefully before selecting a soft blue color.

Eualla watches her for a second, trying to appear calm and normal, then she slowly walks away, scanning the floor, the furniture, the walls as she moves softly, looking for clues, as though the drapes might know what's happening, spring to life and tell her.

Through the living room, to the tiny hall, left down to her parents' room. Eualla knocks, barely making a noise. The door isn't closed and the light touch of her hand pushes it open.

From where she's standing, she can see the bed is made, the old white bedspread hanging evenly on each side. The blinds are drawn, but sunlight falls through the cracks of the old slats. She moves further into the room, watching, listening, as though her mama might appear and demand to know what she's doing. She and Minnie don't go into their parents' room. Even when Minnie is scared at night, she crawls in with her.

Eualla walks to the tiny closet where Mama keeps her clothes. She knows she'll have an answer when she opens the door. She waits, unsure what to do.

Please, Mama, don't have left me and Minnie. Please.

But even before she opens the door, she knows. She holds the handle, for a second, maybe two, like a small delay can change what's happening. Then she opens the door.

Some old hangers. An empty shoe box without the lid. And swaying gently in the vacuum created by the opening door, the dress she was wearing that first day of summer that made her look like a ghost.

Eualla is sure she's stopped breathing.

Turning, she closes the door and looks at the dresser. Her mama's silver brush and mirror that she got from her own parents when she turned sixteen are gone. She opens the drawers and sees an old cashmere sweater, Eualla's favorite because it's so soft, an old pair of black pants. Heavy clothes, winter clothes. She wonders if Mama left them because she plans to come back when the weather changes. But she doubts it.

She sits on the edge of the bed, looks around the room. It feels like twilight, maybe because of the way the blinds are filtering the light. Maybe because her life as she knows it has changed.

She hears a noise from the kitchen. Minnie wanting something. She gets up and goes to her sister. Minnie is standing on a chair looking in the cupboards.

'What are you looking for?'

'The gun Mama keeps behind her bread bowl is gone.'

At first Eualla isn't sure she's heard right.

'What did you say?'

'The gun. It's gone.'

'Minnie, you're talkin' crazy. Mama never had a gun.'

'She did. The one her daddy brought back from the war.'

'Show me where she kept it,' Eualla says, heart racing for a new reason.

Minnie gets up on the chair and then climbs onto the counter. Eualla moves behind her, afraid she might fall or the counter collapse. Minnie picks up the big orange bowl Mama used when she baked bread. She lifts it out and hands it to Eualla, then stands on tiptoes and peers into the cabinet.

'See? Empty.'

'Get down.'

She lifts Minnie to the floor, staggered by how little she weighs, and stands on the chair herself. She opens all the cabinets, looking for a gun she's not even sure exists. There's nothing but some old dry lining paper. But she can see where something has disturbed the dust.

She steps back down to the floor.

'When did you see a gun?'

'Lots of times.'

'Like when?' her voice is firm, demanding.

'Why you mad at me, Eu? I'm just saying what I seen. Mama kept the gun there. She said it was to keep us safe when Daddy was away. She said not to tell anyone where she kept it. And I didn't, neither, till now.'

Minnie has tears in her eyes and Eualla feels like crying herself. Mama gone and now she finds out she hid a gun in the kitchen. Why? Minnie was tender, fragile, unlike others. She saw things, knew things. Eualla always thought it was because she was so small, people forgot she was there, or that they thought her size meant she was powerless. Even though it seems crazy, if Minnie says Mama had a gun hidden in the kitchen, she believes her.

'She's gone, right, Eualla? She's upped and went and she took the gun. Now how we gonna be safe?'

Eualla thinks hard. Whatever she says to Minnie will knock around in that small head of hers for years.

'It seems that way, Minnie. But she might come back. You never know.'

Minnie picks up one of the crayons lying on the table and, grasping it in both hands, snaps it in two. It seems to take all the strength she has to snap a simple wax crayon. Eualla knows it will fall to her to keep them both safe.

'It's OK to cry, Minnie. Cry as much as you want tonight. But tomorrow, when we go to school, don't tell a soul what's happened. Smile and pretend everything's perfect. You hear me?'

Minnie nods. 'Just promise you won't leave, Eu. Promise you won't leave me alone in this terrible place by mahself.'

'Ah, this place ain't so bad.'

She says ain't deliberately. Mama hated when they used that word. Said it wasn't a real word and it was low-class. Eualla uses it thinking if anything pulled their mama back, it would be to tell Eualla not to use that word.

But nothing happens.

'When will Daddy be home?' Minnie asks.

'I dunno, Minnie. Let's just worry about ourselves right now, OK?'

Minnie nods and goes back to drawing. Eualla watches her. She can tell when Minnie is concentrating, absorbed in one of the little worlds she creates of fairies and dragonflies and dancing elves. While Minnie is occupied, it gives her space to think.

Eualla takes some food out of the refrigerator and fixes two plates, one each. Then she covers the rest up tight, knowing it might have to feed them for a spell.

5

June, Maine, Present day

'What are your plans for the summer?' her mother asks one early morning when Peyton is pouring herself a cup of coffee.

She's been home for almost two weeks. Too long for a houseguest but not quite a settling in period for a new roommate. She figures her mother wants to put her in a category of some kind. Her mother was big on organisation and labelling things. And people.

Peyton has rarely left her room, other than for meals. She spends her time looking at her old belongings, things she never took with her but were too important to throw out. Yearbooks, cards and letters she's held on to. Mostly she looks at her scrapbooks. Funny, since she had almost forgotten about those. They feel important now, in a way. She finds them comforting.

Peyton looks out the window. She hadn't really thought

that far ahead. Getting on a plane, getting to Maine, felt like such an achievement. Like all she had to do was change coasts and everything would sort itself out. She looks away from the window, almost surprised to see her mother looking at her. Waiting. Right. She'd asked a question. What was it?

'I hadn't thought that far ahead. I guess I can get a job. Maybe something at the yacht club?' Peyton starts to add milk to her coffee, then stops. She likes how dark it looks in the mug.

'Good lord Peyton, getting a job? How long do you plan to be here?' Her mother is shaking her head. 'No, you don't need to get a job. You need to get your health sorted, regroup, and move forward. You need a plan for the rest of your life. Not just the summer.'

Her mother turns on her heel and starts to walk away.

'And you really need to get a haircut. Do that. This week.' Her mother commands. 'And buy some better clothes. Everything you own is black. That might work in Seattle, but not here.' She feels her mother studying her. 'Buy something pretty, in blue. Your legs still look good. Show them off.' She opens her bag, the same Chanel bag she's carried her entire life. Peyton remembers playing with the chain on it when she was young. She takes out some cash, counts it, and leaves it on the counter, between them. Peyton has enough money in her account to buy some clothes. She just doesn't have any desire to go shopping, to get anything new. But she knows, by the way her mother is looking at her, that this is part of the deal. Yes, she could move home, but she has a role to play now. And it's not of the crazy hermit daughter with the wild hair.

Peyton feels nervous at this. At everything. She hasn't left the house since her crazy night swim. It's like she's getting used to the space again, the creature comforts she didn't have at her condo. The bathroom here is like a spa, with a jacuzzi, a shower with three heads. The floor is heated. The shower curtain had fallen off the wall at her place in Seattle months ago, and she'd never bothered to have it reinstalled, just turned the nozzle toward the wall and put towels on the floor. She thinks for a second, wondering if she left them there. She can't remember.

She can't imagine putting her mother's towels on the floor.

'I'm serious, Peyton. A haircut, and stop dressing like the grim reaper.' She points to the French doors that lead outside. 'There's a big, long beach there, I'm sure you remember it from your recent swim? Get outside and go for a walk. A long walk, on the sand. It's good for your bottom half.' She pauses. 'And buy yourself some lipstick. You need some color. You're all washed out.'

Her mother turns on her heel, walks towards the door. Peyton hears it shut behind her.

Bad hair, pale, out of shape. Yup, she's home.

She finishes her coffee, pours another cup, then takes a shower. She pulls on a pair of jeans and a black sweatshirt and heads down to the beach.

Her father has had the steps fixed, ready for another year. She never saw or heard the workmen, but then, she'd been sleeping a lot.

The sand feels familiar and foreign under her feet. She tries to remember the last time she walked this strip of shoreline as an adult. It's been years. Two or three at least.

She remembers having had big plans to bring Marco for a visit, in the early days when she was smitten. She doesn't want to think about that now.

She feels herself start to sweat, can feel the change in her breathing from pushing through the sand. God, her mother is right. She is out of shape. She didn't realise. She knew she'd put on weight, but she'd always been so thin, she didn't think it mattered. But that's not the issue. It's being out of shape. She's surprised, and as though she can magically fix the issue all at once, she walks faster, heading toward town, where the beach will soon be busy, filling up more and more as the heat builds, hits, driving people to seek the comfort of the ocean breeze, the cold water. The beach by their house was never busy. People thought her family owned it. Or maybe they just had the good sense to stay away.

She is sweating as she hits Sunset beach, the name given the main area around the pier. She sees it now, rising from the water, a behemoth of structure. In guidebooks it's called a quay, but to locals it's just the pier. A tourist trap with a casino, video games, restaurants boasting the best view in Maine. Every place with an ocean view made that claim. She laughs as she walks past it, smelling the cotton candy, the doughnuts, the sugary sweetness from the bakery she knows is next to the arcade. She slows, her sudden resolve evaporating like the foam on the water. She pictures the cinnamon buns, gooey and moist and slathered in thick frosting. She can feel herself moving toward the aromas, like she's being pulled there. But then, something happens. She's never liked the pier. Her father called it an abomination. Her mother called it vulgar. Maybe that's why she turns away, resumes walking. But deep down she knows the real reason. Her mother might be on her way to Portland, sixty miles away, but Peyton knows if she goes to the bakery, she will know. Her mother knows everything. Always has. It's like she has spies following her. Following all of them.

Crossing the beach, she moves up the stairs that lead to the town. There's a hair salon she remembers. She went there a few times in high school. It's open, and she walks in. She might as well get it over with, both the haircut and meeting people from her past. Two birds with one stone.

'Peyton Winchester! As I live and breathe! I heard you were back.'

She can't be certain, but she thinks it's the same woman who cut her hair, all those years ago. Her mother would remember. Peyton likes to forget.

'I need to get a few inches chopped off,' she says.

'Take a seat.'

Peyton sits in the familiar blue vinyl chair.

'So, you here visiting your folks?'

Peyton can feel herself tense. She's going to get a lot of this, people chatting, asking after her family. That's what they did, in the Fort.

She suddenly misses Seattle, and the guy who cut her hair who never said anything that wasn't hair related. The Fort may have its charms, but there's charm in anonymity, too.

'I'm here for the summer,' she says. 'I just couldn't survive without another Maine summer.'

As she says it she realises it's the truth.

★

She feels lighter, after her haircut. When she catches sight of herself in shops windows as she walks by, she can't get over how different she looks. Her mother, as usual, was right. A good haircut would make her feel better. A walk on the beach, too. There's a small shop her mother likes, doesn't cater to tourists. No tacky T-shirts. Owned by a woman who is married to her dad's architect, or something like that. She finds the shop easily, and lets herself in.

'Peyton Winchester! Is that you?'

Here we go again, she thinks.

'You got your hair cut,' her father says, when he sees her. Men, she's been told, don't usually notice such things. But her father is not most men.

She's wearing a new soft blue sweater and a pair of loose trousers the woman at the shop picked out for her. She hadn't wanted to go shopping, but once she was there, she had fun. It was nice, being fussed over, having someone help her choose styles that suited her. Her outsides are looking better, but her insides are still as tangled up as a string of old Christmas lights.

'I did,' she says. Her father is back from Portland, settling in with his stack of books on his favorite chair in the lounge. There's a golden kind of light spilling in through the windows, a light she knows won't last much longer, the honey light of late Spring.

'I'm going for a walk on the beach, dad. When I get back, I'll figure something out for supper.'

He looks up from his book. 'Sounds good, sweetheart.'

6

Eualla

January, Tennessee, 1966

Eualla was cold. Very cold. The house hadn't been built for cold weather. It wasn't built for strong winds or harsh rains, either. Nor was it built, she thought, to house a happy family. If it was, it must have been sorely disappointed by its current inhabitants.

It was January, first day after the Christmas vacation, and Tennessee was having a brutal cold snap. There was no fire in the stove. Mama was still gone and she had no idea where Daddy and Jimmy were. Maybe off hunting. Maybe off drinking. The fact that it was a cold winter's morning made no difference.

Eualla sighs and gets out of bed, already wearing wool work socks and long johns under her flannel nightgown. The floor feels to have stiffened in the freezing night air and she wonders if it'll splinter under her. She needs to light a fire. The one from the night before has gone out. She wishes now she'd gotten up to keep it going. It's easier to keep a fire burning than to light one from scratch.

She moves quietly, not wanting to wake her little sister. Her breath falls in a cold mist, hanging like a bad omen in front of her as she makes her way to the kitchen. She opens the door to the wood stove and pokes the ashes, even though they're stone cold, still hoping they might spring to life. No luck. She sets in some balled-up newspaper, strikes a match and says a prayer it'll light. She looks around for some kindling and some wood. Of course, there isn't any. She feels a spike of anger in her heart.

She pulls on the rubber boots by the door and steps outside. The air is white with frost, the ground, too. It would be beautiful if it wasn't so cold, a sparkling world best observed through a window in a warm house with a mug of something thick, sweet and hot.

She trudges to the shed where the wood is stored, shoves at the door with all her might. It's frozen shut and she pushes hard until it gives with a suddenness that has her stumbling forward, landing on her knees in a frozen puddle on the uneven wooden floor. The pain shoots through her, reminding her that things that hurt, sources of suffering, are everywhere.

She scrambles to stand and takes a deep breath, greeted by more cold and dead air. The smell of decay she associates with the shed isn't as strong as usual and she wonders if the very stench has frozen. If so, she's grateful the cold has deadened some of the smell.

Cobwebs, stale air and the rusty patch in the middle of the floor from where her daddy guts his kills loom in the gray void around her. She looks away, walks toward the stack of wood in the corner. She pulls up three pieces, all she can carry. She can feel splinters digging into her arms, through all the useless layers she's wearing, but she doesn't care.

Back across the yard, to the house, her sister now waiting for her at the door. Eualla is certain the girl can sense when she's more than ten feet away. She drops the wood with a bang, then trudges back for another armload, and another. Might as well do it all now. It'll be dark after school.

When she's done, she kicks off the rubber boots with a defiant flick of her foot. The noise they make hitting the floor surprises her. Minnie's beside her, eyes wide in alarm, in fright.

'Go back to bed, Minnie. Stay warm until I get the fire going.'

'But I wanna help.'

'You can help me most by not gettin' sick.'

Minnie turns and runs back to her bed.

The little bit of kindling is burning and it gives her hope. She throws the wood into the stove, praying it catches, considering how damp it is. Then she goes to the kitchen and boils the kettle. There's a bit of instant coffee left. She mixes it with sugar and makes two mugs, carrying them to the bedroom she shares with her sister. Minnie's too young for coffee, but it's all there is. Daddy's been gone for six days now, clean through New Year's Day. No dancing with Mama on New Year's Eve. She missed that the most. She sighs. There's not much to eat and they've been all alone. What a merry Christmas it was.

She thinks about taking the day off school – it's a long walk and it's so cold. But school will be warmer. And she likes to learn, likes to read. She loves numbers, how exact they are. She likes to be at school. And she wants Minnie to be at school, too. She looks around the tiny room she remembers her mother once calling the parlor. A pretty word for an ugly space, she thinks now. Yes, school is definitely better.

They drink the hot liquid, share the last slice of stale bread. There's no butter, nothing to put on it. It's too cold for much of a wash, since they can't get hot water.

'Get dressed – warm as you can. It's time to go,' Eualla says.

'It's so cold,' Minnie repeats, walking close to Eualla. 'You sure we won't see bears? What about polar bears?'

'Bears is sleeping. Polar bears live by Santa Claus and in Canada, I think. You'll never see a polar bear here – they like it real cold. Like freeze-your-arms-off cold.'

'You sure?'

'I am. Besides, don't think about that. Look at how pretty the snow is, how it sorta shines under the sun.'

They wait and wait but the bus doesn't show. They're the only ones who use this stop and she thinks the driver forgot. He probably doesn't care, either.

'We gotta walk. No bus today,' she says.

They trudge along, getting warmer with each step. They're sweating when they reach school. Eualla drops Minnie off and makes her way to her own class. Some of the seats are empty, the snow keeping kids at home.

Debbie is already in her seat, hair smooth and perfect, a new pencil case on the corner of her desk. Her daddy probably drove her. He has a shiny new truck. Eualla waves to her and of course Debbie sees, but she dips her head, like she's looking for something. Eualla gets a funny feeling in her belly. Could be hunger. She moves to her desk. But something happens. Her old friend moves away from her, recoils.

'Hey, Debbie,' she says, confused, but Debbie just nods, like she's an old acquaintance she can't place, wasn't once her very best friend ever.

As Eualla takes out her workbook, she feels something at the back of her head. Someone has thrown a pencil at her.

Suddenly, she's scared. She doesn't know what's happening. Things have been different since school started, Debbie making different friends, but they still talked, sorta. This feels different. Like she has a target on her.

Eualla slides Debbie a note saying, 'Did you have a nice Christmas?', but Debbie crumples it up and drops it beside her desk without reading it.

Eualla looks around the classroom. Everyone is wearing new clothes. Santa brought them, or parents pretending to be Santa. There wasn't much at their house. Some drawing pads, cheap, from Rexall's. Some pencils. A pair of mittens for Minnie. A box of hard candy. Whatever Daddy picked up at the last minute when he was drunk.

At lunch she waits, just for a second, to see what Debbie does. But Debbie takes off like she's trying to outrace a fire and Eualla knows enough not to follow. In the small gymnasium that's also the cafeteria, she sits alone, trying to figure out what's happening. She's known these kids forever. They've all been at school as one big group. But no one's looking at her. No one speaking to her. About her, yes, she can tell that.

When she returns after lunch, Debbie has moved her desk.

Now, Eualla is sitting alone. She tries to smile at her friend, who turns her back on her. She sees her teacher's eyes dart from her to the other students and back to her throughout the day. Eualla knows something is wrong. She's heard talk of a party over Christmas. She wasn't invited. Did they all decide to shut her out, then? But why?

She tries again to talk to Debbie after school, but the other girls, Pam and Darlene, all seem to form a circle around her, laughing. She thinks she sees Darlene sneer. Darlene's never been nice. Eualla feels like she's gonna cry.

She turns away from the girls and goes to collect Minnie, who waits in her classroom for her each day. Eualla takes her hand. They never hold hands and Eualla tries to be calm, normal, not wanting to upset Minnie. She walks slowly, deliberately, so they can miss the bus. She can't face anymore today.

Minnie talks and talks about her day. How they got to use clay. How they painted with sponges. How nice it was to see everyone after the Christmas vacation.

'I have new letters to practice, too,' she says.

'Sure,' Eualla says, hearing her but not really processing what Minnie is saying.

She's confused about what happened at school. At what happened with Debbie. Before long, though, she stops worrying about Debbie and starts worrying about what's happening at home. Worries about both things, together. She's running out of space to worry.

She looks for tracks in the snow, to see if Daddy is back. She can't see nothin'. Anything. Oh, God, she's tired. And hungry. And upset. There's no truck in the yard, and Eualla is both relieved and angry. They need food, but she hates when Daddy and Jimmy are home. Daddy's been drinking more since Mama left. He's a fool, but Jimmy is a mean drunk, and she hates them both.

She doesn't need to open the door to know the fire has gone out. She pushes it open. It's colder than ever.

'I'll start the fire. We'll have soup.'

Eualla gets the fire burning hot and opens the can. She adds more water than it says, wanting to make it last. She hunts through the refrigerator and the cupboards, looking for something, anything, to add. Then she sits Minnie down and in the quiet, with the fire blazing, they do their homework. For the first time, Eualla finds it hard to concentrate.

After Minnie goes to bed, Eualla goes through her own books, looking for her favorite bookmark. She got it at a fair in Pigeon Forge. It's bright red, with a black bull charging, as if coming out of the cardboard it's made of. There's a red tassel and black studs along the borders. One is missing. She strokes it, fingers the silkiness of the tassel. Then she puts it in her bookbag and starts writing a note to Debbie.

In the morning, the house feels cold enough for the walls to splinter. The sun hasn't appeared and the sky is dull and dark. The fire is smouldering; Eualla had gotten up in the night to feed it. She'd curled up on the old couch as she prayed for the flames to come to life, to burn hot and keep them alive. Why, she's not sure, except there's gotta be something good coming soon. Can't be worse, she thinks. She feeds it more wood and hopes, hard, for a better day. Then she wakes Minnie.

She feels a knot in her stomach about going to school. This is new to her. School has always been safer than home.

Eualla walks into class and feels the silence of her entry, like everyone stops what they're doing to stare at her. She feels herself shaking and hopes no one sees how scared she is.

Then she sees it.

Her desk is completely on its own today, the other ones moved away, a little protective fort around Debbie. She feels sick to her stomach as she sits by herself. She opens her bag and sees the note she wrote to her friend – the one she spent long days in the sun with, had imaginary tea parties with. The friend who gave her pretty blue stationery for her birthday just last year.

Eualla's hand touches the note, written on that paper, and the bookmark, her favorite possession. She stuffs it down inside her bag as she takes out her math books. Her hands are shaking and she drops her pencil on the floor. It rolls ahead. She leaves it where it is and takes out another.

Math class is always the same. The teacher spends the first ten minutes showing them something, then they work on their own as the teacher moves up and down the aisles, studying what they're doing. The teacher generally spends little time with Eualla, who's very good at math. Today she lingers, studies what Eualla is doing, even though she knows it's correct. Eualla gets the feeling she's standing close not because of her work, but out of worry. Kindness? The teacher knows something is happening. Eualla is embarrassed.

The lunch bell goes and Eualla thinks for a second, then she takes the note and the bookmark and puts them in

Debbie's desk. Hopes her friend sees them and tells her nothing is wrong, and everything goes back to normal.

In the cafeteria, she eats lunch by herself, then goes to the tiny library in the school and pulls out a book. She looks at the words but they seem to swim – she can't nail them down. Her heart is beating so hard, it's like it wants to jump out of her chest. It's the longest lunch break in the history of the world, Eualla is certain.

The bell goes at last and she closes her book and walks slowly back to the classroom. She takes her seat, walking past Debbie and Pam and Darlene.

On her chair is the note she wrote Debbie, crumpled into a ball. Beside it, cut into four pieces, is her bookmark. It feels for a second like her heart might come out of her mouth, like her eyes are on fire, her skin, too. Hurt, embarrassment, shame, a horrifying mix, bubble through her, like chemicals reacting in a beaker. She is the glass vessel.

She's sure everyone is watching as she picks up the notes and the pieces of her bookmark and pushes them inside her book bag. That afternoon, for the first time, Eualla Tompkins wishes she is anywhere but in her classroom at school.

7

Eualla

January, Tennessee, 1966

Eualla doesn't do her schoolwork that night. She doesn't make Minnie do hers, either. There's no food in the house. In the morning, the house is bitter cold. She doesn't have the energy to start a fire. She doesn't want to go to school.

Minnie is standing at the door, both their bags ready, an anxious look on her tiny face. They're both hungry and cold, but Minnie knows something is wrong with Eualla. In the deep fog of her brain, Eualla knows she must keep going for Minnie. Eualla wants to claw back time, to the start of the summer. Go to Pigeon Forge and look at clothes, if that's what her friend wants. She wants to beg Mama to stay. She wants to pull back everything that's disappeared.

She dresses in the warmest clothes she can find, makes Minnie put on another layer. They set off. She's carrying the same bag she had the day before, but it feels so heavy, like it's going to break her back. She can feel it rubbing against her spine.

She drops Minnie off, as usual, but her baby sister hesitates. Usually, she runs right into class. Today, she looks at Eualla like she's trying to stare her back to life, to read her mind, her heart.

'Go to class, Minnie,' she says. 'I'm sorry there's nothin' for lunch.'

Walking to her classroom, she thinks about leaving, heading into the woods, staying there until Minnie's bell. But it's too cold. She walks into the classroom and sees it immediately.

The girls are all wearing identical fluffy pink sweaters and bright yellow sweatshirts. Skirts and boots and light blue turtlenecks. Eualla is wearing a red-and-black check hunting jacket with green cord pants her mama used to wear when she was young. She felt fine when she put them on – now, she feels like a Christmas tree.

Shame crawls over her, like those wriggling white maggots she saw on the dead fox near their house. She tried to bury the poor animal but wasn't strong enough to pierce the ground with the shovel, so she threw some broken branches and leaves on it, thought about setting it on fire but didn't like the idea of burning things.

Now, she feels like that dead fox. No one wants to see it, smell it, know about it. People stare at it, fascinated, horrified, not like it was once a living thing. She puts her head down, making herself small – small so no one will look at her. But it doesn't work. The more she shrinks, the more they attack. She's hungry. She's scared. And she misses her friend. The one she used to play dolls with. The one she told all her secrets to. Except the one about her mama leaving. No one knew that.

Eualla leaves school quickly, grabbing Minnie by the hand, racing to the bus. If Daddy hasn't come home, they'll have to have water for dinner. There's nothing else in the house. They're fixing to starve.

When they get on the school bus, Eualla sits up front with Minnie, not at the back with those who were once her friends.

When she gets home, there's a bag of grits, some cornmeal, a loaf of bread on the counter. She makes the grits, sits Minnie down. Minnie's hair is in a state and as she eats, Eualla tries to fix it with her hands.

Eualla wishes she had someone she could talk to about her friends. About what's happening. She wishes Mama would come back and cook dinner and tell her how pretty she is. She remembers her first day of school and her mama walking her into class. Eualla was wearing a pale blue dress with little pink flowers and tennis shoes. Her hair was in a long braid. She was so excited to have a desk, a pencil box. In her school bag she had an orange *and* an apple. What she wouldn't give for an apple now.

She looks at Minnie and feels even worse. She's so little. How can Eualla protect her when she can't protect herself?

Eualla has stopped counting the days of how long Daddy and Jimmy have been gone. Maybe this time they won't come back, she thinks. Maybe they'll just leave supplies. That would be fine – if they left more.

For the second time, she's not done her homework. She was too tired and hungry.

She's shuffling into her classroom when the teacher says, 'Eualla, can you come with me for a moment?'

Eualla knows she hasn't done anything wrong. Nothing at all. Other than not doing her homework. Still, she's scared.

'Yes, ma'am,' she says, following behind.

The teacher is wearing a pink dress, just past her knee, with stockings and heels. Eualla thought it must be nice to have such pretty clothes. She has her purse over her shoulder, like she's leaving school. Eualla wonders if she's being kicked out.

She waits for her teacher to say, 'You don't fit in, no one likes you. You don't have pretty yellow sweaters. You need to go.'

She walks faster, even though it hurts her feet. Eualla isn't sure where they're going. As they pass the little office, she sees the secretary share a look with her teacher. What made adults think kids her age were stupid, and didn't see such things?

Her teacher opens the door to the break room. Eualla stops. They're not supposed to go in this room.

'Come on, come on,' her teacher urges.

The room is warm and smells like coffee, the real kind. She bets they have cream, too. She inhales deeply, pulling the aroma into her very lungs. Her teacher sees what she's doing and pours some into a cup, laces it with sugar and cream.

'Here, have some.'

As Eualla takes the cup, she sees the rings on her teacher's fingers, the pink polish on her nails. And she sees that her teacher, who she likes very much, is careful not to touch Eualla's own hands as she passes her the cup. Eualla has dirt under her nails. Shame wraps itself around her, a heavy blanket left out on the cold ground, needing to be washed.

As she watches, her teacher pulls a hairbrush out of her bag. It's wrapped in plastic and she tears it off.

'Come by the window, Eualla,' she says.

Eualla, still holding her cup, does. She's unsure what's happening.

Her teacher takes the brush and says, 'You're such a pretty girl. But your hair is in a state! My, my. You just can't go around looking like this, sweetie.'

Eualla wants to crawl under the school, curl up in a ball under the earth and flat out die. Hot tears form in her eyes, in her belly. In her heart.

The teacher starts to pull and it hurts, but not as bad as whatever has just entered her, consumed her body.

'Now, I want you to tell me. Is there food at home? Do y'all have enough to eat? Your sister, sweet little thing, she's at school here, too, I know. Is she OK?'

'Yes, ma'am. We have food, ma'am,' she lies.

'You're a very smart girl, Eualla. You can go anywhere. Do anything. This place is just a stop on the road for you. But presentation is important, too. How you look, what you show the world, is important.'

Eualla tries to nod, but her head is hurting from the pulling – and the rest of her is hurting from the shame.

'Now, I have a few other little things for you, too.' She hands Eualla a small white paper bag. 'Tonight, at home, clip your nails nice and short, like this.' She shows Eualla her own nails. 'Give them a good scrub.' She indicates a back and forth motion, as though Eualla doesn't know how to clean herself.

Eualla doesn't want to take the bag. She wants to turn and run out into the road. She wants to run into the cold until her skin blisters and peels from her very bones. Anything, anything would be better than the burning feeling of shame that's smothering her now.

'After school, come see me, OK?'

Eualla nods.

They walk back to the classroom, her teacher talking non-stop, a nervous chatter to fill the awkward space around them. Eualla gets back to class, takes her seat. They spend the afternoon learning about the American Civil War. The teacher reads, shows places on the map. People raise their hands. It's like any other afternoon, except Eualla feels the looks of her fellow students. She knows they're wondering what happened. Why they were gone so long. Why her hair looks different. What's in the little paper bag she shoved into her book bag.

Eualla knows, as she sits in her classroom, she'll forever be the girl who had her hair brushed by the teacher.

'What's in the bag, Eu?'

School is mercifully over and Eualla is picking up her sister. Her teacher has given her a large bag of things, closed at the top. It weighs a lot and is hard to carry.

'Something from my teacher. I'm not sure.'

'Why did she give it to you?'

'Don't know that, neither.'

They walk along. Eualla is tired and wants to take the bus, but it's worse than school, with everyone in a tight space, egging each other on to be mean. She says they're walking. The sky is gray but the deep freeze is breaking. It'll be easier to keep the house warm now.

'You're awful quiet, Eualla,' Minnie says as they're walking the long dirt road to their house.

Her sister is looking at her with wide, frightened eyes. Eualla feels mean to the core, to the bone, but she can't be mean to Minnie. She's sweet as molasses and weak as a kitten. Eualla knows she isn't meant for this world. She switches her bags to the other arm.

'Hush,' she says. And then she feels bad. 'I'm just thinking.' She hopes Minnie doesn't ask what about.

With each step, the earlier shame of the day changes – morphs, slips and slides until it hardens into something new. Resolve, touched with anger. Determination. A plan is forming. New ideas are coming. She can feel herself changing, becoming something different. Someone different.

When she gets home, she builds a fire, staring in the dirty glass door of the stove until it catches, feeding it until it roars. In the bathroom is a tub and she scrubs it clean, using baking soda because that's all they have. There's only cold water in the bathroom and she boils water on the stove, using a big cauldron she vaguely remembers her mama once used to make jam. It takes four trips, but she fills the tub, the steam warming the room.

'Alright. I'm getting in. You stay on the other side of the door until it's your turn.'

'It's Wednesday afternoon,' Minnie says. 'Why we taking baths? It's cold.'

'Hush now and close the door.'

Eualla steps into the bathtub. The water is hot, too hot. It burns, but she lowers herself carefully, holding her breath as though that'll help.

She tries not to think about what happened with her teacher, even as she looks at the contents of the paper bag she dumped on the old wooden chair by the bathtub: a nailbrush. Small scissors – for her nails, as well. Soap and a washcloth.

She picks up the soap and the cloth. Dips them both in the water and sets to scrubbing away the sweat, the dirt – and something else, too: the embarrassment of what's happened and the anger at what her life is. For the first time, Eualla truly understands how different they are, and she hates it. Hates her daddy for being a fool, and her mama for leaving and not taking them with her. She feels the anger and the hatred snap into place, like a new bone in her back, making her feel taller, stronger. She knows they'll be there forever, she can feel them become a part of her. She dunks under the water, holds her breath. Lathers her hair. She picks up the scissors and begins to cut her nails.

The water is a murky gray when she's done. She drains it, telling herself the old Eualla is floating down the drain. Then she wipes the bathtub, wraps her hair in a threadbare towel and boils more water for her sister.

'Your turn,' she says.

'But why, Eu? It's only Wednesday and it's so cold,' she repeats.

'Because from now on, whenever we leave this house, we both look clean and proper.'

Minnie has tears in her eyes, her response to pretty much

everything, but Eualla knows her little sister is scared. This is new and different, and Minnie isn't good with things being different. Eualla softens.

'Minnie, this isn't forever. One day, we're gonna leave this place. Have a nice house in a nice place.'

'You mean like Nashville?'

'Course, Nashville. Maybe even Texas! Or California!'

'Like where the stars live?'

'Exactly like the stars. There's no difference between them and us, except they all live in a nice place. Now scrub good, with soap and the cloth.'

Eualla goes to her bedroom and opens the bag her teacher gave her. There's more soap, a couple of bars. A couple of toothbrushes, one pink and one green, and toothpaste. She tips the contents on her bed. Counts four pairs of socks – two for her and two for Minnie. She moves them aside, stacking them neatly. Thick tights for her and long johns for Minnie, and undershirts.

She sees what was making the bag heavy – three tins of Spam. A bag of grits. She can feed Minnie for almost a week on what she sees, and a tiny bit of relief fills her. But it's what she sees next that makes her gasp. A pink sweater and a yellow turtleneck. She holds them against her chest. They're so beautiful.

She opens the chest of drawers in her room, puts the socks and the tights away. She looks at the food, takes out a precious tin of Spam and wishes so hard they had eggs. She hides the rest of the food under her new clothes. Then she goes to check on Minnie.

*

The kitchen is full of the smoky smell of frying tinned meat. Eualla is cooking it in a big dollop of lard, figures the extra fat will be good for Minnie. She divides the meat up, giving Minnie a bit extra. They'll have grits for breakfast. One less thing to worry over.

She banks the fire, sits with Minnie while she does her homework. Tests her with her spellings. Then she puts her to bed.

'When are you going to sleep?' Minnie asks.

'Soon. I have some things to do. Now sleep.'

When Minnie has settled, Eualla walks to her mama's room and opens the door. There's an eerie glow from the overhead light and the smell of her mama, some sort of flowery perfume and cold cream.

She makes her way to the old chest and opens the drawers. She takes out a cream cashmere sweater she saw the day her mama left. It'll do nicely in this cold weather. She finds a pair of jeans that may fit and some capri slacks that will be good come spring. Eualla thinks she must have left them for her.

She carries the clothes to her room and puts them away. She sits on her old bedspread, thinks about Debbie and how much she misses her, and how much she hurt her. Eualla had fallen once and broken her ankle. The pain of it as her mama dragged her up the steps had made her faint. Then, she was sure nothing in this world could hurt as much as a broken bone, but she knew differently now. The pain of being shunned by her best friend is worse. The friend she played with during summer vacation. The friend she shared stickers and books with.

She remembers going to Debbie's house and playing

with her doll collection. In her bedroom she had two big shelves of them. The ones on the top shelf were china dolls and they weren't allowed to play with them. Eualla was fine with that, as the dolls scared her, standing rigid in their boxes.

Sitting in her empty room now, she feels them looking at her, disdain in their black plastic eyes. One thing is certain: she'll never see Debbie's house or her china doll collection again. As of this moment, Debbie Hyde no longer exists for Eualla Tompkins. The part of her that had loved her friend is now gone. She won't be sad over what's happened anymore. Sadness is a germ, she's sure. Despair is lethal.

She crawls into bed and goes to sleep.

In the morning, Eualla makes breakfast, making sure Minnie eats, then brushes her teeth, brushes her hair, pulls it back in a neat ponytail. She's wearing Mama's cashmere turtleneck and she feels warm and pretty. It's a nice feeling. She uses the washcloth the teacher gave her to scrub her face again, leaving it pink. She makes sure Minnie does the same.

They walk to school, the same way they have hundreds of times, but today is different.

'Now you remember, Minnie. Be nice to everyone, but not too nice. No one deserves to be treated badly and no one deserves to be treated too good, either. The person you treat best in this life is you.'

'Whaddya mean, Eu?'

'What do you mean,' she corrects, then: 'People at school, some of them is mean.' She thinks for a second. 'Are mean. Mean because we don't have the same things they do. Mean for lots of reasons. That's fine. That means they don't like themselves.'

'Why would they be mean because they don't like thesselves?'

'It's hard to explain. I'm just working it out myself. But other people, they are who they are. You can't change that. Just be good to yourself. You're a good girl and you deserve it, OK?'

Eualla stops walking and looks at her sister, her small face, her big eyes. Her heart squeezes. It'll kill her if anyone treats Minnie the way Debbie's treated her.

She drops Minnie off, then walks slowly, purposefully to her classroom. She walks into class, head high, shoulders back. Her ponytail is loose after her walk, but she'll fix it when she sits. Timothy Johnson, who she's known since she was five, does a double take when he sees her. This makes her lift her head more, pull her shoulders back.

In class, when the teacher asks a question, Eualla knows the answer and says it without putting her hand up. At lunch, she goes to the library and reads, selecting a book from the shelf. Her teacher's word echo in her ears. She's not going to be here forever. When she looks out the window, she sees the girls in her grade gathered in a circle, laughing and giggling. Most are watching the boys play baseball. But once when she looks, she sees Debbie is looking toward the library. Toward her.

Eualla looks away.

After classes finish, she moves past the girls who were once her friends without a glance and is leaving, when her teacher calls her name. Everyone watches as she hands Eualla a book.

'You might like this. It was a bit much for me.'

'Thank you, ma'am. I'll read it tonight and get it back to you.'

'Keep it. I'm unlikely to read it.'

Eualla tucks it into her bag and heads out.

On the bus, Eualla sits with her sister, ignoring the girls in the back.

Minnie shows her a sticker she got on her worksheet.

'Isn't it beautiful, a flower of some kind,' Minnie says.

Eualla looks. It's some sort of lily, she thinks, remembering the days when getting stickers was a big deal.

'Very pretty,' she says.

Minnie is smart, like her. They're both going places, she knows. But right now, she's got to figure out what to feed them for dinner. Spam again, she guesses.

The bus drops them off at the stop and they start walking home. They haven't gone far when she hears it, the old engine labouring in the cold. The muffler that needs replacing. Their daddy drives right by in his pickup. Minnie runs ahead, excited. Eualla stands for a second and says a prayer to God he's got food and money. Then she follows Minnie to their home.

Eualla opens the door and sees both Jimmy and her daddy, sitting at the table, cans of beer stacked in front of them. Her heart sinks.

Minnie runs to Daddy and jumps into his arms. Eualla can't suss why she loves him so much. Course she did then, too, at her age. She'll learn.

She sees bags on the floor, food waiting for her to put away. Good. At least they can eat.

'Hey, girl,' her father says. 'How you two getting along?'

'Fine,' Eualla says.

'Fine, sir. Don't you talk to Daddy with no respect.'

'Hush, Jimmy,' Daddy says.

'I won't hush. Girl needs to learn her some manners.'

Eualla ignores her creepy older brother. Daddy brought eggs. Good. She can scramble some. She puts the food away and tells Minnie to start her homework. And she waits, watches. Hoping Jimmy will leave and she can talk to her daddy. About food, and money for school supplies, clothes. There's so much they both need.

The minutes tick by, then hours. They're both drunk.

Eualla goes to her bedroom, shoves towels at the bottom of the door to cut the noise. She checks on Minnie, who's sound asleep, hands clasped under her cheek like an angel. She climbs into her own bed, pulls the blankets over her and tries to think of better days until she falls asleep.

8

Peyton

May, Maine, Present day

Peyton is walking to the library when a police car pulls up beside her. Was she jaywalking? Do they ticket for that now?

She turns to look and her heart sinks. The blond hair, slightly long but pushed back, gel keeping it in place, the head ducked down to look out the rolled-down window.

'Peyton? Is that you?'

The deep, familiar voice.

'John Langley,' she says, her voice unnaturally high and cheerful.

They went to school together, but he was three years ahead of her. He was the nicest guy. Always smiling, affable. Got along with everyone. The guy who sat with the new kid, the outcasts, as easily as the hockey captain, who, Peyton remembers, was usually an asshole.

She waits as he pulls to the curb, turns off the ignition,

steps out and walks toward her. His uniform is pressed, a white t-shirt peeking out from under the button-down gray shirt. His name plate slightly tilted. She never took John for a uniform type.

He lifts his arms, just a bit, holds her elbows as he leans forward and kisses her on the cheek like an old acquaintance. Like a long-lost friend… like a gentleman. She feels a warmth spread through her at this gesture and realizes how lonely she's been.

'I heard you were back in town,' he says, stepping back.

'Can't keep a secret around here,' she laughs, too loud, wondering what exactly he's heard.

'How are things? You look good.'

'Thanks. You're a police officer here?'

'I am. Runs in the family, I guess.'

It takes Peyton a second to remember his father had been a police officer. The chief of police, when they were at school.

John was smart. Class president, going places, she remembers. She doesn't see him as a cop, more an FBI agent. Or a human rights lawyer. She's surprised he never made it out of the Fort.

'How is the family?'

She remembers, too late, his father is gone. A heart attack his last year in high school, she thinks. John probably stayed to be close to his mother. She braces herself for the list of calamities that seem to start befalling friends soon after university graduation.

'All good,' he says. 'Do you have time to grab a coffee?'

Peyton realizes she has all the time in the world. She'd been on her way to start researching a case that was almost twenty-five years old. Another few hours won't hurt.

They walk down to a café by the water, the sun shining in their eyes, bright despite her sunglasses. Peyton can hear the seagulls. Some people like them, but they've always made her nervous. They're too big and too loud. Her mother would say that they know their place.

'What will you have?' John says, taking his wallet from his back pocket.

'Black coffee, please.'

'That's it?'

She nods.

He returns with their order. They sit at a small table at the end of the pier and look out at the water.

'I heard there was a shark spotted nearby. That's new for this area,' she says.

'There was a fatal attack a while back. Global warming.'

'I like the idea of warmer winters here, so I guess the sharks are a trade-off.'

'You plan on being here when the snow falls?'

'No. Summer revamp only. I'm a total wimp when it comes to the cold.' It was one of the things she loved about Seattle. It rained a lot, but you didn't have to shovel the rain.

The coffee is hot. She sips slowly.

'Are you still dating... what was her name? Her family came over from Australia,' she says.

'Rani. No, it didn't work out. Nice girl, though. She's gone back to Oz. We keep in touch. You were in Seattle, weren't you?'

'I was.'

'So, this just a long visit?'

'Here for the summer. Spending time with my parents.

Trying to figure out some stuff. It doesn't sound too taxing, but it's a full-time job for me at the moment.'

He nods as though he understands and it makes her feel better. Lighter. Understood.

'What's Seattle like? I've never been.'

'It's nice. Fun. Urban. Hip. Not like the Fort. It's not cozy; it's polished.'

'Even with all the grunge music?'

'John, John, John. Grunge has been over for decades,' she laughs.

'I still like Pearl Jam.' He shrugs.

'I don't even know what's hip in music anymore.'

'I'm surprised. You were always into music. Artsy, always reading.'

'Was I?'

'That was your reputation.'

'I had a reputation?'

'In the best sense of the word.' He winks at her, and she feels a warmth not connected to the overhead sun.

She tucks this bit of information away to think about later. People probably thought she was spoiled, because of her family. Maybe she was. It depends on what you'd call spoiled.

They finish their coffee as the sun rises higher, making the day feel like it's really underway.

John looks at his watch. 'Duty calls. Do you want me to run you home?'

'No, thanks. I want to walk the beach as much as possible while I can.'

He takes out his phone. 'Let me get your number. You may want to get out of the house one evening.'

'I still have a Seattle number. Add me on WhatsApp.'

She doesn't have her phone with her. She's been trying to spend less time staring at the screen, hoping to hear from Marco, her boss, saying they made a horrible mistake, that sales had dropped off a cliff since she left, that her customers miss her, but there's been nothing.

She watches as John keys her number into his phone, his hands strong, his nails perfectly trimmed. Peyton always thought how a man kept his cuticles said a lot. Even with his head dipped, he's much taller than her, and she's five foot eight. His hair is thick and straight, and he pushes it back. She wonders how he'd look with a bandana or a headband. She thinks he'd look great. Or in a nice suit. But not a police uniform.

'It was nice running into you. Let me know if you need anything.' He brushes his hand along her arm.

Peyton feels a jolt, from his touch and from his words. His kindness.

'You OK?' John asks.

'Yea, fine,' she says. But something's happened. His voice. His words. She's heard them before. It's like another memory that is hiding from her, showing itself long enough just to frustrate her.

She walks to the beach, looks out at the water. Memories from high school stumble around her, banging into her before running away.

She stares at the water, trying not to think. She doesn't want to remember, not now. It's felt like that since she got back but running into John makes it more so. She got out. Now she's back. Did all the time away not mean anything?

She thinks about renting a boat. They used to own one,

but her father sold it a long time ago. It would be nice to be out on the water now, away from everything. She may not be going out at night, she may not be in contact with many people, but her memories are keeping her company. And like company you don't really want to visit, they seem to be everywhere now, with no intention of leaving.

Funny, she doesn't feel like going to the library now, or city hall. Her list of things to do can wait. She feels like going for a swim, but the water is still too cold. Her mother will be furious. She starts to walk home. She'll go, anyway.

9

Eualla

June, Tennessee, 1966

Eualla wakes with Jimmy standing at the foot of the bed. She can tell by the slouch of his shoulders he's drunk. And the only thing worse than sober Jimmy is drunk Jimmy.

Heart thumping, she looks over at Minnie. She's either asleep or pretending to be, her light cotton blanket still. There's barely a shape under it. Minnie seems even smaller since Mama left, almost a year ago, as small and fragile as the water sprites she likes to draw.

'What are you doin'?' Eualla hisses.

'I wanna sandwich. Get up and make me one.' He kicks the bottom of her bed, making her jump.

Eualla gets up, not wanting to wake Minnie, and walks to the open door, blood boiling with hatred and fear increasing with each step. She waits for Jimmy to follow her, stumbling as he does, and then closes the door behind her sister.

In the kitchen, she opens the cupboards, makes a show of looking for bread, taking her time, hoping he'll fall asleep.

'No bread. I can't make a sandwich. Why don't you have a glass of water and go to bed?'

'Fix me some beans, then.'

'We don't have any beans. Look for yourself.'

'Then fix me summat else.'

She gets an egg, adds water rather than milk, not wanting to waste food on him. She takes out one of the biscuits she made earlier and gets a plate. She wishes he were dead as she scrambles the egg and sets it on the fluffy white biscuit, slides the plate in front of him. She can tell by his eyes he's on something, but it's fading now. He's tired. She must remain calm until he falls asleep. This isn't the first time he's woken her to cook for him.

She turns her back on her brother, starts to walk away. Quick as a flash he grabs her arm, pushes her against the cheap wooden kitchen counter. She can feel it digging into her back.

'You think you is so good. You ain't nothin'.'

She keeps silent, knowing any response will antagonize him.

'You walkin' around here like you owns the place, but it's me an' Daddy what feeds you.'

'If that's the case, you might want to up your game, seeing as there's no bread for a sandwich and milk is a delicacy in this house.'

'What you say?'

He presses his arm against her shoulders, pushes her

further into the counter. She can't move. She's frantic, trying to figure out what to do. But she won't let him see that. She must stay quiet – she can't wake Minnie.

'Out of my way,' she says, pushing him off.

'What's happening? Whatcha doin', Jimmy?'

Minnie is standing behind them. When Jimmy looks at her, Eualla scrambles away. Pushing Minnie ahead of her, they go back to their room.

'What was Jimmy doing?'

'Hush,' Eualla says, putting her back to bed.

'But I don't get it.'

Eualla leans over her sister, her face unnaturally white in the darkness of the room, the only light the illumination from the glowing moon.

'Alcohol makes people do stupid things. Promise me you'll never drink.'

Then Eualla pushes a chair in front of the door, tries to calm her heart, and after a while, from pure exhaustion, she sleeps.

When they get home from the library the next day there's food on the table, including milk and also orange juice, the frozen kind, but Jimmy is nowhere to be found. Eualla exhales and starts organizing the food, so they eat the freshest first. She's worried about Minnie getting enough vitamins. She gets some potatoes and starts to cut them up. She boils them and fries them with bacon and onions. Next, she makes cornbread.

She and Minnie have eaten when Jimmy and their daddy pull up. She thinks about it for a second, then puts some grease in the pan and heats up what's left for them. She hates doing it but serves them their meal. Anything to keep the peace so she can spend the evening reading.

When she hears the pull tab on a can of beer, she knows a quiet evening isn't on the cards. Still she continues, like it's a normal house. She puts the skillet in the sink, washes it. Then she takes their dishes from the table and washes them.

'What you doin', girl?' Jimmy slurs.

'Cleaning up,' she said.

Jimmy responds by throwing a half-full beer on the floor. Daddy is slumped on the table, head on his arms.

'Clean that up, then, while yer at it,' Jimmy says, laughing.

As she puts some food in the refrigerator, her eyes fall on the ice pick. She takes a breath.

Eualla thinks about how things have changed at school since that godawful day her teacher brushed her hair. She has the highest marks in the class. No one messes with her. No one messes with Minnie, either. She knows people are slightly afraid of her, slightly in awe. She likes it that way. She's gone to school hungry and tired and still she's done so well, she's skipping a grade, will be in a new class in September, leaving Debbie behind. That feels good, too.

'D'you hear me?' Jimmy persists.

Still, she's silent. She can't hide any food with them sitting there. She starts to leave the room.

'Girl, I'd like a cheese sandwich,' Jimmy says.

'We don't have any cheese.'

'Well yous is sooo clever, go figure it out.'

'I can't create cheese.'

Daddy stirs, wakes. Looks around in a daze.

Eualla takes a deep breath. She looks at her father, a look of such hatred she sees his eyes widen.

'Alright, boy. Let's go inna town. We can get something there.'

As the door closes behind them, Eualla hopes they drive into the great big oak tree at the turn in the road.

The next night, it happens again. She hears them when they come in. People in Nashville could probably hear them, but Minnie sleeps through it all.

Jimmy bangs on the door. 'Git up, girl. We brung cheese.'

Eualla gets up quietly, so Minnie doesn't wake. She walks over and looks at her, not sure if she's sleeping or dead. How could this chaos not wake her? Maybe she's pretending to be asleep, the way Eualla pretends everything is OK for her.

On the table she sees eggs, Spam, potatoes, bread. There's so much food, she thinks for a second she's dreaming. Sighing, tired, fed up, she takes out the skillet and on some sort of autopilot, makes eggs, toasts bread, slices cheese.

As her brother and father eat, she puts away the rest of the food, hiding some in the back of the cupboard. Later, when no one is around, she'll take it to her bedroom, where she's hidden three cans of beans, two cans of soup and five tins of Spam, as well as cans of peaches her teacher gave her. She's preparing for winter.

The next night Eualla makes a big supper thinking it might keep Jimmy full. But it happens again, the pounding on the door.

She gets up and makes sandwiches wordlessly. In the back of her mind, a plan is forming. A good plan. A terrible plan. It takes shape in her head, even though she knows it's wrong. But what's wrong about wanting to survive?

On Saturday, she tells Minnie to stay in her room.

'Why? Where you going?'

'Minnie, for once, can you please not ask any questions?'

Her eyes widen and Eualla sees tears form.

'Please? Just sit in here and read. After I leave, push the chair in front of the door like I showed you. OK?'

Minnie nods.

Eualla closes the door behind her, then she walks into her daddy's bedroom. She opens the closet and takes out the shotgun she knows is there. It's a deer rifle, not a duck gun. A duck gun won't do what she needs it to. She opens the cabinet and takes out a box of shells, puts six in her pocket.

Carrying the rifle over her shoulder, she walks through the hunting cabin they call a house, out the back door and into the field. She walks and walks. They're isolated, but she wants to make sure no one happening by on the roads hears. The only fear she has left is the state taking Minnie from her, although there are some days she thinks that might be for the best.

In the field, she turns in a circle. Then she sets up the old cans she brought with her on the trunk of a fallen tree. It's uneven, but she's not training to be a sniper. She's not sure what she's training for. But she feels certain one of these days, she's going to need to use a gun.

Standing with her feet apart, as though bracing for the inevitable trauma of life, she stares at the cans in the distance. She tries to remember seeing a character on TV firing a gun, but she can't. The only place she ever watched TV was at Debbie's and that was a long time ago.

That simple thought of her old friend makes her squeeze the trigger.

She lands with a hard thump on her bottom, her shoulder on fire with pain.

It takes her a minute to stand. When she looks in the distance, she can't see the can. She walks toward where it was, but it's not there. A few feet away, she sees what's left of it. She picks it up, sets it back where it was and tries again. This time she misses and figures the first hit must have been a fluke. She tries again, carefully, knowing shells cost a lot. Praying Daddy doesn't count them. Her shoulder is throbbing. Holding up a rifle, keeping it still, is harder than she thought it would be.

After eight shells, she's managed to hit two cans. She's disappointed, but what she plans to hit is a hell of a lot bigger than a bitty little can.

When she gets back to the house, she's relieved that Minnie has done what she asked.

'Open the door, Minnie. It's me.'

She hears the chair being pulled away and she turns the doorknob. She takes the gun and puts it in the closet. Minnie doesn't ask what she's doing with the shotgun and Eualla is both shocked and relieved. Relieved not to have to answer and shocked because Minnie is now old enough. She understands.

*

The second time she brings the gun into the field, she brings ten shells and ten cans. Having set them up in a row as uneven as a set of bad teeth, she turns and starts walking away. One step, two, three... seven, eight, nine, ten... nineteen, twenty. She turns and looks. She can still see the cans. She keeps walking.

As she moves through the growing spring grass, she organizes her thoughts. Outside, in the warm air, the soft breeze carrying the scent of so many living things, she wonders what Debbie and her old friends are up to on this Saturday afternoon. She bets one of their parents have driven them into Pigeon Forge to go shopping. Or maybe they're all at Debbie's house, listening to records. Eualla is sure she has tons of records. One thing she knows for certain: none of them are in a field, teaching themselves how to use a gun because they're afraid of their brother.

When she turns again and looks back, she can barely see the cans. It's the furthest shot she's ever tried. She loads the gun. Holding the rifle at her shoulder, preparing for the recoil, she breathes slowly in and out, in and out, and then fires.

Immediately she hears the ping, sees the can explode in the air. She reloads, takes aim and fires another shot. Success. Smiling, overconfident, she reloads, aims and misses. She stops, sets the rifle down and rubs absently at her shoulder, feeling the pain now. She looks in the distance, then picks up the gun. Taking her time, she aims. The sound of the bullet making contact with the can is gratifying. It's the sound of success.

Eight out of ten. That's pretty good for a second attempt. She walks back to the cans, picks up what's left of them and all the cartridges, and puts them in the bag she has with her. Then, putting the rifle over her shoulder, she walks back home.

It's Thursday night and Eualla is tired. She's been studying every hour God sent while taking care of Minnie, who's been sick for days. Eualla wakes at the sound of the truck in the drive, always alert to the noises that mean Jimmy is near.

She tells herself to get up and lock the door, having been back and forth to the kitchen for water, cold cloths. She's worried about her fever. She can hear them in the kitchen and knows by their voices they're both drunk. What kind of man drinks with his son? The kind who was sixteen when he became a father himself, she guesses.

She looks over at Minnie, covered in blankets and snoring slightly. Eualla is worried about the congestion in her chest. She closes her eyes. She has an English test in the morning. She needs to sleep.

And then she hears footsteps. Not evenly spaced, normal steps but lurching ones. She counts them off, knowing exactly where they are. A scrape on the floor and she knows he's stumbled into the coffee table – a heavy old wooden monstrosity her father dragged back from the dump.

The doorknob starts to turn. She throws off the covers, trips on the books by her bed, forgotten in her race to the door. She doesn't want him to wake Minnie.

The door springs open, hitting her, and Jimmy appears, glassy-eyed and swaying, stinking of stale beer and sweat. She wants to throw up.

'Make us summat t'eat,' he drawls.

Spinning round, she sees Minnie stir. She reaches out with both hands and pushes her brother from the room, closing the door behind her.

'Hey…' He stumbles.

'Shut up! Minnie's sick. Don't you dare wake her.' She keeps pushing, even though a voice inside tells her to stop.

Daddy is sitting at the kitchen table, a can of cheap beer open in front of him. Judging by the puddle around it, he's spilled some. She hates the smell of beer.

'Girl,' her father says, holding up his arm in some sort of salute.

God, she detests him.

She looks at the food in bags, all over the floor. She's been feeding Minnie Spam fried with lots of water, creating a vile kind of ham soup.

'There's cheese,' he says, as way of instruction, she guesses.

'Minnie's sick. I'm tired and I have an exam tomorrow. I want to go to bed.'

Behind her she can hear her brother laugh.

'Daddy, she's tired. She wants to go to bed.'

He pushes her, catching her shoulder with his hand, and for a second she thinks he may have dislocated it.

Her father says nothing, just takes another pull of beer. Usually he drinks moonshine out of jars, so she knows he's made some money, enough to go to the store and buy a six-pack. She has two choices: make sandwiches or go back to her room. She has to be smart. Life, she's learning, is about knowing when to speak up and when to hold your tongue.

She walks over to the stove, picks up the cast-iron skillet, still with a layer of Spam congealed in the bottom. The smell makes her want to vomit and she drops it back in the sink.

'I'm tired. I want to go to bed,' she says.

Jimmy's in front of her, angry, looking like he might hit her, but Eualla stands her ground. Then he pushes her.

For a second, she can't see straight. And it's not from being pushed – not physically, at least. It's from anger, hatred, exhaustion.

She grabs the handle of the skillet and swings it like a baseball bat and she's Babe Ruth.

She hits his jaw. The impact rings through her body. Blood sprays toward the ceiling, arcs around the kitchen. He staggers and falls. Eualla watches like she's in a dream. He's on his knees, hands reaching out to grab something for support.

She hits him again. He's on the ground now, blood pouring from his nose. He spits blood from his mouth. Her father looks at her with his watery eyes, eyes that appear darker, his skin white with shock.

'I have an exam to write tomorrow. Minnie is real sick. Come near me again and next time, I'll shoot you. Both of you.' She steps over her brother, bleeding on the floor. Looks at her daddy. 'No wonder Mama left you.'

She goes to her room, lets her knees tremble only once the door is closed. When she's calm, she pushes the bureau in front of the door.

'Study hard. Hold your head high. You're bigger than this town,' she says to the room.

★

Eualla is surprised to see Daddy sitting at the kitchen table in the morning. She figures he simply didn't go to bed. She isn't as scared as she figures she should be. Blood still splatters the walls, the floor. She wets a cloth and starts to clean it, not wanting Minnie to see.

'It ain't proper, what you done last night, girl,' he says.

Eualla runs the many ways this can play out in her head. She can be contrite and apologetic, and he'll know she's scared. If she's scared, she loses.

'It ain't proper,' she spits, 'for a man to go out drinking with his sad excuse for a son while his two daughters do without. It ain't proper for me to be acting like Minnie's mother. It ain't proper that I'm afraid to go to school and leave my baby sister with her father and her brother.'

She sees her father change color in front of her, the white of shock, pink of embarrassment. A purplish flash of rage.

'It's a sad excuse for a man who drinks while his children go without.' She twists the knife. 'I have a test today and I can't go to school cause Minnie is sick. So don't you talk to me about what's proper. I'd kill you both if I could.' She pauses, frightened by the realization that she would, easily.

She knows she would, if she could get away with it, in the eyes of the law. She doesn't believe in any great spiritual reckoning. She turns and walks back to her room, afraid of how she feels. Afraid of the things she knows she could do.

Afraid.

10

Peyton

Summer, Maine, Present day

It's still standing. The Stick House. It's smaller than Peyton remembered, but things in your hometown always are when you return. Except her parents' house. That seems to keep getting bigger and bigger.

She stands outside, staring, as though an answer will come like a puff of smoke from the chimney. It's early morning and cool, the sky still holding the memory of night. She's wearing shorts and a light fleece, the unofficial uniform of the Fort. She feels a chill but knows it will warm up soon, be hot outside by eleven. She knows the weather in Maine. Knows this type of day.

She ran into her mother in the kitchen, before setting out. Both of them surprised to see each other.

'I'm going out walking,' she'd said. It was almost the truth.

'Exercise is good for you,' she replied, like she was sharing some great wisdom. She'd been pleased, Peyton thinks, that she was going outside, moving.

Peyton knows she wouldn't be if she knew where she was going, what she was doing. Every time someone brought up the disappearance of Daisy Wright, her mother changed the subject. Caroline had noticed it years earlier.

A plan is forming, but its nebulous, skirting around her at the moment. She's not sure how she can solve the Daisy Wright case when so many others have tried and failed, but she plans to give it her best shot.

That's why she's where she is now, standing, in the middle of the street, staring at an old house left to rot. The only part of the town not being gentrified. There has to be a reason. And she thinks it's connected to Daisy. She's just not sure how. Or why. Maybe she's wrong, but it's a start.

With a final check to see if anyone is watching, she moves toward the drive, close to the house, a nervousness she's never felt in the light of day taking root inside her. The house scares her, has since she was a child. Scared her even when she sat there with her high-school friends, drinking beer in the little patch of trees behind the house. She turns her ankle, gasps at the unexpected flash of pain. Looking down, she sees tire marks in the dirt drive, hardened with time, so old and established even her weight makes no impact.

She waits a second, shaking her foot as though that'll empty the pain somehow, then keeps walking. Something is pulling her forward. The house is hunkered down beside her, a moss-green monster with faded burgundy trim. The matching carriage house is at the end of the drive ahead of her. She moves toward it, her back to the house now, like this small outbuilding is easier to face.

The paint is faded and peeling. Some of the windows broken. She can't see it being vandalized – her hometown wasn't like that – and she wonders if the glass shattered in the cold. She looks in the windows, remembering all the times she's been here in the dark, being quiet so the neighbors didn't hear but giggling under the effects of the beer. Memories start to poke at her, uncomfortable and half formed, but she doesn't want to pull them forward. She has enough to deal with and she swats them away. But like a group of flies, they scatter then reform, attack, coating her against her will. Memories from high school. Kissing Todd Harcourt, his breath like an Anheuser-Busch brewery, his lips too wet, his hands inside her shirt. Somehow it was both vile and wonderful. A high school rite of passage, drinking beer and making out at The Stick House,

But she'd been there many times before that. That's what's making her feel off, strange, slightly frightened right now. Not what happened, but the memory of what happened. It's poking at her, like an annoying child wanting her attention.

Her sister brought her here. Often. Caroline was always in trouble with their parents and looking back now, Peyton realizes Caroline used her as a shield. Their parents didn't think she'd drag Peyton along and leave her unattended while she drank beer and smoked stolen cigarettes. But she did. She feels a fresh burst of anger for Caroline, at how she treated her all those years ago. She was selfish and difficult from a young age, still is now.

Memories return. She was six at the time and the day

was overcast, the skies filled with rain. It was a haunted sort of day and it felt off. She wasn't sure why they were out walking when the rain was coming. Where was her mother? At work, probably.

She took Caroline's hand in the drive. Caroline had looked down at her and laughed, shook it off, took her to the back of the carriage house. Milk crates from the local dairy were piled against the outside wall. Something smelled bad. She didn't want to be there. But she couldn't tell Caroline. She'd laugh.

'Sit here for a while, OK?'

Peyton tried to say she didn't want to but couldn't. She felt tears form and tried to blink them away.

'For fuck's sake. What's wrong with you?' Caroline grabbed her by the arm, pushed her onto one of the crates.

Peyton was young, but she knew what was happening. Caroline gave her a stick of gum as a treat. Peyton didn't like gum – she wanted taffy. Funny, how both clear and foggy the memory is now.

She walks to the back of the carriage house. The crates are still here. Now, it smells like the trees, the damp earth. What she was smelling back then she later learned was urine. The guys used to urinate behind the carriage house.

Anger grips her, at Caroline for abandoning her to this spot, for her parents who worked all the time. Peyton wishes she could go back to that little girl and pull her out of there. Tell her nothing was going to grab her. She'd be OK.

Only, she's not. Not really. She's pushing thirty, unemployed. Living at home. Scared, still, of what's out there. What comes next.

She walks slowly, trying to look in the windows

without getting too close, afraid something will snatch her. That was the feeling the house gave off – then, now. She remembers being terrified that day, wanting so badly to go home. Peyton hadn't thought about it in a while, but standing here now, flashes from the past seem to be dancing around her, pushing at her and running away. She doesn't like this house. Never has.

Still, she stays. It has a secret and she wants to hear it. Needs to hear it. At least, she thinks she does.

She starts to walk around, toward what they called the woods but was just a band of trees, maybe twenty feet deep. Seeing this now, she laughs. What she thought was some sort of dense forest is a few trees left behind when the land was cleared for the house. At least, that's what she thinks. The air cools even more once she's under the canopy created by the old growth limbs. In the middle it appears – the Stonehenge of the Fort – a clear space of ground surrounded by milk crates. The place where they'd sat on coolers, lawn chairs stolen from home.

In the dirt she sees the remnants of a bonfire, a few crushed cans of beer. Kids still gather here, she guesses. It seemed so isolated and remote at the time, but really, the nearest house was round the corner, down the hill, a quarter mile but a world away. Peyton shivers. The trees, the house itself, blocks both the warmth and the light from the sun. She walks the circle once, twice, then heads back to the sunlight.

There's no grass, there's never been any attempt at landscaping that she can see. It's like the house rose from the earth and the land made space for it. The back porch sags as though under the weight of some unseen force. The wood of the steps is rotted. She sees a 'no trespassing' sign in the window, but really, there should be a fence around the place.

A twig snaps underfoot as she makes her way around the house, startling her.

If she turns now, will someone be there?

She sprints across the baked earth, the overgrown front yard, to the quiet street. The brightness of the sun makes her feel safer, but she still feels like she's a kid again, afraid of what's in the closet, under the bed.

She's had enough intrigue and fright for one day and turns from the darkness, walks quickly to the street, turns to go downhill. There's a man is in his yard, watering flowers. He waves. Peyton is so grateful for this random connection she walks toward him.

'Hi,' she says, waving politely from the curb.

He turns off his garden hose and sets it down.

'Hello. What can I do for you?'

'I've just come home – I grew up here – had forgotten about that creepy old house. Do you know its story?' Even to her own ears, what she's saying doesn't make sense.

'How do you mean?'

What she wants to say is, '*It feels evil. What can you tell me? Any ghosts coming from the chimney? Slime appearing on the walls? Any screams of young children?*'

'It doesn't make sense with all the new building going on that it's just left to rot,' she says.

'It's been empty a long time. An eyesore, if you ask me.' He pauses, looks her up and down. 'And a magnet for the local kids to get up to no good.'

'You're Peyton, the Winchesters' girl?'

She's startled by his comment. He knows who she is.

'Yes. Did I go to school with one of your children?'

He shakes his head. 'No, no kids. Just know your folks is all.'

'I'll tell them you said hello.'

He shakes his head again and laughs. 'They won't know me.'

'Oh. OK. Well, thanks. Enjoy the beautiful day.'

Peyton backs up, wanting to remove herself from the awkward exchange she initiated. She makes her way down the hill, past the same summer homes and to the new boardwalk. Then she heads to the plaza, so she can buy a new scrapbook. It's time to start taking notes.

11

Eualla

June, Tennessee, 1969

On her sixteenth birthday Eualla walks to the diner in town and asks for a job.

Wearing her only nice summer dress, she walks in, goes straight to the counter and says, 'I'd like to apply for a job.'

Dot's eyes, heavily lined in blue and with what looks like road tar on her lashes, nods.

'Would Mr. Owens be here?' Phil Owens owns the diner. He's also the brother of her English teacher. Eualla is certain he will know who she is. Miss Owens had told her to apply.

'Hey Phil,' Dot yells, her booming voice at odds with her frail appearance. It almost makes Eualla laugh.

The kitchen door opens and he appears. Eualla sees the same brown eyes as Miss Owens, but while she's mousy in appearance, Mr. Owens is... dapper. A clean white shirt, a pen in his pocket. Navy pants.

He smiles. A warm, easy smile. She feels the solid matter

in her back that's carried her through storm after storm soften. Relief. She knows she's going to get this job.

'Hello,' he says, the word oddly formal in the small country diner.

'This here's Eualla. She's looking for a job,' Dot says.

'Take a seat.' He gestures to the counter. 'Can I get you a drink? Coke?'

'Coffee, please.'

'Sure.'

Dot pours the coffee into a heavy mug. Eualla adds cream, a luxury they can't afford at home. She thinks cream is the best thing she's ever tasted. And when she has her own big house, she'll always have cream in the refrigerator.

Mr. Owens sits on a stool beside her.

'I hear you're a good student,' he says.

'I try.'

'You're a hard worker?

'I am.'

'Friday nights are busy. You can come then. May end up clearing tables and cleaning. We do a bit of everything here.'

'Fine.' Does she have the job?

'Minimum wage and tips. One evening a week and Saturday. Can you do that?'

'Yes, thank you. When can I start?'

He looks at her, studying her, and Eualla's skin puckers with discomfort.

'You're about a medium, I guess. Grab a dress and an apron from the back. Might be short on you. Make sure they're always clean. That's up to you – no washing here,' he says firmly.

'Great.' She stands and pulls her cardigan around her. 'Thank you for your time.'

'Why don't you take a piece of pie home for your sister?'

'Well thank you. She'd love that.'

Eualla gets her dress, a nylon-and-polyester affair in a shade of orange that somehow manages to look muddy, while Dot cuts the pie and puts it in a box for her.

'See you Friday, hun,' she says.

Eualla feels herself soften at the woman's kindness. She picks up the box and the dress and apron and begins the walk home. Soon she'll be making money, which is good. Minnie will be on her own more, but she'll have to get used to it. She'll be on her own when Eualla goes to college. Her stride shortens and her pace slows. There's no reason to rush home.

Eualla has been working for six weeks when it happens. Debbie and her friends come into the diner after the football game. The door opens and suddenly, the place is heaving with people, noise, sweat and energy.

Eualla has been dreading this. Ever since she skipped a grade, she's been able to avoid Darlene and Pam. Now, here they are – and Trent Jones, captain of the football team. She

watches, as they don't just sit in her section but sprawl all over it.

She pulls in a breath, walks over and says, 'What'll you have?'

She's supposed to say, 'What can I get you?' but she's not saying that to them.

A level of quiet descends, broken by some nervous laughter.

'Well, hey. I'll have a beer. And a whisky!' Trent says.

The group laughs, a sound so loud it's like the big windows that make up most of the diner seem to shake.

'Sweet tea it is,' Eualla says. 'For everyone,'

She's bombarded with shouts of 'Dr Pepper,' 'Coca-Cola,' 'Juniper juice,' and too loud, too energetic laughter.

Debbie looks at her and asks for French fries and gravy. Eualla nods. Darlene asks for a cheeseburger platter. Eualla writes it down, even though she knows she'll remember these orders for the rest of her life. Then it comes to Pam.

She looks Eualla up and down and then says, 'I'll have the fried chicken. But not if you touch it.'

Eualla thinks she may be sick. Then she says, 'I don't touch greasy, fat, ugly things. Why do you suppose I'm standing so far away from you?'

Pam's daddy works at the local bank. They have what passes for money in Bolt's Ferry. But everyone knows her daddy's a drunk with a mistress in Pigeon Forge and her mama lives on pills. Standing here, Eualla realizes something. Money cloaks even the saddest stories in a certain level of respectability. But poverty is poverty, through and through.

Pam's face is red. 'Get the owner. Right now.'

'Knock it off, Pam. She got you,' Trent says.

Eualla takes the orders, face burning, then goes to the kitchen to get the drinks. She carries them over on a tray and starts handing them out. There are two tables and six people at each – twelve kids her age. She hands Pam her Dr Pepper.

'I ordered a Coke.'

She didn't, but Eualla doesn't bother to argue. She hands out the rest of the drinks and gets the Coke for Pam. Pam takes a sip and pretends to choke.

'You put something in my drink. No! You touched it!' She claws at her throat theatrically, laughing and gasping at the same time.

One of the men, a farmer in a John Deere hat, looks over and says, 'You kids should quiet down and show some respect.'

Eualla smiles at him and his Santa Claus beard, stained with black dribble from chewing tobacco.

A temporary silence falls, but only Trent and Debbie look at all chastised. Pam and Darlene are too full of themselves. What's happening has gone over most of their heads.

Eualla walks away from the tables. The drinks are sorted. Now, the food.

She brings out Debbie's fries, setting them down in front of her. The cheeseburger platters and fried chicken all take a little longer.

She's waiting, when Dot says, 'Hun, you want me to take that section for you?'

'I'm fine. I deal with them all day, every day at school.'

Dot looks over at the group of kids. Shakes her head.

'You sure, hun?'

'I am.'

'I went to school with some of them's parents. Apple doesn't fall far from the tree,' she says.

Eualla waits, watches. When it looks like they're done she goes to clear the table and Pam hands over her plate, as though she's being kind. Eualla is reaching for it, when Pam flips it over, covering Eualla with the half-full bowl of gravy and the bones of well-cleaned fried chicken.

'Soorrryyy,' she draws out, loud enough, Eualla guesses, so everyone can hear her.

Eualla looks down at her uniform. She's working in the morning and will have to wash it when she gets home tonight. She prays the gravy doesn't stain. She'll have to buy another uniform and why would she want two such ugly things?

Then, just when Eualla doesn't think things can get worse, she takes a step back, not seeing the gravy on the floor, and slides, her left leg slipping out from under her. Pain shoots through her knee as she grabs the table for support. She has good reflexes and steadies herself quickly.

The farmer in the John Deere hat is up from the table. For a short man with a beachball for a stomach, he's light on his feet and he's beside Eualla in seconds. So is Dot.

'Y'all pay your bill, tip good and get outta here.' He points to Trent. 'I'll be calling Coach Wilkins tomorrow. Sure he'll be proud of how his players behave off the field.'

'But I didn't...' Trent stammers.

'Not payin' no mind to the company you keep,' he says, his belly bouncing in anger.

'I bet your mamas and daddys will be real proud to hear about how you behave. I'll be sure to tell them when I see 'em at service tomorrow,' Dot adds.

Eualla walks to the bathroom and looks in the mirror. Her hair has fallen out of her ponytail and she's breathing funny – fast and slow at the same time. She takes some paper towel and dabs at her uniform, sure it's going to stain.

She does her best to clean up, taking her time, wishing them all gone when she finally re-emerges. She fixes her hair, splashes her face. And vows to get even.

She repeats the words that have pulled her through the dark times. Head up, shoulders back.

'You're too good for this place, Eualla,' she whispers to the mirror.

Then she opens the door and steps into the diner.

The farmer winks at her. Dot is cleaning up the mess. She's old and limps, and Eualla is furious.

'Sorry,' she says to Dot.

'Hush. Ain't your fault.'

She hands Eualla an eighteen-dollar tip, apparently collected by the farmer. Eualla counts it twice, not knowing if she should be pleased by the sum or pissed off. They'd have even more to say about her now, as the man had made them dig deep. She's mad at him, too. Mr. John Deere. Because even though he stood up for her, she knows he pities her. And Eualla hates that more than anything.

12

Eualla

June, Tennessee, 1969

You get to a stage in life where you can't cry anymore. Where you don't want to cry anymore. The broken bits that slice away pieces of you start to, if not heal, scab over. And one day you find the things that made you cry now make you angry. For some people, people who have had it OK, it can take years to get to this point. Decades. For people who grow up fast with no one but themselves to depend on, it doesn't take so long.

Eualla is just sixteen years old when she decides the days of tears at the pain of life are over. She works, she saves and she plans. But what will she do about Minnie?

It's a Monday afternoon, the start of another long week, when it happens. Eualla can feel something different when she walks up the dirt road to their house. Her heart seems to beat faster with each step until she's at the back door.

Whatever's happening, she's glad Minnie is at her friend's house. Maybe she can fix it before Minnie comes home.

It's the scent she recognizes at first. A subtle floral aroma that hits her like an anvil.

She opens the creaky screen door slowly, like something might jump out at her. And then her mama appears. Wearing a purple dress. She's thin – impossibly thin. She looks sad and old and wonderful all at the same time.

Eualla feels like a weight falls from her shoulders for a second, before being replaced by a new and heavier one. Why is she here? What does she want? Is she going to stay?

'Hello, Eualla,' her mama says.

Eualla stands and stares, speechless, her mind both racing and somehow stopped at the same time. Her daddy is standing in the front room, as far away from his wife as he can get while keeping her in his sight. It's like the air is made of glass and could shatter any second.

'I know yous is surprised to see me.'

It's been almost five years since she left. Almost four since Eualla stopped saying prayers that she'd come back. Three since she stopped thinking about her every minute. Two since she stopped thinking about her every day. One since she'd started to hate her.

That's what she feels, looking at her now. Hate. Her mama whom she'd once loved so much. Who she tried so hard to make laugh when she was unhappy. Who she missed so much when she left.

'Hello,' Eualla says.

Her mama stands unsteadily. Her legs seem too thin to hold her up. Part of Eualla wants to go to her and hug some life into her, the way she has with Minnie. The other part wants to turn round and run out the door.

Mama stands still, looking at her. 'You're so tall. And so beautiful.'

'Thank you, ma'am,' she says, because that's what you say when someone compliments you, isn't it?

She goes to the refrigerator, gets out the pitcher of tea. Same thing she does every single time she gets home. Pours a big glass and drinks slowly. Buying time.

'Do you want some tea?' she asks her mama.

'Please.'

Eualla pours.

'Where's Minnie?' Mama asks.

'At a friend's house. I'll have to pick her up soon.'

'I'll take you,' her daddy says.

His normally tanned skin, brown from working outside chopping trees and doing groundwork, is pale, almost white. She sees the shock written on his face. For the first time, they're on the same page, her daddy and her, sharing the same experience. They could look to each other for support, but Eualla glances away. She knows enough not to let her guard down with him.

Eualla sits at the table, across from her mama, trying not to look at her deeply lined skin. Her horrible dry hair, pulled back in an elastic. Maybe, Eualla thinks, she's come back to die.

'How's school?' her mama asks.

'Eualla skipped a grade. Gets straight As. She's a good student,' her daddy says.

'That's wonderful.'

The old clock she never notices anymore seems to be

making the chiming sounds she imagines Big Ben makes with each second that ticks by. The room is somehow both empty and full.

'Trailer's new,' she motions to the back, where Jimmy stays. It appeared after she attacked him with the skillet. He doesn't step foot in the house.

'We need to go get Minnie. Mama, you staying for dinner?'

'I am, yes.'

There's a pause while she wonders at what those three words mean. Maybe Mama and Daddy know. Maybe they talked about it before she got home.

Mama stands, goes to the stove like she never left, takes out the old skillet. Eualla thinks for a second. If Mama cooks and cleans, she can study. Then she has another thought – one that makes it feel she might split down the middle with joy. If Mama is back, Eualla can go. She's free. Someone will be here for Minnie.

'There's chicken in the refrigerator,' Eualla says. 'And some greens, too.'

As she heads to the door, her daddy following her, they hear the familiar sounds of Mama shuffling around the kitchen.

The truck doors have barely closed when Eualla looks at her daddy and says, 'What's happening?'

'I came home and there she was, sitting on the front porch, legs crossed, suitcase beside her like she'd returned from an overnight trip and lost her keys. Thought for a second the sun got to me. Blinked a good few times. Saw spots in front of me. But she was still there, solid as a tree.'

'Solid? She's so thin you could spit through her.'

'You know what I mean,' he says.

'What happened next?'

'I stops the truck, sit there a second, then out I get, and walk to the step. She says, "Hello, Donnie."' He pauses, reliving the moment, she thinks. 'I says, "Hello, Mona," and we stand there a spell. Then I asks if she wants a cold drink. She was sweating. Must have walked from the bus stop. She follows me into the house like she's never seen it before. I pour her a drink and she says, "How are you?" I say fine, never asked after her. She asks after you girls.'

Eualla feels herself grow hot and cold, choking back all the things she'd like to say happened to the girls since she left.

'Jimmy?'

'Hasn't said a word about him.'

'And then?'

'I told her you was doin' great, good at school, and Minnie so talented she could give Mikey-Angelo a run for his money.'

'What did she say to that?'

'She said she knowed you'd do well.'

'Knew.'

'Say again?'

'She knew. No need for a "d". It's not knewed.'

Eualla knows she shames her father when she corrects his grammar. He's been better since he quit drinking, but then he shames her, too. With his lack of ambition, his dirty truck. He's weak and Eualla has no time for weakness.

'Do you think she means to stay?'

He nods.

'Did you ask why she came back?'

'No. Can tell to look at her she's no place else to go.'

This surprises Eualla. She had no idea her father was this intuitive.

'So, what are you going to do?'

'What'll you have me do? She's still my wife.'

Get a real job. Buy a nice house. Wear decent clothes.

'I'm going to college soon. I don't plan on coming back.'

He seems to shrink when she says this.

'Might be good for Minnie to have her back. Someone to cook and clean and mind her when I'm gone.'

'I think she's fixin' to stay, but it's not good for Minnie if she stays a spell and leaves again. So I'll have to say my mind.'

That, Eualla thinks, shouldn't take long.

'There,' Eualla says. 'That's the house where Minnie's at.'

He pulls his truck alongside the curb, puts it in park.

'What we gonna tell her?' he asks.

'I don't know, but we'd better think of something fast.'

Minnie is walking towards them, her hands full of papers and books. Things fall, blow from her grasp, and Eualla gets out the truck to help her gather her things. Minnie has a Hansel and Gretel approach to her belongings, leaving a trail of them behind her. Except when it comes to her art supplies. They're kept in pristine order. Except for the crayon she broke so long ago. Funny that Eualla is thinking about that now.

'Hey, Eu!'

The way she says that, sounding like "Hey, you," hits at Eualla's heart. No matter what happens, now that Mama's back, their lives are going to change again.

Eualla grabs Minnie in her arms, giving her a quick squeeze, surprising them both. Eualla isn't one for demonstrating any sort of emotion, good or bad. She lets her go and picks up the papers she dropped.

'OK. Got everything? Get in the truck. Daddy and I want to talk to you,' she says.

'What about?'

Eualla hears fear in her voice.

'It's OK. Just get in the truck.'

Eualla opens the door and Minnie scrambles in, sitting on the bench seat between them.

Daddy puts the truck into drive and is moving away from the curb, when Eualla says, 'Minnie, do you remember Mama?' her voice slow, soft, deliberate.

The truck jerks as Daddy misses a gear. Eualla grabs the dash, and Minnie grabs her.

'I remember Mama,' she says. Eualla hears fear in her voice. Could be from talking about mama, or the truck jerking. Everything scared Minnie.

'Well, you remember she went away, right?'

Minnie nods, but Eualla can see her biting her lips, a tell-tale sign she's nervous. She knows her baby sister's mannerisms inside and out. Eualla looks at her father, hesitating. What if they tell her Mama's back and by the time they get home, she's changed her mind and gone again?

'Mama's been in touch,' Daddy says, as though reading her mind.

'She's alive?'

Eualla stares at her sister. 'You thought she was dead?'

'Why else would she leave us?'

Dear God, Eualla thinks. This is going to be harder than she thought.

'She's alive,' Daddy says. 'And she wants to see you.'

Minnie has a drawing she did in her hand. There's lots of yellow and blue, and Eualla assumes it's a sky with a sun but can't tell by the way she has it folded. Her drawings have become more ornate, more intricate. She uses a lead pencil to sketch when she's home. Eualla is happy to see her using color.

'When?'

'Now. She's at the house,' Eualla says, holding her hand, the two of them in it together, as they've always been.

In the drive, Daddy turns off the engine, looks at Eualla, and she sees him pull in a deep breath. For the first time, she thinks about what Mama leaving did to him. But she hardens her heart.

Here we go, she thinks.

It's easier than they think it's going to be. Mama has set the table. Minnie is polite to her but doesn't run into her arms. Mama doesn't hold them open, knowing innately perhaps how her daughters might be with her.

Minnie washes her hands, the way Eualla taught her, and then they all sit down to eat. Mama has made mashed potatoes and Eualla's only thought is that she hopes to God she never has to peel another potato in her lifetime.

'How's school?' Mama asks as though she's never been gone, like it's any other day.

'Fun. I like it,' Minnie says. 'Most days.'

'I hear you draw a lot.'

Eualla watches closely. Mama picks at her food, doesn't really eat. It's like she's in some sort of daze.

'Show her some of your paintings,' Eualla says.

She clears the table while Minnie sits with their mama and shows her some of her artwork. Eualla watches for a few moments, ready to pounce if the woman does anything crazy, stupid, but she just sits and exclaims over her daughter's talent. Eualla goes to her room and tries to study, but she can't concentrate, trying to figure out what everything means.

Eualla is at the library reading. Or trying to. Mostly, she's looking out the window at the bare trees, waiting for the cold weather to settle in. She doesn't fear it as she usually does. Since Mama has come back, Daddy has been doing more to keep the place going.

The case of the missing mama has been shelved, no resolution to the drama, as they all go about their days like she never left. The first night back, her parents slept in the same room. Eualla had turned the radio on to drown out any potential noise – and her own thoughts, too. How on earth could her father just accept her back like that? How could the woman have the temerity to come back? She remembered all the fighting and braced herself, but it never came.

'Principal wants to see you,' her homeroom teacher says, appearing beside her. Of course she knew where she was. The cubicle at the library was more her home than any other place in Bolt's Ferry.

'Yes, ma'am,' she says, gathering her things. She wonders

what fresh hell has befallen her and is surprised when she goes into his office and finds him beaming.

'My best student,' he says.

'Thank you, sir.'

'Your marks are excellent. You have a bright future, Eualla. You could be a teacher or a nurse.'

When Eualla was young, she'd always thought she'd be an English teacher. But things have changed. She has other ideas now.

'You can get financial help, you know?' he pauses. 'I'd like to talk to your parents about options.'

Her heart sinks, right into the ugly beige carpet under her chair, in this depressing little office in this depressing little town.

'Daddy's busy and Mama's still poorly,' she says. 'You can talk to me.'

'I'm scheduling an appointment for Wednesday evening with your parents. The school will be open for the children's craft fair,' he says, ignoring her.

'Really, there's no need,' she says. He must know what her parents are like. Why is he doing this to her?

He hands her a letter. 'See that they get this.'

'But—'

'Eualla, do as you're told.'

This makes her insides burn.

It takes her two days to tell her daddy what's happening.

'Why does he want to see me?' he asks.

'Because I have options he thinks I need parental help with to navigate,' she scoffs.

Her father looks <u>ashamed</u> and she feels bad for a second. But the memories of his drinking with Jimmy will never go away. They're as much a part of her as her black hair, her long fingers.

'Just come with me and let me do the talking,' she says. 'Tell Mama the same thing, please.'

She's nervous the entire day before the meeting, walking home from school rather than taking the bus in an effort to calm herself.

'You need to take a shower. And wear your tan pants and blue shirt,' she tells her father.

She's looking at his shoes when Mama appears, wearing a purple dress that would have been suitable for a cocktail party once, but was now faded and depressing to look at. Eualla stares at Mama's twig-like arms and legs. Her hollowed eyes.

'You look nice, Mama,' she says, and brings her a pink cardigan to cover her arms.

They drive to the school in the truck, Eualla in the middle, wearing a dress she bought with her wages from the diner. She feels each bump in the road. Feels each bump of her childhood. All she can do now is pray they don't somehow ruin things for her.

The principal, Eualla thinks, has dressed for the event, in a suit and tie. He shakes hands with her father, nods and smiles at her mother.

'I'm right pleased you could come tonight,' he begins. 'You must be so proud of your daughter.'

Eualla looks at the principal and sees that he's playing a role, pretending her life is normal. Pretending she is normal. She's oddly grateful for this.

'Eualla's marks are top-notch. We suspect she'll win the county scholarship, which will help her with tuition. I'm also putting her forward for other awards. So, she needs to decide what she wants to study. I know she'd be an excellent teacher. It would be wonderful to have her back here, working with us.'

Eualla is glad she's sitting when he says this. Her smile tightens.

'Nursing is a good job, too. Always a need for nurses,' he adds.

Daddy is nodding so much, he looks like he's having a spasm. The principal looks from her mama to her daddy, like they're going to decide for her.

Finally, Eualla says, 'I don't want to be a teacher, or a nurse. I want to be a doctor – a psychiatrist.'

She prays her daddy doesn't ask what a psychiatrist is.

'A what, now?' the principal says.

'A psychiatrist. It's a medical doctor who deals with mental issues.'

On the other side of the desk that divides them, the principal appears so stunned, Eualla wants to laugh. She watches as he folds and unfolds his hands before lacing his fingers together.

'I know what it is. It'll take a lot of years of studying,' he says.

'So I'll need a lot of financial help,' she says.

'It's a long road to becoming a doctor, Eualla,' he says.

'Twelve years, give or take. I plan to do my undergraduate degree in three.'

He looks at her and shakes his head. 'You can't go wrong with a science degree. And you're smart enough... but...'

She watches him twist, searching for the right way to say doctoring is a man's job.

'Just think how good it would look for you if I became the first female psychiatrist from this area.' Eualla now knows sometimes you have to stroke egos, and other times you have to bury them.

'We'll apply for every scholarship we can find,' he says, rising from his chair.

'Thank you, sir.'

Mama stands, looking more like an apparition than a person. Eualla takes her arm.

On the way out to the truck, her daddy says, 'What say we go to the diner and have a slice of pie?'

It's the most normal thing he's ever suggested they do as a family. Her mother lifts her hand to her throat, the way Eualla has seen her do a hundred times. Her own signal of distress. This is the first time she's left the house since she's returned. The diner would be too much for her.

'I don't think we should leave Minnie on her own much longer,' Eualla says.

Her father nods and gets into the truck. The sun is yellow in the bright pink sky. Splashes of purple break up the medley of colors jockeying for position. The back field seems to be glowing when they pull into the dirt driveway. Daddy opens the door for her mama. Eualla slides out his side and then walks her mama to the house.

'Why don't you sit outside, Mama, and I'll bring you a drink?'

Eualla watches Mama for a reaction. She's quiet, as if trying to decide.

'Yes, I think so,' she says.

Eualla goes inside, gets a chair. Minnie's sitting at the table drawing.

'Pour some tea and bring it out for Mama,' Eualla says.

For once, Minnie doesn't ask why. She simply sets her pencil down.

Eualla and her mother sit on the kitchen chairs she brought out, Mama covered in a blanket, although it's not cold. Silence sits with them. Not awkwardly – more like it's aware of the fragility of the moment. It's the strangest, most extraordinary evening. Thoughts are tumbling around in Eualla's mind, trying to find space. She feels tingly, alive. Free. Or almost.

She looks out at the field, sees where the pole from the villa she made all those years ago with her friend is still standing.

'Daddy,' she says. 'Can you pull that pole out of the ground? Cut it up for wood?'

'Sure.'

'Shouldn't you be in school?' her mama says.

'It's evening, Mama. I'll go in the morning.'

Eualla isn't sure if her mama is confused or tired.

'This final year of yours, your senior year – you must do your best.'

'Yes, Mama, I will.'

Her father gets up and walks into the field, toward Jimmy's trailer and the stake.

Mama leans over. 'You make sure you get out. And you take Minnie, too.'

Her eyes are alive, more alive than Eualla has ever seen them. She sees flashes of better times, when her mama read to her, when they danced in the kitchen. But just as quick as it comes, it goes.

Minnie appears with their drinks, as if summoned by her name. She sits on the old porch at Mama's feet, buddha style.

'What about you, Mama? You can come, too,' Eualla says.

Her mama puts her hand on Eualla's arm. She reaches forward and puts her hand on Minnie's shoulder. And just like that, the three Tompkins women are connected, however briefly.

13

Peyton

May, Maine, Present day

'Do you remember the day Daisy Wright disappeared?' Peyton asked.

She and her father are driving to the town hall. Her mother won a basket in some fundraiser and they're picking it up for her. Peyton was going to go alone, but her dad decided to tag along, handing her the keys to his old Jag in the driveway. What was an errand has turned into an event, as her father never let anyone drive his car. She's moving carefully, the hood larger than she anticipated, her father in the passenger seat. He has his hands in front of him, his fingertips pressed together like the actor Marlon Brando in *The Godfather*. She's never seen her father do this and finds it unsettling.

'Of course I do,' he says.

'I mean in detail. Not that it happened, but the actual day.'

'What made you think of this now?'

'I've been thinking about her a lot. I know I was young, but I remember things.'

'It's a sad case. Very.'

'What do you think happened?'

His pause, she thinks, is unnaturally long.

'I don't know, but I suspect someone on vacation grabbed her, got her in his car and was gone. It's the only reason why a body has never been found.'

They drive for a few more seconds in silence, Peyton staring at the road. There's twists and turns and logging trucks and animals that dart about, but the day is clear and the road now empty. She senses her father turn his head to look at her.

'What's on your mind, Peyton?'

'Can I tell you something?'

'Ye-esss.'

She hears the hesitation in his voice.

'Caroline used to ask Mom if she could take me to the playground, when really she wanted to meet her friends and drink beer and smoke.'

'What?'

'She used me for cover. The hood of this car is awkward.'

'You want me to drive?'

Peyton shakes her head.

'I remember Caroline's wild days, if that's what you mean. What else?'

His voice is thin and weary, worn out by the memory of the time, perhaps, or by thinking of Caroline.

'The day Daisy Wright disappeared, Caroline took me for a walk. Mom was nervous, pulling at her pearls. She was gone a lot, too. I remember Scott playing with me in the pool. I knew something was wrong.' It's all snapshots, snippets. She wishes she could bolt them into place, but they are fleeting. Being scared. Knowing something was wrong. That's what she remembers most. How do you solve a crime based on feeling?

'I remember seeing the news when I was doing rounds.'

Peyton knows he's remembering that day. Who he operated on, what he was wearing, what he had for breakfast. Her father remembered everything. She pictured his mind like a card catalogue in the old library in town. Between her father being a plastic surgeon and her mother a psychiatrist, Peyton once joked her parents could build any person they wanted, from the inside out. She can't remember them laughing. Funny, the things coming back to her since she moved home.

'It was overcast and gray. One of those heavy days before a storm, when it was going to rain any minute. You know – the kinds of storms where we'd sit in the gazebo and watch the lightning on the water. Where the air was so thick right before it rained that you felt it press down on you.'

She can sense her dad nod.

'I remember not wanting to go out. Caroline dragged me. And the story was we just went down to the beach, if anyone asked. That we were close to the house.' Peyton feels a flicker of anger at this. 'Later, my friends told me their mothers brought them inside, locked the doors, drew the drapes that day.'

At sleepovers, Daisy Wright always came up. Attempts to scare each other as they curled up in sleeping bags on the floor of someone's living room. Stories like she'd been abducted and was living in the woods with a new family who wanted a little girl.

'We didn't go to the park. We went to the old, abandoned house on Cabot Lane.'

Peyton hesitates, not wanting to get her sister in trouble, even after all these years. Her father puts his hands on his knees, like he's getting ready to launch himself out the windshield, or maybe hold himself in place.

'Caroline and her friends used to drink beer and smoke there. She took me and sat me on a milk crate behind the carriage house.'

Her father is silent for a moment, and then: 'What house?'

'The Stick House, Dad. Everyone knows The Stick House. You're the one who told me what it was called.'

He laughs, a short laugh, not in keeping with the feeling in the car.

'Stick is a style, not the name of the house.'

'A style?'

'A precursor to shingle style,' he begins as he tells her about the features of stick style.

She pictures them on the creepy old house that was obviously a big deal in its day.

'Caroline took you there? When Daisy Wright disappeared?' he asks.

'She took me there a lot. And I think she took me there the day after Daisy disappeared, too. It was July 4th, right?'

'She disappeared that night. The news hit for most people on the 5th. Drive by on the way home. I want to see it.'

Peyton is surprised by this. 'I don't think Caroline's there now,' she jokes.

But her father, who's always laughed too easily at her jokes, doesn't react. They're silent as they drive to the town hall, pick up the basket for her mother. It's huge, filled with things like locally produced soaps and candy that Peyton knows her mother won't use or eat. She thanks the ladies there, talks about the weather and how her parents are while her father waits in the car.

Peyton sets the basket on the floor in the back. 'Mom's not going to use any of this stuff. I wonder if we should ask them to give it to the runner-up.'

'Best not. Feelings might get hurt.'

'What do you mean?'

'Someone put a lot of energy and care into making that basket. If your mother turned it down, they'd be hurt. And the runner-up would feel like a charity case. As it is, there's probably enough people making snide remarks she won it – the person in town who needs it least.'

Peyton puts the car into first, then second, eases out of the parking lot. As she pulls onto the road, she sees the water, a perfect blue, a clear patch of shimmering light where the sun hits. Peace fills her – peace and something else... A joy at the simple beauty of the moment, of the day.

'Drive by the house on Cabot Lane,' he repeats.

She nods and turns in the direction of the house she both does, and doesn't, want to see.

The same man she asked about the house is in his yard again when they drive by. He's on his knees using a trowel, but he sets it down as the car approaches, lifts both his hands in greeting. Peyton and her father wave back. What he said about her parents not knowing him comes back to her.

'Do you know him, Dad?'

'He was a foreman at Donnelly's for a long time. Barry's his name.'

She thinks about telling her father about their conversation, but already they're at the bend in the road. The large shingle house appears, like an apparition summoned forth.

'Place creeps me out,' she says.

'It's got an interesting history. Built by a man who made his fortune in silver mining. His third wife moved Donnelly's here from Ireland. This town owes them a lot. The woman who came over from Ireland was a Donnelly and her husband was a Ford. It would be the old Ford–Donnelly house now I guess, with your generation so fond of hyphenating names. Then it was lost in the Depression.'

'You know everything, don't you, Dad?'

'It's a curse, Peyton. Now, park the car and let's go take a look.'

Peyton pulls to the side of the road.

'What are you doing?'

'Parking.'

'Use the drive.'

'It's private property.'

'It's fine. I know the owner.'

'Someone broke a window,' he says when he sees the carriage house. He says it like it's a personal attack on him.

Peyton looks up and sees him study the window, the same one she noticed was broken.

'Property is being developed all around Fort Meadow Beach. They're cramming condos everywhere. This is such a nice patch of land – high enough you can see the water. I don't understand why it's not being developed, why it's being left to rot,' she says.

'It's a beautiful representation of an architectural style not seen much around here,' he says, not answering her question and staring at the broken glass as though he has some sort of superpower and can fix it with his mind.

They're at the top of the drive, the same path Peyton had walked just a few days before.

'The trees are so beautiful here. The view from the top must be spectacular in the fall.'

Her father doesn't seem to be listening, mostly looking around, studying the house. Paying attention to the ground, careful not to mark his shoes, she guesses.

'So your sister used to bring you here,' he states.

'I came here, too, Dad. Later. In high school. It was like a rite of passage to see who could hang out back here the latest.'

'So much for me knowing everything.' He shakes his head.

Peyton laughs softly at this, as though a loud giggle might antagonize whatever surrounds this old house hidden among the trees. It's a bright summer day. Her tall, fit father is right beside her and still she feels uncomfortable. She's afraid, she just doesn't know of what. Peyton has always had an active imagination, to quote her mother.

'And you came here when Daisy disappeared?' he asks.

'Yes. I was scared of the house, of being here. No one told

me about Daisy, but I knew. I'm not sure how. Maybe the radio. It's all running together, the days, but I know we were here. Caroline's friends were talking about it.'

Her father nods. 'Everyone says the town felt eerie that day, some people out searching all night, others waking to the news.'

Peyton thinks for a minute. 'But you weren't here?'

'I was in Portland, for work.'

Peyton tries to slot this information into the bank she's creating.

'What was Caroline thinking? What was Lydia thinking?' he asks.

Her father using her mother's name jars her. He's never called her Lydia before. It's always 'your mother'.

'Maybe Caroline was doing her a favor. Maybe Mom was hoping I'd be snatched. She's never really loved me.' And as she says it, out loud, in this area with lush trees and the living, breathing ocean so close but blocked from sight by the once opulent mansion now falling apart, she knows she's speaking the truth.

She looks at her father, who doesn't miss a beat before saying, 'Your mother is a very closed and guarded person. Don't mistake her distance for a lack of love. She never had it herself.'

'What?' Peyton stops, stares at her father.

Her father waves it away. But he doesn't deny it and she knows it's true. It doesn't hurt as much as she thought it would, having her long-held belief confirmed.

Her father starts walking, not wanting to talk about it anymore. She can tell by the way he dips his head, lost in thought. They turn the corner and she takes one last look at the house. Sees her father, silent, staring through the window. She looks around, making sure it's just the two of them.

'This should be boarded up.' He moves toward the car. 'I'm livid with your sister for doing that to you.'

His words have an edge to them, an edge she's only ever heard in relation to Scott.

'It wasn't easy having her as an older sister growing up,' she says.

Her father puts his arm across her shoulders, briefly.

'What say we go have a nice dinner, just the two of us, someplace on the water?'

'Can I have dessert?'

'You can have whatever you want.'

14

Eualla

September, North Carolina, 1971

'I wish you weren't going,' Minnie says, standing at the foot of the bed.

Eualla is packing for college. She has a full scholarship to a university in North Carolina, 200 miles and an entire world away. She can't wait to get out of here. Her only concern is Minnie.

She sits down on her sister's bed and pats the space beside her.

'I want you to know, and this is very important, that I'm not leaving you. I am *not* leaving you.' She says it twice, with more emphasis the second time. 'Remember that. I'm only going away so that I can make a better life for myself, and for you, too. That's what we've been working for.'

She sees the shotgun in the corner of the room. Mama's back. Jimmy isn't around much. Daddy's been better. Still, guilt eats at her.

'Let me get settled this year. You'll come visit, a lot.'

'You mean it?'

'I do.'

She knows she won't have a traditional university experience. She wants to graduate early, on the dean's list, get into med school, intern in New York. Minnie can go to art school. She has it all planned.

Daddy says he'll drive her to school, but she doesn't want to be seen in his truck. She says she'll take the bus.

'I don't have much stuff,' she says.

The night before she leaves, she works her last shift at the diner. Dot works the same shift.

'So, you off tomorrow?' she asks.

'I'm on the noon bus.'

Dot reaches under her counter, to where she keeps her behemoth of a handbag. As she takes out a card, she leans to the order window and says, 'Y'all come on out for a second. You stay put.' She points to Eualla, a smile on her face and a hand on her hip.

Eualla promises herself that when she's making money, she'll give some to Dot. Help her out. She's one of the few people who have been nice to her in Bolt's Ferry. In her own way, Eualla loves her.

The cook and his helper come through the swinging door, both wiping their hands on once white towels.

'Now, as we all know, Eualla is off to college,' she says. 'We're proud of you, girl. And we sure are gonna miss you. Here's a little something from all of us to help you out.'

Dot hands her a card showing a green cartoon worm with big glasses sitting at a desk, reading a big book. She opens it and sees a fifty-dollar bill.

'This is so generous. It's too much,' she gasps.

'Some of the regulars pitched in.'

Eualla puts the bill in her pocket and reads the card, all the nice things they've written. It's a card for someone younger than she is, with the cartoon worm, but she loves it just the same. Loves them for standing up for her when Debbie and her friends showed up, which was almost every Friday night. After that first time, Dot served them. They never stepped out of line again.

When Eualla's done her shift, Dot packs up the leftover pie for her. The farmer with the John Deere hat drives her home. He came in to say goodbye.

She's sitting in his truck, pie on her lap, when he says, 'I know your mama and daddy. I know you got worries. I'll keep my eye on Miss Minnie for you.'

She looks at this kind man, covered in scars, both visible and invisible from the Vietnam War and says, 'Thank you. That helps put my mind at rest.'

Before she gets out of the truck, she kisses him softly on the cheek, making him blush. Then she goes inside, one last time, and eats pie with Minnie at the kitchen table.

Eualla's roommate, Katie, is a girl from Texas. Blonde, big smile, unrelentingly cheerful. She puts the state flag above their door and fills her small closet until she runs out of space, throwing everything else on the floor. Eualla neatly hangs up her own clothes, arranges her four pairs of shoes. Places her T-shirts and underwear in the drawers inside the closet. There are more drawers under the bed, but she doesn't need them all. She thinks about offering one to Katie but decides against it. She already feels like she's failed her as a roommate, by not being decked out in fashionable clothes.

'Let's go to the meal hall,' Katie says, and before Eualla can react, they're walking across the quad, arm in arm.

Eualla gets baked fish and salad, revelling in the fact that there's good hot food ready and she doesn't have to make it. Katie gets a cheeseburger and fries, and a piece of chocolate cake for dessert. Eualla can't believe such a small person can eat so much, but then Eualla's never had much of an appetite.

'Tell me about Tennessee,' Katie says.

'No, you tell me about Texas. I've never been.'

'I grew up on a ranch, forty miles from Houston, the best city in the world.'

'I thought that was Paris,' Eualla jokes.

'It's Houston. For sure,' she nods.

Eualla eats slowly, talks carefully and studies Katie. This is a girl who's been raised with money and love, confidence, makes friend easily but doesn't have a clue who she is. Eualla knows she can learn how to interact with other students by following her example. There won't be much time for socializing, but there's always time for learning about human behavior.

She gets a job off campus as a server at a fancy retirement home. Some mornings she serves breakfast, some evenings she serves dinner. Some weekends she does both.

'You study a lot,' Katie says, looking in the mirror as she models her new suede vest.

It's mid-October and Katie seems to be sleeping when she should be in class.

'Isn't that why we're here?' Eualla says.

'We're here to learn about ourselves, what we want in life, too.'

Eualla thinks about this. It makes sense and she thinks Katie's a lot smarter than she lets on. She looks at the clothes and bags and shoes all over the room.

'Please tell me you know what you want,' she groans. 'We don't have space for anything else!'

Katie picks up one of the stuffed toys on her bed and throws it at Eualla.

'Study, Katie,' Eualla says. 'Nothing you can buy feels as good as getting an A.'

'Right.'

Katie gets off her bed and goes down the hall to where all the noise is coming from.

It's Christmas vacation. Her first semester of university is behind her, and she's heading back to Tennessee. Daddy and Minnie pick Eualla up at the station. Minnie, shining with excitement, runs to her as she steps off the bus. Eualla throws her arms around her sister, delighted to see she's grown, even if it's a tiny bit.

'Daddy,' she says, handing him her bag and not giving him a hug.

They climb into his truck. Minnie sits in the middle and talks to Eualla.

'I can't wait for you to see the tree. And we have presents. And Mama made cookies, too. Shortbread.'

At first, Eualla doesn't think she heard right. 'Mama baked?'

'She's doing better, Eualla. You gonna be surprised, girl,' Daddy says.

When it comes to her family, she didn't think anything could surprise her. But Mama, baking? That's more than a surprise. That's a shock. She vaguely remembers her making fried pies, but it was so long ago, she's not sure she didn't dream it.

From the road, their house still looks like a shack. And a small shack, too. But there's something new about it. Daddy has fixed the step and put up a railing. And there's light coming from inside. A warm light, created by something more than a lamp.

Eualla steps from the truck into the familiar rutted drive. Minnie takes her hand, pulling her into the house.

The first thing Eualla notices is the scent. Burning wood mixed with something sugary and sweet. A touch of cinnamon and pine, perhaps. It's festive. Welcoming but alarming with its unfamiliarity.

Mama is standing at the sink. She has her back to Eualla and it takes a second for her mind to process the image, but it is her mama. She's wearing a nightdress that's been washed more times than it should and slouchy wool socks. An old raspberry-colored cardigan is draped over her thin shoulders, completing a look that'll never make *Vogue* magazine. Still, she's standing up, and that's welcome.

Her mother turns. Her face is flushed, her eyes watering, and she's so thin she appears translucent. Eualla moves toward her and directs her to a chair. Sits her down.

'Hello, Mama,' she says.

'Look at the cookies!' Minnie says.

She seems so much younger than her twelve years and

Eualla wonders if the years of being hungry has stunted her growth – something else, something new to worry about.

'Come see the tree,' Minnie says.

The tree is real, something Daddy cut down from the woods that surround them. It has a string of lights, could use two or three more. And a paper chain Minnie made, alternating red and green, and a popcorn garland. It's more than they had those years mama was gone.

'You did all this? Nice!' Eualla says.

And it is nice, in an old-fashioned, simple sort of way. She tries to relax, but that is not something she can do in that house.

Eualla puts her bag in her old room, the one she shared with Minnie. It feels different and she looks around. The wall next to Minnie's bed is painted a bright purple. She has no idea where Minnie got the paint.

'Do you like it?' Minnie asks, thrusting a cookie at her.

'Love it. Let's go have some milk.'

She hopes there is milk. She wants to ask about Jimmy, but he'll show up soon enough.

Eualla has presents for Minnie but nothing for her parents. Putting the university sweatshirt she bought her and the books under the tree, she sees three parcels for her. She has no idea what they could be.

Minnie is so happy, seeing presents, sitting with her, that Eualla lets herself feel good. Her sister is doing OK. She needn't worry so much.

At nine thirty, she makes Minnie go to bed. Sitting up in her old bed, she reads for a few hours before she calls it a night. Lying in her old room feels both familiar and strange, like she's never been away, yet she can't quite remember her life here. Maybe that was because she didn't really have a life. She was always in survival mode. Now, she just has to survive the holidays.

Christmas morning is pleasant. There's juice in the refrigerator, and her mother makes scrambled eggs and toast. Eualla helps, of course.

The sweatshirt she bought Minnie is way too big for her but Minnie is wearing it anyway, which makes Eualla happy. Minnie's given her a pen and pencil set from the local drugstore.

'I love it!' Eualla says. She's always on the scrounge for school supplies.

Her parents give her a black sweater and some wool socks. Eualla is surprised to find she likes the sweater. Daddy gives Mama talcum powder. No one got anything for him. It's not normal, but it's as close to normal as this family has ever been. For a few moments, Eualla is glad she came home.

Then the door opens.

She can sense him before she sees him – fifteen feet away, half hidden by the door, still she knows he's drunk. All the air leaves the room as she grabs for Minnie, wanting to get her out of there. She sees their mama wrap her arms around herself. She, too, is afraid of Jimmy. Eualla's heart starts racing.

'Hello, Eu,' he slurs. 'Back from coll-edge!'

Eualla feels like a fool. For a moment, a second, she

thought her family might have a normal, happy Christmas. She sees Minnie's eyes well.

'C'mon, Minnie. Grab a book and we'll go to our room.'

But then Mama looks at Daddy and he nods. Eualla watches it all, trying to figure out what's happening. Daddy stands, moves toward Jimmy. Minnie is hiding behind Eualla. Mama is looking away, the light in her eyes fading again.

Daddy pushes Jimmy out. Eualla hears the door open, close. Jimmy saying something unintelligible. She lets go of Minnie's hand and walks to the kitchen, looks out the window. Daddy is walking a step behind Jimmy, heading toward his trailer. Eualla feels her insides harden. Then she goes to the kitchen, gets the tin of cookies and carries them back to her mama and little sister. They unwrap the rest of the presents, but the veil of normality, of peace, of festivity has been lifted.

There's a soft dusting of snow on the 26th. Eualla tells Minnie to bundle up; they're going to walk into town and have pie at the diner. Minnie dresses quickly, and Eualla looks at her and tells her to go back and wash her face.

'Get the sleep out of your eyes,' she says.

They walk in silence in the cold, Eualla remembering that long ago day when she reassured her sister they wouldn't run into polar bears on the way to school.

'So, how are things without me?' she says.

'We miss you a lot.'

'I miss you, too. But that's not what I mean.' She's trying

to think of a way to ask if she's being fed, cared for, without really asking.

'It's good. Daddy builds the fire. Mama cooks, most of the time.'

'And Jimmy?'

'He's not around much.'

Eualla feels herself relax at this information.

The diner is warm, the big windows steamed. Eualla is surprised to find she's missed the place. Dot comes over with a hug, the farmer, too. After they sit down, Minnie says he's dropped by with food.

'Stuff from his garden. And then jams and stuff he makes. He's real nice.'

Eualla remembers his promise to her, the night before she left for school.

They order pie and hot chocolate. Eualla is relaxed, happy to see her sister eating, when the door opens and Debbie appears, with Trent and the rest of her old school crowd. When Debbie sees Eualla, some of the color drains from her face.

'Eat up, Minnie. Let's go,' she says.

The warmth of the diner, the simple pleasure of being back, seeing nice people, has gone with Debbie's appearance.

They walk back home, Eualla counting the minutes until she can leave for North Carolina.

After dinner, they have the few cookies that are left, the edges starting to go stale. Her father carries in more wood, gets the fire going.

'Gonna be a cold one,' he says, reaching his hands toward the heat.

She's leaving in the morning. She'll miss Minnie but is looking forward to going back to her life in North Carolina – seeing Katie and being Ellie once again.

Eualla's woken by a banging sound. She sits up in bed, heart hammering in her chest. But there's no more noise. Minnie is still asleep, but then, nothing wakes her.

Maybe it was a bad dream. But no. Moving her pillow, she lies back down and then hears a thud. It's right outside her bedroom window. Something heavy falling. She hears a grunt and knows what it is, who it is. Jimmy. He's back.

She gets up quietly, unlocks her bedroom door. She doesn't remember locking it and guesses she did it out of habit. The hall is warm, almost hot. She hears the snap and crackle of the fire, knows it's recently been fed, knows it's blazing, and she feels the heat of it as she opens the front door and lets in the bitter cold, cancelling out the heat from the flames.

The sky is thick with unfallen snow, with crystals of cold. She feels it in her lungs as she takes a breath and looks down. Jimmy's on the ground beside the steps. He must have fallen trying to open the door. That's what she heard – the thud. Even in the cold night air, the open space, she can smell the stink of alcohol and cigarettes on him, and something else she can't place. A smell of decay, something dying. Not rancid but rotten. Maybe something died under the porch but she hadn't smelled it before. No, it's coming from him.

He looks up at her, his eyes blank, empty, the blue she knows so well darker in the inkiness of the night. Despite the darkness she can see the scar on his forehead, from when she hit him with the skillet so long ago.

She sighs. Thinks about waking their daddy. She looks around, wondering if anyone sees what is happening.

Why did he come to the front porch and not the back door?

She looks for tracks in the snow and sees where a truck has passed. Maybe someone from town dropped him off.

She steps toward him but changes her mind. A thought colder than the frozen air enters her mind. It should startle her, but it feels so natural, makes so much sense. Carefully, she moves behind the door, using it as a barrier, a shield, as she looks at her brother from behind the warped wood. How much better their lives would be without him. Without his drunken foolishness.

As she watches, he makes another attempt to stand, but the ground is slick with ice. She thinks about what to do.

There was a time when she'd have helped him in, put him on the couch, but that Eualla is long gone. It's Ellie now, thinking about the useless man lying in a heap in the snow. Ellie who wants to keep Minnie safe until she can rescue her, permanently. Ellie who thinks Mama deserves better than a son of whom she's afraid.

She closes the door and locks it, goes back to her bedroom, locks that door, too. Putting the pillow over her head, she rocks herself to sleep.

Before the first rays of light fall through her window, Eualla is woken by a commotion outside her door. She remembers what happened in the night. Wait. Did it happen, or did she dream it?

No, there's no way she left him out to die in the snow. Did she?

She opens her bedroom door and feels the heat from the fire competing with the cold from the open front door. And she remembers. She knows.

Minnie is sitting up in bed.

'Stay here,' Eualla tells her, closing the bedroom door.

Daddy's dragging Jimmy into the house. His skin is white. Frost covers his eyes.

'Boil some water. Get some whisky.' he orders.

'What's happening?' she asks, pretending she doesn't know.

'Damn fool passed out in the snow.'

Eualla knows you don't put someone with frostbite into a hot bath. For a second she's conflicted. If Jimmy was gone, she wouldn't have to worry about him around Minnie. Wouldn't have to deal with him ever again. Maybe she could get Minnie and her mama to move closer to her. But she doesn't want that, either. He's a human being. Not one she likes, but that's beside the point.

'Run a warm bath, not hot. You must warm him gradually.'

Her daddy looks at her with something like respect. 'How d'you know that?'

'I just do. Now scoot.'

'Should he go to the hospital?'

'You have the money for that?' she snaps.

Maybe she should have just let him in the house the

night before. Maybe he should have made his own damn sandwiches all those years ago.

'Warm him gradually. No whisky. A warm drink, not hot. And take off his wet clothes.' She barks orders. 'Put him on the couch for now.'

She takes a warm washcloth and dabs gently at his face, repulsed by the person, not the mottled skin under the ice crystals.

Minnie appears with a milky coffee. The scent of it causes a sharpness between her shoulders. The simplest, strangest things take her right back to that time. Being hungry. Being cold. Instant coffee the only thing to drink – and then, watery.

She sets the cloth down. 'Take his clothes off. Put him under the blankets. Minnie and I'll go wait in our room. Call me when he's covered.' She starts to walk away, then turns round. 'Let me know if you see any discoloration in the skin.'

'What's that?'

'Patches of skin that are a different color. Look for darker shades, but I doubt you'll see any.'

Her daddy nods and she takes Minnie's hand, like she's a small child once again, and walks her to their room. Inside, she closes the door, starts to push the shelves in front of it out of habit, but stops, shoves them back into place.

'What's wrong with Jimmy this time?'

Eualla hears something new in Minnie's voice. Fear, yes, but that's not new. Resignation. That's the one that bothers her most. Her baby sister is somehow both too young and too old for her age.

'Jimmy had too much to drink and fell asleep outside. It was stupid of him. He's stupid. Sounds mean, and we're family and all that, but it's true.' She pauses, collects herself. 'Sometimes you have to look at those around you and say, I'm better than this, whether you're related or not. Because you get one shot at this life, Minnie, and you can't let anyone push you around, bully you. Biology might say I'm Jimmy's sister, but I don't.' She pauses. 'You don't have to, either.'

'Is he gonna die?'

'No.'

'I don't like Jimmy.'

'He's not a likable person.'

'I wish he'd go live someplace else.'

Eualla thinks for a second.

'You gotta just hang in there for now. Soon, I'll be done school and you can come live with me.'

'That's years away.'

'Well, maybe you can come for a summer.' She can't see how this will work but wants to give her some hope.

'Really?'

'Maybe. But, Minnie...' She hesitates. 'I'll always be here for you, but you've got to take care of yourself in this world. If Mama and Daddy taught us anything, it's that.'

Minnie appears to crumple and Eualla wishes she'd kept her mouth shut. Maybe she needs to be the kind one now. Maybe she can make her stronger later. She's trying to figure out what to say, when their daddy calls for her.

'You stay here. Draw me something to take back to school with me,' she says.

Jimmy's on the sofa, covered.

'What's his skin look like?'

'Some white patches, that's about it.'

'Did you check his toes?'

'White and kinda purple.'

Eualla lifts the three blankets and checks his feet. His toenails could scare the hell out of God Himself.

'It's stage one, stage two. He wasn't out long.'

'You can tell by his skin?'

'Yeah,' she says, but there's more. She knows he came home at three fifteen and that her father found him at six. She knows how cold it was outside. 'Cause of how his skin looks. If it was black, it would be dead and he'd have gangrene.'

Despite being told to stay put, Minnie appears and is standing a few feet from her. Eualla thinks Minnie knows exactly what her sister did. Funny, but she's not in the least ashamed.

Eualla is packing her small case. She has to get back to work and she has to study. Katie won't be back until the New Year, and she can get a lot done on her own.

Mama appears and sits on Eualla's bed, watching her. Slowly, she starts to talk.

'When you're young, you think all you need is each other. You can live on love and, I dunno – pixie dust. Yeh can't. You're smart. You got a bright future. Don't blow it on some guy who isn't worth your time. Get yourself a career, make a life for yourself.'

Eualla is quiet.

'I was so young when Jimmy was born. Named him after my daddy, hoping he'd forgive me, talk to me again. He never did. Young when you were born, too. Thought the name I give you was classy. Now, when I hear it, it sounds like some sorta noise a donkey would make.'

Eualla is too shocked to laugh.

'Don't make my mistakes, girl.'

Eualla studies her mother's face as she speaks. Sees the grayish skin, the yellow of her teeth. The dullness of her eyes. And she realizes her mama is only thirty-seven years old.

'It's not too late, for you and Minnie.' She puts the new black sweater she got for Christmas in her small case. 'And I go by Ellie now.'

An idea starts to form. When she goes back to North Carolina, she's going to investigate changing her name. For real.

15

Peyton

Maine, July, Present day

Peyton is alone in the house. She sees a summer storm brewing and carries her notebook and pen downstairs. She pours a glass of wine and pushes the door open, so she can sit outside and watch the lightning. She hasn't been sitting for long when she hears the doors slide open and her father joins her. The ice tinkles in his Scotch as he takes a seat beside her.

'When did you get home?' she asks.

'Just now. What are you doing?'

'Watching the sky,' she says.

'We're in for a storm,' he says.

'The sky is almost black to the right, over the water.' Peyton motions with her glass, like she's toasting the approaching storm. 'Where's Mom?'

'Book club in Portland. She'll stay there tonight.'

The house always feels different when it's just the two of

them. Gentler, even now, despite the storm. She's grateful
her mother is away.

'What's on your mind, Peyton?'

'I was thinking about how I wanted to be a reporter
when I left high school.'

A crack of lightning brightens the sky before disappearing
into the water. She can still see the shine in the clouds
when the thunder sounds. The rain begins, drops splashing
into the pool. She watches the circular waves each droplet
creates.

'Why are you thinking about that now?'

'Because maybe if I'd been allowed to do what I wanted,
my life wouldn't have just fallen completely apart.'

Her father dips his head. 'I never knew you wanted to be
a reporter,' he says.

Another flash of lightning.

Peyton looks at him. 'She didn't tell you?'

'No.'

'When I told her, she said I needed to find a good job.
Stopped speaking to me until I took psychology and English.'

'Your mother means well.'

'There's an epitaph.'

'You do have a way of expressing yourself.'

'You know, Dad, when I was sixteen, she looked at me
and said, "I've known from the moment you were born
you were different." Then she looked me up and down and
walked away. And I've been wondering what she meant by
that ever since, because every sixteen-year-old alive wants
to think they're different.'

'I didn't know any of this,' he says, and Peyton thinks she
hears a note of regret. That's something.

'You were too busy making the world beautiful.'

Her father says nothing and she thinks she may have gone too far. They sit in silence, the memories, the anger, like another person with them.

Peyton sighs. Then she gets up and goes inside to refill her glass.

On her return, her father hands her his tumbler and she takes it, without looking at him. She's angry now, that he was never around. That he left her with her mother and Caroline.

'What do you want for dinner?' he asks as she hands him his drink.

She's silent. She wasn't prepared for the little bursts of rage she's had since returning home. She's always loved her father, but she's older now, she sees his failings. And they bother her.

'We could order in seafood chowder and lobster rolls from Tully's?' he pushes.

'I'll call them,' she says. 'Before they lose power.'

Peyton gets up and goes into the house, leaving the door open so she can hear the rain. It's different here than it is in Seattle and she can't figure out why, so she keeps listening as she goes to the sideboard in the breakfast room and opens the drawers, looking for a menu.

She's rifling through old junk mail and receipts when she finds a card addressed to her mother, Dr Lydia Winchester. Judging by the stamp, it's a Christmas card. Peyton flicks it over and sees it hasn't been opened. Curious, she peels the envelope flap. The glue is dry and gives easily.

The card depicts the Three Wise Men following a star, but it's a modern reproduction, the strokes thick and bold. The desert a harsh purple sky. The star a jumble of angles and spikes. Whoever sent it obviously didn't know her mother well, as Lydia is an atheist through and through.

She opens the card, curious. Inside, in lovely clear writing made with a very fine pen it says:

Dearest Eu,

Thinking of you and your family. Please call. I'd love to hear your voice.

Love from Minnie.

Peyton brings the card closer to her eyes, as though that will suddenly make the message clearer. Who's Minnie? She flips the card around, looking at the back. There's nothing. No price. No barcode.

She slips the card under her arm, finds the menu and goes back to her father.

'So, lobster rolls, chowder... I'm getting a salad. Anything else you want?' She hands him the menu.

He's flipping through it as she says, 'I found an old Christmas card addressed to Mom. Who's Minnie?'

He lifts his head to look at her and she knows she opened a can of worms by how his eyes narrow.

'Let me see it,' he says.

Peyton hands him the card.

He reads it, turns it over in his hands, like she had done, as though there might be something telling on the back. He looks at the envelope again. Peyton knows he's buying time while he thinks of what to say. She knows, because she often does the same thing. It's caused her mother to snap at her to answer on more than one occasion.

'She's your mother's sister. They had a falling out many years ago. Put that back where you found it. And I'll have a side of potato salad, too.'

The rain is dancing on the clear water of the pool. The sky is a swirl of gray and black, with tiny shards of soft blue, just enough to give someone hope for a clear sky. The stifling, oppressive heat of the day is starting to break but is lingering. Peyton stands still, sure he's not joking but thinking he must be.

'Are you kidding?'

'No. Your mother has a sister. She lives in Tennessee. She has a brother, too.' He doesn't add any details about her mother's brother. Her uncle. 'Your mother doesn't like to speak of her childhood, or her family, so you're not to mention this to her. Put this back where you found it.' He hands her the card.

Peyton takes it and sits. 'What else don't I know? Was I adopted? Is Scott really her son?' Peyton's voice is too loud, confused, and it mixes strangely with the cooling air, the thunder.

'Unfortunately, Scott is her son.'

Peyton turns her head to her father, who looks at her guilty. 'Never mind. I didn't say that.'

'Yeah, that's not how words work, Dad.'

They're quiet for a second, her father staring ahead at nothing.

'Family isn't what it's cracked up to be, Peyton. Your

mother had it rough growing up. I think that's why she went into psychiatry, to try to understand everything that happened to her. Now, just let it go, OK?'

'But I have an aunt,' Peyton protests. 'And an uncle.'

'You also have a half-brother and a sister, who are both strangers. Don't add to your mother's grief by suddenly thinking family is sacred.'

Peyton looks at the card, tries to remember what she was going to do before all this. Food. They were going to eat. She picks up the phone to call Tully's, places the order.

'Do you want that on your family account?' the guy taking her order says.

They have a family account? This makes her laugh, given the chat she's just had with her own father.

'Sure, go ahead.'

'You give my best to your mom and dad,' the guy on the phone says, and she's reminded everyone knows her family. Except her.

'Thank you,' Peyton hangs up.

A family account... She wonders how many people have access to it.

She takes the card, puts it back where she found it. Then she goes and sits with her father and watches the storm.

Peyton gets up early to walk the beach before the tourists take over and the sun is too strong. Despite her liberal use of sunscreen, she has a few patches of sunburn and her father tells her again and again how bad the sun is for the skin. She's not sure if he's worried about skin cancer or his daughter looking old and weathered, while he expounds on the virtues of perennial youth. Look good, feel better. That was his ad for a while.

She adjusts her sunglasses, puts on her sunhat. Thinks about everything she learned the night before.

Her mother has a sister. She tries to picture her mother as a young girl with siblings. Are they younger or older? She knew her mother came from Tennessee, that her parents were long gone. She always thought her mother was an only child. Now, she doesn't know what to think.

She cuts up to the road. The sand is still heavy from the rain and it is seeping through her trainers, making her feet wet. It's uncomfortable.

On the pavement, she stamps her feet, trying to dislodge the sand. She's about to resume walking when a police car pulls up alongside.

John appears as he rolls down the window in his cruiser. 'Having trouble with your feet, Peyton?'

She laughs. 'Sneakers are soaked. Who knew the beach would be wet after a storm! How about I buy you a cup of coffee? I owe you.'

'Sounds good. Hop in.'

Peyton crosses to the passenger door, climbs in and buckles her seat belt.

'Any place you have in mind?' he asks.

'You pick.'

He turns a corner and she knows where they're going – a diner just on the edge of town. She can feel the engine in his car pull as he heads up the steep road.

'May I ask you a question, as a police officer?' she asks suddenly.

John smirks. 'That's the Peyton I remember – speaking well and asking questions.'

She's surprised he knows this about her. She's not sure she knows it about herself.

'You know the Daisy Wright case? From when we were little?'

'I do. Very well.'

'Maybe I'm crazy, but I've thought about her over the years and how the case was never solved. It's got me curious, now that I'm back.'

'About what happened to her?'

'About why it was never solved, I guess. I mean, we're older now. We know there are predators everywhere. But back then, the population was smaller. And the Fort is so contained. How did someone get away with it?'

John pulls into the diner. They're silent as they both get out of the car. John holds the door for her as she steps inside.

'I see they've set the air conditioner for arctic breeze,' Peyton says.

'We can go someplace else?'

'I'll be fine once I have some coffee.'

'We'll sit in the window, so you get some warmth from the sun.' He looks at the woman behind the counter. 'Is that OK?'

'Sit where you want. Breakfast crowd won't start for a spell. Coffee?'

'Please,' Peyton replies.

The coffee comes in thick beige mugs. The waitress puts down a saucer filled with small creamers and Peyton peels one open, pours it into her coffee.

'You took it black last time,' John says.

'Very observant.'

'I'm a cop.'

'I like the cream that comes in these little pots.' She adds a second one. 'So, the Daisy Wright case?' she begins.

'What do you want to know?'

'Is it still an open case?'

'Absolutely.'

'Do you think it'll be solved?'

'I hope so.' He looks away from her when he says this, toward the old cigarette machine in the back. 'But off the record, I doubt it.'

'Are there any strong suspects? Leads?'

'No.'

'Does that happen a lot, no suspects in a case?'

'You'd be surprised how often we pretty much know the culprit but can't make a case. But that's not what's happening here. There are theories about what happened. That's it.'

'That must be frustrating. You hear of so many cases of people being wrongfully convicted, you never really think of it going the other way.'

'You'd be amazed at what comes into play. What money can buy, and what politics take place, even in a place this small.'

Peyton is startled by what he says, about what money can buy. Her parents are one of the wealthiest in town. Did he mean them?

She starts to think about Scott, about what her father said about him unfortunately being her mother's son. Scott went through his own rebellious stage, butted heads with her dad many times. But he wasn't a murderer, or a pedophile. She'd loved him growing up. He was good to her. But once he went to Hong Kong, she stopped hearing from him. She wonders about this now, why he doesn't want to stay in touch.

'Can you share some of the theories?'

'You thinking about joining the force?'

'No. I couldn't do what you do, dealing with domestics and drunks and child abuse.'

'Some days it stinks. You see the worst in people. Other days, it feels pretty good. People know me, trust me. I love the Fort.'

'Y'all having breakfast?' The waitress appears, refills her cup.

'Do you have time?' John asks.

'I do. And I want the blueberry pancakes.'

'We're going to need more creamers, too,' John says. 'Can I ask you a question now?' he asks when the waitress is behind the counter and out of earshot.

'Sure.'

'Why the interest in the Daisy Wright case?'

'I think about it a lot. Don't you? I mean, you were living here when it happened.'

'I do, yes,' he says softly.

'I remember the weather. And I remember being really nervous.'

John doesn't say anything and she keeps talking.

'I just find it unbelievable they've never found a body. Bones, teeth. Something.'

John still doesn't say anything. Peyton waits. Nothing.

'Have they found something?' she asks.

'No.'

'Why do you suppose that is?'

'A great big forest on one side and a great big ocean on the other.'

'I'm not buying it. The earth would have returned her by now. Something would have washed up on the beach.'

'The earth would have returned her by now?'

'Sounds a bit gentler than hunters would have stumbled on her skull, don't you think?'

'I guess.'

He seems different, quieter. Peyton can't figure out why. It's an old case. Maybe he can't talk about it, professionally.

'I wonder if her family is still here,' she says.

'Just her mom.'

'How do you know? Do you give her briefings? How is she?'

John looks at her, studying her.

'Peyton, I was there when it happened. Daisy was my cousin.'

16

Ellie

Summer, North Carolina, 1972

The second semester passes in a blur. Ellie, as she now calls herself, maintains her perfect grades and after her finals, sleeps for an entire weekend. Katie is going home to Texas for the summer, but Ellie's staying in their dorm room, taking two classes and working two jobs.

Katie's father shows up on their last weekend. He's a nice-looking man, with thick gray hair and an olive complexion. He doesn't look like a father. He looks like one of the cowboys you see on the covers of romance novels in Rexall's. Ellie finds herself stealing looks at him.

When he offers to take them both to dinner, she declines the invitation. 'I'm sure you want to catch up,' she says politely.

'Oh, you're comin', darlin'. Consider it a thank you for keeping my Katie on the straight and narrow.'

Ellie agrees, hoping they don't go someplace too fancy

as she pulls on a simple blue sundress and tan sandals. The shoes don't quite match the dress, but they'll have to do.

They end up at a steakhouse. It has dark walls and a dark wood floor, and it feels three hours later in the day inside than out. The maître d' seats them at a table and Mr. Davies orders a Scotch, neat. Katie orders a gin and tonic. When the waiter looks at Ellie, she has no idea what to order.

'I'm not much of a drinker,' she says, embarrassed by her lack of sophistication.

'I told you, Daddy. She studies and works all the time.'

'Scratch the order,' Mr. Davies says.

'I'm fine with water,' Ellie says.

'It's a celebration. We'll have a bottle of champagne,' he says.

'Yum!' Katie says. 'Have you had it before?'

'Yes, at an event with the chancellor,' Ellie says.

'Were you at this event, Katie?' Mr. Davies raises one eye.

'No, Daddy. It was for people on scholarship, like Ellie.'

Ellie feels embarrassed by the way Katie says scholarship.

'Good for you, getting a scholarship.'

'Thank you.'

She looks around the restaurant. It's the most elegant place she's ever dined. She studies the vases of white flowers, the candles in brass holders. The soft glow from the lights.

The champagne arrives and the waiter pours them all glasses. Flutes, Ellie knows, from reading books. They're so pretty.

'Congrats, ladies, on a successful first year at university. Cheers,' Mr. Davies says.

They clink glasses. The champagne is ice-cold and

delicious. Ellie thought it would be sweet, but it's not. She takes another sip.

'Careful, sweetheart. This stuff is potent, especially if you're not used to the demon drink.'

Ellie laughs and sets down the glass.

They have shrimp cocktail to start. Katie and her dad get steak, but Ellie has a seafood casserole. She's always wanted to try lobster and scallops and crab. She's always wanted to live by an ocean, in a big house with a bedroom that looks out onto the water. Ever since she read *The Great Gatsby*. To wear dresses and ride horses and have a husband who drives a fancy car. This restaurant, the casserole, feel like a nice first step.

They have a second bottle of champagne, Ellie barely drinking any, as she has work in the morning. Katie has chocolate soufflé for dessert. Ellie demurs. She's almost certain she won't have to pay her share, but she's so used to being frugal, it doesn't feel right to splurge at someone else's cost.

'Girl, you need some vices,' Katie's dad says, giving Ellie a wink.

'I'm sure I'll find some when I have time.'

He laughs, orders himself a Scotch.

'You're nineteen years old. You have all the time in the world.'

Ellie is eighteen. But she doesn't say anything.

'Dad's gonna buy a place as an investment. He likes North Carolina,' Katie says the next afternoon, as she packs.

'Nice,' Ellie says, looking up from her book.

'Daddy was thinking it would be good for us to be roommates again.'

Ellie thinks for a second, trying to find a tactful way to say no.

'I know, I know. You think I'll be partying all the time. I can't. Daddy says if my grades don't go up, he's pulling the plug and I'll be living at home. Then I'll be marrying some local boy, living on Valium and vodka like Mama's friends.'

Eualla scrambles to think of another excuse. She can't see Katie settling down.

'No rent. Daddy just wants us to study. He won't let me live on my own and he says you're a good influence.'

Ellie starts to think. With her scholarship and no rent to pay, she'll be able to work less and study more. Put some money aside for Minnie.

'Do you want to be my roommate, or is this a directive from your father?' Ellie asks.

Katie laughs. 'You don't borrow my clothes, you don't use my stuff and you've never thrown up on my bed.'

'Can't say the same for my roommate.' Ellie laughs.

She can laugh now, but the night Katie threw up vodka and orange juice on her bed, she'd wanted to hit her. So badly it had scared Ellie.

'Yeah, don't let my Daddy know that happened,' Katie says.

'I'd never do that to you, Katie. You're the only friend I made this year. The only person who checks to see if I've eaten. You never complain when my alarm goes at five. And I've never heard you say a bad word about anyone. I hit the lottery when I got you as a roommate.'

'Ah, girl. You're gonna make me cry!'

A year of sleeping eight feet away from each other. Turning your back while the other changes. Running to the cafeteria in the rain under one umbrella. But with this simple exchange, their friendship is solidified, becomes real. And they both feel stronger for it.

17

Peyton

July, Maine, Present day

It's been a few weeks since her breakfast with John and Peyton is walking into town to the library. The early morning cloud cover will burn off, and more and more people will gather at the beach. It's gonna be a scorcher.

Peyton wants to tell him how often she thought of Daisy. If someone went missing in her family, she'd want to know people still thought about them, at least she thinks so. But she doesn't trust herself not to say something else wrong, to make another mistake. So she's kept quiet. She still feels sick when she thinks about her comment to him, about finding the skull.

It's getting hot by the time she gets to the library and she can feel herself sweating as she lets herself in the big wooden door.

There's a woman shelving books, wearing nylons with

reinforced toes and sandals. Only in the Fort could this pass for a good look.

'Hi,' Peyton says, walking toward her. 'I'm wondering if you have any newspaper clippings on a missing person case from twenty-four years ago?'

'The Daisy Wright case?'

'That's it.'

She looks Peyton up and down. 'Did you go to school with her, or are you one of those internet detectives?'

'I grew up here and I remember the day she disappeared.'

The woman puts down the books she has in her hands and signals for Peyton to follow.

'It was a sad day,' the woman says. 'Dear thing. And no answers after all these years.'

There's a table in the back corner, next to the local history section. The woman opens a wooden filing cabinet of some kind and takes out a stuffed folder. She sets it on the table and then pulls out another. And another. In the end, there are six files.

'It got a lot of press attention over the years,' she says.

'Thank you.'

She sits down and the woman says, 'Copies are ten cents.'

'Thank you.'

'You're one of the Winchesters, aren't you?'

'I am.'

'The daughter who went out west?'

'Yes.'

'Your parents have given a lot of money to this library. We're grateful.' She pauses. 'No charge if you need to make copies.'

Her father's probably given thousands of dollars. She'll have to make a lot of copies to make it worthwhile.

The files are frayed and Peyton has a small internal laugh at the idea of suggesting they spend some of the money on some new ones. She opens the one dated the summer of her disappearance and sees clippings, long turned yellow before they were finally laminated. She scans the headlines:

Local Girl Goes Missing.

Gone on the Fourth of July.

No Updates with Missing Girl.

Police Believe Someone Knows Something.

Of course someone knows something. But do they understand the significance of what they saw? Are they not coming forward out of fear? Does anyone ever come forward and confess to something after twenty-odd years of getting away with it?

She makes little piles, putting everything in chronological order. It's formulaic – what she was wearing, where it happened. But then something catches her eye.

Daisy is the niece of Fort Meadow Beach Chief of Police Tom Langley.

There it is, in print. Confirmation. Not that she needed it. John had no reason to lie. But it feels more solid now, more real. Daisy is a story and a life. Sometimes that gets forgotten.

She resumes reading, as though the answer might be in the pile of old stories. After a while, she realizes there's not one instance where police say there's a person of interest in the case. A suspect. There would be no DNA to test as she was never found and the entire beach was the crime scene. It was the ultimate cold case.

She tries to remember what it was like, being that age. Would she have gone with a stranger? If she saw something now, a man walking with a crying child, would she simply assume it was a parent with a difficult kid?

Growing up, she thought the beach was enormous. But each time she walks it now, she marvels at how close the houses are to the path. The beach is long, but it isn't wide. Could someone from one of the houses grabbed her, hidden her?

She keeps reading as the story moves from the front page to the second, the third. And then the milestone stories start. It makes the front page again on the one-year anniversary of the disappearance. 'One Year and No Answers' reads the headline. Under that is a photo of Daisy.

Peyton reads the recap of what happened and then turns the page, where the story is continued. There, in a collection of photos from the memorial held at the town hall, is a photo of her father. His head is dipped. He's walking with her mother, her face a grim show of how to behave in the situation. Caroline is beside her. Then Scott. And there, in the corner, holding her brother's hand, is Peyton.

None of them thought she could understand. Except Scott. He knew she was scared. She crawled into bed with him. That was when his room was still upstairs, before he moved to the dark room in the basement.

She pulls the old grainy photo closer. Even though it's colorless, Peyton sees the short black skirt and black tank top Caroline's wearing.

'You look like a big crow,' her mother had said when they were leaving the house. 'At least wear a scarf for some color and to cover your shoulders.'

Caroline had ignored her.

Peyton remembers it so clearly now. The July 4th celebration had been cancelled that year. It was an economic hit to the town. It also took away some of the fun – the event that bound them all through love of this little patch of earth they called home. A patch that had betrayed them somehow by being the site of this terrible thing happening.

It had been such a pretty night. A perfect July evening. She remembers it all, now. Well, not all.

The nearby beach should have been heaving with celebrations, families, life, but the only people out this July 4th are summer people, vacationers, people who somehow don't know about the tragedy the year before.

It's just Peyton and her parents in the car. Caroline and Scott went on their own. Peyton is humming to herself.

'City council really needs to do something about this building. Paint can't cover its multitude of sins,' her mother says. 'Peyton! Stop making that noise!'

'It does need some work,' her father says.

They park and Peyton jumps to the ground, then walks over to Caroline nearby. She's not sure exactly what's happening. She knows it's about Daisy. She's scared. She's always scared when she thinks about Daisy. Someone took her, right from under her parents' nose.

She tries to take Caroline's hand, but she shrugs it off.

Will they get cake? It is July 4th, after all. There are a lot of people about, wearing nicer clothes than normal. The steps are crowded and Peyton feels Scott take her hand.

There's lots of seats set out, the folding kind. At the front, there's a stage that isn't usually there. There's chairs on it, too. And in front, pictures of Daisy. In one, she's graduating from kindergarten, wearing a white cap and gown. In another, she's eating ice cream on a swing, wearing flip flops that are far too big for her. In another one she's reading a book with an old man.

Her dad stands to the side of a row of chairs, waiting for them all to move in and take a seat. Peyton is between Scott and Caroline. She puts her hand on Scott's knee to push herself up so she can see. It makes her chair move, creating a scraping sound, and she can feel her mother stare at her. Scott puts his hand on her shoulder, guiding her back to a sitting position and using his other to straighten her chair.

There's lot of whispering, which surprises Peyton. Daddy always said whispering isn't polite. The occasional squeak of chairs punctuates the low hum of voices. Peyton can hear the air conditioning whirring. Daddy leans across her and tells Caroline and Scott to be quiet.

A man wearing a funny collar and a robe takes the stage and everyone stands. People bow their heads. Peyton has no idea what's going on and dips her head but looks around, right then left. She can't see much this way. People say something together, then everyone sits. Someone new walks to the microphone. The mayor. He's been to their house for dinner. Peyton looks out the windows at the cars shining in the golden early evening light. She looks at those around her. She swings her feet.

Scott leans down and says, 'Try to be still, just for a while, OK?'

Peyton stops swinging her legs.

Some people at the front start to sing and they all stand again. Peyton would sing, but she doesn't know the words.

When they finish, everyone sits again. Peyton's chair moves and Scott grabs the back, steadies it, then takes Peyton's hand.

Everyone is very, very quiet. And then a woman stands up. Peyton watches her walk to the front of the stage, where the microphone is. Despite the warm night, she's wearing a navy cardigan. She is very, very skinny and even from where Peyton is sitting, she can see the woman shaking.

'Thank you for coming tonight.' Her voice trembles.

Peyton wishes they'd sing another song, a happier one. 'You Are My Sunshine' is her favorite.

'It's been a year since I last saw my sweet girl. A long, hard year. If someone had told me I'd be standing here tonight, not knowing what had happened to her, I'd have said that was impossible. That there was no way I'd still be able to stand, still be able to walk, to move, to live, with the agony. But here I am – standing here. I have to. Because I have to get my baby back.'

There's a pause. The room feels different now. People shift in their seats and drop their heads. It looks like the woman has stopped speaking, but then she starts again.

'My daughter loved the beach. Loved her rainbow sprinkles on ice cream. I once asked her why, saying I didn't think they had any taste. She said she liked the way the colors cheered up vanilla ice cream. I thought she'd be an artist. She always liked bright colors.'

Her voice breaks and it feels to Peyton like everyone in the big, hot room wants to run out the door.

'She *will* be an artist, one day.'

Silence.

'Someone knows what happened,' she says. 'Someone saw something. Please, please come forward. The police are working so hard. They need some help. Please...'

Another pause. She takes a tissue from her pocket. The silver microphone somehow amplifies the pain in her silence as well as her words. Peyton can see her hands shake as she holds the tissue.

'We love you, darling. And we won't rest until you come home.'

She moves away from the microphone, toward the chair. One or two start to applaud, a few claps of nervous hands before realizing it's not acceptable.

'My God,' Peyton's mother says.

There seems to be some murmuring among those onstage. People shift in their chairs. The man in the robe stands and addresses the crowd.

'Let us pray.'

As everyone rises, Peyton takes Scott's hand again. She's not scared, exactly, not like when the wind blows the branches of the tree against her bedroom window, makes shadows on the walls. When her nightlight goes out and she's sure there's something walking down the hall outside her bedroom. It's not monsters – it's not knowing what's happening. It doesn't make sense, the singing, the woman crying, people all looking so uncomfortable despite the sunshine outside.

Scott gives her hand a squeeze. She squeezes back.

'I'm leaving now, OK?' Scott says to her dad, not looking at him.

'Go straight home,' her dad says.

Scott steps back, presses his lips together.

Before he can say anything, their mother says, 'Do *not* make a scene here, either of you.'

Her father walks away and starts talking to the mayor.

'Not the place to talk business, is it?' Scott smirks.

'You don't know what he's talking about, Scott,' Caroline says.

'Go. Both of you,' their mother says.

Scott looks momentarily surprised. Then he walks quickly to the door.

A woman is talking to her mom. Peyton studies her face – it looks like her lipstick is melting. Peyton laughs and her mother pinches her shoulder.

It's just the three of them, again, on the drive home.

Her father is pulling onto the hill that leads to their home, when her mother says, 'What were you talking about with Mayor Williams?'

'I told him the town hall was an eyesore and something needed to be done.'

'And what did he say to that?'

'He said there was no money for it. I said I'd finance some of the work.'

'Why would you do that?'

'Why do you think, Lydia?'

They pull into the drive. Her mother doesn't say anything, just looks out the window.

'Where's Scott?' he asks.

'Gone out with friends.'

'I told him to go straight home,' he says loudly.

'You didn't tell me that,' her mother says.

'Would it have made a difference? You let him do whatever he wants and at the rate he's going, I'll have to recreate The Colosseum to make amends in this place. You know, where we live? Where my family spent summer after summer with no issues?'

'You could have told me.'

'Lydia, they both need reigning in.' He sighs. 'It's one damn thing after another.'

He opens his car door and unfolds himself, removing his tie as he walks to the house. Peyton isn't sure what's happening. Her mother is sitting in the passenger seat. She opens her purse, looks inside and then seems to remember Peyton is in the car.

'For heaven's sake, get out and go get ready for bed,' she snaps.

Peyton struggles with the button on her seat belt, then runs into the house. She finds her dad with a glass in his hand looking out the window.

'Can I go in the pool?' she asks.

'Of course, sweetheart.'

Daddy's sitting by the pool while Peyton floats on her back. She's thinking about the little girl who disappeared. How do you disappear? And why doesn't she come back?

Her mother appears and says, 'I told her to go to bed.'

He doesn't reply.

*

Peyton feels someone nearby and the memory disappears, like a startled bird taking flight. Once again, she's adult Peyton, in the Fort. Her parents still spending most of their time apart. Her brother and sister with lives of their own, gone. Daisy Wright still missing.

'Do you need anything, dear? I'm taking my break,' the woman says.

It takes Peyton a second to remember where she is. Sitting in the library, surrounded by old newspaper clippings. The memory of what happened was so strong, she's surprised she isn't drenched in water from the pool.

'I'm just going to make some copies,' she says. 'Don't worry about me. Can I come back tomorrow?'

The librarian laughs. 'You don't have to ask permission.'

Peyton is careful with the old newspapers as she fits them on the screen of the copier. It feels strange, to be looking at a photo of her younger self so long ago.

As the copier scans and whirs, the blade of light moving back and forth, she thinks about calling John and inviting him out for dinner.

She gathers up the clippings, hands the file back to the librarian. Then she starts to walk home. She takes the long way, along the beach, past the tacky new pier. It's made to appeal to visitors, and she realizes, standing there, that is the issue for her. The Fort isn't a tourist destination for her, it's her home. Like it or not.

This is where it happened, on this piece of land. The old pier collapsed and a little girl disappeared from the sand where she now stands.

She walks closer to the water, listens to the lapping sound it makes, constant as the sun rising and setting, the comforting repetition of it. The sun she takes for granted, the water she loves. For its beauty. For its sound.

She turns her back on it now and looks at the houses, a line of witnesses to the events. Most of them were there at the time, but not in their present incarnation. They've been built up, remodelled, changed hands and been upgraded as the Fort became more and more of a tourist destination. But someone looking out the window on the second or third floors, on the roof terraces, might have seen something...

She takes one last look around, as if some new clue will present itself. The sound of a boat grows louder and she turns to watch as it speeds by, the frothy white wake it leaves disturbing the shimmer on the water before its absorbed again into the waves and the water is once again flat.

It's past four when Peyton gets home. Too late for lunch, too early for dinner. She sniffs the air, certain she smells cigarette smoke. Someone must have been visiting.

She opens the refrigerator, looking for a snack, and grabs an apple, then she gets out her phone. She opens WhatsApp, finds the note John sent her after they met by the marina.

Hey, John. Just wanted to say again how sorry I am to have brought up Daisy the way I did. I'm not sure how I forgot your family connection, as I've thought about her often over the years.

Peyton stops typing and looks at the note. She thinks for a moment, then types:

I owe you a meal. Let me know if you want to get together.

Peyton sets her phone down, then opens the refrigerator again, starts digging around for something to make for dinner. She thinks about what she sent to John and what she wanted to send, but didn't:

I really want to know what happened that day – and not just for Daisy. For myself.

That was the good thing about getting older – knowing most of the time what to say and what not. And being able to pour yourself a glass of wine whenever you wanted. Unless, of course, your mother is around.

She's sipping her drink by the pool when her phone beeps. She feels nervous picking it up.

Dinner sounds great. She was such a beautiful little thing. Kind and smart and funny. I try to remember her life more than her disappearance. Not solving the case killed my dad.

Peyton reads the note twice. She gets not wanting to talk about things. She might not understand having someone you love disappear, but she knows what it's like for your family to be a subject of gossip and interest, other people dissecting your life for sport. Like when Caroline was arrested for shoplifting. And Scott for drunk-driving. Peyton wonders if those cases made it to the Langley's dinner table.

Let me know when is good for you. And again, I'm really sorry that I brought it up and grilled you like that.

A smiley emoji appears:

I'm sorry, too.

Peyton looks at the text, wondering for a second what he's sorry for. But that's not what makes her the most curious. It's the realization that with everything Marco put her through, on the rare occasions she told him how she felt, he never apologized. He twisted it to make it look like she was at fault. If she swapped Marco for John, she knows the text would have read:

I tried to indicate to you it wasn't something I wanted to talk about, but you didn't pick up on the clues. You need to respect people's boundaries.

Another realization hits Peyton. Her mother does that, too.

18

Ellie

August, North Carolina, 1972

It's the last day of August and Ellie is moving into the house Katie's father bought. She and Katie will share the ground-floor apartment and a professor has the upstairs. It's a five-minute walk from campus, down quiet tree-lined streets, with houses with wraparound porches and big flower beds on the lawn. For her it is paradise.

Ellie buys a mattress and puts it on the floor in the smallest room, a lamp next to it. She makes a desk out of milk crates and a sheet of plywood a man a few streets over was throwing away. She buys towels on sale and three new pieces of clothing for school. A miniskirt, a turtleneck and a blazer.

Looking around her room, she wishes she had a bookcase and thinks about the one her daddy made, his idea of atoning. She can do without. She neatly stacks her books on the floor.

She hums to herself as she puts some groceries in the

refrigerator. She's happy – the happiest she's ever been, in her entire life. She has a perfect grade point average and is on track to graduate early. Then med school, then a big house of her own.

At noon, she walks to the mailbox at the end of the walkway. She's not really expecting anything, but she has been using the address for a while.

She has a letter and it confirms her new name: Ellie Anna Tompkins. She stops with it in her hands, thrilled by the magic of how easy it's been to recreate herself. Katie gave her the name Ellie, but Tolstoy christened her Anna.

A truck pulls up and she knows Katie is here with her stuff. She's excited to see her old friend, who sent her exactly two letters all summer. Ellie heard more from Katie's father, who needed her to pick up keys and let in the cleaners and hire a gardener. She'd laughed and said she'd offer to do it herself, but she had no idea how to start a mower and didn't know a rose from a daisy.

He'd chuckled and said he didn't want her working any harder than she already did.

'You remind me of myself,' he'd said. 'I grew up dirt poor and worked like a fool to get where I am. I like your gumption.'

'Thank you,' she'd said, mostly because she couldn't think of anything else to say, and embarrassed he saw her poverty.

'Girlfriend!'

Katie comes running toward her, arms outstretched, and Ellie realizes how much she truly likes Katie and her big heart, her enthusiasm for pretty much everything. Her friendship. They hug in the middle of the lawn.

'Hello, Miss Ellie!' Katie's father says before giving her what she thinks is a standard Texas-style hug, lifting her off her feet.

Ellie feels light and safe and happy, and something else, in his embrace.

'Hey, Mr. Davies,' she laughs.

'Daddy, put her down.'

'Call me Dan,' he says.

It feels nice, to be part of this normal happy-family interaction, even if only on the periphery. And she feels bad, for a second, that she hasn't seen Minnie since a two-day visit in July. Mama was still standing, thank God. Daddy gave her money. Jimmy was nowhere to be seen and she prayed the whole time she was home he didn't show up. Minnie was well and happy and drawing and painting. That was all that mattered.

'I can't believe you guys drove all this way. You must be exhausted,' Ellie says.

'A few days driving through this pretty country with my best girl? We had a great time.'

Katie, standing behind her father, rolls her eyes.

'Alright. Let's get this truck unloaded. I'll take a shower and then I'll take my two favorite girls out for dinner.'

'I'll help unload, but then I have to go to work,' Ellie says.

'You're kidding!' says Katie.

'Sorry. I didn't know what day you were coming, or I'd have changed my schedule.' Ellie's surprised at how disappointed she feels, remembering the last meal they had together. She can almost taste the crisp, citrussy Champagne, the creamy casserole. It was the best meal of her life.

'Aw, that's too bad. But I'll be here all weekend.'

'I took the small bedroom up front and left you the big one off the kitchen. Is that OK? I have a bigger window but you have a way bigger closet.'

'She'll need it.' Katie's father appears with a large suitcase in each hand.

'We brought beer!' Katie says.

Ellie hears the bottles rattling. What the heck! she thinks.

She clinks bottles with Katie and her father, who insists, again, that she call him Dan.

Dan Davies, the cowboy, she thinks. Dan Davies of the Houston Davies.

'OK. I'll see you guys later. Enjoy dinner!' she says.

She's running late and moves quickly down the street, head bent trying to make up time. She's brushed her teeth and is chewing mints but still she worries about the smell of beer on her breath, even though she only had a few sips. She may have another later, if everyone's awake when she's finished work. But it's a long shift, and late when she gets home, she lets herself in quietly, closes the door softly. The click when it catches echoes in the still night air. She pushes her bedroom door open and turns on her overhead light.

There, neatly set up against the wall, is her bed. Only now it's in a frame, complete with headboard. A small nightstand is beside it, her lamp and clock sitting on top.

She sits on the edge of her bed, her heart hammering in her chest. And she starts to cry. She's not sure why at first. Maybe she's tired... But no, that's not it. At least, it's not a physical tired. She feels worn out not by all she does, but all she carries. The bad memories of childhood, the anxiety, the fear. And the feeling something was wrong with her. Why didn't her parents stop Jimmy? Why didn't they care what happened to her? That's the hardest bit to carry. Sitting here, the memories taking swipes at her, she can't remember the last time she cried.

There's a knock at her door. Her head snaps up in the direction of the noise as it opens and Dan appears.

'Hey now. What's going on in here?'

Ellie wipes her eyes with her hands, embarrassed to be caught in this state. She jumps up, embarrassed, too, for some reason, for being caught sitting on her bed by Katie's father.

'My mattress seems to have grown a frame. And a nightstand.'

'I took Katie out shopping and we came across a deal. You need a good sleep with all you do, young lady.'

'This is really sweet of you, but you've already done so much, what with covering rent...' She falters.

He waves it away. 'It's an investment. I don't believe in wasting money on rent. The tenant upstairs brings in money and the place is paid for.'

He pauses, looks at her, a blend of concern and interest and... something else?

'Now tell me why you're crying. It hurts my heart to think of you in here crying by yourself.'

'I'm not sure why I'm crying, really. Just felt a bit overwhelmed by everything.' She gives a nervous laugh.

'You're burning the candle at both ends. That's not good. You're so young. You should be enjoying yourself.'

Ellie doesn't say anything, mostly because she can't think of anything to say. She's not about to tell him she doesn't have anyone she can rely on. That she has no idea where the little bit of money her daddy gave her even came from.

'Do you have to work so many shifts? Can you scale back?'

'I'm going to have to. School is becoming more and more demanding. I'll have to live on bread and water.'

He gives her a hug, holding her gently against him. Ellie feels her heart beating faster. It feels nice.

And wrong.

'Get some sleep. We'll go for breakfast in the morning.'

He leaves her room, closing her door behind him.

Dan Davies is such a nice man. She just loves him.

19

Peyton

July, Maine, Present day

It takes three full days at the library, but Peyton has now read every single article written about Daisy Wright. She's also poked around at some of the articles written about her own family and is starting to think that every time Scott or Caroline got in trouble, her own father made a large donation to some public work within weeks. She can't be sure, as their names aren't used in the police blotters – just generic notes about police responding to noise complaints, shoplifting. The only case that made the news was Scott being charged with impaired driving. She can't believe that. No one drinks and drives anymore, do they?

She never did anything herself so bad he had to write a check. She never did anything bad. She wishes she had, now. It seems to have worked for Scott and Caroline, who have big careers and family, while she sits at home, with neither.

Scott's been in Hong Kong for years. Caroline never

comes home. And here she is, using the place to regroup. When she finally does leave, will she not look back, either?

She thinks about her father saying her mother had a tough childhood. Maybe it all started there. There's no way she can ask her. Peyton barely knows her mother, but she knows she'll say it is none of her concern. She's curious about Minnie, since she found the Christmas card. When she's done with Daisy, she'll work on that mystery.

It's four o'clock. She has an hour before the library closes. She opens up her pad and starts to make notes.

The population of the town that summer was just over six thousand. Take out those under twelve and over seventy-five. No, eighty.

It would have been heaving with summer vacationers and tourists there just for the weekend. She flips through her notes where she listed the hotels at the time. Assuming maximum capacity, she adds another 800 people to the figure. How many children, elderly, incapacitated could she take from that number? How many people were on the beach where it happened?

From reading the newspaper clippings and talking to John she knows Daisy was with her parents, John, his aunt and uncle and their son, John's cousin Richard. She'd scribbled his name down after seeing something on John's face. He didn't like his cousin, she could tell. He lives in Tucson now. Peyton made a note to Google him. She sees the note now and circles it to look at later. Returns to the task at hand.

Add another 400 staying with family. She adds it up. The figure looks both manageable and overwhelming.

She wishes she could see the police files. She wishes she

could tack everything up and look at it chronologically, make a timeline. But her mother would hit the roof if she marked the walls.

She shuffles everything into a pile and stuffs it in her bag, then starts to walk home. It takes less time than usual, her leg muscles more powerful now as she pushes through the sand.

The house is quiet when she lets herself in. She hopes she gets some time alone to think, but the sound of papers shuffling means one of them is home. She finds both her parents sitting at opposite ends of the conservatory, each reading a newspaper. She takes a deep breath. Her mother already thinks she's crazy. She doesn't need to push her father into thinking that as well, but she feels driven to make a timeline, to solve this case.

'Is there a wall I can use in the house to create a timeline?'

Both her parents look up, startled – either by her presence or her question, she's not sure which.

'What *are* you talking about?' her mother asks.

'Is this about the Wright girl?' her father chimes in.

'Yes. It is. I just need someplace to set out my notes,' she says, pressing her feet into the floor, standing her ground.

'Peyton, you're being ridiculous,' her mother says.

'Lydia…'

'What, Octavian? She's over thirty, living here, and she's obsessed with a twenty-five-year-old case?'

'Obsessed is a strong word. I'm curious. Most parents would encourage that with their children.'

'You're hardly a child anymore.' Her mother returns her attention to her paper.

'So, back to my question. What room can I use?'

'What's wrong with your own bedroom?'

'Can I tape things to the walls?'

'No!'

'Peyton, use Scott's old room downstairs. No one will bother you and the walls need repainting.'

Scott had moved to a room in the basement, next to the pool table and the ping-pong table. It was his way of saying he wasn't part of the family, by moving into the basement. Part of it is sort of finished, part of it not. The rooms are all cut up and it feels like a maze. So much different than the house above, with its sleek lines and flow, its elegant emptiness.

'Is it necessary to be so difficult?' she hears her father say.

'She needs to get her life together.'

Peyton doesn't hear what her father says. She scoops up her photocopies and heads to the kitchen, finds tape and a marker and some thumbtacks in the junk drawer. Then she heads downstairs, to Scott's old room. She puts everything on his old bed, then picks the biggest wall, the one without the window.

How do they do it on cop shows? She wishes she had a whiteboard. She'd like to put a picture of Daisy in the middle of the wall. She has a small photo with an article she copied. She folds it so the grainy black-and-white picture is all that shows and tapes it to the wall. Standing back and staring at the little girl, head tilted up, a mass of curly hair, her mouth open wide in happiness, Peyton feels a new sense of sadness. For her, it's a mystery. Something she's carried with her all her life but only taken out occasionally while she went about her life.

When she hears about stories of abduction or someone

posts a missing photo on Facebook, the feeling she gets reminds her of that day. Sometimes, too, when the sky is heavy with rain that has yet to fall, in the sweltering heat of a July day. But she's been able to walk away from it in a way others couldn't. In a way Daisy couldn't. She's gone. All the potential, everything that could have been, taken away. It's just not right that her story has no ending.

Looking at the photo, Peyton promises to do her best. Although her best these days isn't much.

She tapes some paper to the wall and starts charting everything she knows about what happened that July night all those years ago. The picture of her family at the memorial goes up and a thought starts to form.

On a piece of paper next to Daisy's photo, she draws a picture of a house. Like something a child would create. She doesn't have the skill to draw The Stick House, but she's almost certain that Daisy's disappearance and the old mansion are somehow connected. She just has to figure out how. And then, maybe, a way to prove it.

20

Ellie

April, Texas, 1973

It's Easter weekend and Ellie is traveling to Texas with Katie.

Katie's father sent plane tickets for the two of them. Ellie has never been on a plane and is both excited and nervous. She holds the armrests of her seat the entire time, pulling up on them as though it'll help keep the plane flying.

Dan picks them up at the airport. Ellie's heart gives a funny little lurch when she sees him, tanned and in blue jeans and a blue shirt, topped off with a Stetson cowboy hat.

'Hey, Daddy!' Katie hugs her father, looking over his shoulder.

Ellie notices Katie scanning the crowd, hopeful and scared at the same time.

'Mama not with you?'

'She's gone to Branson in Missouri to see some singer. Didn't she tell you?'

'No,' Katie says. Ellie sees her friend's perennial good nature falter.

It's a forty-minute drive to their house, so they stop and get burgers and shakes, eating in the car as they drive. Ellie is finishing her last fry, cold now, when Dan turns down a tree lined lane, and a sprawling stone mansion appears. It's like nothing she's ever seen, with what looks like entire walls made of glass.

'Wow, Katie. Is that your house?'

'Yup.'

'It's gorgeous,' Ellie gushes.

'Well now, thank you. We're happy here,' Dan says.

'How could you not be?' Ellie sighs.

The house seems to glow in the early evening light, the gray stones taking on a ghostly sheen. There are walls of glass, and through them you can see the inside staircase. She knew Katie had money, could tell by her complete disinterest in it, as well as all of her clothes. Seeing the house she figures she must have money like the Vanderbilts, the Rockefellers. She feels too poor to even enter.

Katie's dad grabs their bags, and Katie opens the front door.

Ellie can almost feel her jaw drop. It's even more beautiful inside, with a huge fireplace dividing the kitchen from the living space. The ceilings must be thirty feet high.

'Where shall we put Miss Ellie? In with you or the spare room?' he asks.

'Whatever's easiest,' Ellie says.

'Give her the spare room. She's gonna wanna study.'

Katie's dad laughs. 'You're gonna study over Easter?'

Ellie nods, too taken with the house to speak.

Dan takes her bag and walks up the staircase, the girls following. The stairs open onto a landing with another fireplace and a sitting space, with a couch and table and three chairs. A big window. The landing is bigger than the diner back home, she thinks, wondering why she's making that particular comparison. She feels like she's in a dream or a movie. Yes, it feels like the setting for a big romance movie, with a cowboy and a woman in need of attention. The only romance novel she's ever read plays out in her mind.

Katie moves to a door and opens it. 'This is my room. You can bunk next door.'

Katie's father carries her bag into the room. There's a huge four-poster bed in the middle with a lovely peach bedspread barely visible for all the cushions and pillows. She's never seen so many in her life, set up in row upon row, and decides she doesn't like them. They're too busy, and she thinks they make the room look cheap and showy, like too much lipstick on a woman or a cheap suit on a man.

'Bathroom's through there.' Dan points to a door in the corner. 'Come down when you're ready and we'll throw some steaks on the grill.' He winks and closes the door.

Ellie looks around the guest room. The thick brocade drapes covering enormous windows, the framed print of a bridge in the mist on the wall. Ellie walks closer to see if Dan painted it or maybe his wife. It says Monet. She wonders if Minnie likes his paintings.

Minnie.

She thinks of the little shack she was raised in and shame

covers her again. Because she's here for the weekend, in a mansion with a pool, while Minnie is at home. She goes into the bathroom, flicks on the light and washes her face as though that might remove some of the guilt.

Katie's nowhere to be seen when Ellie makes her way to the kitchen. Instead, she finds Dan standing looking out the window. He turns to face her as she approaches and she sees a glass of some amber liquid in his hand. There's a bottle of Jack Daniels on the table.

'I'm celebrating your home state,' he says. 'Care for a belt?'

She shakes her head. 'I'm not much for hard liquor.' She's never tasted Jack Daniels and has no plans to. She imagines it smells like Jimmy.

'Can I pour you a glass of wine?'

There's a rack behind him and he pulls out a bottle.

'Um, yes, please,' she says. 'Where's Katie?'

'She's at the stables, visiting Clive, her horse. First thing she always does when she gets home. I can walk you down if you want to meet him.'

'Who?'

'Clive. Her horse.'

'Um...'

He laughs. 'Don't tell me you're a girl who doesn't like horses?'

'I don't think I do. I'm not sure. I've never been around one.'

'Nor had Katie. Saw one in a book and never let up till we got her one.'

Ellie can't imagine what it must be like to want a horse and get it.

'Let me show you around.'

He pushes the patio door open and she feels the hot Texas air cancel the cooler air from indoors as she steps onto the stone patio.

'The pool is beautiful,' she says.

And it is. Instead of being a rectangle, it's kidney-shaped, curling in toward the house. There's a waterfall at one end, made from the same stones as the house.

The land seems to roll on out back, but in the distance she can see something. Stables. She notices it now, the faint scent of hay and horses. Country wealth, she guesses, is what it smells like. Anger catches her, sets her jaw hard for a second. She went hungry to feed her little sister while Katie grew up with horses and a pool.

'Everything OK, Ellie?'

Dan's voice catches her off guard. Has he been watching her?

'Just thinking about how much fun it must have been to grow up with horses in your backyard. And a pool.'

He continues to study her, not buying it.

Careful, Eualla, she tells herself. People notice more than they think. Then she catches herself. Ellie. She's Ellie now.

Ellie wakes early, as is her habit. She forgot to close the blinds and the penetrating Texas sun has jolted her to life. She knows it's too early to go downstairs, so she takes a shower, brushes her teeth, then, hair still wet, crawls back into bed with a textbook on abnormal psychology. She reads until a knock at the door startles her.

'Come in,' she says, and Katie appears.

'Hey, babe,' she says, crawling into bed.

Ellie sets her book down as Katie curls up beside her. She still has sleep in the corner of her eyes.

'How are you?' Ellie asks.

Katie shrugs without opening her eyes.

'You didn't say much at dinner last night,' Ellie adds.

'Didn't have much to say.'

Ellie curls up on her side, facing her friend.

'Is it your mama being in Mississippi?'

'Sorta.'

Ellie waits, not wanting to push.

'She and Daddy are never in the same place at the same time anymore.'

'What do you mean?'

'Mama's usually at the apartment in Houston or her daddy's place in the Gulf Shores and Daddy's on business or here, making sure the horses are fine.'

'Maybe they just need some time on their own to figure out their new roles now that you're older.'

'Maybe. I know I'm a grown-up, but I can't believe she won't be here with an Easter basket for me.'

'I've never had an Easter basket in my life,' Ellie says, unthinking. 'Well, maybe one when I was really young.'

Katie opens her eyes. 'Never had an Easter basket? Golly.' She thinks. 'Well, neither of us will have one this year.' She leans over and kisses Ellie on her cheek. 'You're gonna be a great therapist. I'll be your first patient.'

'I'll give you a discount.'

Katie smacks her with a pillow. It's a small moment in time, a moment of connection, but she'll remember it forever.

'Hey!' Before Ellie can grab a pillow and retaliate, Katie perks up.

'I smell coffee,' she says. 'Daddy's been up for hours, chomping at the bit for us to get up and go horse riding or swimming or into town or something.'

'Coffee sounds great. And I want to pet a horse. Never done so before.'

'You grew up in Tennessee!'

'Trust me, no self-respecting horse would be caught dead in my hometown.'

'I'm gonna shower,' Katie says, sliding back under the covers.

'You look like you're gonna sleep.'

'Hush. I'm showering.'

Ellie waits for a second, then pulls her hair back in a clip and heads downstairs. There's an enormous painting on the landing of Dan, Katie and Ellie guesses, her mother. It screams wealth, not happy family portrait. Ellie looks around, making sure no one can see her staring.

She finds Dan sitting with a newspaper.

'Morning, Ellie!' he says, sliding off his reading glasses.

She likes how he looks with his glasses. Intelligent, pensive. But without them you see his blue eyes better.

Dan pours a mug of coffee for her and slides the cream toward her. She adds a dollop, watching the white liquid turn the black coffee sandy. She stirs it with her finger, making Dan laugh.

'I know we're pretty rural, but we do have spoons here

in Texas.' He passes her a spoon, and their hands touch briefly. It warms her in a way the hot coffee doesn't. She takes another sip. It feels different, the air in the room, the shadows of the early morning light. Something new is here, with them. Something real but unseen. Something alive.

'Is that daughter of mine awake yet?'

'Yes and no. She woke up and came into my room, where she promptly fell back asleep.'

He laughs.

'She seems a bit sad, which isn't like her,' she says.

He nods. 'Her mama. She likes to… how d'you say it? Do her own thing, lately.'

There's nothing she can think of to say to that.

'Why don't we get you fed and we can walk the property? What'll you have?'

Ellie has a slice of toast and takes an apple with her as they set out.

What a beautiful day. Already, she loves Texas.

On Easter Sunday, Ellie wakes early and decides to go downstairs to grab a coffee. She hopes no one sees her, in bare feet, wearing an oversized sweatshirt and a pair of shorts.

When she opens her door, she stumbles on something. An Easter basket waiting for her. She looks down the hall and sees one outside Katie's door, too. She wants to wake her, but it's barely six o'clock. She picks up her basket and carries it back to her bed. There's a chocolate bunny, wrapped in foil. A fuzzy stuffed blue bunny. She picks it up and hugs it. It's soft and cuddly and already she plans to send it to Minnie. In a box in the middle is a gold necklace with her initial, E. She's nineteen years old and this is the first Easter basket she's ever received.

Without thinking, she heads downstairs. Dan is sitting at the table with a newspaper in front of him.

'Morning, Miss Ellie.'

'Thank you for the Easter basket.' She can feel her eyes shining, excitement and happiness thrumming through her.

'How's that?'

'The basket outside my door.'

'The Easter bunny found you.'

'Found Katie, too. She's just not awake yet. Did the bunny find you, as well?'

'My baby girl is here and you're here, so I guess it did.'

Spontaneously, happily, she throws her arms around him. She can feel his hand on her back, a fatherly pat, and then he's rubbing her back, softly. Gently. Pulling her in close. Holding her. And then she feels his hand cradling her chin. He looks into her eyes. She can feel something all through her body. Then he kisses her. A deep kiss. A long kiss. Thorough. It's her first and it's magnificent. Right down to the tickle from his moustache.

They hear steps and break apart. Katie appears in a similar outfit to Ellie. She has a pair of bunny ears on her head. It's both cute and sad, and very Katie, who has so much but seems so empty to Ellie.

'The bunny has been. What did you get, Ellie? And why are the two of you always up so early? It's not normal.' She kisses her father on the cheek. 'Thanks for the basket.'

She throws her arms around Ellie, almost knocking

her off balance. As the two girls, entwined, stumble Dan steadies them with a hand.

'Oops!' Katie says, kissing Ellie's cheek.

There's a lot of kissing in this kitchen this morning, Ellie thinks, her heart racing. What does it mean, this kiss?

'Daddy, let's saddle the horses and go for a ride.'

'What say we have breakfast first?'

Katie turns to get coffee and Dan runs his hand across Ellie's back. Something is happening. She's just not sure what.

After horse riding and lunch and another trip to town and a game of lawn darts and a BBQ, Katie crawls into bed with Ellie, like they're young girls at a sleepover. But her friend doesn't want to sleep. She wants to talk. And talk. And talk. Ellie is distracted, still thinking about the kiss. About all the times during the day when Dan brushed by her, touched her arm. All the times they found themselves looking at each other.

'Katie, I can't keep my eyes open,' she says. The clock says it's just after two in the morning.

'Have it your way. I'll leave you to it.'

She can feel Katie slip out of bed. Outdoor lights go on. Ellie falls asleep thinking about Dan kissing her. She feels warm and comfortable. She feels tingly and safe. She feels alive.

21

Ellie

May, North Carolina, 1973

Another school year is over. Katie's going home for the summer but Ellie's staying put, same as ever. She's asked Katie if Minnie can come visit and she feels a certain lightness at knowing her sister has something to look forward to. And that she's keeping a promise to her.

'When's your dad coming?' she asks as she helps Katie pack.

She tries to sound casual, but Dan Davies is a constantly in her thoughts.

'Tomorrow night,' Katie says. 'I don't know why. I'm leaving everything here. I can fly on my own.'

'Maybe he wants to inspect the property, worried about his crazy tenants.'

Katie throws the clothes she was folding into her bag. 'Let's go for a pizza and a beer.'

Ellie looks at the clock out of habit, figuring she needs to be somewhere, doing something. But she's not working and doesn't need to study anything.

They walk to the local student bar – a place Ellie has hardly been to but is a second home for Katie – where they order pizza and a pitcher of beer. Ellie isn't keen on draft, but it's cold and the day is hot that the two work together to make her down her first glass and start on her second. One pitcher turns into two and Ellie finds herself playing darts with some guys she's seen around campus and she realizes it's OK to have fun. Nothing bad will happen if she lets loose once in a while.

They stumble home at one, arms linked, singing 'Age of Aquarius'. Ellie knows maybe a dozen words at most, Katie even less, so they make up the lyrics.

In the street outside their apartment Ellie says, 'You left the lights on.'

'No I didn't.'

The main door opens and there's Dan, jeans and a long-sleeved shirt, despite the heat. Ellie's heart gives a flip and she both instantly sobers and becomes more drunkenly giddy.

'Well now, what have we got here?'

He fills the doorway and Ellie, even in her beer-induced euphoric giddiness, is struck by how solid he is. Tall, nice shoulders. He shakes his head, but she can tell he's laughing. Ellie has never been intoxicated before. It's nice. She likes it. Nothing to worry about… nothing at all. Really. Why has she always been so worried?

★

Ellie wakes with a headache and a sense of unease. She needs to brush her teeth. Dan, who usually stays at a hotel, is asleep on the sofa. Or at least she thinks he is, until she hears, 'Good morning, Miss Ellie.'

'Oh, hi... Mr. umm ... Dan.'

He sits up, swings his legs so his feet are on the ground. She sees the crease on his cheek from the cushion, wants to trace it with her finger.

'Come talk to me,' he says.

'Sure. Just give me a second.'

She walks to the bathroom, brushes her teeth. She has sleep in her eyes and washes her face, puts on some lip balm and checks on Katie. She's out cold, sprawled on her bed. Ellie doesn't think she's changed the sheets all semester. Once she leaves, she'll do it for her.

Her heart is thudding wildly when she walks back to the living room.

'You girls have fun last night?'

'We did. An end-of-year celebration. Your daughter thinks I'm boring.'

'My daughter is wrong.'

He puts his hand on her bare knee and she feels that same jolt run through her.

'I've been thinking about you,' he says.

'Me, too. About you, I mean.'

'Doesn't feel right, you being so young, but there's something between us.'

Ellie doesn't trust herself to talk. She looks at Dan, the way his skin is so tanned. The blue of his eyes. The gold watch on his arm.

On the morning of her first hangover of college life, she sits on the sofa and kisses the father of her roommate, the only friend she's made in college. It feels right. And normal, exciting. And safe.

And dangerous and scary and very, very wrong.

22

Ellie

July, North Carolina, 1973

It's hot as hell and Ellie is so excited, she's finding it hard to concentrate on both her studies and her job. Dan is coming to visit, her second visitor, as Minnie has just been. Spent a week with her. It'll just be the two of them for three whole days. They've spoken on the phone. He calls her from his office line. She wants to write him a letter, but he says that's not a good idea. He sends her flowers. Big yellow roses for Texas.

She races home from work, wanting to cook dinner for him. She has a bag of groceries under her arm and is trying to open the door when it pops open, and there he stands.

She drops the bags and goes to him. He wraps his arms around her.

She's almost twenty years old when she has sex for the first time. It's not what she thought it would be. It feels more like she's hovering above herself, watching things happen to her. It's painful for a second and then it's like she guessed it would be, if a little fast, a little frantic on his part.

But the kissing... The kissing is nice. The feeling of being wrapped in his arms is nice. After, he lights a cigarette and hands it to her.

'I don't smoke,' she says.

'Was that your first time?'

She sees his smile.

'You're so innocent,' he says. 'You shouldn't be with an old fool like me.'

She starts to say she loves him but holds back, knowing it's wrong. She sits up in bed and kisses his shoulder. He wraps his arms around her. It's better, the second time.

By the time he leaves, she's certain Dan is the man of her dreams. She's madly in love. So in love, she tells herself this is good for Katie, she'll be a good influence on her. A better stepmother than Katie's own mother has been to her. After all, she raised Minnie. She knows what she's doing. But then, she wouldn't be a stepmother. She'd be a friend. And when she comes to visit her and her dad, Ellie promises herself she'll always meet her at the airport.

23

Peyton

July, Maine, Present day

Something wakes her, a noise she's not heard before. A thump of some kind. Did she feel something shake? It's not like her to wake at noise. Silence... and then a shout, as though for help. She throws back her blanket and cotton sheet, twisted from her sleep, but doesn't get out of bed. She must be dreaming. She can't seem to move. Someone is banging on the door.

'Peyton, get up! Get up! It's your father.'

Peyton's heart is out of bed and across the floor before the rest of her. Pulling open the door, she sees her mother wild with panic.

'Mom?'

Peyton's father is on the floor, making an awful gasping, wheezing sound. She moves to him, crouching in front of him, her hand on his knee. She can feel her mother disappear from the doorway.

'Dad. Dad, are you OK?' It's clear he isn't, but she can't think of anything else to say.

He's rubbing his chest, winded.

Her mother appears beside her with a robe for Peyton. She's in shorts and a tank, kneeling over her father.

She throws the robe on. Her father is rubbing at his chest with one hand, the other supporting him upright off the floor, where he's fallen out of bed. She rests her hand on his shoulder. She feels the cold of him through the thin pajama top material and it terrifies her. Not her dad. Please. Not him. Not now.

'When did you call 911? They should be here.'

'I didn't,' her mother says.

'Why not?'

'I yelled for you!'

Peyton sprints to her room, grabs her phone, calls for an ambulance as she rushes back to her father. She pulls a blanket off the bed, wraps it around him.

'It's OK, Dad, it's OK. Help is on its way.'

Peyton hears sirens and races down the stairs to let the paramedics in.

'Upstairs, hurry. Please.'

Peyton runs up the stairs and they follow.

They move past her mother, who's sitting on the floor by her father. One of the paramedics grips her arm and pulls her up, sliding into her space. Peyton watches as they lift him onto a sheet, then onto a stretcher. Peyton starts to follow them out the house, but her mother grabs her, telling her to put on some clothes.

'You can't go to hospital like that!'

Somehow, her mother has managed to change into another breezy pantsuit.

Peyton stumbles into her room, adrenaline, fear, shock making her body seem just outside her control. She pulls on a pair of trackpants, a tank top and a sweatshirt and races downstairs, sees her mother waiting for her in the hallway, the door open.

The blinking blue-and-red lights of a police car fill the entranceway. Peyton looks out as she pulls on her shoes and sees John coming to a stop. She runs out to meet him, to tell him to move his car, that she has to get to the hospital.

'I heard the call for an ambulance on the scanner. Are you OK?'

She sees his concern, genuine and real and very welcome in the middle of this terrifying night.

'Dad's having a heart attack. I think. The ambulance just took him.'

'Oh, Peyton. Come on, get in. I'll take you and your mom there. You're not driving in this state.'

Peyton turns to run back to the house, but her mother is beside her. John opens the front door and helps her mother in while Peyton climbs into the back. He follows with his flashers on but no siren, driving slightly over the speed limit. Peyton wants to tell him to hurry up, as though being close to her father will somehow will him to be OK. Will everything to be OK.

John has barely stopped his car when Peyton is opening the door.

'Easy,' he says.

She feels his hand on her arm.

She waits until he parks, then jumps from the car. She

flies into the hospital and then comes to a stop, unsure what to do next. She looks around the room and wonders why everyone is so calm when her dad is dying.

Then John and her mother are beside her. Peyton feels ridiculous, rushing forward yet not knowing what to do next.

'Pull yourself together, Peyton. The drama isn't helping.' She pulls two masks from her bag and hands one to Peyton. John pulls one from is pocket.

Peyton sees John's eyes widen, briefly, at her mother's words.

Then her mother walks toward the information desk. Peyton turns to John.

'This was really nice of you. Thanks,' she says, like he's taken her out for ice cream.

He reaches out and gently touches her forearm. The hospital is cool and Peyton is embarrassed that she's not wearing anything under her sweatshirt but the thin tank she slept in. She wraps her arms around herself.

Her mother beckons her and she and John move forward, the naked lights bouncing off the white floor and walls. It feels bright for a building that sees so much darkness.

'They're working on him now. The nurse said she'd let us know when there's any news,' her mother says.

John shepherds them to seats. 'There's coffee in the vending machine, but it's not very good. I can run out and get you some?' He looks at his watch.

'We're fine, thank you, John,' Peyton's mother says.

Peyton was going to ask for a hot chocolate. She's cold, feels like she may start to shiver. But she keeps quiet.

A radio on John's belt cackles to life and John grabs it in

a quick motion. He nods as he moves to the door, talking into the radio.

'He's a nice young man,' her mother says.

'He is.'

'Very sweet of him to come when he heard the call.'

Peyton nods, guessing her mother is talking out of nervousness.

'What happened? Did you find him on the floor?'

'I was reading and I heard a thump. I called his name and didn't hear anything.'

Peyton knows her mother is a lousy sleeper, that she often wakes in the middle of the night and reads. It's one of the reasons her parents have separate rooms, she thinks. One of the reasons, at least.

'He said he had indigestion earlier. I thought he must have eaten something spicy when he was in Portland. I asked if his arm hurt, asked if he was in pain. He said it was indigestion, not to worry. Don't look at me like that! He's a doctor, too. How was I supposed to know?'

Peyton sits in silence, knowing her mother is talking more to herself than to her.

John comes back in. 'I have to go. I have a call. I'll check back later. Call me if you need me.' He bends and kisses Peyton on the cheek. Then he leans over and takes a hold of her mother's hand.

'Thank you, John,' she says.

Peyton asks her mother if she has any change.

'Pardon?'

'I didn't bring my bag and I want something hot.'

Her mother hands Peyton her wallet. 'Get me something

hot, too. Coffee. I wish they had brandy in that vending machine.'

Peyton takes the wallet, shakes out some quarters.

They sit quietly, waiting for their drinks to cool, the steam disappearing into the air-conditioned air. Peyton takes a sip, the chocolate thin and lacking taste but hot. The minutes pass painfully as they sit, as they wait.

'The coffee is terrible.'

'Hot chocolate isn't much better.' Peyton looks in her cup.

'Do you think we'd have heard by now if something had happened?' Peyton asks.

'I don't know, Peyton. Just try to be positive.'

Her mother's words shock her. Lydia Winchester isn't a warm soul. Nor does she believe in positive thinking.

Peyton has no idea how long they've been sitting, her drink now cold sludge in her hand, when a doctor appears.

'Doctor Winchester?'

Peyton's mother sits even straighter.

'Yes?'

'We've found a blockage and we're moving him to Portland for surgery,' she says.

Her mother stands, nodding.

'May I see him first?' Peyton asks.

'Of course you can.'

Peyton takes her mother's empty plastic cup and throws it out with her own, then they follow the doctor down the hall. She isn't sure what she expects to see, but her father looks better. Pale but with a tinge of pink. Not the awful gray color he'd been when she found him on the floor. His eyes are closed and he has tubes in his nose, in his arms. She tries not to cry.

Her mother stands on one side of the bed and Peyton watches as her mother smooths the hair from his forehead. The simple action both warms and surprises her, scaring her, too. Makes it seem like her mother is saying goodbye.

'Hey, Dad,' Peyton says, lightly holding his hand.

'Sweetheart,' he says. 'Who's the little man on your top?'

Peyton looks down, although she knows she's wearing a 'Life is Good' sweatshirt, the stick figure waving. She found it in the back of her closet, long forgotten. Funny that she's wearing this on one of the worst days of her life.

'They've given him drugs,' her mother says. 'He's a bit loopy.'

Orderlies appear and Peyton and her mother move away from his bed.

'We'll be waiting when you wake up,' her mother says.

Peyton bends and whispers, 'I love you, Dad,' in his ear.

She can count on one hand the number of times she's said this to him. She's never said it to her mother. They're not that kind of family. He closes his eyes and she thinks she sees him smile.

Peyton waits for her mother to say something about her being romantic or foolish, but she says nothing. Simply watches her husband disappear down the hall.

'We should have driven here. We need the car now.' Her mother starts walking to the exit. 'The surgery will take at least six hours. We can go home, have something to eat, bathe. Pack the car to go to Portland.'

Peyton stops, thinking. They should be there during the surgery. In case something happens. What if a doctor comes out to tell his family and there's no one to tell? She wants to ask her mother but is afraid to say those words, to put them out into the fragile space around them.

'You coming?'

She follows her mother down the hall. It had seemed so bright before, but now, the day breaking outside seems to have dimmed the inside lighting. She sees the wear and tear, the gray floor that was bleached white before.

Peyton is looking for a phone to call a cab when John appears, coffee in his hand.

'Hey. How is he? Any news?'

Peyton can't talk.

Her mother appears and John hands her a coffee, pulling sugar out of his pocket.

'Thank you,' she says. 'They're taking Peyton's father to Portland for surgery.'

It feels strange, standing still, drinking coffee, with everything that's happening.

Peyton sees John square his shoulders at the news.

'Good doctors, excellent hospital. I've been there a few times myself. Do you need to go home? Or I can take you straight to Portland,' he says.

'We need to go home, get a few things. Then Peyton can drive. We'll need the car when we get there.'

John looks at Peyton, as if searching for confirmation. Peyton nods.

'Let me take you ladies home,' he says, opening the main door for them.

Peyton scans the heavens, looking for a sign, a celestial note saying her father will be OK. But the stars have disappeared and the sun isn't up yet. It feels empty. She takes a deep breath and walks robotically to John's police cruiser, gets in.

'Call your sister, tell her what's happening,' her mother says.

They're still in the parking lot and her mother has switched into practical business mode.

'I'll call from home. I don't have my phone.'

John starts to hand her his.

'No, John, it's fine. We'll be home soon,' her mother says.

The car moves silently through the empty streets of the Fort. The houses are dark, the streetlights dim, barely glowing. Peyton remembers when they used to hum before they were replaced with environmentally friendly lights. She misses that sound now.

John pulls into the drive, gets out the car and opens the passenger side for her mother.

'Call me if you need anything.'

He waits as they walk to the door, until they're in the house, as though they may be attacked in this bit of land on the edge of the Fort, where nothing ever happens. Well, almost nothing.

Peyton opens the door and suddenly feeling the dark, switches on every light on the ground floor of their home. She goes to the kitchen and picks up the phone. It's just before five in the morning. A stupid time to call.

'Hello?' Caroline's husband answers the phone, his voice groggy and full of sleep.

'Hi, Conor. It's Peyton, Caroline's sister.' She's not sure why she adds the last part.

'Peyton.' He pauses as though trying to sort out if he's asleep or awake.

'Is Caroline around?'

'Sure, I'll get her. Is everything OK?'

'Not really. Our father's had a heart attack. He's in surgery.'

'Oh, shit.'

She hears him stumble, like he's walking around. Do they not sleep in the same room?

Peyton hears him call for Caro. She can't imagine her sister being called Caro or any husband of her sister's saying shit.

'Peyton? What is it? We never use the landline.'

She feels she's being admonished for calling it.

'Dad collapsed earlier and we took him to hospital. He's had a heart attack and he's on his way to Portland for bypass surgery.'

Peyton knows from the silence that greets her that Caroline is thinking, rubbing the tip of her nose with the nail on her right thumb the way she does.

'How does it look?'

'Scary.'

'How's Mom?'

'OK. Taking a bath and packing so we can drive to Portland. We'll stay at the condo there.'

'Call me when you know something.'

'I will.'

Peyton ends the call, looks around the kitchen. Should she make tea?

She opens the refrigerator and the cabinets like she's never been here before. Like an answer will be hidden among the spices. Nothing.

She goes upstairs to shower and pack. Then she goes to

her room, pulls out the only carry-on she moved home with. She pulls out some clothes, sets them inside. Walks to the bathroom and turns on the shower. Then she undresses, dropping her trackpants and sweatshirt in the laundry, even though she's only had them on a few hours. Hospital germs. Lingering fear of disease. Not wanting to see what she was wearing when she said goodbye to her dad before he went to surgery. He's the only thing keeping this family together. If he doesn't make it, they'll each go their own way. She knows this.

She's blow-drying her hair when her mother appears at the bedroom door.

'Did you reach your sister?'

'I did.'

'When's she coming?'

'She said to keep her posted.'

'We need to get going.'

Hair still wet, Peyton grabs both their bags.

She loads her mother's Cadillac and starts to get into the passenger's seat, when her mother says, 'You drive, please.'

Her mother is using her phone, not paying attention to Peyton as she pulls out of the drive.

'Text your sister when we get to the hospital, let her know where we are.'

Peyton is wondering who her mother is messaging on her phone, if not Caroline. Then it dawns on her. Scott.

Peyton turns the air conditioner down, suddenly cold. Her phone buzzes beside her.

'Check my phone and see if that's Caroline,' Peyton says, looking over her shoulder as she changes lanes.

'Please,' her mother says.

'Really, Mom? With everything going on? Give me a break.' Her voice has an edge she's never used with her mother before, and Peyton knows her mother is startled by her reaction.

Her mother picks up her phone. 'What's the passcode?'

'Two-two-five-five.'

Her mother punches in the code and waits as the screen fills with messages.

'John telling you to drive safely and call him if he can help.' She pauses. 'And Marco, saying hi. Asking if you're still in Seattle.'

Her mother turns to look at her and Peyton wishes she could jump out of the car, right here, on the interstate. Run for the hills, away from everything that is happening. All the nights she stared at her phone, wanting him to call. All the texts she sent that went unanswered. And now, on this terrible night, when she's finally stopped thinking about him, he texts.

'Not sure why he sent that,' she says.

'Who knows what men think,' her mother says.

'Remind me again what you do for a living?' Peyton jokes.

She feels her mother look at her.

'Nothing from Caroline,' her mother says, setting Peyton's phone down. Her mother closes her eyes, leans back into the headrest. Peyton looks over at her, sees the lines around her eyes. They seem new, brought on by what is happening. She looks away, back at the road.

'Do you want to stop for anything?'

'No, let's just get to the hospital. We're going to be here a while.'

*

The surgery takes seven hours. Peyton is starting to sweat when the doctor comes out and tells them it went well.

'He should make a full recovery, Lydia.'

'Thank you, Michael,' she says to the surgeon.

'When can we see him?' Peyton asks.

'He's in recovery. It'll be a few hours. Why don't you go get something to eat, have a rest? When you come back, I'll take you to him.'

They drive to the condo, unload their bags.

'Let's go for brunch. Someplace has to have brunch.'

There's a restaurant in walking distance to the condo, a high-end chowder house. Peyton's mother orders a fruit and cottage cheese plate and a Bloody Mary. Peyton orders eggs Benedict.

When the waiter leaves, her mother says, 'You won't keep the weight off that you've lost for long, eating like that.'

'I've been up since three. I held my father's hand while his heart failed. I sat in a cold hospital without a bra while the hottest guy in this town held my hand. And I'm living with my parents. I've earned these carbs.'

Her mother tilts her head, studying Peyton as though she's someone new who's just sat at their table.

'You do have a way with words,' her mother says.

The food comes and Peyton dives in, but after five or six mouthfuls, she's full.

'Is it not good?' her mother asks.

'I feel full already.'

'Your stomach has shrunk,' she says. 'You look so much

better than you did when you landed. I was worried about you. So was your father.'

Peyton takes a sip of her water, processing the fact that both her parents had been worried about her.

'You were concerned about the wrong things,' Peyton says.

'What?'

'Of all the problems I've had in my life, putting on fifteen pounds doesn't even make the list.'

'I don't think we need to talk about your problems now.' Her mother orders another drink.

'No,' she says. 'I guess we don't.'

24

Ellie

December, Texas, 1974

'When will I see you over Christmas?' Ellie asks.

They're in bed, in her new apartment in Houston. Dan is smoking. She's tracing hearts on his shoulder with her index finger. He doesn't answer right away and she knows before he says anything he has plans with his family.

'I was thinking,' he says, sitting up and stubbing out his cigarette, turning his back to her. 'Maybe your sister could come. Be good for you to see her. I can buy her a ticket, a Christmas present for you.'

Ellie sits up, holding the sheet to her chest, a cotton shield against her sudden feeling of vulnerability.

'I'd love to see Minnie, of course I would. But what about you? When will I see you?'

'Well now, I'm off to Telluride in Colorado, skiing,' he says, still not facing her.

'By yourself?'

'Hell no. Do you think I'd be flying down a mountain in the cold when I could be here with you?'

'Katie and her mother?' She never calls them his family.

He nods, then wraps his arm around her. 'I'm sorry, baby, but we won't be back until New Year.'

'You promised we'd be together this year,' she says, trying to keep her voice steady, neutral.

'I know, baby. And I'm sorry. But one day, Katie will be all fixed up and we'll be together.'

Ellie closes her eyes, the words so familiar, the only bond they really have. Ellie's in her first year of med school in Houston, chosen so she could be close to Dan, while Katie was still in North Carolina, playing at getting her undergraduate degree. Dan said when she finished he'd buy her a ranch and she could teach kids to ride. He'd told Ellie when this happened, they'd be together.

'Maybe you can meet Minnie, if she comes early enough? Or stays until January?' she says.

'Well now. Would that be a good idea? She knows Katie,' he says, his voice different. Reserved. Nervous. Distant.

Ellie is shaking her head, more forcefully than she needs to. 'She won't make the connection,' she says. She wants someone she knows to know about Dan, however tenuous it might be.

'I don't think it's a good idea, darlin',' he says.

She is disappointed, again. But it's OK, she tells herself. They'll have lots of Christmases together. Lots of time with Minnie. Besides, medical school is busy. For the first time, she really has to work to maintain her place. It's good Dan's going away. At least that's what she tells herself.

'I'll get the ticket this week. Christmas will be here before you know it,' he says.

'Hmmm,' she says.

It's sunny and cool out, the sky blue and the air crisp and clean. Ellie's favorite kind of day. She can feel the festivity, the joy in the air unique to the holiday season, her first Christmas in Texas. At the airport, she checks the arrivals board. She's the first one at the gate, as close as she can get. Maybe it's the holiday lights, the excitement in the air, but she feels good. Excited, even.

'Eualla… Ellie!' Minnie calls.

It's the loudest she has ever heard her baby sister's voice.

Ellie hugs her sister, so much smaller than her. So different. She's the only person on Earth besides Dan who she genuinely loves. Dan, who rented the apartment for her, saying he just wanted her to focus on studying. Who had helped her move from North Carolina to Texas, who sent her flowers until she told him to stop, to save his money, for when they are together. She remembers how he laughed as this.

She loves Katie too, but it's complicated, thinking about her friend.

'Welcome to Texas!' she says.

She watches Minnie looking around the huge airport, the oversized, over-the-top decorations.

They catch the bus to her apartment and Minnie stares out the bus window at the tall skyscrapers, gleaming in the late afternoon sun.

'It's a great place,' Ellie says. 'And it has some fantastic art schools.'

'Can we go see the Museum of Fine Arts?'

'Sure we can. Let's go to my apartment and drop off your bag first.'

The bus drops them almost outside her building. Minnie tips her head back as she takes in the apartment building, all nineteen floors.

'You live *here*?'

'I do.'

'Golly. How big were your scholarships?'

Ellie feels a jab of embarrassment at this and a sudden flare of anger toward her sister, even though she knows it's not fair. Minnie doesn't know. And it's her guilt. About the apartment. About Katie. About Katie's mama. But then Dan isn't happy. He deserves to be happy. She deserves to be happy.

They walk into the lobby, the floor she thought was marble until Dan had laughed and said, 'At these prices? Not even close.'

Ellie heads to the elevator and presses the button. They move swiftly to the fifteenth floor.

The hallway is lined with green carpet with gold trim.

'Golly. This is so pretty!' Minnie says.

She opens the door to her home and ushers Minnie inside.

'I can't believe how nice your apartment is, Eu.'

Ellie smiles to herself. The apartment is beautiful, with one wall made up entirely of mirrors, making it look bigger. The others are a peach color and there's a gold chandelier in the ceiling. It's bright and shiny and new, and she loves it for these reasons.

'And look at this,' she says, leading Minnie to the sliding patio doors.

They step out onto the balcony and there, spread out before them, is Houston.

'Wait till you see it at night when you can see all the city lights. It's beautiful,' Ellie says.

'Wow, Eu...'

'OK, Minnie. You've got to stop calling me Eu. Please, call me Ellie.'

Minnie looks at her, as though this simple request has made her a stranger. But she knows there's more to it than that. She's in medical school and living in an expensive apartment. Minnie's not stupid, but once she meets Dan, she'll understand. There's no one else in the world like him.

Minnie is standing on the balcony looking at the city when there's a knock. Ellie flies to the door. He's standing there, in a suit and tie, a cowboy hat. He has an enormous bouquet of flowers tucked under one arm.

'Hey, darlin',' he says.

It's how he always greets her and he steps quickly inside to the foyer.

'What are you doing here?' she says.

'Flight doesn't leave for a few hours.' He grabs her, pulling her to him.

'Minnie's here.'

He's holding her, kissing her neck like he didn't even hear her.

'Stop. My sister.'

She's so small and quiet, they hadn't noticed her. But Minnie is right there, watching them.

Dan drops his arms, stands straight, as though at attention, as though small Minnie is inspecting him.

'Dan, this is my sister, Minnie. Minnie, this is my friend, Dan.'

Minnie stands still, looking at him. Her already white skin pales. Ellie knows something isn't right.

Dan steps forward. 'Pleased to meet you, Miss Minnie. How are you liking Texas?'

Minnie continues to stare. Ellie feels her heart start to thump.

'My sister's an artist. Watch out, or she'll be studying you to see how you'd look in a portrait,' Ellie says, scrambling to figure out what is happening.

The movement seems to jar her into action.

'Hello,' Minnie says.

He hands the flowers to Minnie. 'Welcome to the Lone Star State – greatest state in the union!'

Minnie takes the flowers, the crinkle of the paper they're wrapped in the loudest noise in the room. They stand there, awkwardly, the three of them like points on a triangle. Minnie continues to stare.

'Take a seat in the living room, Dan. Minnie and I'll put these in water.'

In the kitchen, Ellie throws the bouquet in the sink.

'What's up? Why are you behaving this way? Dan's my friend.'

'I know him from someplace,' Minnie says.

Ellie feels like someone has let the air out of her, just for a second. Then she thinks maybe it's good, that someone else knows about Dan. It makes it more real, at least for her. It's what she wanted.

'How could *you* know him?' Ellie asks.

'I know him.'

With those words, he appears at the door.

'Hate to run, but I have to get to the airport. Miss Minnie, it was a pleasure.' He tips his hat.

'I'll walk you to the door,' Ellie says.

'Is everything OK?' he asks, his voice low.

'Yes.'

'Does she know about us?'

'She does now.'

'Does she know Katie?'

'They've never met. You're safe,' she says, even though she doesn't feel it.

'OK. Good.'

'Merry Christmas. I love you.'

'See you soon,' he squeezes her bottom, and is gone.

She closes the door behind him, scrambles to figure out how to deal with Minnie.

In the living room, she finds her sister sitting with an open can of beer. Ellie is shocked by the sight.

'I know I know him from somewhere,' Minnie says. 'I'm trying to remember where.'

Ellie feels herself grow cold. How can she know Dan? It's not possible.

'I've seen his picture, in Katie's room. When I stayed with you. He's Katie's father.' Minnie's eyes widen.

Ellie can't believe what's happening. She prides herself on being the smartest person in the room, any room. Every room. But now she remembers when Minnie visited her that summer in North Carolina. Ellie can picture the photo in her mind. She scrambles, wondering what to do. She can lie, tell Minnie she's wrong. But Minnie will remember, when she and Dan eventually get married. It'll always be between them.

'Yes, he's Katie's father. But he's my friend. He helped me a lot when I had no one, those first few years at university. It was hard,' she says.

And the feelings come back, the constant sick feeling in her belly, worrying all the time. She feels herself slump, suddenly exhausted by the life she led years ago.

Minnie must see this too, as she says, 'I won't say anything.'

Ellie nods. She goes into her bedroom. At first she can't see anything. Then she notices the pillows on her bed have been moved. She lifts one up and sees a long flat box, wrapped in foil. It's from Houston's Jewelry Store. It's not Christmas, but she sits on the bed and opens the box.

A diamond bracelet. A tennis bracelet, she thinks they're called. It's beautiful.

She puts it back in the box and moves to the closet. She takes down the cardboard box where she puts all the gifts he's given her that she can't wear, in case someone sees, asks questions. She sets it inside, then goes back to the living room and sets about planning to show Minnie Houston.

She looks out the patio doors and sees the sky is still the same perfect blue. She's surprised by this because it feels like it should be starting to darken. Be darker. When you know it's not a passing cloud but the start of them gathering, and you wonder how long you have before the rain begins.

25

Ellie

July, Texas, 1979

Ellie can't remember the last time she was this happy. She doesn't think she's ever been so happy. It's been a long four years, but medical school will soon be behind her. She's made it, almost. Soon, she'll begin her residency and a new part of her life.

As he has done almost every Friday night for the past four years, Dan is coming over for dinner. They need to talk about the future. Katie has finally graduated and Dan has set her up on her own horse farm. It seems to be working out. Ellie's is certain Dan has been waiting for her to finish med school and is going to propose. She can't wait to see her ring.

She's wearing a low-cut, sleeveless, clingy black dress and the ruby necklace he gave her for her birthday. Her hair is long and loose, not piled high and enormous the way most women are wearing it now. She doesn't have the time or the interest. Besides, Dan said she looked like someone from the golden era of Hollywood and that he liked that about her.

She's looking in her bedroom mirror at her reflection when she hears the familiar sound of his key in the door. He makes so much noise wherever he goes.

'Baby!' he says, 'Where are you?'

She races to him, can't help herself.

She launches herself into his arms.

'Medical school grad-u-ate!' he says, lifting her from her feet.

Then he's setting her down, heading to the kitchen, where she's set the table. He pulls a bottle of champagne from a bag and shoves it in the freezer.

'It'll be ready in twenty minutes,' he says.

Ellie sees the bag is from the corner store, clearly bought on the way in. It doesn't sit right with her, the last-minuteness of it. Shouldn't he be better prepared? Shouldn't he have had something planned?

She takes off her black heels and walks into the kitchen barefoot, the red polish on her toes stark against the white of her skin and the black of her dress. She sees how pale she looks. She needs some sun.

'I can't wait to get a tan,' she says. 'Do you know how long it's been since I've sat there and done nothing, just soaked up the sun?'

'Maybe we can get a weekend in Galveston this summer,' he says, pouring a glass of the red wine she has on the table. 'Where's the steaks?'

He looks around then opens the refrigerator, pulls them out. He slaps his hands together, seemingly more excited by the sight of red meat than her, and turns on the indoor grill.

She hadn't planned on eating so early and drains a glass of wine as she throws potatoes in the oven to roast.

Dan walks over to the balcony and opens the door, steps out into the night air.

'I made a good deal today. A lot of money for the company.'

She's lost count of the times he's said this to her. She nudges his arm so she can cuddle in next to him. He looks at her and pulls her in.

'I love this city,' he says, looking out at the endless lights.

Most are businesses, she knows, but around the edges, the suburbs, each of those lights is a home. She likes to think one day, one of those lights will be theirs.

'So, I have to make some plans,' she begins.

She feels him stiffen slightly.

'Well now, of course you do. Of course you do. A pretty young doctor? Female? You got the whole world ahead of you.'

This isn't going to plan. If he had a ring, now would be the best time to give it to her. But Dan has always been unconventional, she tells herself. Maybe he has a different plan.

'I have to finalize my residency,' she says. 'I've had a few offers.'

'Well now, where are you thinking of going?'

Ellie tells herself to be calm. It would be just like him to play her, get her going, then tell her she's staying right where she is, with him, and pulling out a ring.

'I've narrowed it down to Boston, Houston and Raleigh,' she says.

'What would be best for your career?'

Of course. He'll want what is best for her career. She sighs.

'They're all good,' she says.

'Well, you liked North Carolina. And you have people in Tennessee.'

People? What's he talking about? Dan is her people.

She turns away, steps back into the apartment. He's not following her. She can tell. She feels nervous and stoops to put her shoes back on, like she's going to have to run somewhere. She pours another glass of red and drinks it while she checks the potatoes.

Dan appears in the kitchen.

'I'll open the champagne. It's a celebration!' he says.

Ellie nods as she takes the salad from the refrigerator. She'd spent so much time and money getting everything ready for this evening. A new dress. A pedicure. She looks at the clock. She thought she'd be engaged by now.

The pop of the champagne cork makes her jump. Dan laughs as he pours himself a glass, and then her.

'A toast,' he says, raising his arm.

He's taken off his jacket and she can see patches of sweat, like Rorschach tests, inkblots under his arms. It makes her cringe. She knows she's looking for reasons to dislike him, to be angry with him. She's just not sure why.

'To the lovely and beautiful Ellie Tompkins. The sky is the limit for you, darlin'.'

As far as toasts go, it isn't much. She drinks her champagne. A nice brand, but not Cristal. Not Dom Perignon.

She opens the oven and spears a potato, then turns up the heat.

'Five more minutes,' she says, putting the steaks on the stove.

Dan pulls her into his arms for a waltz around the kitchen and she melts. He's always made her feel safe and they've had so much fun together. He's the only person since Debbie she's ever been silly with.

'We need to buy you a hi-fi,' he says.

'They're called stereos now,' she says, wondering if this means he's planning on spending more time in this apartment, with her.

He stops dancing and pours himself another glass of champagne.

'Steaks are done,' she says.

Ellie has cooked this same meal for them so many times, she has it down to a science.

Dan sits at the table and she slides one on his plate. She gives him the biggest baked potato and watches as he loads it with butter, sour cream and bacon bits.

'So, I was talking about my residency,' she says.

'Where has the last four years gone?' he asks, shaking his head.

Dan is devouring his meal, but Ellie hasn't touched hers. She picks up her knife and cuts up her steak, pushing it into a neat pile. Dan reaches over and spears a piece.

'We should have had asparagus, with hollandaise,' he says.

'Then we should have gone to a restaurant.' She downs another glass of champagne, knowing she'll feel terrible in the morning.

They finish dinner and take their drinks onto the balcony. He kisses her gently, sweetly, telling her how proud he is of her. The kisses grow deeper and they end up in the bedroom. When they're done, he gets up and walks, naked, to the living room.

When he returns, he has a long flat box in his hand. Sitting up in bed, she wishes, hopes there's a ring inside. That he put it in a different box to surprise her.

It's a diamond tennis bracelet. A familiar diamond tennis bracelet. He's already given her the exact one, that Christmas when Minnie visited. Funny, but she'd almost worn it tonight.

'Congratulations, baby,' he says.

Ellie puts the box down on the bed. 'How much jewelry have you bought me since we started… seeing each other?'

'I dunno. Why?'

'You bought me a gold necklace – my first piece of jewelry – for Easter. Then you bought me a diamond necklace. And the ruby one I'm wearing right now.' She stands, walks to her closet, takes down the shoe box where she keeps her jewelry. She removes the twin diamond bracelet and shows it to him. 'You bought me this.'

It takes him a second to realize what he's done.

'Oh, baby. I'm sorry. Tell you what, you tell me what you want and I'll get it for you. How about a nice emerald? Or a sapphire? I didn't see one of those in the box.'

'I want a ring.'

'Sure thing. Whatever you want…'

He looks at her and she sees the reality of what she wants hit him.

'Katie has her ranch. Your wife is always in New York or Alabama. And you've made promises to me,' she says, keeping her voice even.

'Ellie, baby. Katie, well, she still needs me and my wife, well, just give it time.'

She can see a line of sweat forming on his forehead.

'Why do you need more time? What will that accomplish?'

'My wife, Katie's mother. Her daddy gave me my start. I'll lose so much.'

'But you'd have me, you'd gain me,' she says.

'I already have you,' he says.

Ellie feels calm, despite everything that's happening. He was never going to leave his wife. It was all a lie. He's played her for a fool.

He's sitting on the edge of her bed now, pulling on his boxer shorts, looking over his shoulder at her. His back is bare. She's staring at his shorts. He always wears the same color, white, the same style. She's never given it much thought before, but tonight, she's repulsed by the old man shorts, by the freckles on his back.

'This is how it's going to work. I'm staying here until I start my residency. I don't want to see you or hear from you. Pull any tricks, and I sit Katie and your wife down and tell them everything.' She would never do this, but he doesn't need to know that.

'Ellie, baby. Please.'

'I move, you don't follow me, and none of this ever happened.'

'You don't mean this.'

'Unlike you, I always mean what I say.'

'Try to understand—'

'Get out.'

He doesn't move. She picks up the closest thing she can find, one of her black heels, and throws it at him. It bounces off his chest, making no impact other than some shock value. She scans the room again and picks up a bottle of perfume, also a gift from Dan. She launches it at him. It bounces off his forehead. He staggers, slightly. She's barefoot, naked, looking for things to throw at the man she loved until this moment.

'Jesus, Ellie,' he says, touching his head.

She watches as he scrambles to pull on his pants as she hurls another bottle of perfume at him. Also a gift from Dan. Medical students pick up the smells of illness, death, decay, formaldehyde. He's bought her serval bottles of scent. Now, she sees it as a mask – masking not the smells but her accomplishments. He's just told her his father-in-law made him what he is. This is new information. Ellie is self-made.

He's scrambling for the door, pulling on his shirt. She follows him, naked, hurling another bottle at him. He's moving like the building is collapsing around him.

'You're crazy,' he says.

She tosses another bottle as he pulls the door shut behind him. The sweet, heavy smell of perfumes inches toward her, envelops her like a heavy fog.

She thought it was love, but she'd been his whore.

The smell of the fragrance is overpowering. She opens the patio doors. Opens the windows. She hunts for the black heels she was wearing earlier and pulls them on. Crouching, naked, she cleans up the mess she's made. Only one bottle broke, and she wraps it in paper and then two plastic grocery bags before pulling on her trench coat and making her way to the garbage chute. No one sees her. She doubts she'd care if half the city had.

She takes a long shower, scrubbing hard at her skin.

Erasing the lingering smell of his aftershave. Of him. She finds it strange she isn't crying, isn't more upset. She's gone from being in love to being filled with hate in less time than it takes to run a bubble bath.

She steps out of the shower, wraps herself in a towel and wishes, for the first time in her adult life, that she had a friend to talk to.

26

Peyton

August, Maine, Present day

Peyton is sitting with her father, doodling in her diary as he sleeps, when her mother appears. Peyton looks at her watch. She wasn't expecting her mother so early.

'What's up?' she asks, standing.

'My patient cancelled – at the last minute – so I thought I'd come over and see your father.'

Her mother is at the foot of her father's bed, looking at him like he's a science experiment.

'Well, if you're going to stay, I might go back to the Fort.'

'Why?'

'I need some clothes. My electric toothbrush charger. I want to get my laptop.'

Peyton walks over to her father, bends and kisses him on the forehead. He feels warm again. Sweaty. She presses her cheek against his forehead, like her mother used to, but has no clue if he has a fever.

'Dad still feels warm.'

Her mother looks up from where she's taken a seat, already pulling out a newspaper. She looks at Peyton, walks over and rests her hand on her husband's forehead.

'He's fine.'

Peyton hesitates, but her mother waves her away.

She walks through the corridors, saying hello to her father's nurses. Smiling at patients, the other people visiting sick loved ones. Then she steps out into the light of day, pulls in a deep breath, wanting to clear all the hospital germs from her lungs, wanting to pull in some energy, some life. In the parking lot she finds her mother's car, sleek and glistening in the sun. She opens the door, slides inside. The leather seats are hot, from sitting in the sunshine. She doesn't turn on the air conditioner. She likes the feeling of being warm, of being hot. It's always so cold in the hospital.

Traffic is light as she hits the interstate, heading to the Fort. She turns on the radio, scans until she finds something she likes. Finds herself singing along to Elton John. The sun is shining. She's always loved driving. And she's warm. Her father is in the hospital, but just for right now, she lets herself feel good.

She pulls into the drive of her family home. She finds herself happy to see the great white behemoth, perched on the hill above the water. She lets herself in through the garage, bypassing the entrance she hates.

It feels good to have the place to herself, and she walks along like she's exploring something new. She feels the peace in the quiet, in the emptiness. It's just her and her thoughts, and she plans to make the most of these few hours.

In the kitchen she grabs a bottle of lemonade from the

fridge, then walks to the basement, to the timeline. She gives herself an hour to look at the familiar photos, the old newspaper clippings, the timeline on the wall. She's flipping through them, hoping for some answer to jump put at her, when she sees a note she'd scribbled to herself. She'd almost forgotten. John's cousin Richard. He was two years older than John. He'd been hurt in the collapse and she wonders where he was standing in relation to the rest of the family, all of whom were uninjured.

Picking up the paper, she heads to the kitchen, to the light. She seems to think best in different places in the house. She can't think at all in her bedroom, but the kitchen counter has helped before. Maybe it's the way the light shines in the patio doors. She opens them now, looks at the pool. She'll go for a swim before she goes back to Portland.

She reads the note again, and an idea starts to form. Picking up her mobile, she calls John. When he doesn't answer, she leaves a message on his voicemail. Then she heads to her bedroom to find a swimsuit, thinking with every single step.

27

Ellie

September, Boston, 1979

Ellie is unpacking a box of books in her new apartment in Boston when she feels sick. It hits her like a wave, making her grab hold of the shelf for support. She goes through a list of things it could be until she realizes she hasn't had a period in a while. She's never been regular, so she hasn't given it much thought. Now, she's reaching for a calendar even as she tries to keep her lunch down.

She won't think about it now. Can't think about it. She has too much to do. And it can't be happening. It just can't.

She's on a hospital rotation when she takes a test. She doesn't want to be pregnant. Can't be pregnant...

She goes about her day, waiting for the results. Ignoring it. Hoping it will go away. But she knows. She's tired, and she's never felt tired in her life.

The test is positive. She goes to the bathroom, closes the lid on the toilet, sits and tries to think. She should tell Dan. Should, what does that even mean? She has to do what is best for her, and for this tiny being now living inside her. Dan Davies is not the best at anything.

It takes a week to make the decision to call him. She uses his office number, the line that went just to him.

'Sweetheart,' he says.

'Don't call me that.'

'I'm surprised to hear from you. I didn't think—'

'I'm pregnant.'

She can hear him breathing, can picture him sweating.

'Ellie, everything I have, I can lose. My father-in-law owns all of it. I can't give up my life for you. I'll have nothing.'

She isn't surprised. Even her own daddy married her mama when she was pregnant. She never thought Donald Tompkins would turn out to be a better man than Dan in her eyes, but he is, at least for this moment.

'I don't want you back. But my child is not going to be raised in poverty. So you'll have to support him… or her. Have a lawyer set up a trust, or whatever men do in this sort of situation. Have him contact me. I don't want to hear from you again.'

'I'll be in touch.'

'Aren't you listening, or does your father-in-law do that for you, too? I only want to hear from the lawyer who handles the money. I have enough on you to ruin your life. Don't forget that.' She hangs up before he can respond.

She needs to think. To have a plan.

She makes a cup of tea and heads outside to the

communal garden. Her apartment is one of six in a red-brick building. It felt solid and cozy, the opposite of what she had in Houston, which is why she chose it. Ellie sits in one of the chairs. A woman appears. She's very tall, with long red hair, wearing green capris and a pink shirt.

'You must be the new one in five.' She sits beside her.

'Sorry. Five?'

'Apartment five. I'm six. I knew you were new because no one ever sits in Lydia's chair.'

'Lydia?'

'She was five before you.'

Ellie laughs. It feels good to laugh.

'I'm Gayle,' she says. 'I'm moving out, too. Back to Alabama. But wanted to watch one last sunset. Do you have a glass?'

'Um, no. For what?'

'It's cocktail hour!'

She pulls a plastic cup from her bag and a thermos of some kind. She pours a drink and hands it to Ellie, who feels light-headed at the very fumes.

'Thanks.' Ellie sniffs it.

'It's a Singapore sling. Lydia made better cocktails. Had her own glass. She always sat there.'

Gayle looks at the chair Ellie is sitting in, like she's considering whether or not she's worthy of Lydia's chair.

Ellie takes a drink. It's sweet and summery, not like the alcohol she's used to.

'We've had some good times sitting here. Great people in this building. They're all leaving, moving on to different lives. Me, too.'

'Like what? New life, I mean. Why are you leaving?' It's been so long since she's made aimless chit chat, she's forgotten how.

'Me, I'm starting over. Clean state.'

Ellie thinks she means slate, but keeps her mouth shut. The woman has a story she wants to tell, and Ellie is too tired to listen.

'And Lydia?'

'Getting married. Found a great guy, she's happy.'

Ellie nods, acknowledging the rarity of this.

'Cheers. Drink up. You're gonna have fun here.'

Ellie watches as Gayle gulps at her drink as the sun starts to set. A pale peach color marks where the blazing yellow sun had been, and then a cotton candy pink and a swirl of brilliant orange and fiery red. The sky is positively operatic as it cedes to the evening, then night. It feels like a proper end to the day.

'Now wasn't that spectacular?'

Gayle stands up, wobbles slightly as Ellie watches, uncertain if it's her kitten heels, the slope of the lawn or the booze. Probably all three.

'Nice to meet you. I hope you have fun here!'

Ellie stands, feeling she should follow Gayle inside, make sure she's safe. The stars are starting to come out. It feels good to sit, and simply look at the sky, but she has things to do. Decisions to make.

She makes her way back inside as the last vestiges of day give way to the true dark of night. Back in her apartment, she closes the door and looks around, starts thinking about a woman she's never met. Lydia. Who found a nice man.

Who has a great job. Whom everyone liked. Ellie was the name Katie gave her. It no longer fits. She's not that person anymore.

Lydia Anna. But not Tompkins. She's never liked that name. Thomas. She looks into the mirror above the small bathroom sink and says, 'Hello, Lydia. Nice to meet you.'

28

Peyton

September, Maine, Present day

It's the first night that her father is home and Peyton is wide awake, afraid something will happen in the middle of the night. She stares at the ceiling and listens for what seems like hours, but when she looks at her phone, she sees it's barely past midnight and she went to bed at eleven.

Peyton pads carefully down the stairs. When she turns the corner and moves into the kitchen, she sees a light through the patio doors, by the pool. Someone must have left it on.

She moves to the bar and pours a glass of wine then heads back to the kitchen. The patio door is open and Peyton hesitates, looking out at the pool, the cool, glassy surface of the shimmery blue water so clear and perfect in the cooling night sky. But it's not the chlorine or the distant suggestion of fall in the air she smells but cigarette smoke.

She turns and sees her mother, sitting in a chair she's

moved closer to the house, closer to the door. She's no doubt listening in case her father needs help.

'Peyton,' her mother says.

Peyton's not sure what to do. She keeps her back to her mother so Lydia can hide her cigarette, and they can pretend Peyton has no sense of smell, but she hears her mother inhale.

Peyton sits and takes a sip of wine. 'Can't sleep?'

'No.'

'It's September,' her mother says.

Peyton remembers the conversation they had, soon after she came home. About making a plan.

'Are you heading back to Seattle?'

'I hadn't really thought about it,' Peyton says, truthfully.

'Perhaps that's for the best.'

'Pardon?'

'It'll be good for your father to have you about while he recovers.'

'Oh.' Peyton can't figure out what else to say. 'Do you want me to get a job? Should I sell my condo?'

Her father had made the last mortgage payment for her, when she'd run out of money. She hadn't thought about her bills since.

'I'll have my accountant look at your mortgage. Do you have any idea how much you owe?'

'Most of it.'

'You've always been better with words than numbers.'

It's one of the nicest things her mother has ever said to her and Peyton wonders how much she's had to drink.

'Do you think Dad's going to be OK?'

'Medically, yes. But it'll be hard for his ego, and I doubt he'll have the same success with his practice.'

'He's a surgeon. Shouldn't he be retired now, anyway?'

'Yes. I should, too. But we both worked so hard for our careers, it's hard to think of them as being over. It's hard to move on.'

Peyton looks at her mother, surprised to be hearing something so personal from her. She wants to ask why she became a psychiatrist, why she works so much. She wants to ask about Minnie, her family. Scott's father. She has so many questions, but she's afraid to start. Afraid of the answers, or maybe not being answered at all.

'He can teach and work on his restoration plans. He's always seemed more interested in buildings than people.' Peyton hadn't realized this until she said it out loud, but it's true.

'Your father's a good man,' her mother says.

'I never said he wasn't.'

'I don't want to argue with you, Peyton. I'm tired.'

Peyton sits there, ignoring the smoke from her mother's cigarette, the fact that she can't speak without being accused of being argumentative.

'Maybe we should have a timeline for when I leave.'

'What do you mean?'

'I mean, I owe you and Dad. I want to help. But I also don't want to be where I'm not wanted.'

'What do you mean by that?'

'I mean I'm tired, too. I know I'm not the brilliant Scott or the genius Caroline. But I don't see either of them bothering much with Dad now, do you?'

'They don't need to come because you're here.'

Peyton looks at her mother. Her neck still tight and taught – Peyton wonders now if her father gave her a few free tweaks. Her tasteful clothes. Even sitting here by the pool, she looks like she's been styled by someone from *Vogue*. 'Successful After Sixty' or 'Looking Good at Every Age'. Articles she detests. Then she notices something else. The only jewelry her mother wears is her wedding ring and diamond studs. It's her mother's style, has been forever, but she wonders about it now. She's sure she used to wear a single strand of pearls.

Peyton stands up, picks up her glass. 'Enjoy your cigarette.'

Then she walks back inside and goes back to bed.

'I'll take your father for his check-up on my own today.' It's the first thing her mother says to her when they meet in the kitchen the next morning.

'Fine.'

Peyton pours a mug of coffee and takes it outside, closing the door behind her, a glass wall sealing her off from her mother. A few minutes later, the door opens.

'Put your banking information on the table, for my accountant,' she says.

'OK.'

Peyton finishes her coffee, then goes in to see if her father needs her help on the stairs.

'Stop fussing, Peyton,' he says, with a smile. He still looks pale to her, unwell, and she's worried. Once he's in the car, she goes to her parents' room. She looks around the bathroom, checking to see what medication her father takes.

Lydia Winchester would never have something as tacky as a medicine cabinet in her home, so Peyton opens the drawers in the large vanity that houses two sinks ten feet apart.

The first drawer has her toothbrush, toothpaste, dental floss. The next has all her little pots of serums and creams.

The next drawer is a shock.

Pills. Bottles and foil packs of more drugs.

Diazepam. Also known as Valium. Why is her mother on Valium?

Peyton looks to see who wrote the prescription. Her mother prescribed it for herself but had it filled in Bangor. So no one knows, Peyton guesses. A shrink on Valium would hardly inspire confidence.

Ambien, to sleep.

Ativan, for anxiety.

Peyton looks at her watch. Looks out the window and opens it so she can hear a car if one pulls up. It would be just Peyton's luck for her parents to forget something and her mother to appear as she's going through her drawers. The very thought of it has her heart galloping. She knows what she's doing is wrong, but she also feels a sense of exhilaration she hasn't felt in a long time.

There's not much else in the bathroom. Her father's pills must be by his bed. She looks out the window, makes sure there's no car, looks in the hall, just in case, then heads to his bedroom. There's no medication to be seen and Peyton figures her mother must have taken it with her to the doctor's appointment.

She moves to her father's den, to his desk, and starts looking for other things.

Peyton rolls the drawers open slowly, afraid to make

noise. She doesn't find anything. But she's not even sure what she's looking for anymore. Her mother doesn't have a desk, doesn't have a workspace. All of her secrets must be kept at her office.

Disappointed, Peyton heads down the stairs to Scott's old room. She stares at the photo of Daisy, willing the small photo to tell her what happened. If she could solve this mystery, it would give meaning to her time at home. She could write about it and go to journalism school. She pictures herself in a newsroom, on a plane heading somewhere to cover a story. But Daisy is more than a story, and she deserves a happier ending than the one she got. But that's true for many people.

Still, she's going to try.

29

Lydia

November, Boston, 1979

Lydia has a loop of questions that run constantly in her mind. What if he'd given her the diamond bracelet first? If she hadn't had two glasses of wine and two glasses of champagne? If she'd had a different roommate? If she'd been smarter – known that she wanted a father figure, not a lover? She's angry with herself, but what's done is done. She just never thought this would be her life.

She was going to be different, successful. No way was she going to end up like her mama. But here she is.

She writes a letter to Minnie, in art school in Atlanta. She can't picture her fragile sister in a big crazy city, but Minnie loves it. When she is done she writes a letter to her mama. Inside, she puts two twenty-dollar bills, enough for her to take a bus to Boston, as she won't fly. She doesn't say she's pregnant and needs their help. She'll save that for when they arrive. She simply tells each woman they have to come, now.

She waits two weeks, then she writes another letter, puts in more money.

She's starting the third letter when there's a knock at her door.

She's standing there. Her mama. Still unnaturally thin but healthier, more solid-looking than Lydia has ever seen her. Like being summoned by her daughter has galvanized her.

But then Mona Tompkins takes one look at her daughter and for the first time in her life, Lydia Thomas sees she has disappointed her mama.

'I see,' is all she says, letting herself in.

Eualla closes the door behind her. For she's no longer Lydia, standing here with her mother.

Minnie arrives the following day, happy to see Eu, as she still calls her.

'Wow. This sure is different from your place in Houston!' she says.

It's only when Minnie sees their mama sitting at the small kitchen table, cradling a teacup with both hands in a way neither of her daughters has ever seen, that Minnie realizes something is wrong. Lydia can almost see her studying the scene. Her sister, who can draw anything, paint anything, who sees light and color in a way that staggers her, has to be told.

'I'm going to have a baby.' She pauses, the following words harder to say out loud. 'And I'm going to need your help.'

Lydia had wanted Minnie to come earlier, to prepare her, afraid she'd connect the dots and know who the father of this baby was. That will have to wait.

'What do you need us to do?' she asks. Then she sits at the table, across from Mama.

Lydia takes the other seat, the three women facing each other, the teapot and life between them. And they make a plan.

It's four days before she finds herself alone with Minnie. She's sitting on the sofa, looking at paint samples, trying to figure out what color to paint the nursery. Lydia takes a seat, settles in, but before she can say anything, her sister speaks.

'I won't say anything,' Minnie says, head bowed, eyes never leaving the samples.

'What?'

Minnie's not asking Lydia to repeat herself. Not asking her for clarification. The 'what' is one of astonishment.

'The baby's father…' She seems to need to confirm they're on the same page.

'He's not in the picture anymore. He was a mistake. The biggest one I've ever made. I don't want to ever think about him, ever again,' she says.

If only it was that easy. But at least now, she isn't completely alone.

Lydia works as hard as every other person on the program. She hides herself in dark colors and flowing fabrics. She's grateful that it's an easy pregnancy, that the extra weight she carries is all baby.

She gives birth on her due date and goes back to school three days later. She thought she got away with it all, but in front of her locker she finds a small pile of baby gifts. She's touched and ashamed in equal measure.

She's a single mother, living with her mama and her sister, who are caring for Scott while she works. Mama looks so frail, Lydia is afraid she won't be able to lift Scott, but she does, easily. Her grandson has brought her to life. It's something, she supposes.

She hates Dan Davies with everything in her, until she doesn't anymore. Life can only hold so many things. And Dan Davies isn't one of those things worth holding. She says that now, but some days, when she's tired, when things are difficult, the hate comes back. With such a force it almost knocks her off her feet. But Lydia squares her shoulders. She'll never let anyone hurt her ever again.

30

Peyton

September, Maine, Present day

Peyton and her dad are on their own. Her mother is in Portland. They're sitting by the pool when he says he's craving a root beer float.

'I'll go buy the ice cream and soda, if you promise not to have another heart attack while I'm gone?'

'Scouts honour,' he laughs. If he dies on Peyton's watch, her mother will kill her. It takes twenty-two minutes and she feels aged by the trip.

She makes him sit at the counter, where she can see him, while she finds an ice-cream scoop. When she's done, she puts his float on a napkin, adds a bendy straw and a long spoon, and pushes it toward him.

'Ta-dah!'

'I feel like I'm at a soda counter!' he says.

Peyton sits across from him and takes a sip of her float,

remembering quickly that she's not a fan of ice cream and soda.

The house is quiet, a safe quiet. There's no tension or animosity in the air. The two people sitting in the kitchen have no ill will toward one another. Peyton's sure it changes the very atoms in the air. Her mother is so uptight, so quick to criticize. It feels so much lighter, not having her here.

He pushes his glass toward her. 'I'll have another float.'

Peyton thinks about it for a second. She bought low-fat ice cream. There's maybe a cup of root beer.

'A small one,' she says. 'Mom will kill me if you croak on my watch.'

He laughs. 'You do have a way with words.'

She remembers her mother saying that to her, while they had breakfast, while he was being operated on.

She makes the float, pushes it toward him.

'When was the last time Mom saw her family?' she blurts, surprising herself.

Her father looks up at her, a bit of ice cream on his upper lip. She hands him a napkin.

'Why do you ask?'

'Because all the secrets are driving me crazy.'

'What secrets?' he asks, pushing the ice cream under the root beer with his spoon.

'There's so many, Dad. With Mom. With Scott. With this family...' She pauses. 'With this town. With Daisy.'

'Lots of secrets, Peyton, or just people dealing with life?'

'What do you mean?'

'Your mother had a bad childhood. She doesn't talk about it. Not a secret – a coping mechanism.'

'Scott?'

'His father didn't want to be in his life. Do we keep dragging that up to hurt him? To remind your mother she once was in love with a cad?'

Peyton feels her heart start to beat faster, like she's on some sort of alert, the information coming at her like baseballs at a batter.

'They're not your stories, Peyton. So drop it, OK?'

She feels herself blush, embarrassed by his admonishment.

'Ok. I'll drop the whole mom thing. But not Daisy.'

'Have you learned anything new?' he slurps his ice cream.

'I think whoever grabbed Daisy was staying at The Stick House. And I think her body is there.'

Saying the words, putting it out there, she realizes this is what she does believe. She had to say it out loud, to make it real, even for herself. She has no proof, but in her mind, the two are connected. Have been since she moved back and saw the old house.

Her father pales. Significantly. Peyton reaches her arm out in case he faints, falls off his chair.

'Dad, I was young, but Caroline took me there. I remember a skinny man with bad teeth.'

'Daisy's not at the house.'

'How do you know?'

'Because I do.'

'Did you have it searched?'

'No, Peyton. I can't tell you how I know. I just do. You've got the wrong end of the stick on this one.'

'But—'

'Let it go, Peyton. I can't cope with this now.'

Shame crawls through her. His heart is weak and she can feel her own racing.

'Sorry, Dad,' she says.

She knows that's not enough, so she adds more ice cream to his float.

Her father goes to bed at ten o'clock. Peyton sits by the pool, checking her phone. She thinks about texting John to come over for a swim and goes inside to check and see if her father is sleeping.

In the washroom, she sees her hair is looking lighter and drier from being in the water and in the sun. Her skin is dry. She ties her hair back and grabs some body lotion from her mother's room and heads back downstairs. It's so nice, sitting by the pool, being close to the ocean. Maybe she should just concentrate on getting into journalism school, focus on Daisy's case and forget her own crazy family. But she can't. Because Caroline took her to that house. And then, another thought. Does her sister know something?

She's rubbing lotion on her dry shinbones, thinking, when she hears something. A thump, from inside the house. She knows the thump. Has heard it before.

Terror propels her out the chair, through the kitchen, down the hall, into the entrance.

Turning to run up the stairs, she sees him sprawled on the landing.

'What the hell?' she shouts.

'I wanted to make sure you locked the back doors.'

He's on his back, one hand on his chest, the other trying

to find purchase, as though he can push himself up. Never in her life has her father checked the doors. Peyton's certain the conversation earlier unnerved him, too, and she feels even worse.

'Don't. Just don't. Don't move,' she sputters. 'Did you break anything? I'll call an ambulance.'

'I slipped on something. I didn't break anything. I just need some help to stand.'

Peyton steps back as though some message will appear in the air, telling her what to do. As if somehow she'll be able to use the laws of physics to her advantage. But her father is the biggest man Peyton has ever met and she knows she can't lift him, fit and young as she is. He's just too big.

She calls John. 'John. Sorry it's so late,' she blurts. 'Dad has fallen and I'm wondering if you could come over...'

'On my way.'

Peyton sits on the floor next to her father. 'John's on his way.'

'Peyton?'

'Yes, Dad.'

'We won't tell your mother.'

'Of course not.'

'And Peyton?'

'Yes, Dad.' She puts her hand on his and he surprises her by curling his fingers around hers.

'Get me a glass of Scotch.'

'What about the medication you're on?'

'I'll be fine.'

Peyton thinks for a second. Her father is on the floor, recovering from heart surgery. His wife is in Portland. His eldest children haven't even come home. His youngest is obsessed with a cold case and dismantling the mysteries of a family bound by nothing more than spider webs.

She goes downstairs, opens the door for when John shows up and pours him a glass of Scotch. Then she takes a sip herself and winces. It's like drinking gasoline – not that she has. She spits it into the kitchen sink. Her mother would lose her mind if she saw her do this. Then she pours herself a glass of wine.

She's settling in next to her father, an eye on the open door, when John appears. She waves from the top of the stairs.

'We're up here.'

Her father takes a long pull and hands her back the glass.

John walks up the stairs like he's in the house all the time. Easy, normal, no drama.

'Hey, Dr. Winchester. How much of that have you had?' He nods at the Scotch glass.

'Not nearly enough,' her father replies.

John bends down, crosses her father's hands across his chest, puts his own under her father's armpits and hoists him up.

Peyton stands back to watch, holding her breath. John is six feet, lean, like a swimmer. Her father is six inches taller and at least forty pounds heavier. But it looks effortless as John pulls him up slowly, her father getting his feet under him.

Peyton feels a burst of love for them both. She brings her father a high-back chair to lean on and then the three of them are standing in a group on the landing at the top of the stairs.

'Thank you, John,' her father says.

'No problem. Did you hurt anything? I'm happy to run you to hospital, just to be safe.'

'I'm fine, thanks.'

'I dunno, Dad. Maybe we should. I mean, what made you fall to begin with?'

'There was something on the floor, I think. I slipped.'

All three of them start looking at the floor. Peyton sees a streak of something and she knows. It's the body lotion she took from her mother's room. It must have dripped from the nozzle after she'd used some.

She's wiping it up with her sock and is trying to think of a way to apologize, when her father says, 'Since we're all up, why don't we order a pizza?'

'Not a chance,' Peyton says. 'But how about a drink by the pool, and I'll make some snacks?'

'Sure,' John says.

He walks beside Peyton's father on the stairs, so he can grab him if he trips, she guesses. But her father seems fine. She can hear him telling John to help himself to the bar.

'No more Scotch for Dad,' she yells.

Peyton opens the refrigerator and has a rummage. She cuts up celery and carrots and arranges the contents of the cheese keeper on a plate. She carries it outside and sees her father sitting with John, who doesn't have a drink.

'There's beer in the refrigerator,' she says.

'Thanks, but I'm driving.'

'Have a beer. You can stay here. Is that OK, Dad?'

'Of course.'

Peyton gets him a beer and some baby tomatoes. They contain lutein, which is good for the heart, and her mother has Mary throwing them in everything these days. Then she grabs a bag of chips and a bowl. Balance, she guesses.

'It's so nice, sitting here. No neighbors to complain about the noise,' John says.

'That was one of the things Lydia liked most about it when we moved here.'

Peyton looks at her father, waiting for more. But she remembers the promise she's just made, to stop poking around in her mother's past, and she lets it go.

For now.

It's almost two when her father calls it a night. Peyton walks him to his room, trying to make it seem like she's not.

'I'm fine, Peyton. Goodnight,' he says, closing the door.

Peyton listens for a moment as he settles. He seems fine. He has good color. And it's her fault he slipped.

Downstairs, she pours some wine and grabs John another beer. Sitting side by side, they stick their feet in the pool.

'Feels nice, doesn't it?' John says.

'It does.'

'So, what are your plans, Peyton, as the summer draws to a close?'

'Have you been talking to my mother?'

'What?'

'She's big on me having a plan. But right now, things are up in the air, due to recent events,' she says. She doesn't want to say she missed the deadline to apply for journalism school.

John nods.

Peyton moves her foot back and forth in the water.

'I can't believe your parents had lights installed inside the pool.'

'Yeah, my mom saw it at a hotel somewhere and liked the shimmer it created.' Peyton looks at the round dots that light up the water.

'So, when do you think you'll know if, or when, you're leaving?'

'I don't know. I feel like there are still a few mysteries I'd like to solve.'

'A few?'

'Yeah, a few.'

'Well, maybe I can help you. And maybe I can change your mind about leaving.'

Peyton turns and looks at John.

'I think that's the nicest thing anyone has ever said to me.'

She leans forward and kisses him, softly. And then deeper. She feels his hand on her back. Then she stops, grabs his hand, pulling him to the pool house.

'Peyton, what are you doing?' he asks.

'Shhh. My dad might hear,' she says, walking through the damp night grass. 'He sleeps with his window open.'

She opens the door to the pool house, pulling off her shirt as she walks inside.

'Are we going for a swim?' he asks.

'Nope,' she says.

All at once, he realizes what's happening. Peyton can see the moment in his eyes.

'Um. Are you sure?'

'Mmm-hmm.' She unfastens his shorts.

Smiling softly he reaches out, brushes the hair from her face. A small act of tenderness she didn't know she needed, until that moment.

31

Lydia

September, Boston, 1983

Her son is three years old. Scott Francis Thomas. Named for F. Scott Fitzgerald. She had wanted to name him Fitzgerald, but Minnie had looked at her and said, 'I think the kid has enough to deal with already, don't you?'. She had settled on Scott, as close as she would get to her Great Gatsby dream.

Lydia is now a psychiatrist working in Boston. Mama has gone back to Tennessee, and Minnie takes care of Scott. Each payday, Lydia goes to a bookstore and splurges. Her days are spent between her new job and her son. But each night after he's in bed, she spends an hour or two, depending on how tired she is, reading.

She's standing in line at a bookstore one evening after work, her arms full, when she drops a book on the German philosopher Nietzsche. A man standing behind her kneels and retrieves it for her.

'Thank you,' she says, struggling to keep the whole pile from falling.

He takes three, maybe four steps – his legs are impossibly long, she notices – and grabs a basket.

'Here...'

He holds it for her while she transfers her books.

'Nietzsche? Camus? Some rather intense reading,' he says.

'I know how to have a good time,' she says, and he laughs.

Wordlessly, naturally, he takes the full basket from her and holds it, standing next to her, towering over her. He feels like a sentinel, like a soldier, like a bodyguard. Lydia, who's normally so wary of people, finds herself immediately taken by him.

'Architecture?' he says, looking at another book on the top of her pile.

'Just starting to learn about it, really.'

'Passing interest?'

'I'm new to Boston and have seen so many nice buildings on my walks. Just thought I'd learn a little about the different... styles? Movements?'

'What have you seen so far that interests you? The Stearns Building? The art deco on Congress Street?'

'The Massachusetts Historical Society on Boylston Street,' she laughs, slightly embarrassed. 'I walk by it often and think it's such a pretty building.'

'So, you appreciate colonial revival?'

'Is that what it is?'

'With a bow-front exterior and Doric columns.'

'I knew about the columns. I read about the three types: Doric, Ionic and Corinthian.

'Ionic are too plain, Corinthian too much. I like Doric best,' she says.

'You have fine taste. I happen to agree.'

It's her turn at the checkout and she pays for her books. When the clerk hands over the bag, he takes it.

'That's heavy. I hope you don't have far to go,' he says.

'I'll make it.'

'We could have a drink and I could tell you all about Boston, since you're new and I've lived here all my life?'

'I have to get home... but thank you for your offer.'

'Sure I can't tempt you?'

'I have a son to get home to,' she says, figuring the mention of her son will put an end to his flirting.

She sees him look for her hands, which are hidden by the bag she's holding. She knows he's looking for a ring.

'I'm not married,' she says, mostly to pile on how unsuitable she is for him.

She can tell by looking at him that he has money. He's wearing a cashmere blazer, tailored gray pants that fall perfectly over what she knows are expensive loafers. No ring on his finger, but she sees the band of a nice watch peeking from under a shirtsleeve. But it's not just that. He has a dignity, a quiet class that was missing in Dan.

'Another time, perhaps,' he says.

It's a statement, not a question.

'Perhaps.'

She turns, walks out into the early evening light of Boston. She'll never see him again, but still - it was nice to have such a tall, handsome man show interest in her.

★

Lydia likes to leave early for work. Having Minnie living with them makes it easier. She can leave as early as she likes. It's a long walk to her office, but she loves Boston, the history, the elegance. It's like a classy, established older aunt to Houston's noisy, nouveau riche nephew.

She's walking past the Massachusetts Historical Society, when she sees him, walking toward her. She can't miss him. He's a head taller than everyone.

'We meet again.'

'Is this a coincidence?' she asks.

'Absolutely.' Then he dips his head and blushes. 'Actually, no.'

Lydia tells herself not to get too excited. She's never had much luck with men, after all. Or much luck with people, she realizes, remembering Debbie. All these years and it still hurts.

They're facing each other, standing on the sidewalk, the crowd moving, flowing around them like they're on their own private island. She likes the feeling.

'Did you get a lot of reading done over the weekend?' he asks.

'Some. Not a lot.'

'Must be hard with a little one. How old is your son?'

'Three.'

'Cute age.'

'Do you have children?'

'No. But I like them.'

Lydia wonders if he practiced this conversation in case he saw her. It's easy, genuine, and he's managed to let her know he's OK with children and her being a single mom in a few sentences. That's nice. She's interested.

She starts to walk, pleased to see he falls in step beside her.

'So, what do you do for a living?' he asks.

'I'm a psychiatrist.'

'Really?' He stops walking, looks at her with new interest.

Lydia is intrigued. His first reaction isn't shock that she's a female doctor. She likes that. More than she should, perhaps.

'Where do you work?' she asks.

'Mass General. And I have a private practice, too.'

'What do you do?' she says, walking again.

'I'm a doctor.'

'Specialty?'

'Plastic surgeon.'

'Where do you work out of?'

'Cambridge,' he says.

'Impressive,' she says. 'Perhaps our paths will cross again – professionally, of course.'

She smiles and crosses the street, even though where she's going is on the side she was already on. She's going to make him work for it.

On Wednesday, Lydia sees him again. He's wearing a different coat, in navy blue. He looks distinguished. And Lydia has always thought distinguished to be more attractive than attractive. She likes people who stand out, perhaps because she always has.

'We meet again,' he says.

Not his best opening line, she thinks. But his smile is so easy, so cute, she's still charmed by him.

'Week going well?'

'It is, thanks. And yours?'

'Fine, fine. Weather is lovely and I've met the most charming woman.'

'Have you now?'

'I have.'

'What's she like?'

'Smart. Beautiful. And she has great taste in buildings.'

Lydia laughs. It's been so long since she's laughed and it feels good.

'I hope this isn't too bold, but I was wondering if you'd like to go for a walk through Boston Common on Saturday.'

'I spend Saturdays with my son.'

'Bring him along. That's why I chose the park.'

'Can I think about it?'

'Of course.' He reaches into his pocket and takes out a business card. 'This is me.'

She looks at the card. Octavian Winchester. The rifle she learned to shoot with, kept in her closet all those years ago, was a Winchester. She smiles at his name. It's strong. It's noble. It's perfect.

She tucks the card in her pocket. 'Lydia. Lydia Thomas.'

'Nice to meet you, Lydia Thomas.' He nods, and she's certain if he was wearing a hat, he'd doff it.

He turns and heads to the train, and she continues her walk to work. When she reaches her small office, she sits and looks at his card. Then she slides it into her bag and sets to work. She knows she'll be spending Saturday with him. But she waits until Friday to let him know.

32

Peyton

November/December, Maine, Present day

Summer ends, slowly at first. The mornings dawn cold and the evenings grow chilly, but for a few golden hours each day the air is warm, hot even, the sun burning like it is trying to hold onto its starring role. But no matter how hard it tries, the days shorten, its power fades, and snow blankets the Fort. Looking out at the covered pool, the naked trees brittle with frost, Peyton can't imagine a world where she was warm. Mostly she can't believe she's still home. But it's fine, for now.

She's noticing different things about her hometown, like how the beauty of the Fort is different in winter. The cold may take your breath away and split the skin of your fingertips, but the sun still makes the water dance, the snow glitter like it's laced with diamonds. Somehow winter in the Fort is both vibrant and lazy, the earth enveloped in the pillow of deep snow.

'Life is easier in the summer,' she says, staring out the French doors.

'Aren't you a little ball of cheer this morning,' Peyton's mother says.

'I don't like the cold.'

'Be grateful you have a warm home to live in.'

'Lydia, the girl can have an opinion without being attacked. Leave her alone,' her father says.

For a second there's a stillness in the air, a quiet. Not a peace, but a quiet. Peyton still isn't sure what's happening. Her father has been off, not quite himself. Still, he never speaks to her mother this way.

Her mother picks up her cup and drains her coffee. The room is silent, none of them sure what's happening.

Her mother stands. 'I'm off to Portland. I'll see you this evening.'

They wait to hear the door close and then Peyton opens the refrigerator.

'Dad, I'm roasting a chicken for dinner. Can I invite John?'

'Sure. Tell him to stay.'

John has logged a few nights in the guest room now. He also helped her close the pool for the season and install the new TV after the last one broke. And he's seen the Daisy board. Her father retires to his book in his den and Peyton feels at loose ends. She knocks on her father's door and asks if he'll be OK if she goes for a walk.

'Sure. Enjoy yourself.'

She bundles up warm, but still, it's cold when she starts out. The water is a steel blue, the sky heavy with snow. No way will her mother make it back. The air hurts her lungs at first until she adapts. It reminds her of walking to school when she was young, wearing snow pants and the woosh-woosh sound they made when she walked.

The sky is almost white with snowflakes, the soft, downy kind, and Peyton is certain there will be people cross-country skiing on the main street before long. She passes John's condo, thinks about stopping in, she hasn't seen him in a week now, but knows he's at work. Besides, she thinks better when she's walking. Alone. And she'll see him tonight.

She finds herself on the street heading to The Stick House. The man who's always outside is sweeping the snow from his drive. He stops what he's doing, lifts both arms in greeting. Peyton waves back at him then rounds the curve in the road.

There it is. The Stick House. She stands in the street and stares, willing it to give her some answers. It looks colder, with the dusting of snow, and she wonders if someday it'll simply collapse upon itself, like the back porch.

She thinks about scaling the fence that magically appeared after her visit with her father, but the man is still outside and she'll leave tracks in the snow. The house holds answers, she knows. The man she saw that day – she knows he was there. The snow is coming down on an angle now, the flakes smaller. They're in for a storm. So she heads back home before it is too deep to wade through.

She's cold and her hair is wet when she arrives home, but as she thaws, she feels herself becoming excited. The pieces are there. She will find out what happened. She's humming with a new sense of purpose as she prepares dinner and watches TV with her father until it's time to eat.

The snow is starting to drift outside. John texts and says he'll be late as he's been dealing with car accidents.

'I wonder what this snow will do to The Stick House,' she says.

'You're very interested in that house,' her father says.

'It's an interesting house.'

'Are you still snooping around the old Daisy Wright case?'

'I am,' she says, her heart beating faster. 'I mean, as much as I can. I've had a few distractions of late.'

It's interesting, she thinks, that her father went from her asking about the house to talking about Daisy. Despite being adamant Daisy wasn't there. Maybe he suspects something, too.

'I know my heart troubles threw you off schedule.'

'I didn't mean it like that.'

'No, no. I know. Poor choice of words.'

They eat in silence for a few moments, trying to find some equilibrium.

'I find it hard being around Mom. She's very critical. But I enjoy the time I spend with you. It's like we're getting to know each other as people. I think you have poor taste in spouses, but other than that, you're a very nice person, Octavian.'

Her father looks at her and laughs. 'You've always had a way with words, Peyton. Why did you go into pharmaceutical sales?'

'Because Mom stopped speaking to me when I said I wanted to go to journalism school.'

'I'm sorry about that,' he says. 'I really didn't know.'

'You worked a lot. You didn't even make it to my graduation party at the house. You were always in Portland.'

Peyton stops eating, flashes of memories coming together for her. Her Dad being gone, her mother being home. Saturday nights with just the two of them.

'Were you and Mom separated my last year of high school?'

'It was a long time ago, Peyton.'

'Tell me.'

'We went through a rough patch. It was easier for both of us to maintain distance.'

'That's why you have the condo. It was your bachelor pad.'

He doesn't have to say anything for her to know she's right.

'There were a few rough patches, weren't there? The summer Daisy disappeared, too.' She feels it coming together, not so much a mystery to be solved as things becoming clearer. Childhood memories taking on a different meaning as an adult remembering.

'Wait until you get married, Peyton. Sometimes all you can do is remember your vows and hang in there.'

'Do you love each other?'

'We do, Peyton. But life can beat you up, and it leaves scars. And as much as you try to understand, it can be too much sometimes.'

'Is that why Mom doesn't speak to her family?'

'Only your mother can answer that, and I think you know enough by now to know she'll never tell you.'

The conversation is heavy, like the falling snow coating

the roof of the conservatory, and Peyton wonders which will be the first to make the glass, the room, their lives, shatter.

Still, she can't let it go.

'I know I have an active imagination, but I think The Stick House is connected to Daisy's disappearance. I know you said it wasn't possible, but I'm sure of it. There was a man in that house.'

Her father looks at her shrewdly, eyes narrowing. She feels like he's sizing her up.

'It very well could be, Peyton. It very well could be.'

Peyton is so shocked that it takes her a few minutes to gather her thoughts. She closes her eyes, the memory becoming clearer. She wills it forward. If she can see him, she may be able to draw a picture of the man who took Daisy.

She can't see his face – at least not all of it. But he had bad teeth. Yellow and twisted. An old smoker's teeth. He was wearing a black T-shirt. Or maybe that's a shadow her memory is creating...

'Do you remember what he looked like? This man you saw at The Stick House?' he asks.

Sometimes Peyton feels like her parents don't know her at all. Other times she feels like they can read her mind.

'Bad teeth. A couple missing. And a black T-shirt, with gray or white on it.'

'Did he hurt you?'

Peyton looks at her father and sees he's paled.

'No. I just saw him. But it's weird. Who squats in the Fort? And why was he hanging out with Caroline and her friends?'

'A better question is why Lydia let you out and what the hell Caroline was thinking.'

'Well, Dad, you have to cut her some slack. She only really thinks about herself, so when someone else is involved, it's all new, uncharted territory.'

Her father laughs. 'I should correct you for saying such things about your sister. But you speak the truth.'

She tops up their glasses, draining the bottle.

'Mom would be horrified, us sitting here drinking together. Common, she'd say.'

He laughs. 'You got that right.'

The mystery, the difficulties, the strains, the hurt... maybe it can all be fixed. Maybe this is why she came home. She wasn't strong enough when she was younger. But maybe she is, now.

33

December, Maine, Present day

Memories change.

They grow, develop, like an old-fashioned photograph. Evolve, take on a life of their own. Ripen with age. People do, too, mostly. But does the person change the memory, or does the memory change the person?

It's the coldest day they've had so far and Peyton is out walking. She can't remember the last time she felt the intense bitterness of a winter day in the Fort. She knows it must have been a trip home at Christmas during university which wasn't that long ago, but it feels like it was another lifetime. With each intake of frozen air she wonders how she ended up back in the Fort, and why she is still there, six months after her return. It's like she has failed at being an adult. She walks faster, trying to outpace the maudlin thoughts. She is bundled up in her new winter clothes, bought in Portland and paid for by her parents, walking along the deserted frozen beach. The snow has a frozen layer on top that her boots, also new, crunch through, making her wobble. She stops, her nose running from the cold, and looks at the water. The way the sun is hitting the surface makes it glow, a hollow white color brighter than even the hottest summer day. Even with her sunglasses she has to squint.

It is beautiful, in its own way, winter in the Fort. But for Peyton, this winter it feels cruel, too. When she's out walking and she sees families with small children skating, struggling to get their feet under them as an adult holds them up, or flying down the hills on toboggans, she thinks of Daisy, of all the simple joys she missed. Of all the joys her parents missed.

She goes home, lets herself into the too warm house. Her mother hated the cold. Pouring a glass of wine, she starts to cook dinner. Mary had fallen and broken her hip, so Peyton was now keeping the house running.

She's on her third glass of wine, sitting with her parents in the lounge, when she jumps up and announces,

'I'm going to take out the Christmas decorations and decorate the house.' She's unsteady as she stands. Three drinks is not acceptable and she saw her father's worried look as she'd poured the third one.

'Do we need to bother with all that?' her mother asks.

It's the first Christmas Peyton has been home in three years, and she finds herself wondering what her parents did when it was just them for the holidays. Surely they must have decorated the house. But no, she can see it now. Eggs benedict for breakfast, a bottle of Champagne. Her father giving her something tasteful and expensive. Not jewelry, her mother detested jewelry. Her mother giving him books on architecture and art. An expensive coat. Her father had an entire closet dedicated to sports coats, overcoats, blazers, pea coats, wool jackets. Handcrafted, purchased in Italy, commissioned from tailors. Her mother didn't have a similar compulsion. She had no habits, no hobbies. She was not a collector, although she did have three Chanel handbags. Gifts, she figures, from her father.

'We aren't going to celebrate Christmas?' Peyton says, a whine in her voice even she can hear.

Her father sets down his book. 'It might be nice to get a tree, have an old-fashioned Christmas,' he says, and she sees a certain twinkle return to his eyes.

'Where is everything?' she says.

Her father looks at her mother.

'Where's what?' she says.

'The Christmas decorations,' Peyton and her father say together.

'Are we still talking about this?' she shakes her head. 'They're in the utility room, in the basement, next to where Peyton has set up her crime solving headquarters.'

Peyton feels a rush of something go through her, like her blood has turned to venom. Her mother has taken to mocking her research into Daisy's disappearance. The first time she dismissed it as being a fantasy, that she, Peyton Winchester, could solve the mystery after all these years. The second time, she had asked her how things were going at crime solving central. Each time Peyton felt diminished by her words, but something new happened, too. Once her mother's words would have stopped her, this time they didn't.

'I'll bring them up, Dad. After I check in with my supervisors at Interpol.'

She's in the hallway, heading for the back stairs, when she hears her father say, 'Why hound her, Lydia?' She doesn't wait to hear her mother's response, doesn't want to know.

The door to the room is small by the standards of the house but would be a second bedroom if she had it in her condo in Seattle. Once it was painted an off white, or maybe it was white and this is the effect of time and emptiness on the walls. Peyton looks around. Stacked by the door are boxes with Scott's name on them. He's been gone so long, she can't imagine what must be inside. Stuff he has no interest in, but her mother can't throw away. She's thinking about taking a peek inside when she spies some clear plastic bins in a corner and pulls the cover off one. Some garland appears, Christmas bulbs once wrapped in tissue paper but now loose.

She pulls one out. It's red, still shiny, but not the way it was when she was a kid and they decorated the tree. But she remembers. Each year her mother picked a theme, silver bulbs with white lights one year, red and green another. Once she did the tree in pink and gold. It didn't feel Christmassy to Peyton and when she voiced her thoughts her mother sent her to her room. She was at the age when adults where always telling you to be truthful, then getting mad at you when you told the truth.

Looking into the box she thinks maybe it's not a good idea, decorating for the holidays. A simple container made in China for peanuts has turned into a Pandora's box in front of her. Because it doesn't just hold decorations, it holds memories.

She hears someone on the stairs and turns to look, half

thinking the noise might be a figment of her imagination. She turns and sees her father standing there.

'Ignore your mother, Peyton. Come on. I'll help you with the boxes.'

Her father, always the buffer between them, Peyton and her mother. He must be exhausted.

'I'll carry this one up dad if you start going through it. We'll have to pick a theme to please Her Majesty, and you have a better eye for those things than I do.'

They both know what she's doing, giving him an excuse so he can allow his daughter to carry the boxes, after his heart attack. It's OK, Peyton thinks. She's strong enough now. It's time for her to carry some of the load.

'Your sister's coming for Christmas,' her mother says. Peyton looks up from her cookbook.

'Just her?'

'And Rob and the kids. What do you think, she's leaving her family alone for the holidays?'

Peyton doesn't reply, returning to her cookbook. She doesn't know where these little angry bursts from her mother come from, but she's decided the best way to deal with them is to ignore them.

'The family,' she says, emphasizing the word, 'will be here the 22nd. We'll have to go shopping, buy some presents. Get some food in. I'm not sure how we'll manage without Mary.'

'I'll cook.' Peyton says. 'I can buy presents and wrap them. I'm already cleaning the house.'

'Finally, you've found your purpose in life!'

Peyton feels something slice through her, a pain greater than any knife could wrought. A reason, after all this time, for why she was born. To replace their injured help.

'Oh for God's sake Peyton. I can tell by the look on your face what you're thinking, getting all hurt and twisted again. I was making a joke.' But Peyton sees it, in her mother's face. She knows she's gone too far. She knows her words have struck a blow. And she sees something else. Her mother is speaking the truth. Her truth, at least.

It's Christmas Eve and the house is full. Well, not full, there's still plenty of space, but it feels full. Caroline and Rob are here, and their two children. Peyton hasn't spent much time with them and is quite taken with these small humans. They're funny, and kind, and confident. They must get it from their father's side, as they certainly don't get it from hers.

They have lobster for their Christmas Eve meal. Her father decided it would be easier for Peyton, and a treat for Rob, who loved a Maine lobster. She made potato salad to go with it, and one with artichoke hearts and green beans that turned out really well. They washed it back with several bottles of Champagne, also chosen by her father. Peyton has two glasses and then switches to water. She's cooking a turkey and has to get up at five to get it in the oven. But that's not the only reason. She wants to ask Caroline about The Stick House, and she needs to have her wits about her when she answers.

Not long after the kids go to bed Peyton takes one last

look inside the fridge. She's drawn up a little chart so she knows what time to start cooking everything in the morning. She saw something called a breakfast strata on TikTok and is making one for the morning. It's eggs and cheese and butter and white bread soaked overnight. She's buttering the white bread when her mother appears. She looks at the breakfast casserole Peyton is assembling as though it was a small animal she was gutting, the white bread entrails hanging over the countertop.

'I'll clean up,' Peyton says, thinking her mother is eyeing up the mess.

'We usually have Eggs Benedict,' her mother replies.

'Beyond my skill,' she says.

'I don't know. The salads tonight were very good.'

Peyton looks up from the cheese she is grating.

'Everything wrapped for the kids tomorrow?'

'All done.'

'You've done a lot. Thank you.'

'Sure,' Peyton feels discombobulated, like the floor has shifted ten degrees underneath her. She is not used to her mother offering praise, and certainly not to her.

'I'm not sure about that casserole. Do you have anything else ready?'

The floor levels out, just like that.

'It will be fine. I can't mess up cheese and bread,' she says.

Peyton is up at five, putting the turkey in the oven. She planned to go back to bed, but she isn't tired, and doubts she will be able to get back to sleep. Quietly she makes a pot of coffee, pours a mug and goes and sits by the tree. It's snowing out, soft fluffy flakes twirling down. It won't amount to much, but is especially pretty to watch, on an early Christmas morning.

She hears the toilet flush, and then someone on the stairs. Her father. She can tell by his tread. She listens as he walks into the kitchen, and she knows, somehow, he is looking for her.

She is starting to get up, thinking he might want coffee, when he appears.

'There you are,' he says. 'Up early.'

'Lots to do,' she says.

He stands in the doorway.

'Can I get you some coffee?' she asks.

'I was just looking out the window. It's a pretty morning, so far.'

Peyton wonders about the addition of so far.

'Come into the kitchen,' he says.

Her father takes a seat and Peyton pours him a cup of coffee in a mug depicting dancing reindeer.

Her father sees it and laughs.

'I bought them at the nursery, when I got the tree.'

Her mug has dancing elves.

Her father stands, and she hears him at the bar cart in the conservatory. He returns with a bottle of Baileys. She loves Baileys. He adds a generous measure to both their mugs.

'Let's enjoy the quiet. We'll need the hit of booze once the kids get up,' he laughs.

The turkey is in the oven, the strata is ready to go. 'I need to set the table dad.'

'I'll help,' he says.

The snow is still falling, the air is filled with the aroma of a feast being readied. Her father looks happy as he sets the forks in place.

At that moment, Peyton Winchester is very happy that she is home.

The strata, the presents, the turkey, all turn out perfectly, and Peyton is flushed with success and Champagne.

She is clearing up in the kitchen and Caroline is sitting drinking red wine. Peyton needs to ask her about The Stick House, about that weekend, and figures the time is right, but her parents are in the next room, Rob is playing with the kids nearby. Caroline is as scary as her mother. Maybe more so. Lydia Winchester never loses control. Growing up, Caroline often flew into a rage.

Rob appears and Caroline asks him to do something for her. Peyton can't quite hear. He grabs his jacket and lets himself out the back door. Peyton feels the gust of wind.

'Where is he going?'

'To turn on the heat in the pool house.'

'What for? Wait, what? There's a heater in there?'

'You didn't know?'

'Why would there be a heater for a building we don't even use in the winter?'

'Dad put it in so Scott and I could hang out with our friends in there.'

'That explains the dart board I found,' Peyton says. John had found it, on one of their trysts.

'I ate too much,' Caroline says. 'Dinner was really good.'

Peyton feels another wave of pride.

'I wonder if I can put the turkey roaster in the dishwasher?' she says.

'Soak it first. Run the first load. Then put it in.'

Peyton nods, and turns on the dishwasher. Through the window above the sink she sees Rob, clearing the path to the pool house with a shovel. She likes her brother-in-law. He's one of the good guys.

Rob returns and Caroline grabs a bottle of wine and another bottle of Baileys from the liquor cabinet and pulls on her boots, motioning for Peyton to do the same. Caroline opens the back door and Peyton follows.

The sky looks soft and fluffy, heavy with the snow that will soon start to fall. It feels gentle, quiet, like the world is wrapped in cotton.

'Scott and I used to hang out here a lot.' She opens the door and is barely inside when she lights a cigarette.

Peyton gets it now. They're sitting in the pool house so Caroline can smoke. Peyton doesn't tell her their mother also smokes in secret. Maybe they've both smoked in here together. She's going to need a spreadsheet soon to log all the secrets she's keeping.

'So, why are you still here?' Caroline asks, and Peyton stops moving, halfway between taking a seat and a standing up, slightly lost.

'You motioned for me to follow you?'

'Not here, here,' she waves her arm and her cigarette makes a trail of smoke. 'Living with our parents in the Fort.'

'I'm not sure,' she says. She doesn't trust Caroline and isn't sure how much she can tell her.

'Well, I know I told you not to go back home, but you

look so much better. The lines around your eyes are gone. You look great.'

It's the nicest thing her sister has ever said and she savours it like the expensive wine they're drinking that their father paid for – it's a treat, yes, but it somehow feels wrong.

'But now you need to think about getting your life going,' Caroline says.

Hello? Reality, Peyton thinks.

'That's the plan for this year,' she says. She doesn't tell her she has started filling out journalism school applications.

'I mean you can't stay here, but I don't think you should go back to Seattle.'

'Why? I mean, I agree, but what's your thinking?'

'You looked like hell when I saw you. Not just your hair but your eyes. You looked half-dead.' She takes a drink of wine.

'I made a lot of bad decisions. About work. About men. About myself.'

'You're not the only one,' Caroline says. 'So don't beat yourself up.'

It takes a second for Peyton to process this. Caroline can't be speaking about herself. She's seen the way her sister looks at her husband. And it is with love.

'Do you remember going to The Stick House when we were kids?' Peyton eases into the conversation, trying to sound casual about something that's always on her mind.

'Huh. I haven't thought about that place in a long time.' She lights a new cigarette with the end of the one in her hands before putting the butt in an empty wine bottle.

Peyton watches the smoke in the bottle twist inside.

'What'll we do with it, when we get it?' Caroline says.

'What?'

'The Stick House. Do you think Scott will want it? Or should we sell it for the land?'

'Caroline, you've lost me.'

'When Mom and Dad are both gone and we're divvying everything up. Who do you think will end up with The Stick House? I sure as hell don't want it.'

Peyton opens her mouth to speak, then closes it again.

'Dad owns it,' Caroline says.

'You sure?'

'It was part of Grandfather's real estate portfolio. Dad's had it since he got this place.'

'That's impossible. I went there this summer with Dad and he never said a thing.'

Caroline shrugs. 'Dad's family owns a lot of the Fort.'

'Why didn't he tell me? How did you know?'

'I was here when the police came about kids breaking in. Dad boarded up some windows. Maybe. I think I just always knew.'

Peyton is dumbfounded.

'It's no big deal. Dad owns lots of land.'

Peyton's mind whirrs. If her father owned the property, why isn't he doing anything with it? Why hasn't he said anything?

'Does everyone in the Fort know who owns it?'

'I don't know. It's not a secret.'

For Peyton, it feels like a secret. Another one. Caroline is here, and she's talking. All Peyton can do is dive in. She starts from the beginning.

'Do you know anything about Mom's family?'

'Like what?'

'Like anything. She has a sister, and a brother.'

'I knew she had family she was estranged from.'

'How do you know that?'

'Scott used to mention a woman, Mom's sister. And I think she visited, a long time ago, but I'm not sure.'

Peyton takes a sip of wine.

'We don't know who Scott's father is. Scott doesn't even know,' Peyton says.

'Isn't he dead?'

'Who knows? And don't you think it's strange Mom has no close friends?'

'I never thought about it.'

'She's our mother and she's an enigma,' Peyton says, holding her glass out as Caroline pours them both more wine. 'John says she reminds him of Jackie Kennedy. The twinset and the pearls.'

'What's going on with you and John? You've mentioned him a few times.'

'We ran into each other soon after I moved back. Had coffee a few times.'

'Just coffee?'

'What can I say? I'm having a fling with the most popular boy ever to grace our local high school.'

'Do you think you'll stay here? Be a cop's wife? That mom and dad will babysit your grandchildren?' Caroline laughs, but Peyton hears something in her chuckle. The belief that this is something Peyton might actually do.

'No to any of those things. Neither one of us is in it for

the long haul,' she says. But maybe she should bring this up with him again. Make sure they're on the same page.

'We've been talking a lot about Daisy Wright.'

'Crazy what happened to her,' Caroline says. 'Does John have any idea?'

'From a police point of view, he's not saying much.'

'What other point of view does he have?'

'He was her cousin. Didn't you know that?'

'If I knew, I forgot. Seems like life in the Fort happened a long time ago.'

'Do you remember the day it happened?'

'Of course. I remember listening to the radio when I was in the pool. I stayed home with you, but Mom went out to see if she could help.'

Peyton sits up straighter. She wishes she had brought her phone so she could record the conversation.

'What? Mom went out? To help?'

'Yeah. She told me to lock the doors and not let anyone in. I remember thinking she was overreacting, but once she was gone, I was scared. Turned on every light in the house. She was tired and cranky when she got home. Snapped at me when I asked what was happening.' Caroline takes another drink.

'I can't picture her going out to help search for a missing girl. She's more the write-a-check kind than the get-your-hands-dirty kind.'

'When she came home, she had dirt under her nails.' She stops. 'I just remembered that. Her clothes were dirty, too.'

Peyton feels like something cold has just dropped into her belly.

'No way was our mother digging through sand on the beach or walking through the woods with a flashlight.'

'I can't see it either, but I remember the day.'

Peyton tells herself to think. The Stick House was dirty inside. She remembers that.

'That day, the day it happened. You said Mom went out and we stayed home.'

'Yes.'

'I don't remember it that way. I remember us going to The Stick House. There was a creepy old man there.'

Caroline looks at her like she just sprouted another head.

'You're dreaming.'

'No, I'm not.'

Caroline shakes her head, takes a long pull on her cigarette.

'Never happened.'

They're silent, the room suddenly colder, without life and energy. Peyton figures she can push it and ruin Christmas or accept it for what it is – Caroline's version of events – and move on.

'I remember it clearly,' Peyton says.

But does she? It's hazy, vague. She remembers the feeling more than the image. Could she have the wrong day?

Caroline tilts her head back and Peyton might not know her well, but she sees the signs of her losing patience. She watched for them enough growing up. She knows.

'Are you and Scott in touch much?' She changes the subject.

'We email mostly. Presents for the kids from time to time.'

'He didn't come home when Dad was in hospital.'

'Did you expect him to?'

'I'm not sure. It just seems strange. I mean push comes to shove, we're family.'

'Peyton, you need to stop trying to create something that doesn't exist. We're not the Brady Bunch. Never have been, never will be.'

'That's not what I'm trying to do,' Peyton says. It hurts to hear outright that your family isn't much of a family at all.

'So, back to you. What do you think you'll do next?'

'I'd still like to go to journalism school,' Peyton says.

It's hard to tell who's more surprised by this, Caroline or Peyton herself. She can't believe she's said it out loud.

'Be a bit of a hard road, starting over at this age. But you've always liked reading and writing, and you know everything going on in the world. It's a brave decision.'

'The brave part will be telling our mother.' She gives a laugh, a laugh with the goal of making an unpalatable truth easier to swallow.

'Well don't ask her permission or look for her approval – you won't get it. Just tell her.'

'Thanks.' She pauses, thinks, regroups. 'Caroline, I know we were at The Stick House that weekend. I know we were. You used to take me there all the time, using me as cover when you smoked with your friends.'

'Where are you going with this?'

'There was a creepy man there. I know this. And I think he's connected to Daisy Wright's disappearance.'

There. She'd said it. Out loud. She's trying to figure out what to say next, when the door opens.

'Room for one more?'

Rob is at the door, bottle of wine in his hand and a makeshift cheeseboard in the other. Mostly, it's just packages of cheese from the refrigerator piled on a kitchen plate, a box of crackers under his arm. A blast of cold crisp air comes in with him.

'Close the door,' Caroline says.

'Come on in,' Peyton says, standing and taking the plate from him.

'This is cozy,' he says.

'Kids asleep?' Caroline asks.

'Just checked them. They're out cold.' He pours himself a glass of wine and tops up Peyton's and Caroline's.

Peyton picks up a cracker and spreads some blue cheese on it. 'Yum,' she says.

Caroline nibbles a dry cracker.

Sitting in the pool house under a heavy wool blanket, snow falling outside the small, tinted window, Peyton tries not to resent her brother-in-law for the interruption. She's said her piece. Now, she must wait and see what Caroline has to say. But something tells her it won't be much.

34

Lydia

May, Boston, 1983

Minnie is more excited than Lydia that she's has a date. And the fact that she gets the entire day to herself pleases her even more.

'So, you met him on the street?' Minnie says, washing the dishes. 'Not the best "how we met" story.'

'It's a bit early for that. One date, in the afternoon. And with my son in tow. I doubt it'll go anywhere.'

She hopes she's wrong. Scott needs a strong male role model. He's being raised by two women. And his paternal genetics aren't the best. Hers aren't great, either, when she thinks about Jimmy and her daddy.

On the Saturday, Octavian shows up at her apartment with a bunch of spring flowers. Peonies, not roses. She likes that it's not roses, which are too romantic for a first date. And too cloying in general. He brings a coloring book for Scott. Bert and Ernie from *Sesame Street*. And a box of crayons. Scott has hundreds of crayons, thanks to his artistic aunt and a mother who won't let him do without. Lydia knows she's trying to give him the childhood she never had, that she's spoiling him, but she buys them anyway. To make up for him not having a father... for how she feels about his father.

She watches as Octavian kneels, resting on his heels as he shakes hands with her small son. She sees kindness in the action. And potential.

'This is my sister, Minnie,' she says.

Minnie smiles at him. A smile so different from the one she gave Dan so long ago. Lydia feels good about this smile. She's always treated Minnie as weak and needing protection. But when it comes to reading people, Minnie has her beat.

'Hello, Minnie,' he says. 'I hear you're an artist. I'd like to see your work sometime.'

Lydia watches the interaction carefully. Minnie never shows her art. If she agrees, it'll be as clear as a declaration in skywriting that Minnie sees a good person in him.

'I'm just assembling my first portfolio. I'd love some feedback.'

Lydia swivels to look at her sister so quickly, she feels a ping in her neck. She's never said a word to her about a portfolio.

'I'm not sure how much help I can give, but I'd love to see.'

'Shall we go?' Lydia says, holding her hand out for Scott.

He's parked his car in front of their building. Scott sits in the back, playing with his new toy car, humming to himself. They talk about the weather, how their Friday went, until Octavian points to a building and starts to tell her about it. She listens intently. She may learn something interesting, if the date proves to be a bust.

It's a beautiful May afternoon and the Common is busy. They're walking slowly and Scott walks ahead of them.

'Minnie doesn't let people look at her work. I ask from time to time, usually when I can smell turpentine coming from her room, but she always says she's not ready. I'm surprised she was so amenable to showing you her work.'

'It must be both thrilling and terrifying to show something you've created to the world,' he says. 'Not knowing how people will react, how it'll be interpreted.'

Lydia looks at the little boy walking ahead of them.

'It is,' she says.

Just then, Scott trips over a rock in the path. Octavian scoops him up and holds him so Lydia can check his knees and hands for scrapes.

'What say we rent a paddleboat? Do you want to go out on the water and see the ducks up close?'

Scott nods through his tears.

Octavian's actions are kind and gentle. He's gentle. And both Eualla Tompkins and Lydia Thomas are ready for gentle.

Somehow, the first date turns gently into the second, and then the third, and fourth, until Lydia stops counting how many dates they've been on and starts counting how many months they've been together. Octavian has looked through Minnie's portfolio and given both his feedback and his praise. Watching them together one day, Minnie still small but glowing with health, Octavian towering over her, somehow making his imposing size less so. He is so good with people. Lydia envies him this.

They're having a glass of wine in her apartment one night when he says, 'I'd like to take you to Maine for a week. Do you think you can get away?'

They've been seeing each other for a year and this will be their first trip together. Lydia wonders if this is significant. 'Maine?'

'My family has some property on the water. It's a beautiful spot and I think you'll like it very much.'

'I'm not sure. Scott has school. It's a lot to ask of Minnie.'

Minnie, Lydia can tell, wants to get on with her life. She's been a godsend to her and Lydia knows her son feels a deeper connection with his aunt than with his mother. It hurts, but she knew what she was doing when she put work first. She knows one day he'll understand. At least, she hopes.

'I'm sure we can arrange something with Minnie. Or we can take Scott with us,' he says.

In the end, Minnie stays with her son but says when Lydia returns, they need to talk. Lydia knows what's coming. Maybe she'll hire an au pair.

They fly to Portland and spend the night in a hotel overlooking the harbor. It's not as grand as Boston Harbor, but that's one of the things that appeals to her. It's charming and it feels so safe.

They're having breakfast when she says, 'How come your family owns property here?'

'It's a long story, but both my great grandfather and grandfather were pretty shrewd investors. We have them to thank for a lot.'

She hasn't met any of his family, who live in New York. But then he hasn't met anyone but Minnie on her side. She told him very early on she didn't want to talk about her childhood and he hasn't pushed. If he had, they wouldn't be here today.

He rents a car and they head out along the coast. The sun is shining and the day bright, but there's a cool wind off the Atlantic. It's Lydia's favorite kind of day, sunny and cool. She doesn't like to be too hot, doesn't like to sweat. She doesn't like to be cold, either. She knows it's from when she was at the mercy of the elements in that terrible cold winter in Tennessee, all those years ago.

They pull off the main road and end up on the outskirts of town. Gas stations and diners appear and her heart starts to sink. It looks a lot like the road that leads to her old hometown. And that just won't do. But soon it changes. Homes appear, old and dignified, stately and regal.

'Welcome to Fort Meadow Beach. Or as the locals call it, the Fort.'

'It's beautiful,' she says.

Restaurants and shops pass as he drives slowly down the main street. Then they're on another road, a hill that climbs.

'I'm excited for you to see the house. I spent my happiest summers here,' he says.

A house appears. A large white house that seems to sprawl, taking up all the space – and there's a lot of it – at the top of the hill. It can't be the one he is talking about, she thinks. It's a mansion. But she can tell he is heading towards it.

'When you said property, I thought you meant a little cottage on a lake. I wasn't expecting something so grand.'

He laughs. 'My grandfather bought it during the Depression. He scooped up a lot of property then.'

At the top of the drive is space to park six, eight, ten cars. A large garage is attached to the house.

'It was the carriage house, but we added a piece, connected it to the house,' he says. 'It's cold walking to the house in the winter.'

They walk up the steps and Lydia turns to see the view. The house sprawls on a cliff, overlooking the ocean. There are no neighbors nearby, but if she looks to the left she can see the town, easily reached. Old trees tower above, so she knows the soil is nurturing, the land solid. She isn't impressed by property anymore. The stone house in Texas screamed wealth that was all smoke and mirrors. What she likes about this place is the permanence. It's stood watch, withstood storms and time. She sees herself living here. Can feel herself being safe here.

He opens the door and they step inside. 'I'll get the bags and then let's change and go for a walk on the beach. Then we'll find a place to have a good feed of lobster.'

'A feed?' she laughs.

'That's what we call it here.'

Lydia has never seen Octavian so excited. So happy. He's like a kid and she finds it endearing.

On the last evening, he asks her to sit outside with him. He's moved two chairs and table outside, close to the edge of the cliff. She sees a bucket and the top of a bottle of champagne. She knows what's coming. She's thought about it. She's ready. At least, she thinks she is.

Lydia likes Boston. Walking to work in the early morning, the sun rising, she has a sense of peace that's new for her.

But sitting by the water in Maine with this man is a peace she feels deep in her bones.

She can feel the breeze on her face, hear the gentle swoosh of it through the small leaves, barely unfurled so early in the season. They sit beside each other, the wooden chairs not particularly warm or comfortable but solid.

'I knew, from the moment I laid eyes on you, Lydia Thomas, that you were the girl for me. The way you walked down the street. So confident, so dignified. And I think we could live a very nice life together,' he says. 'I know my life would be better with you.'

He takes a small velvet box from his pocket and opens it.

'I've noticed you don't wear much jewelry, so I chose something simple, but we can always change it.'

She sees a cushion-cut solitaire on white gold. Clean, simple, stunning, solid. It sparkles even under the shade from the trees. She remembers, briefly, the jewelry Dan had given her. Showy, ostentatious. She'd sold it all a long time ago.

'It's perfect,' she says.

He takes it out of the box.

She looks at the ring. And she looks at Octavian. And she makes a decision.

'Before I answer, I have a few things I need to tell you. First, my name hasn't always been Lydia.'

When she finishes speaking, she looks at Octavian, convinced he'll take the ring back.

'I've always known there was something. Could see it in how guarded you were. You don't get that way unless you've been hurt. Traumatized. I knew you'd tell me when you were ready. And none of this changes how I feel about you.' He pauses a moment. 'It does make me wish I could go back in time and protect you, and Minnie.'

She didn't tell him everything, but she told him enough for him to know what he was getting into.

'Well?' he says.

'Yes.'

'Yes?'

'Yes,' she repeats.

He tries to put the ring on her finger, but it catches on her knuckle, so she pushes it in place herself. Holding up her hand, she sees the diamond sparkling in the fading light of day. It is beautiful, the ring, and the trees, and the ocean. At that moment, everything.

'I love it here. I think we should stay.'

Octavian looks at her like he's never seen her before.

'Here? In Fort Meadow Beach?'

'I know you love Boston. I do, too. But this place – it's just so perfect. Scott has space to play. The house is the house of my dreams. Imagine looking at that view each day.'

'The winters are something else.'

'I've lived through winters in Boston. It's all New England, isn't it?'

The wedding is a simple affair, at Boston City Hall. Lydia wears a crisp white suit she bought at Filene's department store. She carries a bouquet of cala lilies and peonies. Mitch, Octavian's best friend from college, stands with him and Minnie stands for Lydia. She wishes she could invite Katie, that things were different, but it's not possible. So much time has passed, but she still can't look her old friend in the eye. Besides, Scott might only be six, but he looks exactly like Dan.

'Don't mention Mama or Daddy or Jimmy to Octavian, or his family,' Lydia says to Minnie.

They're in the motel room Octavian rented for her to get ready. She thought it was a waste, she could use her apartment, but she can't make any more waves. His parents are already disappointed not to be having a country club wedding, but Octavian is divorced and Lydia didn't want questions around the lack of relatives on her side of the church.

'I won't,' Minnie says.

They walk across the street to the city hall. Scott is in a suit, standing with Octavian and Mitch. Lydia walks herself down the aisle and vows are exchanged. She slips a plain gold wedding band on Octavian's finger and he slips a diamond studded one on hers. Later, she'll learn it's called an eternity ring.

Mitchell cheers when they kiss. He's a lawyer in Mississippi and what some would call larger than life. Lydia struggles to like him and his oversized ways that remind her so much of Dan.

They go for dinner after. She thinks again of Katie, wondering if she's married. Wondering if she's still so up and down.

'What's wrong?' Octavian puts his hand on her knee and whispers in her ear.

'Nothing, why?' She's surprised by his question.

'You're pale. And you looked a million miles away.'

'I'm fine.'

'I hope you're better than fine,' he laughs.

She puts her hand on his knee and gives a gentle squeeze. He's a good man and she's lucky. In the morning, they're heading to the South of France. A place called Nice and then Saint-Tropez. She chose the spot, remembering that summer so long ago, sitting under that cotton sheet in the villa behind her house. It feels like both yesterday and a million years ago.

She's made it.

35

Peyton

December, Maine, Present day

Caroline is in her room, packing. They're getting ready to leave. Peyton has one last chance to ask about The Stick House. She's nervous, approaching her sister. She's been fine this visit, but Peyton will always be wary of her sister's mood swings.

'It's been a great Christmas,' Caroline says when she sees her in the room. This makes Peyton pause. Why ruin it? But she has to know. It is driving her crazy. 'I'm a bit sad it's all over. It was nice spending time with my niece and nephew,' she says.

'You can always come visit. We'd love to have you,' Caroline says, folding the black pashmina Peyton had given her for Christmas. She'd given Lydia a camel one. Caroline had given her a black cashmere turtleneck from the whole family, but her niece had given her a bowl she'd painted at one of those paint your own ceramics shops. Peyton loved it. She hadn't gotten anything from her mother, she just realized. She'd given Caroline a handbag, some designer Peyton had never heard of, but made Caroline very happy.

'I know what you want to talk about,' Caroline says, her eyes never leaving her suitcase, the perfectly folded clothes sitting beside it.

'You do?'

'The Stick House. Daisy Wright. You were so young, I didn't think you'd notice. But you never missed anything. You were such a sensitive kid,' Caroline says this last part like being sensitive is akin to being a serial killer. Peyton tells herself not to pay attention to it.

'Yes, I took you to The Stick House. Many times. I shouldn't have, but what did I know? Mom and Dad were always watching me, I think that was why they put the heater in the pool house, to give me a place to go. To keep me and Scott close.'

Peyton is holding her breath, afraid if she speaks Caroline will come to her senses, revert to her taciturn self. Stop talking.

'There was some homeless guy there once. I can't remember if it was the same weekend as Daisy. Maybe. But I really think you should stop looking around in the past.'

'The homeless guy. Skinny. Bad teeth. Black T-shirt.'

'Yeah.'

Caroline sits down on the bed. She looks older than she did a few hours ago, and Peyton can see some bad memory gripping her.

'That house is weird. There was always something off about it. I mean, we all hung out there and drank and smoked, and everyone must have known that, but we were never busted. We used to sneak inside. Sit in a big circle on the floor in the crazy big main room, pass around a bottle of whatever we stole from our parents. I remember the homeless guy because we got him to buy beer for us, and cigarettes, and we shared some of it with him. He was harmless though.'

Caroline stops, seems to take a breath and gather her thoughts. Peyton wills her to keep speaking.

'I can't remember if he was at The Stick House the weekend Daisy disappeared, but I know who was.'

Peyton is certain she can touch the suspense in the air. It feels like cold steel, like shards of jagged glass, like a mushroom cloud.

'Who?'

'You'll think I'm crazy.'

'I doubt it,' Peyton says, although growing up this is exactly what she thought of Caroline.

'Our mother.'

'Jesus,' Peyton says. It's like the shards of glass, of steel, have fallen, piercing her. But what Caroline says. Peyton knows, somehow, she's right.

'Auntie Peyton said a bad word!'

Peyton spins around to see her niece standing there, looking pleased with herself for calling out her aunt.

'Oops,' Peyton jokes, her hand flying to her mouth. 'I did say a bad word. I'm sorry.'

Caroline returns to packing. Peyton can tell by the way she squares her shoulders that the conversation is over.

'Come on,' Peyton nudges her niece ahead of her, gently holding her shoulders. 'Let's pack up some cookies for the drive home.'

*

At the car Caroline says, 'Let it go Peyton. You and I both know Mom had nothing to do with Daisy disappearing.'

'But why was she there?'

'Who knows? But Dad's getting over a heart attack, they're both getting old. No good can come from bringing it all up now.'

Caroline looks at her, a meaningful look, but not menacing, the way some of her looks can be. Not imploring, either.

'Safe drive,' Peyton says, the first to break eye contact. She closes the passenger side door, then leans into the backseat to say goodbye to her niece and nephew once again. She hears the snow crunch and knows someone is coming towards them. Rob, and her father.

Rob hugs her goodbye. 'Thanks again for the spectacular meals,' he says. 'Outstanding!' He rubs his belly and she laughs. Her father is taking out his wallet, handing each grandchild a twenty-dollar bill. They scream in delight. Then Rob is in the car, heading down the drive. He toots the horn and Peyton and her father wave.

She looks out at the Atlantic Ocean and wonders if last May, when she took her evening swim in the frigid waters, she was trying to hurt herself.

She opens the door and walks inside, greeted by the too warm air and the ugly black and white tiles. And something else. A sense of peace. She feels better. Caroline telling her to back off has validated all the crazy feelings she's had about that weekend, not just since she moved home but her whole life. She is certain she has never, not since it happened, gone a week without thinking of Daisy Wright.

'Come into the kitchen Peyton,' she hears her mother call. She feels herself slump.

Her mother is standing at the stove, heating up the last of the strata in a pan. Her mother hated the microwave. And loved the breakfast strata.

'There's an envelope on the counter,' she indicates the manila envelope, sitting in the middle of the empty space. She takes a seat in front of it.

'That's for Christmas. From your father and I,' she says.

Peyton opens the envelope. Inside, paid in full, is the mortgage on her condo in Seattle.

'I don't understand,' Peyton says.

'What's to understand? We've paid off your mortgage.'

'But it's so much,' Peyton says. 'Too much.' She turns the deed over, like there's something more to be learned.

'You shouldn't have had a mortgage to begin with. Your father should have bought it and you paid him back. There was no need for the banks to be making money,' her mother says, transferring the strata from the pan to a plate. She sits beside Peyton, who is still too shocked to speak. Between the mortgage and her mother eating leftovers, she can't quite connect what is happening. She looks around the kitchen to make sure she's in the right house.

'Put it someplace safe. Better yet, now that you know about it, give it back to me, and I'll put it in my safe deposit box.' She sets down her fork and opens her bag. The black Chanel with the gold chain link strap. She played with it as a kid. Asked her mother once if it was real gold.

And she saw it, that day at The Stick House. Sitting outside behind the carriage house. She thought it was a barn at the time. Or was she sitting by the boiler? No, she was outside, she can see someone walking, capris trousers, black loafers with gold buckles. A white blouse. And a black Chanel handbag.

Her mother was the only woman in the Fort who owned a Chanel bag.

She was there. Caroline was right.

'Goodness Peyton, now what? You look like you've seen a ghost.'

'Cramps,' she says. An old excuse but it always worked.

'Have a gin and tonic. Get a hot water bottle,' she says.

She nods, stands. Randomly she bends over, gives her mother a hug. 'Thank you,' she says. She feels her mother squeeze her elbow.

'That's enough now, Peyton, I want to eat my dinner.'

Peyton disengages. She doesn't think her mother had anything to do with Daisy's disappearance. Not really. But she's watched enough crime shows to know anyone is capable of anything and everything.

She moves to the stairs. Her parents bought her a home, whether she wants it or not.

36

Peyton

February, Maine, 2022

The Fort seems to have hunkered down, waiting out the coldest part of the year. Peyton moves a small space heater into the room in the basement where Daisy's timeline now takes up two entire walls but doesn't reveal any new truths.

She was sure she'd have figured it out by now, what happened all that time ago. But then she was certain she wouldn't be in the Fort come September and here it was, January. Her applications for journalism school are mostly completed, sitting on the old desk in a folder, waiting for her to complete the essay portion.

She's getting another cup of coffee, when she hears it.

'Peyton. Come into the conservatory. I want to talk to you,' her mother says.

Here we go again, she thinks.

It isn't sunny out, but it isn't exactly gray. For some

reason the glass in the conservatory has caught what little light there is and magnified it, hurting her eyes. She feels like it's mocking her now. Or maybe she's spent so much time in the small room in the basement she's turning into a mole.

Her mother is sitting with a cup of coffee and her daytimer. Peyton looks at her watch and pictures the entry: Eight fifteen – make Peyton lose the will to live.

'You've been home for almost eight months now.'

Some days it feels like she's just arrived, others it feels like she's been here forever, like all the time away was a dream.

'What are your plans?'

Peyton hesitates, unsure what to say.

'You must know what you want from your life.'

She thinks about saying she wants to go to journalism school. But her mother will probably dismiss her again.

'I'm working on it,' she says.

'Well, work more. Time is your friend in your early twenties, but it's not now.' Her mother looks at her watch. 'I'm going to Portland. Will you cook dinner for your father tonight?'

'Yes,' Peyton says.

'We'll talk again next week. You can tell me your plans then.'

'I have a week?'

'Yes. And I'm being generous. You have time and no responsibilities. And a paid-off condo. You can focus entirely on yourself.'

Peyton feels herself slump, like she's Atlas from Greek mythology carrying the world on her shoulders. She hears her mother's words echo. She just has herself to worry about. Does this mean Lydia worries about her children? Her husband? Peyton can't see it.

'And that shrine, timeline, whatever you call it in the basement... I want it to come down. Today.'

'Why?'

'It's morbid. Maudlin. And disrespectful.'

'Disrespectful?'

'To her family.'

'They don't know about it. Except for John. And he wants to know what happened to her. What do you think we talk about when we're together?' Peyton feels herself blush. A lot of what they do does not require conversation. After her conversation with Caroline she causally brought up that she was still planning to leave as they watched the New Year's fireworks together. He nodded but took her hand when they were walking back to his condo. She knew she had to be careful. She would never do to someone what Marco did to her.

'They will. It's Fort Meadow Beach, Peyton. Sooner or later, everyone knows everything.'

Not everything, Peyton thinks.

Her mother gets up, picks up her purse and walks to the door. Peyton waits for it to close, then goes downstairs, to the basement, to look at her wall again. She's missing something – she just doesn't know what. But the bigger question is why her mother is so hellbent against what she is doing.

'I can cook, Dad, or we can order from Tully's,' Peyton says. It's six o'clock and she's calling it a day after accomplishing nothing. Well, she stared a lot, if that's an accomplishment.

Her father looks out the window, as though the answer is in the clouds. Then he says, 'Let's order in.'

She's pulling out the menu when she sees the card from her aunt Minnie. And she remembers the conversation she and her dad had, the last time they ordered from Tully's. A primary source to one mystery, at least. The mystery of her mother. Minnie. She'd know her mother in a way no one else would.

She picks up the card, runs up the stairs to her room it, hides it in her closet as though her mother will suddenly appear and rip it from her, destroy it. Then she goes back downstairs and calmly orders food, talks to her father. Inside, she's making plans, as she was told to do.

Like going to Tennessee to find Minnie.

37

Lydia

Fort Meadow Beach, Summer, 1991

Life moves quickly – so quickly you miss it - when things are good. Or at least calm. The days, weeks, months, years filled with agony...? Well, you feel every single moment of those. Lydia knows. She felt like her childhood lasted forever. But now, time is sailing by, like the boats she watches from the edge of the cliff near her home. She feels good. Tired but good. Scott is smart and capable, like her, and their daughter Caroline is strong and determined. Two kids. Octavian is a good father to them both. She is happy that part of her life is over. And then she wakes one morning and starts to get out of bed, when the room sways slightly and her stomach turns. And turns again. And she knows.

Seven months and three weeks later, after a pregnancy that's caused gestational diabetes and pre-eclampsia and following ten weeks of bed rest, her second daughter is born. She has no name ready. She'd never quite got her head around being pregnant the third time and at her age – thirty-nine – it's practically a scandal.

She rests in her bassinet, a sleepy, drowsy baby. Lydia stares at her through the Plexiglas – another being she's now responsible for. She can't hold her. The doctors say her strength will come back and Octavian offers to help but she just can't. She's been a mother since she was nine years old. She's tired.

'What shall we name her?' Octavian says, resting his hand on her back.

'I'm not sure.'

He looks at her in surprise. 'You had Caroline's name all ready to go.'

'Caroline knew who she was. *I* knew who she was, the minute I saw her.'

The lines in his forehead appear and she knows he's puzzled, confused. Unsure what to say.

'Are you feeling alright, Lydia?'

She shakes her head. 'No. I feel like I've been beaten up, badly beaten. Everything hurts. I just need to rest.'

'Hospital food's probably not helping and your doctor wants to keep you at least a few more days. What can I bring you?'

'Nothing, Octavian. Thanks. I just need to sleep.'

In the end they named her Peyton because Octavian's mother liked the name. Peyton Lee, which was his grandmother's name. She was a very easy baby, happy enough. Never fussed, never pushed boundaries. Lydia should have been overjoyed, but it made her suspicious. She thought Peyton knew enough not to push the envelope. Knew her place in the family was tenuous.

She tries very hard, but the feelings she had for Scott, for Caroline, she lacks for Peyton. But it's OK. Octavian loves the child. She won't notice that her mother is distant. Her children have everything they need. They have money. It'll all work out, she tells herself. Perhaps Peyton will go to boarding school. Caroline had wanted to go to Switzerland, but she'd said no. If Peyton asks, they will send her. Everything will be fine, she tells herself. She prescribes herself something, just to pick her up. To get through the weeks. It helps. And just when she needs a bit more support, Minnie asks if she can visit. Lydia sends her a plane ticket.

'Your Aunt Minnie is coming to visit,' she tells her children. They're all in the same room, which is so rare she thinks about taking a photo. Caroline is reading a book, which makes Lydia happy. Scott is sitting with Peyton, making shapes with Play-Doh. She never thought Scott would have the bond he has with his half-sister, and it makes her feel better knowing Peyton has her brother's unconditional love. That's something. It's OK, she tells herself.

It's the third day of Minnie's visit. They're sitting near the cliff edge, so Minnie can see the water, cold drinks in hand. Peyton's sitting by herself, playing in the sandbox Octavian built for her. Scott is out with friends. It's the first time they've had to just chat.

'Scott is so big,' Minnie says for the tenth or twelfth time since her arrival.

'He's smart,' Lydia says.

'Caroline's going to be a stunner.'

'She knows it, too.' Lydia shakes her head, knowing something is coming.

She can tell by the way Minnie moves, bending forward and scratching her knee, leaning back and looking around. Fidgeting. The way she keeps looking at Peyton, playing by herself, fifteen feet away.

'Peyton's very quiet for her age. I remember the other two being much more gregarious.'

Lydia feels a flash of anger toward Minnie. A flash of anger that makes no sense, but for her guilt.

'She's small for her age. She's different,' Lydia responds.

'You're different with her. Not as warm, like.'

Lydia turns to her sister. The way she adds like, drags out her vowels… The twang. The fact that she can criticize after everything she did for her.

She can see Minnie move back in her seat.

'You can get as mad at me as you want, Eu. Peyton's the one suffering.'

Lydia watches as she stands, walks over to Peyton, who looks up with an expression of startled delight. Minnie sits in the sand and helps her build a castle in the sandbox Octavian built for her.

Lydia knows her own failings, knows her faults. Knows what she should be doing. But she turns to the ocean, takes another sip of her drink, turning her back on both her daughter and her sister. She just wants to enjoy the summer.

Minnie had been gone a day when the police came for the first time. Caroline opened the door to find the chief on the porch.

'Dad!' she'd yelled, breaking the 'no shouting in the house' rule.

Octavian had appeared, his hands covered in finger paint from drawing ducks with Peyton.

'Chief Langley,' he'd said. 'What can I do for you?'

Lydia was behind her husband, wondering what on earth could make her daughter shout for her father.

'Evening, Lydia, Octavian.' Chief Langley touched his hat, then saw Caroline. 'Could we speak someplace?'

'Of course.'

Apparently, the back door of the candy factory was easy to open, and Scott and his friends had been helping themselves. Mary had found a lot of candy wrappers in his room and Lydia had thought if that was the worst thing they'd have to deal with, him eating too much sugar, she was fine with it. But there was more to it than that. He was stealing. Breaking and entering.

Octavian had been furious, angrier than she'd ever seen him.

'Stealing? You don't get enough from us?' he'd raged.

Scott, sitting in a chair, looking the most afraid she'd ever seen her son.

Things were uneasy in the house the next day, and the next. Octavian was simmering and everyone, even Lydia, was giving him a wide berth, everyone except Peyton, who knew something was wrong and crawled onto his knee and hugged him, night after night.

Time, she was sure, didn't so much heal as deaden the pain. Anger, no matter how strong, how deep, was exhausting to carry and sooner or later it had to be put down. Octavian, she saw one day, was letting go of his rage at Scott.

The summer sun was high in the sky, and as it warmed the land and the water, it melted some of the tension. Lydia let herself relax.

A Wednesday night in August and Lydia thinks everyone is home in bed when she hears a noise. She's a light sleeper, always listening for danger. All these years later, waiting to see Jimmy at the foot of her bed.

She sits up. Listens. There's another sound. Retching. She's been a mother long enough to know when a kid is sick.

She gets up to check if it is

Caroline or Scott. Peyton could not make such noise. She smells it, in the hall. A stink that hits her like a physical blow, stopping her, almost pushing her backwards.

Beer. Whiskey. Stale alcohol and lots of it. She feels herself start to shake, has to tell herself, no, by God, no. She is safe in her own home. Safe. He is not here.

Scott.

Her son is on his hands and knees, vomiting onto the floor. She stops, figuring out what to do. She can't get him to his own bathroom in his bedroom. Her son is a big man.

Someone is behind her.

'Go get a bucket,' Octavian's voice is low, calm. Frightening.

She runs down the stairs, to the closet where Mary keeps

the cleaning supplies, grabs a bucket, knocking over all the cleansers and brooms around it. Holding the bucket she races to the stairs, aware of the cold tiles in the entrance under her feet. She's always hated the entryway, but Octavian won't replace the floor. The tiles weren't made anymore. Something to do with some goddamn bit of architecture that she lost interest in a long time ago.

'Here,' she sets the bucket down. 'You can go to bed,' she says to her husband. She does not want to go through more weeks of anger.

'Now go get a mop, cloths, cleaning fluid – whatever's needed to clean this lot up.'

'Let's put him to bed. I'll clean up,' she says.

'He's cleaning it up. Not you.'

Lydia looks at her husband, who is standing, immoveable, towering over her son, who is on his hands and knees, a pool of vomit on the floor. Her fear of Octavian's reaction, her son's behaviour, wars with revulsion. They all had it so damn easy compared to her. Why could they not simply behave?

'It's food poisoning,' Scott drawls.

In his words, she hears Jimmy's voice. And something inside her snaps.

'Do you think I'm stupid?' she barks. She's cold with rage.

Scott lifts his head to look at her, his eyes red-rimmed and watery.

'I won't have this in *my* house,' she growls.

'Lydia!'

Moments before Octavian had been furious, but now he is admonishing her.

'So only you can be angry?' She turns her fury on her husband.

Caroline appears, eyes groggy from sleep. She's wearing a tank top and shorts. Her hair is long and messy, and Lydia still notices how beautiful she is.

'Go back to bed.'

'Stop yelling at him! He's sick,' Caroline says.

Shuffling and whimpers, and then Peyton appears.

'What's wong?' she says.

No 'r' in wrong. She's too old to speak this way and it irritates Lydia.

'Get back to bed!' she shouts.

'Jesus!' Caroline says, shooting her a dirty look as she scoops up a now weeping Peyton.

Lydia, who prides herself on being able to control any situation, feels the room further fracture around her. Somehow, she's the bad guy.

Until Scott vomits again.

Lydia says nothing as Octavian pulls him from the floor, half walks, half carries him to the bathroom. Caroline takes Peyton with her to her room. Lydia stands alone for a moment, then gets a mop and cleans the floor, giving her time to think, to try and breathe even as she holds her breath against the stench.

Caroline has turned into a beautiful girl, smart and capable, but volatile, difficult, demanding. Lydia has been thinking about getting her counseling, but how would that look, her own daughter seeing a therapist when that's what she does for a living? Doesn't she have a rule book? Shouldn't her family be perfect? It's not even close, but it's so much better than what she came from. She takes comfort in that.

And then there's her youngest daughter. Peyton is at an awkward stage, still very much a little girl but occasionally showing her independence, a hint of the person she might be, could be. Lydia knows she's failing the child. Knows Octavian sees it because he makes much more of a fuss over Peyton than he did Caroline. He babies her, spoils her. Lydia resents this. She never wanted to be a mother to Scott, but she rallied. Caroline is so much like Lydia. She challenges her. Peyton is a sensitive child, like Minnie. Lydia doesn't have the energy to protect Peyton the way she did her little sister. She shouldn't have to. The refrigerator is full. The house is beautiful. Why can't they all play ball?

She gags, cleaning up the vomit. She'll make more of an effort with Peyton, who's a lovely little girl. It's not her fault Lydia was looking forward to being done with being a mother.

38

Peyton

February/March, Maine and Tennessee, 2022

She is nervous, walking to the post office. It feels like her mother is going to appear from behind a shrub. A snowbank. Pull up beside her in that enormous new Escalade of hers and order her in, seize the applications she has hidden in her bag, and demand to know just what is going on with her.

They're all finished, all twenty-seven of them. Schools across the US, one in Canada. Most she sent online, but where she could she applied with paper. She missed the deadline for application for some and is applying for winter sessions and part time enrolment, too. It's time to get the ball rolling. She figures she'll be the oldest student in any class she gets into, but she's going. Somewhere new, someplace she wants to be. Doing exactly what she wants.

The sun is out today, its rays pure and strong, melting the snow so it runs down the streets, into the grates.

It's beautiful, but it's March. There will probably be another storm. The locals will look outside in disgust and close the curtains against it, but it will come anyway.

But today, today is a nice day. She stops and looks at the way the light plays with the icy blue Atlantic Ocean. Soon it will be the first anniversary of her coming home swim. She feels the cramp of cold in her body just at the memory.

There's no one in line at the post office so she moves directly to the counter. A girl she went to high school with – Wendy is her name, she thinks – helps her. She sends them all tracked, filling out all the little forms, and pays with her credit card.

She watches as each manilla envelope disappears into a bag.

'There you go,' Wendy says, handing Peyton the receipt. The long twist of paper looks like a tail, and for some reason she laughs at the sight of it.

Outside, the job done, she takes out her phone and texts John, who has read some of the essays she's written for her applications and cheered her on every step of the way.

She stops and buys a coffee, drinking it as she walks through town. It's such a pretty spot. She's not sure she ever realized that before.

She takes her time walking home, the hill and the winter sand no longer a problem, her legs strong and capable now.

She lets herself in the house, taking off her shoes in the entry, carrying them to the mat under the stairs.

She knows her mother is home, even though she's not making any noise. The place just feels different when she is there.

She finds her in the conservatory, looking out the window, drinking a mug of something.

'Hi,' she says.

Her mother looks up and for a moment Peyton is not sure she sees her. It feels like her mother looks right through her.

'I've been thinking,' she says. Peyton's heart drops.

'If you're still here this summer, you need to get a job. The yacht club should take you back on as an instructor. Do you still have your sailing certification?'

Peyton nods. 'I'm making a plan, mom. I think I've got some things figured out.'

39

Peyton

Spring, Tennessee, 2022

They're on their way to the airport, she and John. Bruce Springsteen is on the radio and the sun is shining in a cloudless sky. It's a beautiful day and Peyton is wondering why she's flying to Tennessee to spy on a family her mother has nothing to do with.

'So you'll be back Monday night?' he says, pulling into the drop-off outside the terminal.

'I will.'

'And I'm not to say a word about anything, just be on alert for issues?'

'You can hardly be accused of boredom in your life. Never a dull moment. Hope you know what you've got yourself into.'

She told her parents she was going to Seattle. John is the only person who knows where she'll be.

He puts the car in park, steps out and takes her bag from the trunk, places it on the curb.

'That's all for three days? You pack light.'

'I got enough other stuff weighing me down. I don't need more.'

He kisses her on the cheek. 'I'll be here when you get back.'

It's the nicest thing anyone has said to her in a long time.

The air feels so different in Knoxville when she lands. The Fort is still a frozen tundra, but it's spring in Tennessee. She rents a car and it takes a few minutes to adjust the mirrors, the seats. She figures out the GPS, plugs in the zip code from the Christmas card now sitting beside her and sets off.

It's only as she's looking for the interstate that she sees flaws in her plan. The card could be old. Her aunt could have moved. She's here now, so she keeps going.

She finds the I-40 and merges into traffic. The area is beautiful, from what she sees. Hills and mountains, sloping land, beautiful old trees. Not as beautiful as Maine. Different to Seattle. But it certainly has something, the hills lush and green, the earth already coming back to life after winter's turn.

The landscape is the same, until suddenly it is not. The closer to Bolt's Ferry she gets, the less lush it becomes. The few billboards that line the road are old, weather-beaten, falling apart.

Peyton looks at the GPS and sees she's only a few miles from where her mother grew up. It feels surreal.

She merges, takes her exit, and instantly she is in another world. At the end of the ramp is a boarded-up gas station. Some of the plywood is missing and Peyton suspects local kids of breaking in. An old sign welcoming her to Bolt's Ferry appears, the wood holding it up rotted, the aluminum bent and rusted. Already she finds the place depressing.

She turns left onto the main street and sees more of the same, boarded-up old businesses, interspersed with ones that are still open but struggling, on the verge. There's something more discouraging about them, like they refuse to accept the inevitable. There's a small diner to her right. It's open, judging by the old pickup trucks parked out front, the only spot on the street with any vehicles.

She thinks for a second then decides to get a feel for the place. She pulls in next to a truck and gets out.

The diner is like something from a fifties movie, the name painted in a semicircle on the door long faded but once red, advertising the Blue Ridge Diner. Peyton wonders if someone was having a laugh, painting it red originally.

She barely has the door open, when everyone inside – eight people, she counts – turns and looks at her. She hesitates, wondering if this is the sort of place that's closed to newcomers. There's a scent hanging in the air, heavy, thick. Grease, French fries, sweat and hopelessness, all vying for the space. Peyton wants to turn and leave, but she can't, won't, because somewhere in the twisted air she feels is the answer to some of her questions. She lets the door close and moves to the counter.

'Take a seat anywhere,' a voice says. 'What can I get you, hun?'

A waitress appears in front of her, wearing an apron

that was once white but is now gray, wrapped around a polyester uniform that she's sweating through, despite the air conditioning. Her coral lipstick looks like she put in on with a butter knife. Peyton can't remember the last time she saw a woman wearing purple eyeshadow. It takes her a second to reply.

'Iced tea, please.'

Peyton watches as she takes a red plastic tumbler from the shelf, fills it with ice then pours tea from a pitcher.

'Anything else?'

Peyton looks up from the menu and orders the chicken salad.

She senses the man beside her watching her. His side glances are hardly subtle and he's a big man. He takes up a lot of space.

'Where you from, doll?' he asks. 'It's not from around here.'

Peyton laughs to herself. She's never been called doll before.

'I'm from Maine. On the East Coast.'

'I know where it is.'

'Sorry.' Peyton is embarrassed and tells herself not to judge.

'What brings you to these parts?' he says.

Peyton loves the accent, the slow drawl. It's charming, sweet, welcoming. As she listens, she realizes her mother has no sign of this accent and fear creeps in that she's in the wrong place.

'Oh, I have family from around here.'

The waitress sets a plate in front of her, a mound of chicken on a bed of iceberg lettuce, a sprig of parley so big she thinks it might be fake. She pokes it with a fork and sets it aside, unsure, and takes a bite of her meal. It's good. Really good. She takes another forkful.

She thinks about the restaurants she went to with Marco. The meals she ate when she was a rep, Michelin-starred and Zagat-rated. This is the best chicken salad she's ever eaten.

'This is great,' she says.

'Aren't you sweet, hun.'

She eats in silence, trying to observe others without looking like she's staring. When she's done, she's full.

'Piece of pie?'

Peyton shakes her head. 'I ate too much, but it was so good.'

The waitress tops up her iced tea as Peyton asks where the bathroom is. The waitress points her toward the back.

The only bright spot in the bathroom is the blue-colored water in the toilet bowl. The room is gray and only the cold faucet works.

She pays the bill and is starting to walk out, when she stops, looks at the waitress and says, 'I'm looking for a woman named Minnie Tompkins. Do you know where I might find her?'

'You kin?' the large man who had been sitting beside her asks looking her up and down like her height might provide an answer.

'Yes, but she doesn't know me. At least, I don't think so.' Peyton hesitates. She's making this sound a lot more complicated than it is.

The waitress is staring at her.

'You Eualla's girl?'

'I don't know that name, either, I'm afraid,' Peyton says. She's not even sure what she said. Yewellen? Ualla?

What little conversation had been taking place dries up. Everyone has turned to look at her. She's certain she sees recognition in the woman's eyes. It flashes bright and then she dips her head and turns away. As Peyton watches, she shares a look with an old man at the end of the counter, eating a slice of peach pie.

'Minnie lives behind the drugstore. It's just a piece down the road,' the big man says. 'Just knock on the side door, toward the back.'

'OK. Thanks.'

Peyton tips the waitress, wishing she'd left more. It seems such a dreary place to have to spend your working life. She walks out to her car, into the empty street, the drab land. She can't picture her mother ever living here.

The drugstore is on a corner and she sees the door the man mentioned immediately. She can't quite bring herself to knock, so she goes into the pharmacy.

Inside, it has the same dull feelings of hopelessness as the diner. Cheap make-up and soap and toothpaste line old metal shelves. She looks for something to buy, thinking she should support the local economy.

'You're not from round here, are you?' The clerk is wearing a white lab coat that's slightly frayed. 'Where are you headed?'

'So it shows that I'm not a local, then?'

He smiles.

'I'm looking for Minnie Tompkins.'

She sees his hand stop as she counts out her change.

'Minnie?' he asks.

'I was told she lived behind here.'

He looks at her over the top of his glasses and Peyton feels herself squirm like she's done something wrong, even though she hasn't.

'Does Minnie know you?' he says.

'She might know *of* me, but we've never met.'

It sounds like a line in an article: *They were blood kin but had never met until she flew to the tiny town where she thought she'd be safe and confronted her aunt about her mother.*

'I'll call and let her know you're coming. Can I ask your name?'

'It's Peyton Winchester. If she doesn't know the name, tell her I'm Lydia's daughter.'

Peyton watches his face closely but sees no reaction.

He picks up a phone, the old kind that sit in cradles, once cutting-edge but now only a means to access to the internet.

'Miss Minnie? It's Trent. How are you today? Feeling good? Weather sure is pretty today.'

In the space of a day, she's driven to the airport, been on a flight, rented a car, driven around a brand-new state and eaten at a diner, but waiting for this man to get to the point is the longest part of her day so far. She waits while he seemingly listens. Peyton is sure time is slowing down.

'Sure, I'm happy to do that. Now, Miss Minnie, I have a lady here who wants to see you. Her name is Peyton Winchester.'

Peyton watches as he nods not at her, but at the voice on the phone.

'OK. I'll send her back.'

'Miss Minnie will see you,' he says, like Peyton's heading out for an audience with the queen.

Peyton looks around the store. 'Is there anything I can take her? Anything from here she likes?'

He moves from behind the counter and walks to the candy section. He hands her a Whitman's Sampler and after he takes payment, he walks her to the door, opens it and points to the street. 'Around the corner, to your left. Door's at the back.'

Peyton walks to the street and turns instead of crossing the sad brown lawn. She steps over the sidewalk cracks, covering the distance to the door in seconds, the chocolate in her hands like she's delivering a pizza.

The door is closed and she waits, thinking Minnie might open it, knowing someone is coming. As she's reaching to knock, a woman appears, a good eight inches shorter than her mother and very thin. Her eyes are a warm brown and seem to dance. She sees nothing of her own mother in this woman and fears, once again, she has the wrong person.

She smiles at Peyton. She's wearing black pants and a brown sweater that Peyton is certain she bought in another decade. But it's her earrings she can't stop looking at. They're a medley of red and blue and green and purple and orange plastic bits, made to look like a bunch of grapes, Peyton thinks. They'd give her mother a heart attack.

'Hello,' Peyton says. 'I'm not sure you know who I am.'

'Of course I do. You're Eualla's girl.'

The same name as she heard at the diner. They can't both be wrong?

Peyton shakes her head. 'No, ma'am. My mother's name is Lydia.' Peyton falters, unsure how best to say why she's come all this way.

'Lydia to you, maybe, but my sister was christened Eualla.'

Peyton feels a jolt at the word sister. She has the right woman.

'Eualla?'

She nods, as though she knows the shock Peyton is experiencing at that moment.

'Come in, sweetheart. We have a lot to talk about.'

Peyton follows her into the tiny entrance, up three narrow stairs that open into an equally tiny kitchen.

'Take a seat. I'll get us some tea.'

Opened, the refrigerator door takes up most of the kitchen. Her aunt pulls out a glass pitcher with oranges and lemons painted on it, an orange plastic lid. Adds some ice from the freezer to two tumblers and then sits at the table with Peyton.

'You don't seem surprised to see me. To know about me,' she says.

Minnie smiles, her thin lips disappearing, the corners turning up. 'I guess I'm not. Your mama said you were curious, always wanting to know what was going on.'

'My mother told me about you?'

'Sure did. And I've met you, too. When you were a little thing.'

'So the two of you are in touch?'

'Not now.'

She looks away, and Peyton can feel the sadness in her words, see it in how she turns away.

'She doesn't know I'm here.' Peyton tries to create some distance between her and her mother, so the woman will know she's friend, not foe.

'I figured that.'

'Why?'

'Your mama wouldn't want you here, poking around in her past.'

'I'm not even sure why I'm poking around. Must be a character flaw.'

Minnie laughs and Peyton likes her immediately. Peyton takes a sip of her tea and tries not to wince. It's more sugar than tea and she's certain she can almost feel her teeth start to decay.

'Tea OK?'

'Yes, thanks.'

'Liar. Eualla always said I made it too sweet.'

Peyton grins. There was that name again. 'I'm sorry – Eualla?'

'Your mother, Eualla.'

Minnie's eyes sparkle and for a second, Peyton worries it's the shine of madness. Her crazy aunt Minnie, hidden away by the family. It happens a lot in Southern Gothic literature. And her mother never drank iced tea, at least not that she can remember.

'I hope I'm not bringing up bad memories,' Peyton says. 'But I'd love to hear more about her. And your family.'

'She was born and raised Eualla Linn Tompkins,' Minnie says. 'So, have you moved nearby? Is that why you've searched me out?'

'No, I haven't. I'm living at home with my parents at the moment. I found a Christmas card you sent my mother and I asked my father about it.'

'How is Octavian? He's precious,' she says, her voice soft and warm, the verbal equivalent of a chocolate chip cookie.

'He's fine, thanks.' Peyton wants to say she had no idea her mother even had a family, but it sounds harsh. The air conditioner kicks in, and she feels a fresh but welcome blast of coolness. She plows ahead. 'Mom has never really mentioned Tennessee, or her past, or her parents. And the card, well, Dad didn't have much to say.'

'I bet Octavian told you to let sleeping dogs lie. He's always been real protective of Eualla.'

'He did. And he still is.'

'They were well suited in the sense that they both enjoyed quiet and being on their own.'

Minnie takes a drink of tea. Peyton can see a sludge of sugar on the bottom of her tumbler as she tips it up.

'Now, before I tell you about Eualla, let me ask this: where does she think you are right now?'

'She thinks I'm in Seattle checking on my condo.'

'You are your mother's daughter.'

'I'm not sure I follow?'

'I want to say cunning, but that doesn't sound nice. I'm not sure I know the right word.'

'How about curious?'

'You could have asked Eualla.'

'And how do you think that would have gone?' Peyton sits up straighter. '"My past, Peyton, is none of your concern."' She tries to mimic her mother's dismissive tone. 'Or maybe,

"I suggest you concentrate on your own life, as *that* is what needs the most work."'

Minnie laughs at first, then sighs. 'She wasn't always like that. Yes, she's always been spirited and feisty, but she had a great sense of joy and fun, which was hard to keep, growing up as we did.'

Peyton feels a flutter of fear. Her mother has a story. One that forged the woman she knows. Maybe now she'll get some answers.

'I don't know any of it. She's pretty much a stranger to me.' As the words fill the small space around them, Peyton realizes that she's speaking the truth. Her mother is a stranger to her. She might know how she takes her coffee, and that she doesn't drink sweet tea – and who could blame her, if this was sweet tea – but she doesn't know anything real about her.

'I'll tell you what I can, but I'm afraid some stories are Eualla's alone to tell.'

'I'll take whatever you can share.'

Minnie finishes her tea. Peyton's is still full.

'I guess things started getting really bad when our mama left. I don't remember it exactly, but it hit Eualla hard. Daddy was a drunk. I dunno if Mama left because he drank, or if he started drinking after, but our whole lives revolved around it.'

Peyton feels dizzy, hearing this. Learning this.

'It changed Eualla something fierce. All she did was study, all the time planning her escape, I see now. But it also made her hard as nails. I saw the change, but even after all this time, I'm still putting the pieces together.' She pauses. 'I can only do it a little at a spell or else I get so sad, I can't get out of bed.'

The only sound is the hum of the old refrigerator. She knows Minnie is quietly reliving the past.

'She took care of me. No one else was going to. Daddy was harmless. Weak, I guess you could say. But not mean. That was our brother, Jimmy, and boy did Eualla hate him.'

She pauses and Peyton knows not to push. Physically, Minnie is right beside her, but mentally, she's in her own world and Peyton knows it's not her place to enter, at least not yet.

Minnie looks up, as though surprised to find Peyton sitting there.

'D'ya have a car? There's no taxis here.'

'I do.'

'I'll show you where we all grew up,' she says, already rising from her seat. 'I have to tinkle first.'

Peyton rises, embarrassed for some reason by what her aunt has said. Tinkle is a child's word and feels odd coming from the mouth of a woman her age.

Her aunt reappears, the faint sound of the toilet flush following her, the apartment is so small. Peyton looks away.

'Let me grab my pocketbook,' she says.

Peyton waits at the bottom of the stairs for her aunt, then she opens the door and steps outside, her aunt a few steps behind. Peyton opens the car door for her, waits until she's seated and closes it. Waits for instructions, feeling antsy. She wasn't expecting to feel so discombobulated by meeting this woman.

'Turn left and go straight until I tell you,' Minnie says.

They've only driven a few hundred yards, when her aunt says, 'You could have written a letter.'

'I thought about it, but then I thought, if you wrote back, it would be the one day my mother got the mail before me, or Mary,' Peyton says, but it's not quite the truth.

You can take your time with a letter, only reveal what you want. Face-to-face, you learn so much more. People can only hide so much.

'Mary still working for y'all?

'She is. Have you met her?'

'When I met you, you was... were... five?'

Peyton can't think of anything to say, trying to remember having met this woman. Does she even remember being five?

'Eualla always said she'd have a housekeeper. Swore she'd never hang clothes on a line or wash another dish once she had enough money to hire a housekeeper. God knows she did enough of that as a child.'

'Well, I've never seen my mother do either of those things, so I guess her wish was granted.'

The asphalt turns to a mix of dirt and stone, and Peyton is worried about the rental car being damaged, the paint being chipped. She slows down.

'You'll want to turn soon... Take a right just there.'

Her aunt points and Peyton puts on her blinkers, even though there's no one around to see them. She turns. The new road even worse.

A building appears – a small barn, Peyton guesses. She figures they must be getting close to her mother's home.

'Here we are,' Minnie says.

A shed? It's too small for a barn.

'My childhood home,' Minnie says, something cold and hostile poking into the last word.

The place looks abandoned. It has the feel of one of those farmhouses lost in the Depression, the soil blowing into the wind and the wood drying and splintering under the relentless sun. Sometimes you can tell when a house has borne witness to unhappiness. The building remembers and loses its soul. Peyton can see that in the faded clapboard in front of them. What she can't see is her polished, educated, sophisticated mother living here.

'Pull into the drive.'

Peyton looks at the dirt path she guesses her aunt means and pulls in. She feels the bump of the uneven dry clay, pitted with old stones under the pristine tires of the rental car. She lets the car roll to a stop, then puts it in park. She waits for her aunt to make the first move. She seems to be hesitating. To Peyton, it looks like she's building up strength.

'Can we go inside?' she asks.

'Yes. I don't know why you want to, but yes.'

They get out of the car, doors closing with soft bangs seconds apart. Peyton thinks she hears an echo, but the earth is too flat. Even an echo wouldn't want to return to this space.

Her aunt stares ahead, not so much at the house as through the house.

'We don't have to do this if you don't want to,' Peyton says. Now that she knows where it is, she can come back on her own.

'I pray each day to forgive, but I hate this place.' Minnie starts walking.

Peyton looks at the way her aunt has crossed her arms across her chest, like she's trying to hold herself together, shield herself from pain. She hadn't thought about how her pilgrimage might affect others.

They step into a porch that looks like a makeshift shelter someone would put up if they got lost in the forest overnight. Dirt coats everything and dust hangs in the air. Peyton wishes she had a mask.

'Brace yourself,' Minnie says, pushing open the door. Peyton steps inside first, and Minnie follows. There's no entry, they're right in the kitchen already. The floor is linoleum and she thinks it may have once been a deep green. An old Formica table, so old it might actually be a vintage find, is pushed against one wall. She walks wordlessly past the unplugged refrigerator and the old stove, into the main room.

The house looks like a blast of bad breath would chew through whatever is holding it upright.

'Watch out for mice. Snakes, too.'

Peyton turns and stares at her. 'Are you serious?'

Her aunt laughs. 'City girl.'

Peyton hesitates, one foot in the air, ready to take a step but doing nothing.

'I'll go first. Scaredy cat,' she says as she passes Peyton.

For a second, Peyton sees what she'd have looked like as a girl growing up with her mother. A woman from whom Peyton is certain snakes would have fled.

'It's all clear,' her aunt reports.

Peyton can hear the amusement in her words and it makes her smile as she follows her aunt through a small front room, past what must be the front door, past a closed door, and down a narrow hall to the back of the house.

'Bathroom to your left.'

Peyton peeks inside at the small room, with a claw-foot bathtub that might be worth something if it wasn't so shabby, a sink with exposed pipes underneath that look like they may disintegrate at the first touch of water. An old toilet under a window looking out over a back field.

Across is a bedroom with a bed. Peyton can see what she hopes are water stains on the mattress and there's an old dresser against the facing wall.

The room gives her the creeps and she's backing out, when her aunt says, 'Mama and Daddy's room. I don't go in.'

And then another room, just off the front room, at the start of the hall. They've already walked past it.

'This was mine and Eualla's room,' she says, moving her arm toward the doorway like a model on a game show, but not looking in.

Peyton steps into a room with filthy windows. There are two beds, a nightstand that's battered but looks solid. An empty bookcase. She crosses to the window and sees it looks out over an empty field – brown, now, but she's sure there will be grass and flowers soon.

Peyton studies the walls, the paint now faded and peeling. She sees an outline where something once hung, a small painting maybe. She'd like to know what it was. She remembers when all her friends had bedroom walls covered with pictures of celebrities. Boy bands, mostly. The one time she asked for a teen magazine, her mother had refused to buy it.

'Don't be so foolish,' she'd dismissed.

Later, her father bought it and told her to keep it a secret. She's old enough now to know she didn't even want it – she just wanted to take it to school so her friends saw it. It was before she was popular because of her house and her pool. Because of their money.

All these years later, standing in her mother's childhood home, it's strange – both what's happening and her thoughts.

She walks into the room, tries to picture her mother, young, poor, angry, growing up in this house. She sees that one of the walls has been repainted, faded now but was once purple. She moves toward it. Her mother hates the color purple. Perhaps this is why.

She looks around the room, walks purposefully, like a loose floorboard might be hiding a time capsule that'll fill in the blanks. Isn't this what she's trying to do? With this trip, with Daisy? Fill in the blanks so she can understand why her life has hit this patch?

Something forced her home. Something made her go to Tennessee. There has to be a reason.

She waits, but the room has no secrets to share. It feels like it, too, is exhausted by its past.

The sun is going down and it's starting to cool, like a late October evening back home. She leaves the room, heads back toward the kitchen, past a small black wood stove. At least they were never cold, she thinks. Although she can't imagine this shack ever being warm.

*

It's been a long day for Peyton but she's not tired – she's buzzing from all she's learned. As she drops her aunt off at her home, she says, 'Can I pick you up in the morning, take you for breakfast?'

'That'd be real nice,' Minnie says.

Peyton gets out the car and helps Minnie with the door. Funny, she's a lot younger than her mother, but she comes across as older. She's frail.

'How is eight?' Peyton says.

'I'm sure it's lovely, but nine would be better.'

Peyton laughs. 'Fair enough.'

She waits until her aunt is in the house and she sees the kitchen light come on before she gets back in the car, heads back to the highway. When she gets to her hotel room, she checks her phone. John has texted her twice to make sure she's OK. She texts she's fine.

How's Tennessee?

So far, I really like it. The way people speak to you, use terms of endearments. I've been called hun about ten times today.

So, are you getting answers to your questions?

I am, but they seem to lead to more questions.

True. Be safe and check in tomorrow, OK?

Will do. Sleep well.

You too.

It's a nice way to end the day.
She turns on the light, takes out a pen and her notebook, and starts to write.

Peyton arrives at her aunt's home at 9:02, according to her phone. She has two coffees with her and her stomach is rumbling. She wants to have breakfast – a big greasy breakfast. All the subterfuge is making her hungry, she guesses.

'Good morning,' Minnie appears on the step, locking the door behind her. She moves past Peyton, heading to the car.

'I brought coffee,' Peyton says. It's from the lobby of the hotel where she is staying. In Styrofoam cups. She hasn't seen small Styrofoam cups in a long time. Minnie seems anxious to get on the road. Peyton looks around and can see why. Her aunt spends her days in this cramped little space. No view. Nothing to do with her time.

'Don't drink it,' she says. 'But thank you.'

Peyton looks around. The coffee is lukewarm now anyway. She drinks hers, then pours out the one she brought for her aunt. Stacking the empty cups together, she sets them in the space at the bottom of the driver's door.

Peyton gets back in the car, thinking her aunt is more excited about being mobile, getting out, than seeing her niece. But then, this trip isn't about her. It's about her mother, Minnie's sister.

'I ate there yesterday. Food was good,' Peyton says, indicating the diner. It was where she was planning to go for breakfast.

'I hate the place,' Minnie doesn't say the words so much as spit them.

'Oh. It seemed... nice... to me.' Peyton flails.

'Horrible place. Horrible.'

Peyton is silent, waiting for a story she knows is coming.

'You remember yesterday, I told you your mama used to be real spirited, fun?'

'I do.'

'Well, before mama left she had a best friend. Debbie. She and Eu were thick as thieves. Best friends. You know, the kind you make at that age.'

Peyton nods as she continues to aimlessly drive.

'Did everything together. We were poor, but kids don't notice that much. Then, Mama leaves. Miss Debbie's family got some money. Her daddy won the contract to build the new wing of the hospital. Next thing you know, they're living in a nicer house. Materials, building stuff, whatever you call it, goes missing, and bam, they have a new truck. Everyone knew he was stealing from his own worksite, but no one said a thing. Folks don't do that in these parts. They should, but they don't.

'Then Miss Debbie is suddenly too good for Eualla. Won't speak to her. Cuts her dead at school. Eualla cried like nothing I've ever heard before or since. And I've done my share of crying, too. That's when she started reading. Lots.'

'I'm not sure how this is connected to the diner?'

'Your mama worked there to buy food for us. Debbie and her friends would come in, treat her real mean. I worked there later, but my classmates were a nicer bunch than Eualla's year. People remark on that, still. Some days I feel Eu got it bad across the board. Lousy family, lousy friends.'

Peyton feels sick at this.

'Debbie is the big cheese at school. Goes to the University of North Carolina at Chapel Hill. Marries herself an accountant, lives in one of them big places. Fancy.

'Next thing you know, she's got three little kids. Her daddy is busted for theft. Her husband loses their money and runs off with a new wife. Debbie has nothing. Moves home with her mama, takes a job at the diner. Waiting on the people she looked down on. Divine justice, I call it. But the day I give up my job there was the last time I set foot in the place. Although I do miss the peach pie.'

Peyton hears something wistful in her voice. And she's sure it's not about the pie.

'There was a large woman, purple eye shadow, horrible lipstick. Was that Debbie?'

'Bosom like a couple of loaves of bread strapped to her chest?'

Peyton tries not to laugh at her aunt's odd description. 'She waited on me. I tipped her well.'

'Go back and get it.'

'If I could, I would.'

'I have two questions for you.'

'Shoot.'

'One, how did my mother get from here,' she nods her head at the vast nothingness around them, 'to where she is now. And two, where do you want to go for breakfast?'

'She won scholarships and went to university, after Mama came back.'

'She came back?'

'Uh huh.'

'OK.'

Peyton is about to ask where she went when Minnie says: 'And I want to go to Pigeon Forge. It's a fair piece by car. Is that OK?'

'Pigeon Forge? For breakfast?'

'There's a lot to do in Pigeon Forge.'

'Do you know how to get there?'

'I do.'

'Then let's go.'

The sun is moving up in the sky, but there's a hazy quality, a milkiness to the light it shines. Like the sun is covered in a veil. Peyton presses the accelerator and waits. She knows this kind of day and knows the sun will burn through the barrier soon enough.

Asking questions, Peyton is learning, has a lot do with timing. With reading a room and reading a subject. Marco always said she wasn't very good with people.

She gives her head a shake. She doesn't want him popping into her thoughts anymore. She's starting to wonder what she saw in him. And she's learning something else.

Sometimes people will bully you, if they think they can get away with it.

She let him get away with it.

Sitting at a restaurant in Pigeon Forge Tennessee, she is suddenly grateful for her mother, for her parents. Because when her life fell apart, they told her she could come home. Not everyone has that.

'So, mom went to university in North Carolina. I knew that. Got a science degree.'

Minnie has ordered a breakfast that could feed everyone in the Fort. The fluffy biscuit alone would be enough to fill her tiny aunt, but she's shoveling in eggs, grits, bacon.

'You girls now, you can do anything. But Eualla going to university? Studying science? Well, that was unheard of then.'

'So my mom was a trailblazer.' Peyton feels a tingle of pride at this.

'In many ways, honey. In many ways. That was when she changed her name for the first time. Ellie, she christened herself.'

Peyton sets her fork down. 'Ellie? I can't see my mom as an Ellie.'

'I think her college roommate gave her that name.'

'Who was that?'

Minnie chews, swallows. Stops. 'You know I said I'd tell you what I could?'

Peyton nods.

'Well, I can't speak much to that time. And even if I could, I wouldn't.'

Peyton feels curiosity spark and crackle and ignite inside her.

'Not even if I said please?'

'Move along, Peyton. I've said my piece.'

Now, she really wants to know.

Minnie resumes eating.

'After North Carolina, she moved to Houston for medical school. Then to Boston for residency. And that's when Scott was born. You think she was a trailblazer for getting a science degree? Single working mothers were almost unheard of then. And no, I ain't telling you, aren't telling you, who Scott's father is. That's a secret I cannot share.'

Peyton wonders how she can get her aunt to tell her the bits she really wants to hear. Alcohol is the best bet. She'll order wine with lunch. It's not ethical, but sometimes you have to cut corners. For the greater good. At least, that's what she tells herself.

After breakfast they go for a walk through the mall.

'Can I ask you something about you?' Peyton begins.

'Sure.'

'The Christmas card you sent my mother. Did you paint it?'

'I did.'

'It's gorgeous.'

'Thank you.' Minnie pauses. 'She still has it?'

'I found it in the sideboard.'

'I figured she threw it out. It's been a lot of years. I try, but Eualla, Lydia, whatever you call her, ain't much for forgiveness.'

'She kept it,' Peyton says, although she's sure her mother shoved it out of sight and planned to throw it away but forgot. 'The card, it's why I'm here. I couldn't ask my mother, and dad didn't have much to say, then he got sick.'

Minnie stops walking. 'Octavian is sick?'

'He had a heart attack.'

'Is he OK?'

Now, it's time for Peyton to share family stories.

It's been a long day, and much has been said. They're in the car, driving back to Bolt's Ferry. Peyton thinks how it is also a stupid name for a town. There's no waterway or place for any sort of boat she can see. She could ask Minnie, but Peyton's not that interested. Besides, she has no plans to ever see the place again.

'So, did you learn all you needed to learn?'

Not even close, Peyton thinks, but says, 'It's good to know a bit more about mom. I think I understand her a bit better, now.

They're moving along the highway, the shadows from the trees that line the road crisscrossing the pavements, the golden light appearing and disappearing in the trees. The air feels like you could pour it into a jar, like honey. Peyton sees a sign for a Cracker Barrel. She hasn't been to one in years but remembers the pies. Remembers what her aunt said about missing the peach pie at the diner. She bets Cracker Barrels are even better.

'Are you tired?'

'No, why do you ask?'

'Want to stop for pie at Cracker Barrel?'

'Oooh. I like Cracker Barrel!'

Peyton is very happy that she remembered the pie. Despite what she's learned, what she now knows about her mother, it is her aunt's excitement at that moment that makes the trip worthwhile.

Peyton parks the car, grabs her bag. As she walks into the restaurant, she puts her arm, briefly, around her aunt's shoulders. Despite the lumberjack breakfast she ate, and the pound of fried chicken she had for lunch, all Peyton feels is the sharpness of her bones. It can't be healthy to be that thin.

Her aunt wraps her arm around her, briefly, until they're at the door, and inside. Peyton watches as she heads for the country shop like a kid in a candy store. It's nice, that they're ending the day with a bit of fun.

Minnie picks up a salt and pepper shaker shaped like corn on the cob. The cobs have little faces – a type of kitsch her mother would hate.

'Aren't they cute?' she asks Peyton, setting them back down and moving on.

They cost twelve dollars. She can't believe with all the money her parents have, her aunt can't afford a set of salt and pepper shakers, and anger for them burns in her. She sees they sell full pies, and buys a peach one and a pecan. And the salt and pepper shakers, too.

They're sitting in the car, outside her aunt's home. There's some golden light in the sky, a shimmering force, and she remembers the hazy veil of the morning. Is it the same force, altered by the time of day, the heat of the air, the stories being pushed out again, into the world?'

'Do you have any pictures, photographs, of your family?' Peyton asks.

'We weren't the type for... How do you call it? Kodak moments. Never had a camera.'

Peyton figured as much but had to ask.

'So, my mother never forgave you, Debbie or her own parents. But you said she hated Jimmy the most?'

The night before, while writing down the things her aunt had said, a thought came to her. A bad thought, one that led to an even worse feeling. But she can't bring herself to ask it. If Jimmy had done that to her mother, Peyton would find him and kill him. But then, if her father had known, he would have a long time ago.

'Yeah, I done made a mess there. Jimmy showed up one day, looking sadder than ever. Was real contrite and sorry. Wanted to make amends. Wanted to know where she was living. I thought maybe it'd be good for him and for her. Mama and Daddy were kids themselves when they were born. He didn't have no room, slept on the sofa. He had it tough, too. But he showed up and I don't know what happened, but she never forgave me. I shoulda known he was full of shit.'

Peyton has to physically keep herself from bursting out laughing at what Minnie says. She pulls in a deep breath.

'Showed up where?'

'You know, that big mansion you call home in Maine.'

It feels like all the air has left the car.

'When was that?'

'Over twenty years ago now. I can't remember.'

Peyton's heart starts to race.

'Please try. It's important.'

'I don't like to think about it.'

'Please.'

'Summer, maybe, no, over twenty years ago. You were small. I remember. I had just visited, felt Eu needed to ... forgive. Show some love. I should have known, with her and Jimmy. What makes us who we are, meanness, cruelty, or kindness, don't change. Doesn't change.

Peyton's mind starts to spin. If she was standing, she thinks she might have whirled like a top as it all fell together. Was he there when Daisy disappeared – this horrible man who beat his sister? What else did he do?

She'll have to ask some hard questions when she's a journalist, so she pushes forward.

'How abusive was Jimmy with my mother?'

'I know where you're headed. And no, it was never like that, far as I know.'

Peyton feels herself nod. Thank God. One less thing to worry about.

'What does Jimmy look like?' she asks.

'Last time I seen him, like a human scarecrow, with bad skin.'

It's not the strongest description. But it's perfect.

Peyton is silent, absorbing all that's been said. Willing the connections, what she needs to know, to appear.

'Pretty sky tonight,' her aunt says, raising her arm and moving it, mimicking the swooping patterns of the light.

'Do you still paint?'

'Not as much as I used to. Paint is expensive. It's hard to get to the supply store.'

'You could order what you need on Amazon.'

'I've never figured out how to use my computer. Trent

picks stuff up for me when he can. He's been so good to me.'

'Trent?'

'The pharmacist. Owns where I live.'

'Oh.'

'He went to school with Eualla. Never married. Charges me peanuts in rent.'

'That's nice of him.' It's all Peyton can think to say.

'Not really. He was mean to Eu, too. His way of making up for it, since she never forgave him, either.'

'I'm sensing a theme here,' Peyton laughs. A nervous laugh, the kind used to make a truth more palatable, less frightening.

'You be careful, Peyton, lest you be next.'

Peyton doesn't bother to tell her that in many ways, her mother never forgave her for simply being born.

Peyton's mind is spinning, conjuring scenarios of what happened with Jimmy all those years ago. Minnie is occupied with her own memories, silently attacking her. Peyton can almost feel them. Peyton gets out of the car, carrying the salt and pepper shakers, the pies, in a bag. She feels heavy with all she's learned and not learned twisting around her.

At the steps, Minnie turns and faces her.

'Look, can you come in for a second? I have something I want to give you.'

'Of course.'

Peyton follows her aunt inside, setting the bag on the table as her aunt turns down the little corridor that she figures must lead to the rest of her apartment. She takes the pie out the bag and starts to open the refrigerator door.

Sees a postcard, attached with a magnet shaped like a pear. There's a photo of a bridge, lit up at night. She knows she shouldn't, but she picks it up and flips it over. She knows the handwriting, the clean, crisp lines. From birthday cards she got when she was young.

Scott.

She looks in the corners for a date, but there's nothing. Still, the card is new.

She scans it quickly:

Auntie Min,

Was walking to work today and thought of you. Wish you'd set up the computer and get on email – you're the only person I know who isn't connected. I'm better at typing than writing – as you can see.

Everything is fine here – I'm busy, as usual. Be good to have you come visit. The girls would love to see you.

Let me know if you need anything.

Love,

Scott

Peyton reads the card twice, dumbfounded.

She hears drawers opening and closing, and then silence. She scrambles to put the postcard back on the door. Her aunt reappears, carrying a small painting.

'Here. For you.'

Peyton takes it. It's a small girl, with blonde hair, wearing a red bathing suit, building a sandcastle. She bends closer to the painting, lifts it closer to her face.

'I know that sandbox. That's our yard at home.'

Minnie laughs. 'That's you. I painted it from memory, a long time ago.'

Peyton looks closer, unsure she sees herself in the little girl, unsure what's happening. She's not even sure who she is. But she is sure of one thing.

'I love it. I absolutely love it.'

Holding it under one arm, she reaches out and pulls her aunt into a hug. And her aunt hugs her back.

'I'm so glad you came to see me, Peyton. I miss Eualla, but she's made up her mind. Having you here has helped.'

She wants to ask about Scott, about the postcard on the refrigerator, but there's a certain poignancy in the air, a feeling of things being wrapped up. It's time for her to leave. Peyton gives her aunt another gentle squeeze. Minnie pats her back and they stand like that for a few seconds. A 'nice to meet you' and a 'I'm not sure I'll see you again' all wrapped up in one small embrace.

She lets go and walks to the door.

'Drive safe,' Minnie says.

'I will. Thanks again.' She lifts the painting.

She's driving past the diner, her mind full of all she's learned, when she thinks about her mother, growing up in that dump, being ostracized at school. An idea comes to her, and she pulls a U-turn, right in the middle of the main road. No one's around, so it doesn't matter.

She stops the car in front of the diner, gets out. The sounds of the door closing makes the locals inside look. She pushed it with more force than necessary.

She walks inside, stops. Sees Debbie, picking up a pot of coffee. She walks over to her, and loud enough for everyone to hear, she says, 'I'm Eualla's girl. And I just want you to know, we live in a mansion overlooking the ocean. Have a second home in Florida. And one of my mother's handbags is worth more than you'll make working here in a year.'

40

Lydia

July, Maine, 1997

It's hot, with summer vacationers clogging the streets. The town is preparing for its annual July 4th bash. Lydia isn't much for crowds and parties but finds herself looking forward to the festivities this year.

It's Mary's day off and she decides to bake. She rummages until she finds flour, sugar, the things she needs to make cupcakes. She'll take Peyton to the store and let her buy candy to decorate them. An early start to the celebrations. Some time with her youngest.

She's mixing the batter, when she hears something, a pounding of some kind. She stops, a funny feeling in her chest. The knock comes again. She knows the pounding. She's heard it before.

'Don't be stupid, Lydia. Don't be stupid. You can't recognize a knock.'

Still, she hesitates. Octavian is at the hospital. Scott is at work. Caroline is out with friends. Peyton is at day camp. It's horse-riding week and Lydia tries not to think about that. All these years later, seeing horses in fields, as beautiful as they are, takes her back to that Easter weekend. Now, she's alone in her own sprawling mansion, but she's never ever alone. No one with bad memories ever is. And a knock at the door has her shaking.

She opens the door. There, standing on the porch, is her worst dream come true. She may not have seen him in years, and he looks half dead, but she'd know the beady eyes and godawful teeth anywhere.

'Hey there, Eualla. Long time no see.'

He looks so old, decrepit, falling apart. He doesn't have lines on his face so much as long gouges.

'Jimmy. What are you doing here?'

'Nice place yeh have here, for sure.' He looks over her shoulder.

His drawl has a bit of Tennessee in it, but mostly it's the voice of someone whose brain is slogged in alcohol and drugs. She will not let him in her house.

'What do you want, Jimmy?'

'Hey now, can't I visit my sister?'

'People who plan to visit call ahead. Suitable times are found. Plans are made.' She pauses. 'And generally, they enjoy each other's company, they want to spend time together.'

'Well now shoot, Eualla! I wanna spend time wi' you. Always have. You, girl, make a great sandwich.'

Lydia feels herself go hot and cold. Her hands turn to fists. If she had a gun, she'd shoot him now, she's certain.

'My husband will be home soon. What do you want?'

'My brudder-in-law? I'd love to meet 'im.'

'Not going to happen,' she says, forcing herself to be calm. But Caroline could come home any minute, or Scott.

'You could gimme a tour.'

He looks at the house. The shed the gardener uses is nicer than the home they grew up in. For the first time since she moved into her husband's family home, she wishes it wasn't so palatial.

'How did you find me?'

'Minnie.'

She shakes her head. 'How did you reach Minnie?'

'Saw her at the diner back home.'

'And she told you where I was?'

'You know that big heart o' hers. Told her I was sick, wanted to make peace. She tol' me your husband's name. Not too many Octavian Winchesters in this world.'

He pronounces it Win-hester. She's surprised he found her. She didn't think Jimmy could write, or that he'd be smart enough to find her if she drew him a map.

'*Are* you sick?'

'Healthy as a horse.'

'So you lied to your sister. Well done.'

'Anything to find my favorite sis.'

'The feeling isn't mutual. Now, I'd appreciate it if you left.'

He grabs her arm, hard. Pain grips her. She thinks it may break, but she refuses to react.

'Let go of me.' She stares right at him, praying her family stays away until she can figure out what to do.

He drops her arm. 'I told ya. It's been a long trip an' I'm hungry.'

'I'll give you money to buy a meal and a plane ticket.'

'You can't make me summat?'

She could kill him so easily and not lose a moment's rest.

He loosens his grip and she pushes him backward. He stumbles. She locks the door on him, leans against it as he starts to pound on it. He won't go away, not now he's seen her. She has to get him out of here. He can't see her kids. Even in her panic, her fear, she's angry with Minnie for what she's brought into her life.

She sees Octavian's spare keys to his rental properties and gets an idea. She grabs them and her purse. Pulling in a shaky breath, she opens the door. He's sitting on the step, waiting for her.

'Get up,' she says.

'Ask me nicely.'

'Get up. I have a place where you can stay. If you move now.'

He stands and she sees his filthy jeans. Her stomach rolls. Please, God, don't let anyone see me driving with him, she thinks.

'Nice vehicle,' he says, getting into the passenger side of her Cadillac.

Her hands don't feel like her own as she grips the wheel, backs the car out.

They're on the road that leads into town when she demands, 'What do you want, exactly?'

'To be friends,' he laughs.

She wants to throw up.

'I don't. I don't want you here. I don't want you anywhere near me.'

She scans the road as she drives, heading toward that old

house on Cabot Lane. She hasn't been there in years. She scours the sidewalks, the other cars as she drives, hoping desperately she doesn't see anyone familiar.

'I can take you to the airport, buy you a ticket anywhere you want to go,' she says.

The airport is in the opposite direction and she looks for a place to turn the car around, even though she knows he won't leave. She doesn't know what he wants but doubts it's a trip to Hawaii. Or down memory lane.

'I wants to stay here with you.' He reaches out his hand like he's going to hold her arm or press it against her leg.

She slaps it away.

Cabot Lane is quiet, the trees creating a canopy protecting them from the sun. At first it looks empty, then she sees a man in front of a home on the left-hand side of the road. She's not sure who he is, but he might know her. She turns her head, but it's the car that stands out. She's the only person in Fort Meadow Beach who drives a Cadillac. Dammit.

She turns the corner and sees the ugly old house. She wanted Octavian to develop it or sell it, but he likes to moon over the architecture, doesn't want to alter it. She gets out the car, tells Jimmy to follow. Her voice is an urgent whisper, like she's trying to sneak a boy into her bedroom, not hide the person she loathes most in this world.

She watches him, standing in the drive, staring at the old house.

'What are you waiting for?'

'Ya expect me to follow you into this dump?'

'It's nice inside. Now move.'

She puts the key in the lock and pushes open the back

door, prepared for damp and coldness, despite the hot day. It felt haunted the last time she visited with Octavian, but now, it's still empty but not as hollow. She moves forward. The fireplace has been used. That scares her. The chimney isn't in good shape. There's a smell of something. Something heavy. Fast food. Cheese? Pizza? Does that make sense?

She hears Jimmy behind her. One problem at a time. One nightmare at a time.

'In here.' She will not show weakness now.

'You plannin' on hittin' me with a shovel and burying me in the cellar?'

'Don't give me ideas.' She turns to face him. 'Now, what do you want?'

'I done tol' you.'

'Oh, shut up. I detest you and I'm sure you feel the same about me.'

There are two lawn chairs set up in the middle of the room. Someone has definitely been here. But who? Squatters aren't likely in the Fort.

'Sit. Tell me what you want. Honestly, if you can.'

'Mama's gone. It's just Daddy an' me. I can't work no more. You got lots.'

'So you've come to practice a little extortion, have you?'

'Say again?'

'Like I said, what do you want?'

'A house, ten thousand a year to live on.'

'Or?'

'Why you gotta be like this? We kin.'

'Then no, I'm not giving you a thing. Now, get out of my life and don't come back.'

'Help us or I say a big fat hello to my bruvver-in-law.'

'He knows who and what you are. I told him before we got married. So try again.'

'Bet he doesn't know you tried to kill me.'

'When did I do that?'

'Time you done hit me with the skillet. Night you closed the door on me, left me outside.'

'If he met you, he'd understand.'

They stare at each other for a second, seeing who blinks first.

'Five thousand, once, and I never see you again.'

'Aw, I'm hurt.'

His voice is mocking, but she sees a flash of something. He is hurt. She could be kind – maybe he's changed. They are blood.

But no. He made her life a living hell. She may have left it all behind her physically, but she carries it with her every single day. It's as real as the floor under her feet.

'Five grand?' He rubs his chin, mocking her. 'You probably got more 'n that in your pocketbook.'

'Five grand, and I never see you again.'

She has money in the house, and her office. She can get him on a bus out of Maine tonight. Whatever happens, it has to be quick. She looks at her watch as the room darkens, the sun disappearing behind a cloud. She has to pick up Peyton from the bus stop. Already, she's late.

'I have to go. You stay right here. I'll be back later, with cash.'

He sets down the old khaki backpack he's been carrying. She can tell he's worn out.

'Stay here,' she repeats.

'I got no place to go.'

'And who's fault is that?'

She turns and walks to the door, driving past the same man, still outside, tending what looks like a perfect lawn. He waves and she waves back. Then she floors it – she's late.

Her daughter is sitting on the sidewalk by herself and Lydia can tell she's crying. It's her fault, she should have been here, but really! She's fifteen minutes late. Peyton lifts her head when she sees the car and stands, picking up her backpack.

She parks in the small lot and gets out the car. Peyton walks toward her, dragging her bag. Her face is blotchy from crying. Lydia wants to cry herself.

'For heaven's sake, Peyton! You must have known I was coming. I could hardly have forgotten you. Now get in the car.'

Lydia is shocked by her own behavior. How hard would it have been to pick her up and hold her, tell her she was sorry? But she doesn't have time for this now and Peyton must toughen up. She opens the car door for Peyton, lets her sit up front. She's so small, she needs a booster seat.

She clicks the seat belt in place for her. Peyton still hasn't spoken. Lydia looks and sees how close she was to the road, to the traffic.

'Why didn't you sit over there, on the bench? It's safer.'

'The bench has bird poo on it. And the trees are scary.'

Lydia reminds herself that Peyton's small for her age. She and Octavian have discussed it, unsure as to why she's so fragile in stature, if they should run some medical test. But

Lydia knows – she gets it from her side of the family. From Minnie.

'OK. Let's go to the store. We'll get some treats.'

She thinks about how she'd been planning to make cupcakes. How quickly her plan, and her life, has changed.

'I have an errand to run,' Lydia says. 'You have to watch your sister tonight.'

'I have plans. Scott can do it.' Caroline says.

'You're both staying in and watching her.'

'What?' Scott looks up from the refrigerator, where he's foraging for his tenth meal of the day.

Every time she sees her son, she's grateful he's tall like her, like Octavian. She knows he looks something like his father, but she can't remember exactly what Dan looked like now. She's grateful for this.

'Why both of us?' Caroline says.

'Because I said so.'

'I have plans!'

Lydia can tell by looking at her daughter that she's getting ready to have one of her patented tantrums and she has no time for it. She walks over to her and looks straight into her eyes.

'Challenge me on this and you won't leave the house for the rest of the summer. And you'll pay your own goddamn tuition, too.'

Scott is standing with a plate of cold chicken in his hand, too stunned to set it on the counter. The only noise comes from Peyton.

Lydia swivels round. 'And why are you crying again?'

Lydia is shocked by her own rage. She hears the plate clatter on the counter. Hears Scott's tread as he crosses the floor, scoops up Peyton and carries her from the room. Hears him saying, 'It's OK, kiddo. Mom's in a mood.'

Somewhere in the forest fire that is her anger, the ocean of her fear, she's proud of her son.

'Don't leave the house. And don't let her out of your sight.'

Lydia turns, walks back to her car. Pulls out into the street. She can hear the rattle of bottles of beer, the six-pack she bought Jimmy, in an effort to keep him from trying to find a bar. The pre-made deli sandwiches, the cold fried chicken. Garbage food she'd never feed her own children. Even the clerk commented on it.

'Having a party?' she asked.

'Unexpected guest,' she replied, then immediately regretted it. She had to get him out of town without anyone knowing.

The same man is still in the yard. Does he ever go inside?

Then she pulls into the drive, walks to the house. Let's herself in. She doesn't see him at first, but then there he is – a pile of rags asleep on the floor, using his backpack as a pillow. Her brother. She watches him for a second, an image of smashing him to bits with a fire poker coming to mind. She prods him with her shoe, hard, until he wakes.

He sits up, somehow both disoriented and ready to fight. Briefly, she's curious about what his life has been like. Just not curious enough.

'Sit up. I brought you something to eat.'

She sets the bag of food on the floor beside him. Doesn't make eye contact, like she's feeding an animal. Lydia watches as he struggles to open the clear plastic container. His hand–eye co-ordination is ruined by years of drink and drug usage. He's pathetic.

She lowers herself enough to open the container, avoiding touching his hands, and stands as he falls upon the food, ravenous. She turns her head to look away, disgusted. He shoves the food in furiously then stops, abruptly. He's eaten a quarter of it. He's full.

'I can give you five thousand if you promise never to come back here again.'

He looks up at her, his eyes vacant. There's sleep crusted in the corners. She notices body odour mixed with the smell of the chicken and the damp of the house. She sways with revulsion.

She was going to call his bluff. She doesn't have the energy for that now. It's simpler to give him money. Enough to stay away, enough not to get in touch again.

'Five thousand dollars, if I don't see you ever again. That's more money than you've ever had. And if you contact me again, I'll have you charged for the all the times you shoved me around growing up.'

He looks up at her from the floor and she sees his thin, drug-addled body. She closes her eyes against the feeling of relief his death would bring. An absence of compassion is a sign of psychopathy. Lydia knows she's not a psychopath. She's just hardened by all that life has thrown at her. She also knows she's not because of how much it hurts that Minnie has betrayed her.

'I'll be back tomorrow, with the money. You stay here until then. Do not leave this house. Do not look out the window.'

'I could stay fer a spell. I am your brother,' he says.

And for a second, she softens. But just a second.

'You were my brother when you woke me up, drunk, to cook for you. When you left me and Minnie to go hungry.' She stops. She doesn't have the energy to recount all of it.

'I made mistakes. Addiction's a disease.'

'I'm a doctor. I know.' She moves a foot away from him, as though something might jump on her. 'And sometimes it's just a lifestyle choice.'

He stares at her, the concept too complicated for him to understand, she thinks.

'I'll be back tomorrow. Don't leave this house.'

She can see his reflection in the glass of the doors. Knows he's sitting on the floor, spindly legs stuck out in front of him. Still she feels uneasy, like he might rush up behind her and attack her. She moves quickly to close the door between them, to lock it.

The heat of the day grabs her, wraps her in its spell. The terror she felt at simply being near her own flesh and blood vies with the promise of the beauty of the day, the sun shining overhead, the sound of the leaves in the soft breeze, gently keeping the day from being too hot. How can anything bad happen on such a perfect day? But she knows it can. Mama left on such a day.

She gets in the car, baking hot inside from sitting in the sun, turns the key, cranks the air conditioner. Octavian always says this does no good, that the engine must cool before the air conditioner kicks in. She starts to drive. She needs to go home. God knows what her children are up to. Caroline at her worst might be hurling dishes on the kitchen floor. Scott could either be sitting quietly drawing with Peyton or have gone out with friends, ignoring her. He's been better since they grounded him for six weeks, better now he's working at the golf club. Octavian had been right about him getting a job. But they don't need the money and she wants her children to have the time to do the things she couldn't.

The house appears. It's still standing. From outside, everything looks fine.

She kills the engine. Sits behind the wheel. 'You can get through this, Eualla,' she says to herself. It takes a second to realize she used her old name.

The house is quiet at first, when she lets herself in. Then she hears splashing. Peyton giggling. She walks toward the kitchen, to the clean, shiny patio doors of her own home that look out on the pool, the sprawling lawn. To the right she can see the Atlantic Ocean. It's everything she's ever wanted.

In the pool her children, all three of them, are playing. Peyton is on Scott's shoulders. He keeps dunking the two of them, making her squeal with delight. Lydia stands and watches, proud of what she's created for her children. They'll never know hunger or fear on her watch.

Caroline looks over to her and says, 'Your secretary called. Said it's important. Some man is trying to reach you.'

Just like that, the veneer of beauty, simplicity, respectability is shattered. But then she stops and thinks. She spoke to Sue Ellen this morning. There's no phone at the Cabot Lane house and no reason for Jimmy to be looking for her now. He's found her.

She relaxes. Probably a former patient.

She goes inside, picks up the phone and calls her secretary.

'I hear someone is trying to reach me?' She tucks the phone under her chin, walks toward the refrigerator. She may have a drink.

'Yes. Just a second... here it is. Texas number.' She rattles it off. 'Name is Dan Davies. Wants to talk to you.'

Lydia is certain she feels all her blood rush to the soles of her feet. Her head feels like a balloon, ready to pop. The glass in her hand slips, but she catches it in time.

'Hello? Lydia? Doctor Winchester?'

Everything, even the shimmery blue of the water in the pool outside the big windows in the kitchen, is hazy. Like a sepia photograph.

'Lydia?'

'I'm here. I'm here. What exactly did he say?'

'That he knew you in Houston and was trying to get in touch with you. Wanted your home number, but I know better than that.'

There's something else she's not saying.

'What else?'

'Is he a friend of yours?'

'No. Not at all.'

'He started off really charming. You know, a good ole boy. Then when I wouldn't give him your number, he turned into a real creep.'

'That's him. If he calls back, under no circumstances give him my number.'

When he knew her, she was Ellie Tompkins. How on earth did he find her? She shakes her head. When you had as much money as Dan Davies, you got what you wanted.

She hangs up. She's hiding her brother across town. On the other side of the country, Scott's father is trying to reach her, after all these years. Could it get any worse? She looks out at the Atlantic Ocean, its cold dark waves drawing her forward, pulling her under. She looks up, as though she can counteract this by reaching for the heavens. There's a small wisp of darkness in the distance, a storm cloud starting to form. And she knows this won't be the Fourth of July party everyone has been planning.

41

Lydia

July, Maine, 1997

'OK, I have your money,' is the first thing Lydia says to Jimmy, who's stretched out on the floor.

'And good mornin' to you, too, darlin'.'

She has breakfast from the local diner in a white paper bag and two cups of coffee. A gym bag she stole from her son packed with bills. Not quite five thousand, but he won't check. She's been awake all night, worried. About Jimmy. About Dan. About what they both really want. She keeps one and sets the other down for him, avoiding brushing hands.

'You own this place, too?'

'My husband's family. Five grand, did you hear me?'

Already he's shaking his head.

'Nope.'

Lydia will pay anything to be rid of him, but she can't show weakness.

'Well now, I think I'll stay put a spell. Seen posters about the July 4th part-ee. Like to see all the fuss.'

'No.'

'I'm a grown man, Eu. I can do whatever I want.'

Her worst fear is now standing in front of her. A sad, pitiful drunken fool with bad teeth and the fly of his pants half undone. She feels sick at the sight of him.

'Six grand if you leave today, or I tell my husband who you are, that I thought you were long dead and you've returned to blackmail me – us.'

'And what do I have to use as blackmail?'

She winces inside. She's overplayed her hand. For the first time, she realizes her brother isn't as stupid as she thought.

'I told him how you treated me and Minnie growing up. He already loathes you.'

'I never done nothin' to Minnie.' His voice is loud, almost a yell. Lydia looks around, afraid the sound will knock down the house. Her heart bangs in her chest. She knows what violence her brother is capable of.

'I want you gone. Now.'

He coughs, a hacking, wet cough that makes her step backward, further away from him.

'Six grand and I stay a few more days. Got no place to go,' he shrugs.

'There won't be any motel rooms left. It's a holiday.'

'Why would I need a motel room? I like this place just fine.'

Lydia looks around. Octavian had had the place inspected, some walls reinforced. His plan had once been to turn it into condos, but he'd decided against it, saying altering the house would be like cutting out its soul. Lydia had stopped paying attention. He'd poured so much money into it and always seemed to be there. To her, it was dark and foreboding. To him, it was an architectural delight.

He turns on a light and Lydia is surprised to see there's electricity.

'Refrigerator works, too.'

She hasn't seen the kitchen since the day Octavian showed her the house. She's never even driven by it since that day. A part of town there's no reason to be in. A building she doesn't like. What would be the point? But looking around now, she sees signs of life. Beer cans that aren't rusted. A bag on the back of a doorknob, being used for trash. A fan in the corner. It looks new.

She turns round, expecting an answer to a question she has no interest in asking. All she wants is Jimmy gone. Permanently.

'I'll be back tomorrow with the rest. Don't you dare leave this house.'

He nods and she can see he's a little more broken than she thought. Maybe this isn't just about money. But she won't buy into that.

She turns on her heel, hoping she looks more confident than she feels. She'll get Jimmy sorted and then she'll figure out what to do about Dan. When the dust settles, she'll get the rest of her family in shape. One problem at a time. First, she has to find enough money to be rid of her brother forever. Tomorrow is the 4th. She'd like to have him gone by then.

They're sitting by the pool, having dinner. Octavian has grilled steaks. He was a blend of happy and surprised when he got home and saw her in a summer dress, cutting vegetables in the kitchen. Peyton is at a sleepover and Lydia is pleased about this. Peyton is an emotionally fragile child and she's trying her hardest to toughen her up. Sleepovers are a good way to teach her how to be on her own, with her own peer group. She's far too attached to Scott and to Caroline, who isn't a good influence.

'Have you been to the house on Cabot Lane lately?' Lydia tries to make it sound casual, even though she hasn't asked about the house in years.

'I drive by fairly often, make sure it's still standing. Why?'

'What's happening with it?' She can't exactly say she's stashing her brother there and, by the way, she thinks people might be hanging out there, too.

'Nothing at the moment. I need to do something. I just need to find the time.'

'Have you been inside?'

'Not recently.' He stops eating. 'Why?'

'I don't know much about houses, but they can't sit empty for long spells, especially in the cold, can they?'

'I turn the heat on regularly in the winter. I was there in April, when we had that snowstorm.'

Lydia takes a sip of wine. She's on her second glass, a rarity.

'Everything OK?' he asks.

'Of course, why wouldn't it be?'

'I dunno. Something feels different.'

'I'm cooking dinner. How often does that happen?'

He laughs and cuts into his steak.

★

The phone rings at midnight and Lydia sits upright, heart beating like it's trying to make its way out of her chest. First, she thinks of Jimmy. Then she thinks of Dan.

Octavian picks up the phone, says a few words. Wipes his face. Says he's on his way.

It must be the hospital. Lydia lies back down, the cool of the pillow comforting her.

'Hospital?' she asks.

'Peyton.'

She rolls over onto her side. 'What's wrong with her?'

'She wants to come home.' He swings his legs over the side of the bed, stands up. Pulls on a pair of pants and a T-shirt.

'Where are you going?'

'To get her. Go back to sleep.'

She sits up, gets out of bed.

'No need for you to get up,' he says.

'Should we make her stay?'

'She's six!'

She nods.

He walks to the bedroom door, lets himself out. Lydia looks around, not sure what to do, then she remembers how close by Jimmy is and it feels like her stomach falls into her pelvic floor. She knows that's not possible, but still, it's how it feels.

She gets up, goes downstairs, waits to see her daughter when she comes home. Now that she's up, she might as well have a good think.

42

Lydia

July, Maine, 1997

He must be leaving today. Has to be. It's July 4th and no one will question a stranger boarding a bus, even one who looks like Jimmy. She just has to get through the day first.

Her office is closed, so even if Dan calls, he won't be able to reach her. She turns on the radio and listens to the forecast, hoping the rain will hold off. Problems seem worse in the rain. There's a malevolence that comes with heavy air and rolling thunder, cloaking mists and hurling downfalls. She doesn't need that today, as well.

Peyton is up and fed, wanting someone to go in the pool with her. Scott obliges and she can hear Peyton giggle as he splashes her. Lydia pours another coffee.

'Can I make you some breakfast, Dr. Winchester?' Mary asks.

Lydia is Dr. Winchester to her, but Octavian is Octavian. Of course, they've known each other for longer. But that's not the reason.

Mary has been hovering and Lydia is certain she can feel her anxiety.

'No, thank you, Mary.' She pauses. 'Why don't you take the day off? Go do something fun. I'm around, and Octavian and I'll be taking Peyton to the beach for the day.'

'I have some laundry in the machine.'

'I'll hang it out. Don't worry about it. Go. Really.'

As she pours more coffee, she can feel Mary glancing at her. It's starting to annoy her now.

Mary goes out to the pool. Says goodbye to Peyton and Scott. The door is closing behind her as Caroline appears, shorts and a T-shirt over her swimsuit, a backpack. Lydia feels an overwhelming urge to check it for beer and cigarettes, but she doesn't. That's a problem that can stay buried; she has enough to deal with right now.

'I want you home by ten o'clock,' she says to her eldest daughter.

'What? Why? Everyone else will be out all night,' Caroline says.

'Ten.'

'Scott can stay out as late as he wants.'

'Scott is older. And he's a boy. And he has to be home by midnight.'

'So what?'

'Less things to worry about.'

'What does that mean?'

'Nothing. Just get home by ten.'

Lydia listens as the door slams. Then she takes her coffee

out to the window and watches her children playing in the pool.

They walk down the steps outside their front lawn, down to the beach. Peyton is running ahead, a tiny figure in pink shorts and shirt, her white-blonde hair glowing in the sun. Lydia scans the area, keeping an eye out for Jimmy, as though she could stop him if he decided to approach. It's not that she's lied to Octavian – he knows she had a difficult childhood. She told him the night he proposed. But she also told him it wasn't open for discussion.

If Jimmy shows up, she fears there will be so many things to discuss. So many things she wants to stay buried. But there's more. It's an embarrassment, having him for a brother.

'Looking for something?' Octavian says.

'Sometimes I can't get over just how beautiful this world is,' she says.

Octavian never misses a trick. Because he was so kind, so affable, such a gentle soul, people tended to dismiss him. But Octavian Winchester was more than book smart. He was street smart, too.

She thinks about telling him. Really thinks about it. It's been so long. And they do love each other. She knows he'll be supportive, kind. But something is holding her back. Shame. Of her past, of her family, of her brother. Octavian's family is so normal, dignified, compared to hers. And how much can she tell? Does she mention Dan? What she did to her friend, Katie – she can't even think about Scott's father without shame. She resents having to relive all of this and she shivers.

'Don't tell me you're cold! I'm roasting over here.' He moves closer, wraps his arm around her. Kisses the top of her head.

It's been a joke between them, almost from the start, how she's always cold. Sitting in air-conditioned restaurants is a form of torture for Lydia.

'I was cold a lot as a little girl.' Her voice catches, starts to break.

Octavian stops moving, looks at her.

'Lydia?'

This is it. She's going to tell him. About Jimmy. About leaving him in the snow to die. Maybe he'll leave her. God knows she's tested herself over the years, wondering if she has psychopathic tendencies, hidden behind her unbridled drive, her perfectly tailored clothing. Maybe he has wondered too. Maybe this will be what pushes him away.

And then Peyton does a cartwheel, lands badly, lets out a wail. Lydia moves toward her, but Octavian is ahead of her, his long legs crossing the sand in three strides. Lydia fears she's broken her wrist.

Peyton sobs as Octavian scoops her up. Lydia doesn't usually approve. Children should stand on their own feet. But tonight, with the sun still high in the sky, the sound of the waves enveloping them, she puts her hand on her daughter's head.

'You OK, sweetheart?'

The look Peyton gives her – surprise, fear, confusion – breaks her heart. She knows even at this young age that her own daughter senses her mother isn't like other mothers.

Octavian checks her wrist.

'Nothing broken,' he says, wiggling it, making her laugh.

Already the tears have stopped. He kisses her nose, sets her down, and she stumbles before getting her footing in the sand and racing ahead of them once again.

More people appear on the beach, carrying coolers, umbrellas, towels and inflatable rafts. They all know Octavian. They know her, too, but it's him they greet. Octavian, who donates to all their causes, paid for the new planters that line the main street, who stops and asks about their children and their grandchildren.

Lydia walks past him, keeping an eye on Peyton, who's scanning the crowd for friends. She's a pretty little girl, but Lydia knows she'll struggle in life. She's too soft-hearted, too much of an empath. She wishes she cared more about herself than others, but there's no way to say that to her.

The whole town is on the beach, it seems. Lydia stops watching her daughter so she can look for the man she wishes had frozen in the snow all that time ago.

They eat lobster rolls and French fries from cardboard boxes sitting on the boardwalk. Octavian goes in the water with Peyton and what looks like the rest of Maine as Lydia watches from her chair. Someone has given her a glass of chilled white wine – she looks down at the ice cubes, already melting. It's too sweet but it helps her relax. She takes another sip.

Peyton and Octavian are walking towards her, Peyton's hair a halo in the light. They're shadows, outlines of bodies seeming to dissolve as she shields her eyes from the sun, watching them.

'Let's start heading back,' Octavian says, toweling off.

'Daddy! I want to see the fireworks!'

'We'll watch them from our house. We'll have the best view of anybody!' he says.

They walk along the beach, back the way they came, the early evening sun lengthening their shadows.

'I'm going to drive to Portland tonight, stay at the apartment. I have to be at work for six.'

'OK,' she says, surprised. 'But you'll wait until the fireworks are over?'

'Of course.'

At home, Lydia runs a bath for Peyton so she can scrub off all the sand and sunscreen. She sets out clean pajamas and rinses her hair.

'Can I have ice cream?'

'If we have any.'

'We do. It's in the freezer.'

Lydia smiles. 'You mean we don't keep it in the cupboard?'

Peyton giggles, a real little girl giggle, and Lydia reminds herself to be silly with her daughter more often.

She opens the freezer and pulls out the ice cream. Takes down a bowl. It's frozen solid, rock-hard, and she can't scoop it. Octavian takes over.

'Enough?' he asks.

'Thank you.' She stands on tiptoe and kisses him.

'What was that for?'

She wants to say because I love you. But those are words she struggles with.

'For scooping ice cream so I don't break a nail.'

He laughs.

Peyton comes racing into the kitchen, her pajama top on inside out. Lydia stops herself from saying anything.

'Can I have sprinkles?'

'Do we have sprinkles?'

She nods so hard, Lydia wonders about her neck.

'In the cupboard by the sink. Mary lets me have them.'

Lydia opens the cabinet, finds the sprinkles. She shakes some on the ice cream and then, feeling silly, shakes some into her wine.

'Want some, Octavian?'

'Why not?'

She shakes some into his drink, too. Then she carries the drinks as Octavian carries a barefoot Peyton down to the edge of the property to wait for the fireworks to start.

Lydia wakes early. She always wakes early, a holdover from university. One look at the clock tells her it's just gone five. She rolls over, surprised for a second not to see Octavian. Buying the condo in Portland seemed like a good idea, but he's been using it more and more and she finds herself missing him in the morning.

She pulls in a deep breath, closes her eyes, tries to relax. But she knows she won't be able to get back to sleep. So she steps out of bed, takes a warm shower, then heads downstairs to the kitchen. Mary's off and even if she was working, it was too early for her to be here. She switches on the radio for some company.

Usually she likes the early morning quiet, but right now, just for a few minutes, she doesn't want to think about Jimmy or Dan. Or how much Minnie has betrayed her. Jimmy is a real threat and Dan is her biggest regret. Minnie's betrayal is new. All she's done for her sister and the only thing she's ever asked is that she never tell Jimmy anything about her life.

Waiting for the coffee to brew, she opens the cupboards. She should know what she has in her own house, she thinks. She picks up the sprinkles. She's never bought them, never put them on a list for Mary. It must be a secret between her and Peyton. She's holding them in her hand, looking at the yellow and blue and pink colors, when the news comes on.

'Police are asking for the public's assistance in the search for a six-year-old girl who went missing last night from Fort Meadow Beach. Daisy Wright was with her family near the old pier when she disappeared.

'The abandoned pier collapsed last night, resulting in a few minor injuries to onlookers and July 4th celebrants. While Daisy and her family were in the vicinity, a search of the water by police has led Chief Langley to say they don't think the two events are connected.

'Daisy is described as being...'

Lydia feels nauseous, like she's eaten something that didn't agree with her. Despite the air conditioner, she feels herself starting to sweat. A little girl has gone missing. Jimmy is in town. She doesn't think he'd hurt a little girl, not like he hurt her. But Jimmy is such a mess, who knows what he is capable of?

★

'Hey, did you hear some kid's gone missing?' Scott comes loping into the kitchen, hair still wet from the shower and wearing the same shorts as the day before.

Peyton is sitting at the kitchen island, an uneaten bowl of cereal in front of her, more interested in her toy unicorn.

'Shit,' Scott says, seeing her.

'Scott said a bad word,' Peyton says.

'Don't be a tattletale.' He ruffles her hair, something she says she hates but always makes her smile. 'And eat your cereal.' He gives her his look, part baleful, part teasing, but with enough severity that she picks up her spoon. 'Good girl.'

'Come outside,' Lydia says to Scott. 'You, eat.'

Lydia takes the radio outside, waiting for the news as she drinks her third cup of coffee. Scott appears and takes a seat.

'Is she eating?'

He ducks his head into the kitchen.

'She is now. What's happening with this missing girl?' he asks.

'They haven't found anything yet. I've been listening since five and there's nothing new.'

It's eleven thirty. The sky is the color of a bad dream. A heaviness hangs in the air, part unshed rain, part shed tears. It's like the Earth, or this part of it, knows.

'There's going to be a storm,' he says. 'A bad one. Do you know the little girl who disappeared? Same age as Peyton – were they friends?'

'They were in day camp together one week. You didn't come home last night.'

'I got home at four. Sorry. I had a few beers and fell asleep.'

He dips his head at the end of his sentence and she knows he's lying. It's his tell.

'Right. We'll talk about it later.'

'They're asking for people to help search the beach. I'm gonna go.'

'Have some breakfast first,' she says.

The phone rings and the sound makes Lydia jump. Scott gives her a funny look and goes inside to answer. She hears Scott speaking to someone he knows and then say, 'Just a sec.' He carries the portable phone and hands it to her. 'It's Sue Ellen, for you.'

'Sue Ellen?' Lydia says. 'Why are you at the office?'

'I left my glasses here. I checked the messages and, I'm sorry to bother you at home, Dr, Winchester, but that man called again.'

'Man?' She tries to sound casual, like she hasn't given him a second thought.

'Dan Davies,' Sue Ellen says.

Lydia hears something new in her voice. Hesitation, fear. Sue Ellen is bold as brass. It was one of the reasons she hired her. She suffered no fools.

'What did he want?'

'He said not to ignore him or you'll regret it.'

Lydia feels like someone has flushed the blood from her body.

'Did you make note of the threat?'

'I did.'

'Is that everything?'

There's a pause. Lydia can picture her straightening the pens and pencils on her desk, the way she does when she's anxious.

'Should you call the police?'

Lydia laughs. 'Over a blowhard Texan I haven't seen in more than a dozen years? No need.'

Another pause.

'Is that it?'

'You told me you had no idea who he was, when he first called.'

Lydia is furious with her mistake. 'I remembered. Anything else?'

'No.'

'Go home, Sue Ellen. Enjoy your day off.'

As she hangs up, Caroline comes wandering down the stairs.

'That was Sue Ellen. I have problems with a patient. You'll have to stay with Peyton today.'

'Again?'

'Caroline, take your sister out for a few hours... In fact, no, don't go out. Stay in. Keep the door locked – just until they find out what happened to Dai... at the beach.'

'Can't Scott stay with her?'

'He's gone out to search for the missing girl.'

It hangs in the air between them. Such a strange sentence to say. Lydia hopes it'll jar her daughter out of her selfishness.

'How long will you be?'

'Caroline, does everything have to be so damn difficult with you? You're fed, clothed, educated, grew up in the lap of luxury. Are you even capable of thinking about anyone but yourself? And who exactly do you think you are to ask me how long I'll be?' The air outside might be heavy with unshed rain, but inside it's crackling with long-held anger finally being voiced. 'Don't push me, Caroline. Not today.'

She looks at Peyton, still eating her cereal.

'Put on your blue shorts and a T-shirt, OK? Caroline will help.'

She kisses her daughter on the top of her head. Then she gets in the car, drives slowly to the bank, takes out more money in case she needs it. One way or another, Jimmy is leaving town today. Once he's gone, she'll deal with Dan. Then, she'll figure out what to do about her family.

The sky is darker, a medley of swirling black and dismal gray, the storm blowing in from the Atlantic overnight. Lydia has been through enough of these storms, in Tennessee and Maine, to know it can build for hours or unleash at any second.

The man who's always on the front lawn is sitting on his step, coffee in hand. Lydia is annoyed when she sees him. Doesn't he ever go inside?

She returns his wave and smiles, then makes the turn. She's certain the sky is darker over the house. She parks, lets herself inside.

At first, she can't see Jimmy. Part of her hopes he's gone for good. She wants it all done today. She thinks about the missing girl and her brother. Forces herself to remember. He never touched Minnie. It was she, Eualla, he woke up, Eualla he smacked. He was nice to Minnie. Standing still, she remembers now. He was nice to small, defenceless Minnie. She never saw the side of Jimmy Eualla did. Maybe that was why she betrayed her.

There's a mess on the floor. The wrappers and coffee

cups she'd brought him. But no sleeping bag. No sign of Jimmy.

She hears something moving upstairs. She makes her way to the stairs, sees the dust has been swept away. On the landing, she sees an open door, makes her way to it.

Inside is a bed, with navy-blue sheets. A nightstand, a chair. The room has been cleaned. Someone has been using it.

'You done had me sleeping on the floor and there was a bed up here all the time!'

Lydia feels sick and it has nothing to do with Jimmy. Something else is wrong. OK, she needs to focus.

'I have your money. And you need to go.'

He looks around the room. 'I'm kinda liking it here.'

He still looks like she could poke a hole through him with her finger, but he looks better. She's fed him. He's slept.

'A little girl went missing last night. Did you have anything to do with it?'

'I never done nothin' to no one.'

'Well that's not true. You pushed me around more than once when I was a child, about the same age as the missing girl.'

She waits. She was older than Daisy and if he defends himself, he'll know this.

'I never hurt no little girl.' Already he's standing.

'Here's the money. You stay out of Maine and out of my life, or I go to the chief of police and you spend what little time you have left on this Earth in custody. Might take years to charge you, but once your name is connected to that little girl, your life is over.'

'You one crazy bitch.'

Lydia shrugs. She has the upper hand again. She knows what she's doing. His words bounce off her like tennis balls off a racket. She's already moved on to a new problem.

'There are roadblocks up, so you can't leave today,' she says. 'Stay here another day or two. Then go. Unless you know where the little girl is. I'll turn you in now if you do.'

Jimmy is a drunk, a fool, a drug addict and a loser. But there's no way he killed the little girl. What did he have to gain? He'd have stood out on the beach. Someone would have seen him. Besides, he wanted money from her. Why risk missing that chance?

Would she really turn him in, if she thought he did it? That's a problem for another sleepless night.

'Do we have a deal?'

'Alright already.'

'Never again Jimmy. Or I put you in jail.'

On the landing, she looks out the window. The sky is darker now. The leaves are wilted in the heat, carrying the heaviness of the air. She sees movement of some kind. People, teenagers, hiding in the woods. Smoking, she figures. How most of them rebel these days. She scans, looking for Caroline. But even if she's there, what can Lydia do? She's not supposed to be there, either.

She'll have to tell Octavian. They can't have teenagers in the woods, in the house. They'd be liable. She waits and can sense people about but can't see them. And she has other problems to sort.

She looks at her watch. She has to call Dan, but she doesn't want to use the phone at home. She can't go to Portland, can't be that far away. She's sure the little girl will turn up, that she slept at a friend's house. Maybe her parents are in some sort of custody dispute. It's the Fort. And nothing bad ever happens here. Well, until this weekend, when he showed up.

She gets in her car and sees the phone she never uses. She is, for the first time, glad Octavian made her buy a car phone. She starts to dial the number, then stops. She hangs up then calls her lawyer, Mitch. Best man at her wedding. She's known him for years. She tells him briefly what's happening, that her son's father is trying to reach her, threatening her, and she doesn't want to speak to him.

'I could call him for you, as your lawyer.'

Lydia thinks for a second. 'I changed my name to put distance between us.'

'Are we talking physical abuse?'

'No. I was young. He was...' Horrible? Lecherous? Amoral? 'Charming.'

'Oh.'

She can hear the relief in his voice once she says no violence was involved. If men only knew – words and actions were their own form of assault, the damage just not visible to the naked eye.

'I don't want to hear from him. And I don't want him to be in touch with Scott,' she says.

'Let's start with me calling him. Texan, you say?'

'Yes.'

'Lots of rich oil men are now very poor.'

'Do you think this is about money?'

'Lydia, everything is about money, one way or another.'

She gives him the number he left with Sue Ellen.

'I know this goes without saying...'

'But don't tell Octavian. You have my word, as a lawyer and a gentleman.'

'So the two aren't mutually exclusive, as I've heard?' She laughs, a strained, false laugh that sounds tinny to her. Sounds wrong. She realizes she's exhausted.

'Don't worry, Lydia. Whatever it is, we'll get it taken care of.'

Lydia hears a noise, a rumble, so loud it takes a second for her to realize. Thunder. She looks out at the dark sky. The skies open and the rain beats down on the car, dancing on the hood. The beauty of the day before is gone, wiped out like it never existed. But there's strength in the rain, its ability to wash away so many things. There's beauty in that, too.

She picks up her phone and calls home. Scott answers.

'Hey. Any news on the Wright girl?' she says.

'Nothing. I walked every inch of this town, twice.'

'What about the water?'

'Nothing, but they're bringing in divers tomorrow, I think.'

'Are you OK? You sound funny.'

'Yeah, just tired.'

If she was looking at him now she's certain she'd see his chin drop. His tell. She knows his voice. She knows his mannerisms.

'Where's Peyton?' she asks.

'With Caroline.'

'And where is she?'

'I don't know. They went for a walk this morning before I left.'

'They've been gone all day?' she can feel herself shouting, it jolts her mind, her body.

'I don't know, mom. I was out. I just got home.'

Lydia looks out the window. It's still pouring, but she can drive in this.

'I'm on my way home. If they come home, tell them to stay put. You, too.'

'They're back now. Hey Squirt.'

She hears him yell to Peyton and then a woof sound and she knows Peyton has barrelled into him. As she listens she knows he's picking her up. He's saying something to Caroline. 'Has she been crying? Why are her nails dirty?'

'Scott. Is everything OK?'

'Yeah,' he says, but she hears the tone of weariness people get when dealing with Caroline. Another problem to sort when she gets home.

'Can we order pizza?' Scott asks.

'Yes, of course. I'll see you when you get home. And Scott?'

'Yeah?'

'I'm proud of you, for helping today.'

43

Lydia

July, Maine, 1997

The day hasn't yet ended. The rain has stopped and there are some clear patches in the sky, but mostly there's darkness. Small slashes of light reflect in the water, but the sky is bruised with unshed rain. The air is heavy, with a metallic smell. Round two is coming.

Lydia gets out the car for what feels like the tenth time that day and walks slowly to the house. Inside, she sees a glow coming from the kitchen. They've lit candles, but the air conditioner is on, so there's power. She hopes they're being careful. The air is filled with the smell of onions, garlic and cheese. Suddenly, she's ravenous.

The kids are sitting at the kitchen island, all three of them. She can't remember the last time that happened. They look up when she walks in, say hello. But there's no joy at seeing her, even from Peyton. That hurts, a little. The look they give her is one of surprise, and she sees Caroline giving her a once over. Glancing down and sees she's covered in dirt. From that goddamn house. Peyton, she sees, has wet hair and is in her pjs.

'Did you let her swim with the threat of lightning?' Lydia feels her voice raise, loud and sharp.

'No. She took a bath.'

Lydia doesn't have the strength to ask why. They're home. They're safe. That's all that matters.

'I'm going to take a quick shower and change. I'll be right back.'

She wants to move quickly, up the stairs, get back to them, but she's exhausted suddenly, each step an effort, like she's carrying the whole house on her back. She showers for longer than normal then stares in the closet, trying to decide what to wear, when she sees Octavian's clothes. She pulls on a pair of khaki capris and one of her husband's blue shirts, which she ties at the bottom, so it's tight on her hips, and rolls up the sleeves. It smells like Octavian, soap and musky aftershave and kindness. She glances in the mirror, knows she looks ridiculous, but for some reason, she feels better.

She walks down the stairs in bare feet, the coolness of the floor somehow a comfort. Taking a seat beside her children, she picks up a piece of pizza, begins eating it with her hands. She can feel them staring at her.

'Why the candles?' she asks.

'Peyton is afraid we'll lose power and not be able to see to light them,' Scott says.

'Oh.'

She's impressed with her two eldest, for sorting this out for her. When she gets all this drama sorted, she'll spend more time with each of them. She sends up a silent prayer: *Keep Jimmy away. Let Daisy be found. Keep my kids safe. Forgive me.*

After a sleepless night, the day doesn't start well. The rain is still falling. News about Daisy isn't good. There's been no sign of the little girl. Lydia knows she should be doing more to help. Octavian has a certain standing in the community that must be acknowledged, but she's struggling to keep the plates of her own life spinning. She's proud that Scott has stepped up, though. He's been searching. He got home so late, the night she disappeared. She wonders if she saw something. She wonders. No. She doesn't. A speeding charge. Some underage drinking. Some theft. It was a normal way of rebelling, right?

She picks up the phone and calls a local restaurant. Tells them to charge their family account to feed those involved in the search. As she hangs up, the phone rings, startling her.

'Hello?'

'Lydia? It's Mitch. I've been in touch with Mr. Davies.'

She tucks the phone under her chin. It is nine o'clock in the morning. What does one drink this early in the morning. Mimosas? That's for a celebration. Besides, she'll need a clear head.

'And?'

'Well, he was adamant he wanted to speak to you. I love these good ole' Texas boys. Hung up on me when I said you didn't want to be in touch with him.'

'Hung up?' That didn't sound like the Dan she knew. But she never knew him, not really. She was a bit on the side. Nothing more.

'Yes.'

'So where do things stand?'

'Oh, he called me back an hour later.'

'And?'

'Seems he lost his money in the recession. His wife left him. His father-in-law has blackballed him in Texas and he wants the money back he gave you for Scott.'

'I see.'

Lydia doesn't know how to take this news. He gave her twenty-five thousand dollars, a one-off payment – not so much for his son as for her silence. But something doesn't sit right. The fact that he'd get in touch now.

'Did he ask about Scott?'

'No. He didn't come across as a real peach, Lydia. More angry and scared.'

'What do you think I should do?'

'He's a desperate man. No money, used to a certain lifestyle. No wife—'

'What about Katie, his daughter?'

'He didn't mention her.'

Lydia thinks. Octavian knew Dan was older, but he never knew about Katie. Scott stopped asking about his father a long time ago.

'Tell him he can have the money on the condition Katie never knows about Scott, or what happened between me and her father.'

Lydia's embarrassed, saying these things to Mitch.

Perhaps she should have used a different lawyer. But really, professional discretion isn't what it once was, and Mitch is old school. She trusts him.

'You sure, Lydia? In my experience, once a bully knows he can push you, he keeps on pushing.'

'He's not a bully. He's a sad little man who defined himself through wealth that wasn't his. I don't want anything from him. I wish I'd never met him.'

'If you're sure...'

'Yes, Mitch. A man who doesn't even ask after his own son? I just want him gone. But his daughter was my dearest friend once and I don't want her to feel the shame I carry.'

There's a pause on the other end of the line.

'We all do foolish things in our youth, Lydia. Scott is a good boy.'

'He's out searching for Daisy Wright again.'

'Hell of a thing. Can't fathom what happened to her. Must have been a summer tourist.'

'Thanks for everything, Mitch.'

'I'll call him and get this sorted this afternoon.'

Lydia hangs up. One crisis sorted. Standing in the kitchen, the house feels quiet. She knows Scott is out. But where are Peyton and Caroline?

They appear with towels, getting ready for a swim.

'You girls stay close to home today, OK?' she repeats. 'And stay out of the pool if there's thunder!'

'Close to home?' Caroline gives her a funny look.

'Home. Do you hear? Scott's out with the search... volunteering. I have to go out, as well. But I'll be back soon. Maybe we'll go to Portland and have dinner, buy some new clothes.'

Peyton is busy pulling on her water wings. Lydia notices she's frowning, not something she usually does, and she wonders how much her small, gentle daughter is picking up on the drama unfolding around them.

'Stay out of the pool if there's thunder.'

'You said that.'

'I mean it!'

'OK,' Caroline says.

She knows her shrewd daughter won't pass up on a shopping spree and she'll behave for that reason alone.

As she drives to the house on Cabot Lane, Lydia tells herself she'll never return to the place. That once this is all over, she'll encourage Octavian to sell it. And if he won't do that, she'll insist he cut down the trees out back and rent it out. She reminds herself to talk to Caroline. But no, Caroline would never hang out in such conditions. Her daughter did not like dirt, or trees. She chose the pool over the beach. For once she's glad her daughter is so particular. Oh, who is she kidding? She's a snob.

He's outside, that man. Lydia waves as she curses him under her breath. Then she pulls into the drive.

She can tell, stepping out of the car. The stillness in the air, in the trees. Like that day so long ago when she didn't have to go into their tiny little shack to know mama had fled.

A bad feeling inches through her, part fire, part ice, as she walks the path to the back door. Jimmy must be gone. But she has to check, to make sure.

She lets herself into the house. It feels empty. She's sure there's no one here. Can tell by the way the house feels, like it's on its own again. Free of some sort of darkness that does not come simply with the day giving away to night.

There's a bag of garbage on the kitchen counter. She knows it is from the food she has brought him. She will take it with her when she goes, or they'll have rats.

She walks slowly to the cavernous main room, her heart beating, afraid something is going to grab her by the shoulders, by the ankles. Pull her down into the darkness with her. She straightens her shoulders. She's fought the darkness before. She knows what she's doing. Besides, Jimmy isn't why she's here. It's that room, with the bed. The familiar sheets. She moves upstairs, unsure she wants to see it again but knowing she must.

She opens the door, hoping the room is empty, that she imagined it all. But it's there. The bed with the blue sheets she knows so well. The end table, the architecture books. The magazines. It's as much Octavian as if he were standing here himself.

She turns on her heel, starts to leave, but something catches her eye. Wine. She can't see the label, but she knows the shape, the color. She walks over and picks up the bottle. It sells for sixty dollars a bottle. There's a case of it in her home. She knows this because it's Octavian's favorite. There's no dust on the bottle.

She feels her insides turn. She sniffs the air. No perfume. No scented soap. She sniffs the sheets. Recoils from the familiar scent of body odor, decay and failure that is her brother, Jimmy. There's nothing feminine. No woman has been here.

But Octavian has.

She stands back and studies the room, as though an answer will appear from behind the drapes. The house seems to be mocking her. And she's had enough. She turns on all the lights, goes from room to room, looking for disturbed dust. Looking, looking. Opening doors, cabinets. She sniffs the air, but it would be too soon to smell decay.

How did her life come to this?

She's frantic now. If she had a bulldozer, she'd use it. Take the house apart. It's so big, but the cobwebs tell a story. What's been moved, what hasn't. She drops to her hands and knees, crawls along the floor, looking for loose boards. She scrapes her knuckles, cuts her palm as she gropes for answers.

And then she sees herself. It's like part of her is floating above her. What *is* she doing? She tries to catch her breath. There's no sign of a woman having been here except the crazy one on the floor, covered in dust. Bleeding. There's no sign of a body being hidden. But a small child? Should she check the cellar? The attic?

No. Jimmy isn't strong enough to carry a child, even one as small as Daisy. And there was no reason for it. She's making him a monster because that's what he was, to her.

She has to get out of here. Away from this godawful house. A house she never liked but now despises.

Lydia stands up, walks down the stairs, to the kitchen, picks up the garbage. Out the door, across the yard. She's not nervous, not scared anymore. She's tired of it all. Tired of being dragged down by the past, by the idea of family. She wants them all gone. Even Minnie, who she's always fiercely loved. Minnie gave Jimmy her address. She still can't believe that betrayal.

She gets in the car, turns on the ignition and starts to drive. As she reaches out to switch on the radio, she sees how dirty she is. She doesn't want to go home. Doesn't want to see her children right now. Doesn't want to expose them to her until she's sloughed off the ugly feeling that's coated her since Jimmy came to town.

She drives to the beach, where they're looking for that lovely little girl. She sits in her car and watches police officers moving around, like the poor thing might suddenly appear. It's been two days now. She looks at the last few posts where the pier collapsed. Surely they must have checked it well, to see if she was caught in the debris?

Forgetting the state of her clothes, she walks over to the chief of police.

'Any news, Chief Langley?'

'Nothing, Lydia.' He shakes his head.

She thinks she sees him do a double take.

'What can I do?'

'Not much, I'm afraid. Your boy worked all day. And thanks for the food.'

She waves him away. 'It's not good, is it?'

'Hundreds of people and the only witness was the sea. And it isn't talking.'

She listens to the familiar sound of the waves rolling in. They're speaking, just not in a way anyone understands.

44

Peyton

April, Maine, 2022

'How was Seattle?' Lydia asks.

Both her parents are in the house – a rare occurrence – which makes Peyton wonder if she's in for another chat. She hadn't heard them when she came in and dropped her bag.

'Good,' she says.

'Condo OK?'

'Fine.'

'Any leads on work?' her mother says.

Peyton can feel sweat start to run down her back. She studies her mother, wondering if she knows. Lydia Winchester knows everything. But for the first time, Peyton sees beyond the polish, the stylish clothes. The veneer. She sees the house where her mother grew up. Thinks of the awful diner and Debbie. Her mother came from nothing and look at what she has now.

'Peyton?'

New feelings stir. Not love. Some understanding, perhaps tenderness.

'Sorry, dreaming. Flying exhausts me.'

'Work?'

'I'm working on it.'

'Work harder, Peyton.'

'I know, Mom. Time isn't my friend anymore.'

Then, before she can talk herself out of it, she does something she hasn't done since she was a small child. She walks over to her mother and father and gives them both a kiss on the cheek. Then she picks up her bag, goes upstairs and takes out a pad of paper.

My mother is a stranger to me ... she begins. *I know her mannerisms, the shape of her fingernails. I can tell you how she will answer a question, even what clothes she will no doubt be wearing on any given day. But that's familiarity, not knowing. Those are things you learn from sharing a house. As a person, she is an enigma who happens to have given birth to me.*

She writes furiously, wanting to get it all out before it disappears. Words, like so many things, seem to float in the ether. You have to get them down in some solid form, before they move on to something, someone, else.

When she's done she's written a little over sixteen pages. Her hand hurts from gripping the pen so tightly. She sets it down, a feeling of something new, some warm feeling coming over her. She thinks it is accomplishment. She holds them up and looks at them,

That feeling? It comes from creating. It comes from knowing you've done something well. It comes from believing, even momentarily, in yourself. She wishes she could bottle it as she stretches, her arms over her head, her chest full with air, with happiness, with life.

Another idea comes to her. A good one, she thinks.

She doesn't need a pen for this one.

In the morning, Peyton is up before everyone. Up earlier than she's ever been. She pulls on a pair of shorts and a T-shirt and grabs the backpack she packed the night before. She lets herself out of the house as the night is still winning the battle between light and dark. She jogs along the beach, up to the main road running parallel to the beach. Cuts up the side road, up the hill.

For the first time, he's not outside. The man who's always gardening. He must be still asleep. She congratulates herself as though this is some sort of accomplishment.

There it is. Looking more decrepit than she remembered. And more glamorous, too. It's a funny old place, The Stick House. Its personality seems to change. It has moods.

She stops in the street, looks around. Then she jogs to the back of the house, into the woods, and scales the chain-link fence at the back. She drops easily to the ground, making a slight thump that she hopes no one hears. Noises carry in the dark. She takes out the small flashlight she brought and the keys she stole from her father's desk and lets herself in.

The first thing she notices is the smell. Damp, decay, cold, sawdust, she's not sure, but she remembers the smell. She hopes it triggers more memories from that long-ago day. She wants to remember. She's ready, now.

She takes out the bigger flashlight she brought with her. It was so easy finding all the things she needed, she feels like it's some sort of sign that she's on the right track. There's an hour before the sun comes up. She'll text her mother that she couldn't sleep and went for a run. She'll catch hell for going out alone in the dark. That's a problem for later.

She figures the basement and the attics are the best places to start. She wishes she had coffee, but all she has is water. She takes a sip.

Daisy, if you're here. Let me know. I want to find you. I want to bring you home.

Covering her mouth with a mask in case there's something terrible in the air, the walls, she sets to work. One way or another, The Stick House is going to give up its mysteries.

'Where have you been?'

Peyton can't believe her luck – or lack of it. She's covered in cobwebs, dirt and God knows what, and meets her mother as she's coming out the house.

'Where's your car?' Peyton asks. She was sure her mother was gone when she walked up the drive.

'In the garage. Your father was tinkering with something. Where have you been all day?'

'I went for a run.'

'Through what? The haunted mansion?'

Peyton catches herself before she starts to laugh.

'What's that in your hair?' her mother asks.

'I don't know. I ran through the woods.'

'You ran through the woods, in the dark? With a pack?

For an entire day? Are you lying to me, or have you entirely lost your mind again?'

'I wanted the weight to work on my stamina. I brought a flashlight,' she explains. 'And food. Why are you outside?'

'The door to the garage is stuck.'

Peyton can tell by the way her mother is looking at her that she doesn't believe her. It's fine. She didn't find anything. She has no story to tell, yet. But it's a big house and she has all summer to search.

They're doing some sort of dance, wary of each other. Peyton wishes she could just ask a question, but her mother has never been one to drag the past out into the light.

'Wherever you were, stay put now. I'm off to Portland.'

'Right.'

'And Peyton?'

'Yes?'

'It's time you got another haircut.'

Peyton nods, lets herself inside. Goes upstairs, yanks off her clothes and pulls on her swimsuit. Then she goes outside and dives into the pool, cobwebs, dirt, and all.

She sits on the bottom of the pool, like she used to with Scott when she was a kid. She knows she was at The Stick House around the time Daisy disappeared. She knows there was a man there. She knows she's done all she can.

Now, she has to figure out if she wants to tell John what she saw, all those years ago.

And if she wants to tell her parents, too.

45

August, Maine, 1997

Daisy has been gone – missing, lost, Lydia's not sure what word to use – for an entire month. It's no longer the lead story on the news. It hasn't made the paper for the last few nights. Still, it's felt all over the Fort. It feels wrong to go to the beach, to sit in the sun, to go to the shops or have lobster. Collective suffering won't change things, but it feels wrong to enjoy life right now.

It's been an appalling summer. And there's still August to get through. And tonight. She has to get through tonight.

She takes a bath, staying in the tub until the water cools. Stepping out, she catches sight of herself in the mirror. She turns and looks, studies her body. Stretch marks from her pregnancies. But she's still slender and her legs looks good, the muscles defined from all the walking she does. She's no longer twenty. No longer thirty. All the hours she spent sitting and studying she makes up for now with being active.

She dries off, then sits on the edge of her bed and rubs some scented lotion into her skin. She doesn't do this often enough.

She slips on her robe, brushes her hair, applies some make-up. Whatever happens, she wants him to see a strong, attractive woman. Her hands shake slightly and she acknowledges that she's nervous.

She does love her husband, more than she realized.

With a final look in the mirror, she makes her way to the lounge. She pours herself a glass of wine. And waits.

It's just after midnight when the door opens and her husband appears. He walks toward the kitchen, passing the door to the lounge.

'I'm in here, Octavian.'

She hears him stop, pause, then resume walking, his steps moving toward her now.

'Lydia! You're up late.'

She picks up her glass of wine and takes a sip.

'Everything OK?'

'I'm fine,' she says. 'Long day at work?'

She can tell by the way his eyes narrow that he knows something is wrong. He walks into the conservatory and pours a Scotch.

'Long day? Yes.'

'You've been away a lot lately.'

'I have.'

'Not always at the hospital. I've checked.'

'What are you talking about?'

His voice is even, calm, it always is, but his eyes widen, briefly.

'I went to the house on Cabot Street the other day.'

'Why?'

'I found myself in the neighbourhood,' she says.

'With the keys?'

'I went inside. I was surprised to see there was electricity. And I started poking around. Imagine my surprise when I found *my* sheets on a new bed upstairs. And your favorite wine.'

They look at each other, six feet and a world between them.

'Are you having an affair?'

He laughs. She's startled by this. She hadn't been prepared for it.

'No, Lydia. I'm not having an affair.'

She was prepared for him to deny it, but she wasn't prepared for his laughter, wasn't prepared to believe him.

'So, why do you have a bed and wine at a house that's all but falling apart?'

'Because, Lydia, as much as I love you – and I do – sometimes I need my own space. It's hard being around you sometimes.'

She drains the wine she's been sipping. She wants another, but is afraid to stand up, to walk to the bar, to pour it. Afraid she'll fall from the shock.

Her husband drives across town and goes into an abandoned home, where he's created a cave, a retreat, from her...

An affair might hurt less.

They're silent, looking at each other. Like he can read her mind, he takes her glass, crosses to the bar and fills it for her. Handing it back, he speaks.

'What can I do to fix this?'

'Fix this? It's not a broken window or door. It's not something you can plaster over.'

She turns in her seat, so she can look out the window. It's too dark to see anything, but she knows what lies outside. The slope of the lawn, the garden furniture she picked. The ocean in the distance.

'This house is the only place I've ever felt truly safe. I thought we were happy here. And now I find out you need an escape hatch. How can I be happy here again?'

She realizes the truth of the statement as she says it. The house, away from all the others, sitting on a cliff. She can see the headlights of any approaching car before they can see the house. An early alarm system. A warning. She had enough surprises when she was growing up, never knowing what exactly was waiting for her when she got home, when she got to school. Not knowing where her next meal was coming from. But she has a different problem now.

'How do I deal with my husband needing an escape from me?'

He's sitting across from her, drink in his hand.

'I've always loved your intensity. Your strength. But now that I'm older, I just find it hard, that you have no soft side. It bothers me to see how you are with Peyton. And I can't figure out how to fix it.'

What's happening, what he's saying, is the most crushing surprise of her life. Dan's betrayal had angered her, in the way you get angry in your twenties, when you have energy and passion. For being made to feel a fool. But this, this feels like she's been kicked in the chest and is now slowly being smothered by a blanket. Like drowning not in water but in air. In life.

But she won't allow herself to be weak. Not in front of him.

'If you want to leave, you know where the door is. I'm not about to beg you to stay.'

Octavian stands. 'I don't want to leave.'

'What *do* you want? For me to be soft? I don't know how to do that!'

She looks at him and sees him differently. There's more gray at his temples. His wrinkles are deeper. And then she has a new thought. He was old, too, when they had Peyton. It was different for him, but he rallied.

'Where do we go from here?' she asks.

He looks somehow ashamed and broken and angry at the same time.

'Sometimes, coming into this house, I felt I had to act. Be the father, the leader. Rein in a boy who's out of control and not my blood. Rein in a daughter who's too damn much sometimes.' He stops.

'What about Peyton?'

'That's the hardest part, Lydia. You haven't even tried to be a mother to her, and that made me feel things about you I never thought possible.'

It feels like something hard and solid has slammed into her. Like her very backbone might disintegrate. She has no words for this. She knows it's true.

She moves to the stairs as though in a bad dream, afraid to look back in case the bogeyman grabs her. In case she sees her husband leave.

'Where are you going?' he asks.

'I don't know.' She starts up the stairs.

'Lydia? Lydia?'

She hears him call, but she doesn't turn round. She puts her hand over her mouth to cover the sob she's afraid will escape her. She hears the door open and close, and knows he's gone. She doesn't know when – or if – he'll come home. She thought it was an affair, but it was her.

46

Peyton

May, Maine, 2022

Peyton is cold. Her feet are freezing from standing on the concrete. She could just go upstairs and grab some socks, some shoes, but she's afraid to move, afraid to break her concentration. She's staring at the timeline, staring hard, even though she has it memorized, can picture it in her sleep. Staring as though in one magical second, an answer will come. After all this time. She sighs, and looks to the right of the timeline, at the big gap where suspects should be listed. There's nothing. Not one. Well, one. But the police don't know about him. At least, she doesn't think they do. She looks at all the paperwork on her desk as though that, too, will hold an answer. She's getting tired of waiting for answers. Tired of pussyfooting around. She picks up a marker, and a piece of paper. Draws a stickman, adds some crazy hair, and a smile with teeth as crooked as a mountain range. She tapes it up. Steps back and looks. Uncle Jimmy.

She walks up the stairs, looking for warmth. Her mother is in Portland, and her father is in the conservatory reading. She doesn't have to look to know this. She can feel where he is in the house.

'Dad, can we talk?'

He looks up from his newspaper as though surprised to see her there.

'Sounds ominous. What about?'

'When Caroline was home she told me you own The Stick House. How come you never told me?'

'I thought you knew?'

'Didn't have a clue. Why didn't you tell me the day we visited it, when I first moved home?'

'I repeat, I thought you knew.'

He's not looking up from his paper, which is unlike her father, who was all about handshakes, looking people in the eye when you spoke. Manners.

'It feels like it's some sort of secret. I remember that day. I remember asking why it wasn't being developed. If you owned it, why didn't you answer?'

'I thought I did. If not, here's your answer now. I didn't tell you because I didn't hear the question, perhaps. I seem to remember being quite upset to learn about you being dragged there as a child against your will. I can tell you now that I haven't done anything with it because I don't know what to do with it. It's a beautiful structure and it needs to be saved but I'm too old to do much rescuing now.'

Peyton feels slightly off-balance at her father's answer.

'You don't like it? Why? You love all that old, creepy stuff,' she says.

'Creepy is a good word.'

Peyton feels a coldness run up and down her spine. 'You think the house is creepy?'

'A lot of bad stuff happened to the people who lived there. The people who built it lost their fortune and the eldest son died in a plane crash. The next family had a daughter who jumped out a window while on drugs. By the time it came to us, it already had a history.'

She waits, but he goes back to reading the paper. Whatever she was hoping to hear, she hasn't heard it.

'It's no big conspiracy. I just don't like the house. So I let it be.'

'So you're just going to let it rot?' she says.

'I'll have to figure something out, one of these days.'

'If you leave it to me in your will, I'm sending a wrecking ball through it.'

'Could be for the best.'

'I think its connected to the Daisy Wright case,' she says, her voice lower, as though part of her hopes he doesn't hear her.

'I don't see how.'

He turns the page, the newspaper making that part whooshing, part crackling sound. He doesn't look up and Peyton thinks this means something.

'I remember that day, Dad. I was young, but I remember. There was a man in the house. A creepy man. And I think I should tell the police. I think they should search the house. Maybe they have mug books I can look through.'

Her father looks up from the paper. 'They already have.'

'What?'

'They've already searched. I gave them permission a long time ago.'

'What?'

Her father looks up from his paper. Looks her straight in the face.

'I gave the police permission to search the house. A long time ago.' He pauses. 'You weren't the only one to see a strange man at the house that weekend.'

Peyton sits across from her father. 'Why didn't you tell me this?'

Her father sighs and she can tell he's trying to decide what more to share. He looks so much older since his bypass, but healthier, somehow, too. He has some color.

'What I'm going to tell you is not to be repeated. Not to your mother. Not to anyone. You are not to write about it in your notebook. And you're not to tell John.'

'OK.'

'I mean it, Peyton.'

Yes, sir.'

'The weekend Daisy disappeared a man was seen at the house on Cabot Lane. So was your mother. You know the man who's always out front? Barry?'

Peyton snaps back to that day she took her first walk to that old house, to the man who knew who she was. 'Yes.'

'He called me. Told me he'd seen a man at the house. I drove over, not sure what I'd find. Looking back now, I should have called the cops, but they were busy looking and I didn't think the two cases were connected.' He stops, no doubt remembering that weekend. 'I pulled up and the first thing I saw was your mother's car. She was driving a Cadillac back then. Couldn't miss it.'

He stops again. It's making her crazy, all his pauses and thinking.

'Have you ever wondered, Peyton, why your mother never wants to talk about the Daisy Wright case?'

She thinks. 'Not really. I mean, she never wants to talk about anything.'

'I parked down the road, watched. Your mother came out. Sat in the car for the longest time. After she drove off, I went over to the house. Let myself in. I saw a man – bit of a stink to him, looked like hell.'

She waits.

'It was her long-lost brother, come to town to shake her down for some money.'

'Old jeans, black T-shirt. Teeth that would throw the fear of God into you?' she says.

Her father nods.

'Did he do it?'

'Of course not.'

'How do you know?'

'Because Chief Langley and a few troopers came to the house and we talked to him. He didn't have the brains or the physical strength to kidnap a cat. I took him to the bus station, put him on a bus and told him if he showed up again, I'd kill him.'

She wishes she could tell him she'd gone to Tennessee, to see Minnie. But she can't. She's learning something about her parents. They're more of a team than she thought. It looks like they live separate lives, but that's not the case. If her mother ever finds out she went to Tennessee, she doubts she'd ever forgive her. The way she never forgave Minnie.

'I've read everything about Daisy's case. There's nothing about The Stick House being searched.'

'Because I paid for the community gym and the new roof at the police station.'

She thinks of all the notes she made, listing all the money her father donated to the town. The answer was in front of her, in a way.

'Does Mom know any of this? What you did?'

'No.' He opens his paper once more. 'Enough is enough. OK, Peyton? You've had your fun digging around, but let it be now. For God's sake, just let it be.'

She waits, but nothing more is said. So she goes upstairs to think. As of that moment, she knows. Family has limits. And she's overstayed her welcome.

She's sitting on her bed, thinking about what she's just learned, when her phone beeps. It's John. Something else she has to think about. Somehow, they've fallen into what's either an easy relationship or a complicated friendship.

She wonders if he knows about her father and his father, and what they did, to protect her mother. He asks if she wants to meet for dinner. This is a euphemism for what they actually do when they are together. This time, they have to talk.

She sets her phone down without responding. She doesn't want to spend the rest of her life in the Fort. She has to get out before she, too, is consumed by all the secrets. But she can't leave Daisy. Not yet.

She hears the grandfather clock in the entranceway she hates. Looks around her room. Part of her wants to pack and leave right away. But she can't. She has to be smart, now. Has to get it right.

She picks up the phone and reads the text again. A simple invitation from a friend and she has an answer. A plan. Finally, she knows what to do.

*

'You're sure this is OK?' Peyton is nervous, sweating in her skirt and short-sleeved blouse. She's dressed for what's about to happen.

She has her phone and a pencil case, filled with twelve brand-new pens bought at the pharmacy the day before. A big pad of paper, like something she had in school. A list of questions she'd started working on, after John's text. Daisy's mother, his aunt, would speak to her.

Her first interview in many years. John had set it up, told her at dinner that crazy night she confronted her father about The Stick Hose. A week ago, but it feels like years.

John. Somehow he saw what she needed more than she did. Saw what Daisy's mother needed, too. To know someone else remembered her daughter. Someone was searching. Someone cared.

'What did you tell her about me?'

She looks at John, who's driving her to his aunt's house. She sees a faint smile, in profile.

'I told her you were a friend of mine, that you'd been trying to figure out what happened to Daisy and that you've thought about her a lot over the past year.'

Peyton nods, accepting what he said. It's true – she has thought about Daisy a lot. Now, with a tinge of guilt, she wonders if all the trauma of her childhood somehow got twisted, thinking it was all about a little girl disappearing, when it was really about events in her own family that same weekend.

'Thanks for talking to her. Thanks for everything you've

done since I came home.' Peyton knows she'll remember this moment the rest of her life.

John pulls in front of a white two-story home on a street that runs parallel to the beach, about a mile inland. Peyton has walked by it many times but never knew this was where Daisy's mother lived. She always thought it was the other side of town, where they went for fired chicken when she was a kid.

'Has she moved?' she asks John. 'Since it happened, I mean?'

'No. She won't pack up Daisy's room.'

Peyton feels her insides twist and reminds herself this is more than a sad story. This is someone's life. Approach is everything. She hopes she gets it right.

She follows John down an uneven stone-slabbed path to the wooden front step that leads to a screened in porch.

As he knocks, he indicates the flowers bordering the path. 'I planted those.'

They smile at each other, both nervous.

A woman appears at the door wearing old jeans and a pink sweater, despite the heat of the day. Her hair is short, she wears no make-up.

Peyton wants to hug her. Instead, she offers her hand and says, 'Thank you for agreeing to talk to me.'

She follows her to the kitchen at the back of the house. Betty Wright offers Peyton a seat. Sitting on the table is a stuffed dog. Old, beat up, much loved.

'That's Barney,' the woman says. 'He was with Daisy at the beach that day.'

★

They speak for four hours. Peyton doesn't ask all the questions she's written. She asks many she hadn't thought of. Mostly, she lets Betty tell her story. It's hers alone now. Her husband is gone. John's parents, she's quick to point out, were wonderful to her, but John's father is gone, too. John's mother spends her winters in Florida. Betty spends her time looking out the window, waiting for a grown woman who was once a young girl to show up.

As Peyton thanks her for her time, for sharing her memories, Betty looks at her and says, 'You're a nice girl, a pretty girl. She'd be a lot like you, if she were still here.'

Peyton feels tears threaten. She's silent, not knowing what to say. This woman is younger than her mother and looks thirty years older. She's like the kind of grandmother you see in Christmas films. Peyton feels a fury go through her that this woman has had to endure such a living nightmare. That after all these years, she still has no answers. Part of her wants to tell her, wants to say, 'I think I know what happened!' But that's just it, she thinks. Her father says Jimmy didn't do it. And she knows, deep inside, her father wouldn't lie. At least, she doesn't think so.

'Your parents have been so good to me, too, Peyton.'

She feels a jolt at this.

'Your father sent his lawyers to help when my husband died without a will. Kept me in my home. And your mother called regularly, I guess she knew I would need someone to talk to. And they let me stay at their beautiful place in Florida when I needed an escape. They're good people, your parents.'

Peyton nods, smiles, holds her tongue. Her father throwing money at a problem makes sense. Her mother being a shoulder to lean on, someone to talk to? Peyton thought that was only for her patients. She files it away to think about later.

'And you're sure, about me writing about this, that it's OK?'

'I'm sure, dear. John says you have a good heart. I trust my Johnny.'

Peyton sees John's car pull up. He'd left them alone to talk. Peyton isn't sure if he didn't want to hear the story again or if he didn't want to relive it. He was there when it happened and she thinks he carries guilt that he couldn't find her, although he was only nine years old at the time. All the people on the beach, and he didn't see anything, either.

She now knows Betty carries guilt that she'd had that third glass of wine that afternoon. That no one was watching Daisy as the pier collapsed. John's cousin, Richard, had been injured by debris, had spent weeks in hospital. His parents had moved not long after. She never hears from her nephew anymore.

Peyton can't help herself. She reaches out and gives Betty Wright a hug. Then she moves along the path, to where John is waiting.

In the car she's silent, not sure what to say.

'Do you want to stop for coffee?' he says.

She shakes her head. 'I either want to cry or write. I'm not sure which.'

He nods. 'Nothing to say you can't do both.'

She thanks him once more and kisses him goodbye, then she goes to her room, closes the door, looks at her notes. And she starts to write.

'That Weekend' by Peyton Winchester

The July 4th weekend that year was very hot. People still remember that. A storm blew in, but it was after the festivities, and it lingered, off and on, for days.

Those who were children at the time remember an ominous feeling in the Fort. They remember not being allowed outdoors to play, even though the rain held off all that day, the dark clouds growing heavier with each passing hour that Daisy was missing and finally resulting in a storm that caused minor flooding in the town.

But before that, people gathered to celebrate Independence Day. Families and locals met on the beach early, anticipating a crowd. By lunchtime, the space around what was known as the old pier was filled with people, blankets, towels, coolers. July 4th in the Fort had always been a celebration, culminating in fireworks over the water. Six-year-old Daisy Wright was with her mother, father, two aunts, an uncle and two cousins. A close family, the cousins kept an eye on Daisy as they played in the water and on the sand. As the sun shone and temperatures soared, no one suspected what tragedy the day would bring.

If not a gentler time, it was a time before 24-hour news was the norm. The internet was in its early days and few people had cell phones. We didn't know the terms predator, stranger danger or human trafficking. That would all soon change.

No one knows exactly when Daisy Wright went missing. As is often the case, the adults present that day could only say that one minute she was there and the next she was gone.

At 7:25, the old fishing pier started to sway. Within minutes the main support beam had buckled, sending splinters into the air.

The collapse of the old pier and the noise it made as it crashed into the sea is what jarred the revellers out of their sense of ease and had parents reaching for their children. But Daisy's mother and father couldn't see their daughter. As the rotted wood filled the water and littered the sand, her father raced into the destruction, thinking his little girl had been hit by debris.

He didn't find her. Cries for help were not at first heard in the melee and no one knows for certain how much time passed before a group of people linked arms and walked into the water, pushing the rotting wood out the way as they looked for the little girl. But she was not to be found.

Most people went to bed that night knowing that a six-year-old had disappeared from the beach on that hot July day. Others woke to the news on the radio the next morning, when the long wished for rain gathered in dark clouds over Fort Meadow Beach.

Tom Langley was the chief of police then. He was also Daisy's uncle. He died not knowing what happened. His son, John Langley, is a police officer in Fort Meadow Beach and says his father carried the case with him every day of his life. Officer Langley says he does, too, for he is Daisy's cousin and was there that day.

'My father believed that someone knew something. Someone saw something. Something kept them from coming forward. They need to do the right thing and come forward now,' he says.

The first forty-eight hours are crucial in a missing person's investigation. John Langley says his father didn't sleep the first seventy-two. He says every lead was followed and every tip investigated.

The state police were called in to assist and everything that could be done was done. But the days passed and nothing turned up. Nothing was found of Daisy Wright's. No piece of clothing washed up on the beach. Nothing was found in the woods that surround the Fort, despite endless searches.

'I used to walk the beach each night, hoping to see something. I'm not sure what,' current police captain Nathan Hill says. 'I was a rookie cop and I had so much anger and determination over this case,' he adds. When asked what he thinks happened he shakes his head, before saying, 'I used to think a car would slow down, stop, drop her off. That I'd see her and grab her up, run her straight to her folk's house. It's crazy, I know, but that's what I thought. Now, I don't know what to think. I never thought we would be here, no answers, all these years later.'

Years went by, and theories and urban legends started to get tossed around. Despite all the man hours and good, solid, old-fashioned police work, nothing new was learned.

Cold cases once considered unsolvable, crimes that confounded police forces for years are now being solved, but when asked about this Hill says, 'That's through DNA. We've got databases, genealogy sites. We don't have any DNA to test. Really, we don't have anything.'

Hill waits a few moments before adding, 'What we hope, what we've always believed, is that someone saw something, and either didn't realize its significance, or didn't want to get involved. What we keep hoping for is for that person to come forward.'

Daisy's mother lives with this hope every moment of her life.

'She was so beautiful, so bubbly. I've missed her every moment of every day since she disappeared. I'll never stop missing her,' she says.

Daisy's father died having never stopped looking for his daughter.

'I have this dream,' her mother says. 'There's a knock on my door and I open it and see a beautiful, strong, happy young woman. We sit down in her room and I learn all about her. It's just a dream, but it keeps me going. I know if we do find her, it'll be what's left of her. But then I could bury her with her father. They could be together again. That would bring me some peace, too.'

It's been twenty-four years since Daisy Jane Wright disappeared on Sunrise Beach, near where the old pier stood. Anyone with any information is asked to please get in touch with Fort Meadow police or the writer of this article.

47

Peyton

May, Maine, 2022

Peyton is sitting in her room thinking when her phone beeps. It's John.

Aunt Betty just read your article. She said thank you.

Peyton feels slightly sick at this. The article has been picked up by the news wire and she's been in touch with a national paper about writing a longer format, including her efforts to crack the case on her own. In a way, she's now the reporter she always wanted to be.

But she can't help feeling her good fortune comes at the expense of others. Of Daisy and her family. Of John.

I hope someone steps up and does the right thing.

Me too. Want to grab a bite?

Yes. I have some stuff I need to tell you.

OK. See you in twenty minutes?

Make it thirty.

They go to the old diner, the place where they had coffee and she asked him about Daisy all those months ago.

'Has anyone called the tip line?'

'No.'

'And you're sure Betty is OK with the story?'

'Promise.' He makes an X over his heart.

She doesn't know him well, but the way he looks out the window, taps the table with his fingers, she knows something is on his mind.

'So, what's up?'

'I was reading your story and thinking about that day. I've always thought Richard knew something. He was so weird after – when he got out of hospital.'

'You think he saw something?'

'I don't know. I can't figure it out. He was just too anxious after.' He tilts his head back. Turns his head from side to side, like he's trying to relax his neck. 'He couldn't have. He was a kid.' He takes a drink. 'It's just a feeling.'

Peyton knows all about funny feelings.

'What's up with you, star reporter. What did you want to talk about?'

'I'm moving,' she says.

She thinks she sees his eyes narrow at this news.

'Back to Seattle?'

She shakes her head in the negative. 'New York.'

He gives a low whistle. 'The big time.'

'Well, a big city, yes.'

Acceptances have been coming in. She hasn't heard from NYU, but even if she doesn't get in, she's decided that's where she wants to be, in New York. She might be able to build on the momentum of her article. She has options.

She waits, unsure what to say. She's conflicted. Part of her can't wait to leave, another part doesn't want to go. She made a sort of peace with her parents. She feels more in control around them now. But she'll miss John. Very much.

'I wish you weren't going, but I get why you want to go.'

'You do?'

'You're too big for the Fort. You always have been.'

She waits for him to ask her not to go, but she knows it's a ridiculous idea. He's a police officer here. He cares for his mother and his aunt. He cares about the community. He's where he's meant to be. Peyton is still searching.

'Will you come visit?' she asks.

'I will. If you want me to.'

'I do. You were the best part of my time home. You made me believe in the myth of the nice guy again.'

'The myth?'

'I thought it was an urban legend, like a Sasquatch or a yeti or a unicorn.'

'So I'm mythological,' he laughs.

'I know you're real. You're just very rare.'

'So are you, Peyton. I'm going to miss you.'

They eat dinner and then he drives her home. Kisses her

before she gets out of the car. As she walks to the house she feels a peace she hasn't felt in a long time. And just for a minute, she is grateful. She'll tell her parents about her plans for New York. Her mother will be delighted she has a plan. She opens the door, and just like that, the feeling of contentment evaporates, like steam from a kettle. Something is wrong. Very wrong. She can smell cigarette smoke, can feel the tension in the air, as crisp and real as the evening chill. For a minute she thinks about closing the door, running back to John's. But that won't work. There's a very clear rule in the house that she does not spend the night at John's. It would not look respectable.

She lets herself in, for the first time in her life not seeing the ugly black and white tile in the entranceway. She is heading for the stairs when her mother appears, coming out of the conservatory. Peyton is speechless, for a second, maybe two, waiting for her mother to speak, when her father appears behind her, a united team.

What could she have possibly done?

'Come into the conservatory, Peyton. Your mother and I need to speak with you.'

Peyton is afraid to move, to react and not to react.

'Now,' her mother says, her voice low and deadly.

Peyton follows, her Converse still on her feet.

On the table next to the window is a small green box. Peyton has seen it before, at a Cracker Barrel in Tennessee. She can feel the change in the room, like the way the earth vibrates before a natural disaster, alerting the animals to seek higher ground.

'The mailman came today, with a parcel. Seems you left some salt and pepper shakers at my sister's house when you visited. She was returning them to you, with a thank you note for some art supplies you sent her.'

Peyton looks at her father, who looks smaller than he ever has, standing beside his wife who is almost a foot shorter. He looks at her and lowers his head, a subtle way of saying he is both disappointed in her, and on her mother's side in this.

As Peyton stands still her mother takes out a piece of paper.

Dear Peyton,

It was so good to see you when you visited in March. We sure did have some fun, and now you can say you had biscuits and gravy.

It was real nice of you to send me the paint. I've been working on a few things and enjoying being creative again.

I wrote Scott a letter soon after you left and told him you visited. I swore him to secrecy. Scott knows how to keep a secret. We've kept many together.

You left these salt and pepper shakers on the table when you left. I am returning them to you. I hope you or Mary manage to get to the post on time. Haha.

Lots of love,

Aunt Minnie

'I don't even know where to begin,' her mother says.

'You better start explaining, Peyton,' her father says.

They stand, the three of them, her parents who are never together, united against her.

'I found a card from Minnie. I asked dad about it. He said you had a sister in Tennessee. I went to see where you lived so I could maybe understand you better,' she says, her voice calmer, feeling calmer, than she thought she would.

'The weekend you said you were in Seattle,' her mother says.

'Yes.'

'So you lied.'

Peyton is silent. Nothing she says will help here.

'You poked around in my life, like you're poking around in Daisy's life, hunting up the past when you should be getting your own life together. You lied.'

But it is not her words that she feels, but the look of hatred her mother gives her. Her mother has looked at her in this way before. She remembers each time, for it is carved inside of her.

Somewhere in her chest, maybe where her soul is, for she believes in souls, Peyton feels something snap. No, not snap. It's more of a poke. Whatever it is, it jars her into life.

'You made me lie! You make all of us lie! None of us can be who we are because you have so many rules, you are so cold and horrible, you have been to me my *entire life*. That's why I'm here, why I'm not working at CNN in Atlanta, or being a doctor in Seattle, or getting married. Because my whole life I've felt something was wrong with me because of how *you* treated me. And yes, I looked into Daisy's case. Because I remember when it happened and I remember being scared and I remember being pawned off on Scott and Caroline because you were at the hospital,' she stares at her father, 'and *you* were just gone. And I came home because I was tired and unhappy and I wanted to figure it out, put it behind me. And I have, and I am, and I'll leave, just like Caroline and Scott. Because everything is a lie, and we might have the nicest house in Maine but it's not much better than the shack you grew up in.'

Until that moment, Peyton had no idea silence could be so loud. She waits for the walls to explode, the ceiling to collapse, the windows to splinter from her words, from what they mean.

She can hear the clock ticking, her father breathing, as they stand there, the three of them, trying to navigate the unchartered waters, to swim in the chaotic waves Peyton has unleashed.

'Did you learn everything you need to know?' her mother says, her voice calm, rational. Deadly.

Peyton could nod her head, but she's started something now and she means to finish it.

'I learned your brother was an asshole and your parents are dead and Minnie would be living in poverty if it wasn't for Trent the pharmacist and Debbie is working at the diner and you are the queen of holding grudges,' Peyton says, her words as sharp as a sword, their point as deadly as a spear.

'Stop it, right now,' Peyton's father is moving forward, past her mother, who looks ten years older in the three, four minutes that have passed. Words can be as aging as the sun, and twice as deadly, Peyton thinks.

Her father moves to take her arms, Peyton has been waving them like a puppet, like she is directing the play she is starring in. She sidesteps him, the words coming out of her like oil from the ground.

'Your brother was a jerk. Minnie broke a promise to you. What the hell did I ever do? My big sin was being born when you already had the perfect little family, a boy and a girl. Was that it?'

'You're out of line, Peyton,' her father says.

'Let her finish, Octavian.' Peyton can tell by her voice she saw the smirk.

'You're a psychiatrist. You know everything there is to know about human development, but you know nothing about being a good mother.'

As Peyton stares, she is sure her mother shrinks before her, but maybe it's not that she's less imposing. Maybe it's that Peyton has grown, now that she is free from the shackles of her mother's judgment.

'I'm going to John's.' She turns on her heel, leaves the conservatory, walks through the entryway. She thinks, for a second, about spitting on the black and white tiles. But her mother would never forgive that. Vulgarity, after all.

She closes the door behind her, walks outside. Looks down the hill that leads toward the town and starts to walk.

She arrives at John's just as the euphoria starts to wane. By the time he has her sat on a sofa with a glass of water she is fighting tears.

'I'm sorry, John. I'm sorry. This is terrible of me.'

'It's fine. We're friends. Don't worry about it.' He hands her a tissue as her phone beeps and she fishes it out of her pocket. She has a text from her mother. 'John does not need to know about this family's business.'

She thought it might be an apology, a declaration of love, a plea to come home. But they're not that kind of family.

She's been at John's for three days. He says he's happy to have her, but she can't, won't take advantage of him. She is trying to figure out what to do, if she should go back to Seattle, maybe call Caroline for advice, when her father texts asking to have dinner at Tully's.

She texts back and says yes, then asks if he can bring her some stuff. Clothes, her notebooks. He does not reply.

She walks to Tully's, nervous to be around him, no longer certain of her father. She always thought he was on her side. The ocean is sparkling with life, the beach filling with people. She stops and watches a young family, a mother, father, two small children. She wonders if they have any idea what happened a quarter of a century ago, on the very land where they stand, beach balls, pails and shovels, blankets and cooler ready for their day on the beach. Peyton looks at the little girl playing and wills her to be safe.

Then she keeps walking, the sun beating down on her shoulders, a pool of sweat on her lower back.

He is waiting for her when she arrives. She sees him sitting in a booth in the corner, overlooking the water.

'You have to come home, now. Enough is enough.'

'The package was addressed to me.' She's not sure where this comes from. She is certain this is not what she had been thinking, been preparing to say.

'What?'

'Aunt Minnie's parcel. It was addressed to me, and she opened it.'

'What do you want me to do, Peyton? She is who she is.'

'Can you imagine the scene if I opened her mail?'

She looks away from him. Even though she's inside, the sun is bright, shining through the windows, powerful, like it is trying to purify everything in its path. She squints, puts her sunglasses back on.

'This came for you,' he says. He hands her a large envelope. She sees the postmark, the school stamp. She grabs it from him, rips it open. Pulls out the letter and scans it. Happiness suddenly fills her: warm, simple, genuine, complicated happiness.

'I got into journalism school in New York.'

'Good for you. I know it's what you always wanted,' he says.

'I wrote my essay about Mom.'

Her father doesn't reply.

The waitress appears. Peyton orders a lobster roll and a green salad. Her father orders the same, and a beer.

'Me, too,' she says. Alcohol. Might not be a bad idea to add it to the mix. Might not be a good idea, either.

'When will you leave for school?' he asks.

'I'm not sure. Maybe I can go for the summer and take a class, lighten my load in the fall.' She tries to make it sound like a smart decision, but they both know it is time for her to move on.

'You have to come home, Peyton. You can't leave like this. Your mother can't lose you, too.'

Nothing is said, when Peyton returns home. She finds the salt and pepper shakers on the desk in her room. When her parents are out she makes a beeline for the basement, convinced her mother will have ripped down her timeline, but it is still there. She pulls out all her notes; they feel comforting, like meeting an old friend, in her hands. She takes one last look at the timeline, snaps a picture of it with her phone, then starts to take it apart, putting it all in a folder. She may not have solved the case, but she won't stop trying. With one last look around, she packs up all her research, turns and flicks off the light. She's decided to go to New York for the summer, and it's time she got packing.

She's been back three days when they meet in the kitchen, a neutral zone in the no man's land that the house now feels like to Peyton. Her mother is stirring some cream into her coffee. Peyton has never seen her take cream before when she says, 'How did Minnie look?'

Peyton's heart is jackhammering in her chest. Talking to her mother was like dealing with one of those snakes that can strike at any moment. Cobras? Or were all snakes like that?

She moves cautiously, knowing she is on fertile ground.

'Thin. Small. She needs a good face cream.'

Silence.

'She was wearing large plastic earrings that looked like grapes.'

'It was a Rexall's when I lived there. Down the street from the diner. A white building on a corner. Is that where she's living?'

'Yes.'

'You met Debbie.'

'Yes.'

Silence.

'I told her you live in a mansion and one of your bags costs more that she'd make in a year at that diner.'

She thinks she sees a smile trying to form on her mother's lips. She waits. She wants to tell her to call her sister. Wants to tell her to forgive, but how can she do that, when Peyton can't forgive her own mother, even knowing her past?

'I'm going to Portland. You'll feed your father tonight?'

'Yes.'

She turns and walks away.

Peyton finds her father and says, 'Dinner tonight is just us, Dad. Tully's, or steaks on the grill with root beer floats?'

'As long as I'm with my favorite girl, I'm happy,' he says.

She's leaving in the morning and still has packing to do. She's sorting through her books when her mother appears in the doorway. She has a thin envelope in her hand and Peyton knows exactly what's inside. A check. She's not sure for how much. She knows she doesn't want it. Won't take it.

Peyton knows there's a reason she's standing in the doorway. The check she could leave on the counter for her. She must have something to say. When she told them she was leaving her father offered her one of his apartments, but she said no, she wanted to find her own place close to campus.

'Is Dad OK?' Maybe her mother is afraid to be alone with her father, but his tests have all been good.

'I know I've been hard on you, Peyton. Maybe I was

wrong. I raised you to be strong. Part of being strong is knowing the only opinion that matters is the one you have of yourself. You're one of the strongest people I know, and you have a good soul.'

Peyton waits for her mother to say she's proud of her, to tell her she loves her. But they're not that kind of family. Her mother walks over and hands her the envelope.

'Thanks,' Peyton says.

Her mother turns and leaves. Peyton listens to her heels on the hard wood in the hall, passing the painting she knows her aunt Minnie made. She thinks of all the things her mother carries with her as she walks away.

Peyton wonders how far back the history will go if she ever has children of her own. What will she tell them about her parents? The people who shaped her, the people who she knew better than anyone else in the world, and who were also complete strangers to her.

She looks out her bedroom window. Through the gap in the trees she can see the Atlantic Ocean. She swam in it as a child. Stood in it playing frisbee with friends. Walked endless miles alongside it. If it could, she's certain it would have whispered the answer to her. She's sure of that. Maybe it did. Maybe the answers were always there, in the shimmer on the water.

Epilogue

Daisy

July, Maine, 1997

She's sleepy and part of her wants to go home, but not before the fireworks. She's excited for the fireworks, the way they light up the sky, all pink and yellow and red and blue. She likes the ones that twinkle as they fall through the sky. Her skin feels warm, on her nose, the tops of her shoulders. They've been outside all day, her, Mommy and Daddy, aunts and uncles, cousins. Everyone is here, at the beach, eating lobster rolls, which are yucky, and hot dogs, which are so yummy! Her mom is giggling with her aunt, sitting a few feet away on the big blanket they've been using all day.

She's trying to build a sandcastle with her pail, but there are too many people around. People keep stepping on it and apologizing, laughing, when they see what they did. She empties the pail of sand and carefully places the seashells

445

she's collected inside, along with her shovel and Barney, her stuffed dog. Mommy said he didn't belong at the beach and told her to leave him home, but she didn't understand and asked why. She saw dogs running on the beach all the time and they looked so happy. Daddy had laughed when she said that and told her of course she could bring Barney. Mommy said something about it being his fault if it got lost. But Barney's safe in the pail.

Her water wings don't have any air now. She'd opened the little stopper and squeezed it out. Deflated now, she puts them in the bucket, too. She looks at her parents, wondering if they're going to leave. But no, they haven't seen the fireworks yet.

Her uncle opens the cooler they brought with them and pulls out more drinks. She hears her father say, 'I'm gonna feel this tomorrow,' and laugh again. It seemed to her that adults are always either laughing about something or angry about something.

Her pail is full now, all ready to carry home when the fireworks are over. She sees her cousin, Richard, walking towards the old pier. She doesn't like Richard. He's always telling her to get lost, saying she's a baby, but then he's nice to her when his parents are around. Her cousin, John, is following him. She likes John. He sits with her and draws. Sometimes he plays dolls, too. He likes stickers almost as much as she does.

She stands up and goes after him. Maybe he'll play with her.

She pushes through the sand in her new blue flip-flops, the sun making funny pictures ahead of her. She hears people laughing, talking. Music is coming from one of the places selling ice cream. She's already had ice cream today, but it's the Fourth of July! Maybe she can have two. She knows John will buy her one.

She runs faster, wanting to catch up to him. He's talking to Richard, looking in the direction of the old pier. Richard walks ahead. He's calling John a chicken, making clucking noises and flapping his arms. John stands still, but Richard's walking up the ramp. They're not supposed to do that!

There are lots of people around, but no one's telling him to stop. Maybe it's OK... Where is John? There are so many people on the beach, someone bangs into her, knocking her down. A set of arms reach down and stand her up.

'Hey, what's going on here? Where's your mommy and daddy?'

She points, although she's not sure where she is.

Her flip-flop came off when she fell. She looks around. She just got her flip-flops and loves the bright yellow flowers on them. She sees it, next to the pier, sitting on top of the water. She walks in after it, steps into the ocean, so cool now. She almost has it, when a wave comes, taking it further out. She chases after it.

She can hear yelling now. Someone saw Richard on the pier above her.

She takes another step after her flip-flop. Why won't it come back to her?

She hears a creaking, breaking sound. People are yelling. She almost has her flip-flop, almost... One more step...

There's a loud crashing. Something is falling into the water around her. Pieces of wood. She's scared now and tries to turn round. Mommy will be mad she lost her new shoes, but she doesn't want to be here.

Something hits her. It hurts!

She's underwater now. Salty water burns her nose. She can't cough. Where's the top?

She kicks her legs furiously, but nothing's happening.

OK. OK.

She remembers to use her arms, but they're heavy and hard to lift. And her head hurts where something hit it. She doesn't have her water wings. Something else has fallen on her. It hurts so much and then...

She stops trying to move her arms and legs and is still for a second, a moment, coated in something sticky, cold. And then she's floating, the golden light of the sun around her.

Looking down, she sees her family. They're running around. She wants to wave to them, tell them where she is. But something is pushing on her. The muddy floor of the ocean is pulling her down, down. She wishes she had Barney with her. Wishes she had her pail. Wishes she was at home, taking a bath, curled up in her soft pajamas watching cartoons.

Daddy's in the water now, screaming her name. Cousin John is telling people to link arms, walk into the water, keep looking down. Are they looking for her? She waves, to let them know where she is.

She's sleepy again, like before she chased her flip-flop. There's no noise anymore. She can't even hear the waves. She takes a last look at her daddy, wishes she could tell him it's OK. Wishes she could tell Mommy she's sorry about her flip-flops.

It's funny – she knows part of her is in the mud, but

another part is warm and safe, skipping over the waves, dancing through the air, moving like a gentle summer breeze into the golden Maine sky.

She does a somersault in the air and laughs when she sees she has both of her flip-flops now.

Acknowledgements

Thank you to my agent, Hannah Schofield, and everyone at LBA. Thank you to Martina Arzu and everyone at Aria and Bloomsbury as well.

I have dedicated this book to my high school English teacher, Joan McNutt. Once while calling roll she stopped and looked up at me and said, 'The poem you wrote about Spring was outstanding.' She then returned to her task, unaware perhaps of how much her simple words of praise encouraged me. I have been blessed with English teachers in this life, including Miss White, Miss Sparks, Seymour Mayne and Peter Klaus Stich. I am grateful for all of them.

Much thanks to everyone who has made the journey so much better, including Marla McAlpine, Asta Sinusas, Andrew Lawrence, Anne Mackie, Nina Puim, Kelly Holloran Grey, Treena Muck Pixner, Diana Marrs, Christina Rowson, Christine Bridger, Catherine Gladstone, Brigitte Lindig, Rod Collins, Simon Frost, Deborah Scales, Andrew Caldwell Lee, Sybil Crawford, Tiffany Jarva, Katherine Armstrong, Simon Ingham, Lee Walton and the fabulous Bill Buckley.

About the Author

MARINA MCCARRON was born in eastern Canada and studied in Ottawa and Vancouver before moving to England. She holds a Bachelor of Arts and a Master of Publishing degree. She has worked as a reporter, a freelance writer, a columnist and a manuscript evaluator. She loves reading and traveling and has been to six of the seven continents. She gets her ideas for stories from strolling through new places and daydreaming.